KT-198-045

Elvi Rhodes was the eldest of five children brought up in the West Riding of Yorkshire in the depression between the wars. She won a scholarship to Bradford Grammar School and left to become the breadwinner of her family. A widow with two sons, she lives in Sussex. Her other novels include *Opal, Doctor Rose, Ruth Appleby, The Golden Girls, Madeleine, The House of Bonneau, Cara's Land* and *The Rainbow Through the Rain*. A collection of stories, *Summer Promise and other stories*, is also published by Corgi Books.

Also by Elvi Rhodes

DOCTOR ROSE
THE GOLDEN GIRLS
THE HOUSE OF BONNEAU
MADELEINE
OPAL
RUTH APPLEBY
CARA'S LAND
SUMMER PROMISE AND OTHER STORIES
THE RAINBOW THROUGH THE RAIN

and published by Corgi Books

THE BRIGHT ONE

Elvi Rhodes

CORGI BOOKS

THE BRIGHT ONE
A CORGI BOOK : 0 552 14057 0

Originally published in Great Britain by Bantam Press,
a division of Transworld Publishers Ltd

PRINTING HISTORY
Bantam Press edition published 1994
Corgi edition published 1995

Set in 10pt Linotype Plantin by
Chippendale Type Ltd, Pool in Wharfedale, West Yorkshire.

Corgi Books are published by Transworld Publishers Ltd,
61–63 Uxbridge Road, Ealing, London W5 5SA,
in Australia by Transworld Publishers (Australia) Pty Ltd,
15–25 Helles Avenue, Moorebank, NSW 2170,
and in New Zealand by Transworld Publishers (NZ) Ltd,
3 William Pickering Drive, Albany, Auckland.

Reproduced, printed and bound in Great Britain by
Cox & Wyman Ltd, Reading, Berks.

This book is for Mollie Prior,
dear friend and fellow-writer

Acknowledgements

Many people, both in Ireland and in this country, gave me help in researching *The Bright One*.

I wish particularly to thank Veronica Steele, who answered scores of questions and also accompanied me to the scenes of her childhood in the West of Ireland.

I also wish to thank Veronica's mother, Mrs Mary Corbett, who looked back for me over a lifetime of more than ninety years, and Mary's son, Paddy Corbett, who shared his reminiscences and sang and recorded songs for me.

I also wish to include other kind friends in County Clare who gave us such warm hospitality.

Once again, I thank my son, Anthony Rhodes, who accompanied me on my research trips. With the utmost patience he took me wherever I wanted to go, and joined in in all my research.

PART ONE

One

She sat on the grass at the top of the cliffs; damp grass, because the rain came and went, came and went, day in, day out, seldom more than a day or two without at least a shower, usually heavy, which was why the grass was of a green which dazzled the eye with its brilliance. In spite of the wind which always blew around the cliff top, the grass never had time to dry out. In any case, the wind was laden with spray from the sea which, at high water, swirled around the base of the cliff, pounding against the rock with vicious intensity, as if determined to smash it.

The sea was roaring in now, great waves as high as walls, which broke on the strand in wide bands of white foam, frothy as whipped-up egg-white. Close into the shore the sea was slate grey, but only a little further out it was the deep, dark colour of blue-black ink, the surface broken, because the wind was fresh, by galloping white horses, ridden by adventurous seabirds.

The sea stretched away in the distance until the sky came down and met it, until you could hardly tell one from the other. It looked like the edge of the world, and Breda had once thought it was; but now she knew differently. The world did not end there because the sea was the Atlantic Ocean, and it went on for thousands of miles. Her Dada had said so and she could not but believe him, though today he had her so annoyed that she would have preferred not to believe a word he said. However, Miss McCleary had also said the same thing. She had pointed it out on the map of the world, which covered a fair-sized area of the classroom wall. Miss McCleary was never wrong.

The waves which left Ireland, Dada had said, finally broke on the shores of America. In which case, Breda had replied, America must be a very wet place, with all that water.

‘ ’Tis not so at all,’ Dada had said. ‘It all comes back again to Ireland.’ When she’d asked how this could work he’d changed the subject.

‘You are too full of questions,’ he’d complained.

America was where her Uncle Fergal and Aunt Cassie lived with her cousins. They had gone over the water more than ten years ago so that, in fact, Breda had never set eyes on them, but there was more than one proof that they existed.

For a start, there was the photograph of her uncle and aunt, with the four children they had had in Kilbally, on the sideboard, flanked by likenesses of the three who had been born to them in America, and a more recent one of Uncle Fergal taken when he had been promoted to sergeant in the New York City Police Force.

There were photographs in almost every home in Kilbally of relatives who had crossed the water to America or to England. ‘And not only in Kilbally,’ Mammy said. ‘ ’Tis the same all over Ireland. You can tell how long they have been gone by how much the photograph has faded. Many are those who have died in a foreign land, God rest their souls!’

Another proof of the existence of Breda’s relatives in America was the parcels of clothing which arrived twice a year, as regular as clockwork; hand-me-downs from Breda’s cousins, one of whom was only a year older than she was. Lovely clothes they were; so smart, so stylish.

Last winter a warm coat, its collar trimmed with glossy, dark fur; for this summer crisp cotton dresses in floral patterns, with fancy touches – braiding and piping, tucks and pleats – which made them stand out a mile from the serviceable, everyday clothes of her friends. All they needed was to be shortened but this Mammy refused to do. 'You'll grow into them soon enough,' she said.

'Twas a pity. 'Twas a pity also that her mother made her wear a pinafore over the dresses. Without it she might have been the best-dressed girl in Kilbally. She would have liked that.

She was wearing one of the dresses at this moment – a blue and white checked gingham with a full, gathered skirt and a white collar embroidered in blue cross-stitch – though she should have been doing no such thing since it was school holidays and for that Mammy said any old clothes were good enough. The best ones, the latest arrivals, were kept for Mass on Sundays, and the second-best for term time, though even then she had to change out of them the minute she was home from school.

'If you want to look smart when it matters,' Mammy said, '– and don't we all know you're as vain as a peacock, the way you prink and preen in front of the glass – then you'll learn to look after your things. 'Tis the way you will always be having some fit to wear.'

'Twas not easy to prink and preen, Breda thought. The only looking-glass in the house was one foot square, and though it stood on the dresser in the living kitchen for the benefit of all, Breda was not tall enough to use it without standing on a stool. Even then she could only see bits of herself, never the whole picture.

Earlier in the summer she had been invited to tea at Deirdre O'Farrell's house and there, in Mrs O'Farrell's bedroom, was an oak wardrobe with a full-length mirror in the door. Breda had gazed upon herself in her full glory, a sight so far only seen by others, frowning critically at her curly red hair, which was common in these parts. She would have preferred it to be black, and dead straight, like Mammy's. She was not displeased with her blue-green eyes, which Dada said were like the sea on a good day.

Seeing the whole picture she realized that she was not as tall as she liked to think herself. Deirdre, standing beside her, was a good two inches taller, though the same age. Also, Deirdre had black hair and a beautiful name, and was that rare thing, an only child. Nor were the O'Farrells, who ran a small farm, as poor as everyone else, else why would they have a wardrobe like this? Deirdre was so lucky!

And my legs are too thin, Breda thought. But still and all she was not totally dissatisfied. Wasn't there a certain something? She struck a pose, head tilted, right arm raised in a graceful curve, toe pointing forward like a dancer.

'Would you come away from that mirror now,' Deirdre said. 'Else it's the Devil himself will jump out and get you!'

But now she was sitting on the top of the cliff, her arms clasped around her knees, her head shrunk into her shoulders, and if she could have seen her eyes they would have shown dark with anger and frustration. She hated her father, and with good cause. Had he not promised that the next time he went to the races she should go with him? And this was the day.

Last night, before going to bed, she had washed herself from top to toe so as not to have to spend time this morning, and as soon as she had wakened, though it was annoyingly later than she had planned, she had put on the gingham frock, clean white socks and her best shoes with double straps across the instep, outgrown by her American cousin, and hurried downstairs.

'Where's Dada?' she demanded.

'He left an hour ago,' Mammy said. She spoke calmly. Only the extra vigour she gave to kneading the dough for the soda bread hinted that she was not as calm as she sounded. She had told James that there would be trouble.

'You promised her!' she had told him.

' 'Twas not serious,' he replied. 'She knew that. I did not promise the day.'

'You said, "Next time I'll be after taking you with me." Today is the next time. You should never had said it, putting ideas into her head!'

It was entirely like James O'Connor, Molly thought. Wouldn't he say anything to please? Would he not charm the birds off the trees or the ducks off the water? Had he not done it to her when they had met eighteen years ago at Ballinasloe Fair in the autumn? And he had been doing it ever since, and she still falling for it. Still, it was wrong to do this to Breda.

'The races is no place for a child of eight,' James said.

'Then you should have said so to the child,' Molly persisted.

'In any case it's fast asleep she is. Why would I want to be waking her?' he asked.

He kissed Molly – after eighteen years of marriage not many Kilbally men kissed their wives on parting – blessed himself at the small font by the door, and left.

'God go with you!' she said.

She watched him stride away down the street, to the corner where his mates would pick him up in the trap. He was thirty-eight and looked ten years younger. She looked all of her thirty-seven years. But then hadn't she borne seven children and raised six, though thankfully it seemed as if Breda was to be the last. The priest had stopped coming around asking wasn't it time there was

15

another to fill the cradle. She did not know why there wasn't. She and James had never ceased to be lovers.

' 'Tis the will of God, no doubt!' she'd said to Father Curran, though not admitting that she was pleased.

'Where is Dada?' Breda repeated.

'He's gone.'

Breda looked at her mother blankly.

'What do you mean? Where would he have gone?'

'To the races. He left an hour past. 'Tis a long way to Galway and his friends were waiting for him. You were asleep.'

'But why would you not have wakened me?' She was shouting now, distraught, unwilling to believe it.

'We thought it better not. 'Twas Dada's belief that the races were not suitable for a little girl of eight. I had the very same thought myself.' She sounded unconvincing even to herself, nor was Breda to be fobbed off.

'But he *promised*, Mammy! He *promised*!' Breda persisted.

' 'Twas not for today he meant it, *dote*,' Molly said. ' 'Twas for some other time, when you are older.' She spoke gently, quietly, her own heart aching for her daughter's disappointment. If I had the man here, I would hit him, she thought – though she knew she would not.

'Will we go for a picnic this afternoon, then?' Molly suggested. 'You and me and Moira? Perhaps the twins?'

'And why should I want to go for a picnic with my sister and my brothers when I was to go to the races with Dada?' Passion rose in Breda to boiling point.

'I hate him!' she cried. 'I hate you all!'

Tears of rage pouring down her face, she ran out of the house, not stopping to bless herself, and away down the long street towards the sea.

'Come back!' Molly cried. 'Not a bite of breakfast have you inside you! Come back!' She freed her hands from the dough and ran into the street.

Her words were wasted, carried away on the air. She went back into the house, set the dough to rise, and went to waken her other four children still at home, though how they had slept through the last ten minutes she could not imagine.

For a minute, before waking them, she paused to look at her children. So innocent they looked in sleep, so good! Butter wouldn't melt in their mouths now, but when they were up and doing it would be different.

Kieran, the eldest of those left, would be the easiest to waken. However quietly she spoke his name, he would open his eyes and be immediately in the world. He slept at the top of the double bed and the twins, Patrick and Colum, slept top-to-tail at the bottom. It had been all right when they were small, but now they were growing like weeds and their legs tangled and kicked half way up the bed, regularly causing trouble. And since the twins were two to one, and Kieran was gentler, they always won, always, too, had the best of the bedclothes.

This morning Kieran's thin shoulders were bare, while the twins were comfortably covered, but wasn't it always the way? And it was summer, so it was all right.

'Time you were up!' she said to Kieran.

Blue eyes met hers, and he smiled.

'As for these lazy lumps . . . ' Molly said.

She included Moira, spread out fast asleep on the second bed, now that Breda had left it. The girl's dark hair spread out across the pillow; long eyelashes lay against cheeks rosy with sleep. Moira was, Molly admitted, the beauty of the family, yet she never felt totally comfortable with her, never felt quite in control as she did with her other children, however naughty they were.

Moira was the difficult one. From the earliest possible age, from babyhood, she had made her wishes known and had managed to get what she wanted.

'And is it not your own fault?' James always said when his wife complained about Moira's selfishness. 'Did you not always give in to her, right from a baby at the breast?'

'You were no better,' Molly said. 'Did you ever say "no" when she was little?'

'It was not my job to be bringing up the children,' James had said. 'It is the mother's job. My job is to earn the living.'

He was right, Molly conceded. It *was* her fault. She had had a difficult pregnancy with Moira and she was tired after the birth. Also she had four other children, the eldest, Kathleen, not yet six years old. They took her energy and needed her attention. Then to her dismay, though not to her surprise, she became pregnant again with Maeve before Moira was six months old.

What could be said about little Maeve, since she had lived less than two weeks? The other children could not remember her, except Kieran just a little, and Kathleen who, like Molly, would never forget.

Very early one morning – James was out fishing – Molly, roused from her sleep after a bad night caused by Moira's teething, took the new baby into bed to feed her. The baby nuzzled into her breast and started to feed. Molly fell asleep. When she waked an hour later the baby was dead, suffocated against her breast. It was Kathleen who had run, in her nightgown, to fetch the doctor, though too late. Everyone said it was not Molly's fault and hadn't it happened before to others, though Molly, when she thought about it, could not but feel guilty. It was this way there was a four-year gap between Moira and Breda.

'Moira!' Molly called now. 'Waken now, Moira. High time you were up and doing.'

Moira groaned and turned over, burying her face in the pillow. With one swift movement Molly pulled all the bedclothes off her, before turning her attention to the twins.

By the time they were all downstairs Kieran had pumped the water and refilled the kettle.

'Where's Breda?' he asked. 'Did Dada take her to the races after all?'

He knew his little sister had been on about it but he had not taken her seriously. Nor, he had thought, had Dada. It was just one of those things Dada had talked about. You had to understand that Dada talked about lots of things which, in the end, didn't happen. He meant nothing by it, but you had to understand, and Breda took him seriously. But had he kept his promise this time?

'Indeed he did not,' Molly said. 'It was never on the cards. Wasn't he gone an hour past when she came down, and all dressed up, the poor child?'

'So where is she?'

'Ran out of the house as fast as her legs would take her, and not a bite inside her. It is my notion she has gone down to the strand. When you have had your breakfast, will you go after her? You and Kathleen were always the best to calm her down.'

She missed Kathleen, her eldest. She missed her sorely, but she had always known that this would happen. It came as no surprise that at seventeen years old Kathleen had joyfully and eagerly entered the novitiate of the Convent of Our Lady of Lourdes and was away in Dublin.

Even as a small girl she had been devout. When she played with her dolls it was to take them to church services, to baptize them, read the scriptures to them. Not that she had ever been a melancholy child, not by any means. The lark on the wing was not happier than Kathleen. But she was closer to God than the other children.

Well, Molly had thought, quite early on, there is no higher calling than for a girl to give her life to God. A Catholic mother must give thanks for having any child with a true vocation. She had not doubted once that Kathleen would be a nun.

Breda was born when Kathleen was nine years old, and from the first there had been a special bond between them. Kathleen had cared for her sister like a little mother. She had all the caring qualities of motherhood.

'It seems sad that she will never have her own children to care for,' Molly had said to James.

'It's too soon to know that,' James protested.

'Oh no it is not!' Molly contradicted him. 'I am certain sure. As certain as that the sun will rise tomorrow morning!'

And so it had been. And so it was Kieran she sent after Breda now. But as she watched him walk away down the road there was pain in her. She knew, as she had known with Kathleen, that one day *he* would walk away from her, for Kieran had a vocation to the priesthood. As with his sister, his future path had shown at an early age. Wasn't it because of that, because it was so clearly recognized, that the Parish was paying for him to be educated by the Christian Brothers in Ennistymon? And would see him through the seminary, for there was no way James O'Connor could afford this.

When Kieran was out of sight Molly turned back into the house. Am I to give all my children to God, she asked herself, not for the first time? It was too much. It was cruel.

When she saw the twins scrapping on the floor, Patrick astride Colum, holding him down, she was momentarily reassured. These two were not for sainthood, that was for certain! As for Moira, was there ever an easier target for the temptations of the Devil? Twelve years old and parading in front of the boys whenever she got the chance!

Breda was different again, different from any of them. She was one on her own. In spite of the morning's tantrums, Molly's heart lifted at the thought of Breda. She was like the sunshine itself, even though, like the sun, she was sometimes behind a cloud. But when she came out she lightened the whole world. And that, thought Molly, was not just the opinion of a fond mother. Wasn't it Father Curran himself who had said, 'When she comes into the room, she lights it up. The Bright One! She is beloved of God.'

But not *too* beloved, Molly thought fearfully. Not Breda!

'Of course, you must never tell her so,' Father Curran said. He was not a man who believed in praise.

Molly had told James.

'The Bright One!' he said. 'Isn't that entirely right!'

Kieran knew just where Breda would be. It was the place they all went, the unofficial meeting place of the children of the neighbourhood. He'd been there himself a thousand times, though less so now than when he was younger. Sixteen was too old for it. Though still at school, to his own mind he was no longer a child. Some of his friends had left the National School at fourteen, others had gone on to the technical school, but in either case they had jobs, or were looking for jobs, to earn a bit of money for the family purse.

It was a sorrow to him that he could not do this, at least not permanently, though he always tried for jobs in the school holidays. He hated watching his mother struggle to make ends meet, to feed and clothe them all on his father's small, and erratic, earnings. His father had no trade; he relied entirely on casual work: farm labourer, drover, fisherman, odd job man. But to give him his due, Kieran thought, when he was in work, he worked hard. He knew that to leave school now would be to deny his vocation. That he could not do, it would be a sin. God had called him, he knew that for certain. Nor would his mother have expected or wanted it.

After half a mile, the unmade road petered out, dividing into two rough tracks, the one sloping down to the strand, to the firm beach with the sand, where the sea had not yet reached it, of so pale a gold that it was almost white, the other track climbing to the cliff top.

He saw Breda before she spotted him. She was sitting on the grass, her knees drawn up to her chin, gazing out to sea. So small she looked against that wide background, and she was too young to be there on her own. Though the wind had dropped for the moment, it could spring up again just as suddenly along this coast, blowing with strong, sharp gusts. She was also much too close to the edge.

Later in the day there would be other children there, but it was still early, not long after nine o'clock, and they would be at their chores, or running messages. Since there was no school some would still be in bed, but his mother did not allow that except for illness.

He quickened his pace, though not calling out. His feet made no sound on the short grass and the second after Breda heard him he flopped down beside her on the ground.

'So what are you doing here, so early in the day?' He asked the question pleasantly, no criticism in his voice.

She looked at him solemnly.

'I was wondering, will I go to America? Will I go to live with Uncle Fergal and Auntie Cassie?'

'And when would this be?' Kieran asked.

'Now, if I could. Has anyone ever swum to America?'

'Not that I have heard of. 'Tis unlikely,' Kieran answered.

'I'm a good swimmer.'

'You are so,' he agreed. 'But it's a long way. What would you do for food?'

He asked the question deliberately. She was fond of her food, greedy almost. It was a wonder with all she ate why she didn't grow faster.

Breda did not need her brother's questions to remind her that she had not eaten since yesterday teatime. In the evening she had been too excited, and this morning too angry. She felt now as though she had a great dark hole in her middle. She wondered if she were to starve herself to death, would her father be sorry for ever? Would she be made a saint? Saint Breda of Kilbally?

'Mammy has sent you some soda bread,' Kieran said.

He took the packet out of his pocket, rather squashed, and handed it to her. Swiftly, she tore off the wrapping and bit into the soft bread, thickly spread with the farm butter Deirdre's mother had given her to bring home – was it only yesterday?

She did not speak until every crumb was finished. Nor did Kieran. His sister would be more amenable on a full stomach.

'I will so go to America,' Breda said. 'As soon as I am old enough.'

'But not swim there?' Kieran said, and saw the corners of her mouth turn upwards at his teasing.

She might well go there, he thought. There was no way the whole family could stay here, even though Kathleen and himself would be away. In every large family – and most were large – someone emigrated. It was the story of Ireland, not just in the time of the potato famine, about which every schoolchild knew, and wasn't there a very old woman in Kilbally whose grandmother had told her about it first hand? It was the way of life. The land couldn't support them. They crossed the water, and sent money home to help those who stayed. But he had thought it would be the twins who would go, not little Breda.

23

'I will travel on a big ship,' she said.

'Or perhaps an aeroplane, by the time you are old enough? But what will Mammy and Dada do without you?'

'Mammy will be sad,' Breda conceded. 'But Dada does not love me, else why did he not take me to the races?'

'Because it is not a thing for a little girl. Besides, won't they have to stay overnight in Galway because of the horses, which will be too tired to go there and back in one day?'

Clearly, Breda thought, no-one was on her side, not even Kieran, who was kinder to her than anyone.

'Will he bring me back a present, do you think?' she asked.

'If he wins,' Kieran said, 'I daresay he will.'

If he won plenty they would all get presents. If he won a little, then Mammy and the girls. If it was a bad day he'd had then he'd turn out his pocket linings to show they were empty, and it would be a hungry week to follow.

'Mammy thought we might bring a picnic down to the strand this afternoon,' he said. 'It will be low tide. You could look for your pebbles.'

Breda was making a collection of pebbles. They must be small, because she hadn't much space to keep them, but they must also be beautiful, unusually marked, uncommonly coloured. Only the very best would do.

'It would not be as good as the races,' she objected.

'It would so,' Kieran said.

'And who would come?'

'All of us.'

'Even you?'

'Yes,' he promised. 'Perhaps Mammy too.'

That was one of the best things about their mother. It was there she differed from the rest. Busy though she was, she would sometimes leave the work to join them

24

in whatever they were doing. In the evenings she would often sing to them in her rich voice. She knew hundreds of songs. She was not like all the other mothers, not at all.

'Would you ever help me with my pebbles?' Breda asked cautiously. She had no intention of being easily persuaded. She had been badly done by.

'I might,' Kieran agreed. 'But we need to go home now. I have to see Mr O'Reilly about a job in the shop. It's important.'

Mr O'Reilly kept the grocer's. He had almost promised that he would find something for Kieran to do: sweeping up, packing and unpacking, delivering. It would not fetch much in the way of money but hopefully there would be extras – sugar, lard, flour, tea – to bring home.

'Anyway,' Kieran added, 'we must do the chores this morning if we are to picnic this afternoon. Would you have fed the hens at all?'

'I forgot,' Breda admitted.

'Then won't they just be hungry? What if Mammy forgot to feed you? You had better come back with me and do it!' He spoke gently, but as one who expected to be obeyed.

Breda sighed, and gave in, and felt surprisingly better. Kieran held out his hands and pulled her to her feet. There were grass stains on her dress which she hoped would not show or she would be in more trouble.

Her hand in her brother's, she started for home. But I will not forgive Dada, she thought. Well, not at once. I will not speak to him for a week, and if he speaks to me I will not answer.

The picnic was good. There were other children on the beach; most of them Breda knew, so there were plenty of games to join in. The older boys, those who did not have holiday jobs, sat apart, Kieran with them, though it would be his last afternoon for doing so since Mr O'Reilly had given him the job and tomorrow morning he would start work in the shop.

At one point he left his group and kept his promise to help Breda look for pebbles. They were lucky, finding at least a dozen which, after being washed in one of the pools, were judged worthy to join the collection.

'I hope you don't think you're going to keep that lot in the bedroom?' Moira complained. 'There isn't enough room!'

'There is so!' Breda retorted. 'They will go in my treasure box.'

Mammy had given each one of them, the minute they were old enough to own things, a cardboard box in which to keep their possessions apart from everyone else's.

'A stupid treasure, old stones!' Moira said scornfully.

'Not as stupid as lipstick!' Breda said.

Moira blushed. She had had the lipstick from a girl at school, and Mammy did not know about it. Would she ever be allowed to use it, she wondered? Mammy was so old-fashioned. She said little girls did not need such things. But I am twelve, Moira thought rebelliously. I am not a little girl.

It was evening, and the sea rolling in, before they packed up and left for home. Breda had recovered her spirits. She is never down for long, Molly thought as she watched her youngest count her pebbles. I didn't want another child after Moira, but think what I would have missed!

'Will Dada be home when we get back?' Breda asked. Not that she had forgiven him; not quite.

'No. I told you. Not until the morning.'

'Then where will he sleep?'

'Who knows?' Molly said. 'There is no money for beds. They will sleep rough, I expect. In a field, or under

26

a hedge. It was one of the reasons he could not take you.'

'I would sleep in a field,' Breda said. 'I would so!'

'Not if *I* could help it,' Molly said.

For a little while after they reached home they played in the street, Breda and Moira with a skipping rope, the twins kicking a ball. It was still daylight, though looking towards the sea there were bands of red and gold across the sky. Presently Molly called them in to prepare them for bed; Breda first, because she was the youngest.

She lay alone in the bed, savouring the space that was hers until Moira came. She could have fallen asleep at once, but there was no way she would allow herself to do that because she enjoyed watching Moira's nightly ritual: the brushing of her hair before tightly braiding it so that it would have some semblance of waviness in the morning; the massaging into her near-perfect skin of the Ponds Cold Cream for which she had saved her pocket money; the anxious search in the small square of mirror she kept in her treasure box for non-existent spots and blackheads. Breda propped herself up on one elbow, enjoying every minute of her sister's *toilette*. But tonight there was a bonus.

From her box, Moira took out the lipstick and applied it carefully to the cupid's bow of her mouth, sighing with approval at her image in the glass.

'You look gorgeous!' Breda said with true admiration. 'But why are you putting lipstick on to go to bed?'

'Because I can't put it on any other time,' Moira said crossly.

'What will Mammy say if she sees it?' Breda asked.

'She'll make me wash it off,' Moira said. 'But she won't see it, because when she comes in I'll hide under the clothes and pretend to be asleep. And if you tell her I'll kill you!'

'I won't tell her,' Breda promised. 'I won't breathe a word.'

'Move over,' Moira said, climbing in. 'You're taking far more than half the bed!'

Breda was asleep before the twins came to bed, and long before Kieran, who was always last. As her eyes closed she thought of the long summer holiday which stretched ahead, and of Dada, who would be home again tomorrow, perhaps with a present.

Molly, coming into the room much later to look at her children, smiled at the sight of Moira's red lips, pulled the covers over Breda, looked with satisfaction at her three sleeping sons. Here were her jewels.

She wished James was home. She hated going to bed without him.

Two

Four days a week Molly went up to the Big House to give a hand with the cleaning. It was always known as the Big House, though by rights it was Adare House. From leaving school at fourteen she had worked there full time, but when she had met James O'Connor in the autumn of 1920, and married him by Christmas, he would have none of that.

'Am I not able to keep a wife?' he'd demanded. 'Is that it?'

' 'Tis just that it would help until the children come,' she had said, blushing at the thought. 'Help us to get set up.'

'I will not have it.' James had been adamant. 'Ours will be a proper marriage; me supporting you, you looking after me.'

In fact, the children had come quickly. Kathleen had been born nine months to Saint Stephen's Day, and although Mrs Adare, not wishing to lose a good worker, had said that Molly might bring the baby with her, James had remained obstinate.

Well, she thought, climbing the hill to the Big House now, hadn't seventeen years and seven children changed *those* fine ideas? And wasn't the money, though only five shillings a week, the greatest blessing? She did not know how she would manage without it. The fact was that James, faced with a hungry brood, had either come to terms with his objections or, for a long time now, had kept quiet about them.

What would be the outcome today, she wondered? Would he come home with his empty pockets turned inside out, or would there be a bit of money in them? Not much, she reckoned. James's gambling was small-time; had to be because he didn't have much to wager, and she was glad about that.

For the next two hours she swept, scrubbed, dusted and polished. Polishing was the task she enjoyed most, especially the great table in the dining hall. More than once, when she had worked full time here, she had seen it ready for a feast: resplendent with fine china, sparkling with Waterford glass, groaning with food. She rubbed at it now until she could see her reflection in the surface, and that was the last of her jobs here for today.

Back in the kitchen, Mrs Hanratty, the housekeeper, said, 'There is a bit of a parcel for you, so. The end of a joint. A few vegetables.'

Mrs Hanratty was unfailingly kind, though never talkative, never one for a gossip about what the Adares were up to.

'How is your Mammy?' she asked Molly.

'Sure, she is well enough for her age,' Molly said. 'I am going to see her on my way home.'

If there was enough in the parcel she would share it with her mother. If not, she would send one of the children around with a dish of whatever she made from it.

Her mother's house, low, whitewashed, with small, square windows, was exactly like Molly's own, as were most of the houses in Kilbally. Entering from the sunny street, it was dark and Peggy Byrne, sitting in the corner, dressed in her usual black, was almost absorbed into the gloom.

'There you are!' Molly said. 'It's dark coming in. I hardly saw you.'

' 'Tis you,' Mrs Byrne said.

'Who else were you expecting?' Molly asked, smiling.

The house seemed more spacious than her own, perhaps because it was so empty. There never had been much furniture, never enough chairs for them all to sit to meals, but it had been crowded with whichever of the nine children were still at home. It seemed strange, now, to see her mother entirely alone.

Michael Byrne had died a year ago. His chair, a cushion on the seat, a rug thrown over the railed back, was still never sat in by anyone else. It was as if his spirit still hovered.

' 'Tis handy you came,' Mrs Byrne said. 'There is a letter from Josephine.'

Josephine was Molly's sister, older by fourteen years, Molly being the youngest of the family. Most of the others were scattered across the face of the earth, in the United States, in Canada, in England – and all doing well if their letters were to be believed. All, that was, except her brothers Sean and Paddy, who had died in the Great War, which had not been Ireland's war, but they had volunteered. Josephine lived in Yorkshire, in Akersfield. Molly was the only one now living in Ireland.

Would the time come, Peggy Byrne had wondered, watching her children leave one by one, when there would be no Byrnes at all left in the county?

'Isn't it the truth that the Byrnes have lived in this place as far back as anyone can remember?' she asked – inconsequentially to Molly, but she was used to that from her mother.

'Indeed it is so,' she agreed.

They were there before the time when the sailors from the Spanish Armada had been washed ashore from the wreckage of their ships in the stormy seas. They were already there even farther back, when the Vikings had scaled the cliffs, or sailed up the estuary.

'I wonder what news Josephine has?' Molly said.

Her mother handed her the letter. It had been opened, but not read, for the simple reason that Peggy Byrne could not read.

'See for yourself. Read it out, and mind you speak up now! Will I not want to hear every word?'

Molly read in a loud, clear voice. Josephine was well, her husband was well, the children were well. Maureen was now engaged to be married, to a teacher. Kate was expecting her first baby.

'So, I am to be a great-grandmother!' Mrs Byrne said. 'Will I ever be seeing the child?'

'Of course you will!' Molly said. 'You know you can visit Josephine any time you have a mind to. She's invited you often enough!'

'I am seventy-five. I am too old to be travelling to the ends of the earth,' Mrs Byrne objected.

'Akersfield is not the ends of the earth, Mammy,' Molly said. 'And perhaps one of them would come over and fetch you.'

'Get on with the letter,' Mrs Byrne said. 'What else does she say?'

'Not much more. "The mills are busy again," ' she read, ' "making cloth for uniforms. Everyone thinks there will be another war with Germany." '

'At least it will not be Ireland's war,' Molly said. 'Ireland is neutral.'

'And so she was before,' her mother reminded her. 'What difference did it make to me?'

'I'm sorry, Mammy. Oh, there is a postscript. Josephine says she encloses a ten-shilling note! I don't see it. She must have forgotten!'

'I have it,' Mrs Byrne said, smiling a secret smile. 'I have it in a safe place.'

Ten shillings, Molly thought! What will she do with it? She never goes out, and she will not spend a penny unless she has to.

She folded the letter and handed it back to her mother, who she knew would peruse it many times, trying to connect the squiggles on the paper with the news she had heard.

'Mrs Hanratty gave me a parcel,' she said, changing the subject. 'I'll open it up, so, and if there is enough to divide I will give you some. If not, I will send you a dish.'

'Take it home,' Mrs Byrne said. 'It will save me the cooking of it.'

That would be as well, Molly reckoned. She doubted her mother ever took the trouble to make a decent meal, not now when she had no-one else to cook for.

'Let Kieran bring it,' Mrs Byrne said.

'If he can, Mammy,' Molly said. 'He is working for Luke O'Reilly in the shop. But one of us will bring it.' She rose to leave.

She had to hurry home. There was the midday dinner to prepare. Kieran would come home for that, with little time to spare, so it must be on the table, and it went without saying that the other children would be starving. Whether James would be home or not she had no idea. With part of her she longed, as she always did, to see him; with another part she dreaded it, for fear of the outcome.

Breda was sitting on the doorstep, apparently doing nothing, though Molly guessed that she was looking for her father, whether to carry on the feud or to make it up, she couldn't guess. Either way, it would be a positive action. Breda was never one for hiding her feelings, good or bad. Of the other children, there was no sign.

'Where is everyone?' Molly enquired.

33

'The twins have gone to the beach,' Breda said. 'They wouldn't let me go with them, which is not fair.'

'And Moira?'

'I wouldn't be knowing where Moira is. She just went off. She is full of secrets!'

'Ah well, I dare say they will all be back the minute dinner is on the table,' Molly said. 'You children all have alarm clocks in your stomachs. Did you and Moira do the potatoes?'

'*I* did,' Breda said virtuously. 'Moira went off and left me to do it. And I've put the pan on the fire.'

'Good girl!'

'But Moira will have to do them all on her own tomorrow,' Breda insisted. ' 'Tis not fair otherwise. She gets away with everything, that one.'

'She will not do so this time,' Molly promised. 'Won't I see to that?'

Potatoes, which they grew on the scrubby piece of land at the back of the house, were the mainstay of their diet, day in, day out. Only on Sundays was there meat, and that in a good week. A rabbit, a boiling hen too old to be productive any longer; on the best occasions, a small piece of beef.

Molly knew a score of ways with potatoes: potato soup; boiled potatoes with onion sauce; potato scones cooked on the griddle to a golden brown, then drenched with butter (for she only made scones if there was butter in the cupboard); boxty – grated potatoes bound with flour and water and fried; potatoes mashed with scallions, or with carrots and turnips; and many others. Today, having stayed overlong at her mother's, she was in a hurry. Boiled, with onion sauce, it would have to be.

Moira walked in at the door, and would have glided across into the bedroom except that Molly put out an arm and held her back.

'You are just in time to peel me an onion!'

'Oh, no, Mammy!' Moira cried. 'Not an onion! Won't it make my hands smell all afternoon!'

'Give them a good wash,' Molly said, 'and at the same time you can wash the paint off your face!'

She was stirring the thickening sauce, the smell of the onion and milk, sharply appetizing, filling the low-ceilinged room, when the twins rushed in, followed immediately by Kieran. Patrick and Colum at once took their places at the table.

'Go and wash your hands!' Kieran ordered.

Grumbling, they moved to obey him.

'And see to it that you bring more water in before you go out this afternoon,' Molly said. 'I have washing to do.'

Breda and Moira were already at the table, both of them seated; Breda because she was too small to stand, Moira because, since her father was not present, there was a spare stool. The twins stood, as always, but Kieran, as the eldest, had a seat. Moira, with a wrinkled nose, sniffed at her hands.

'Disgusting!' she said.

'There is nothing disgusting about the smell of good food!' Molly said sharply, handing out the plates. 'Patrick, do *not* start to eat until I have said grace!'

She said it quickly, not wishing the food to go the least bit cold. They murmured 'Amen', blessed themselves and began to eat. After a moment, Breda said: 'When will Dada be back?'

'Don't speak with your mouth full,' Molly said automatically. 'How can I tell? I will expect him when I see him.'

'Will he not be wanting his dinner?' Breda said hesitantly.

'He will so,' Molly agreed. 'Are you to save him some of yours?'

Breda put down her fork.

'I will too.' She said it reluctantly. She was very hungry. 'But you must make Moira save some of hers!'

Molly smiled.

'You can eat up, Breda,' she said. 'And you also, Moira, if you had thought of saving some. I have kept back enough for Dada. It was a kind thought, Breda, but did you think I would not save your Dada his dinner?'

Though it might well be dried up and hardly fit to eat by the time he decided to put in an appearance, she thought to herself. At least it seemed that Breda had forgiven him, though that did not surprise her. Breda's passions were swift and strong, but in the end her loving nature overcame them.

'How did it go in the shop?' she asked Kieran.

'Well enough. Would you be wanting me to bring you anything back this afternoon?' He rose from the table and cleared away his plate.

'Thank you, no,' Molly said. 'I will be down myself tomorrow.'

It was impossible to embark on her shopping until she knew what James would bring home, something or nothing. Would it be bread and lard they'd be eating the rest of the week, or perhaps rashers, or even, please God, a tin of salmon? In any case, she had a fancy to see Kieran at work. Just supposing he took a fancy to the job, and Luke O'Reilly, who had no children, to him, so that he forgot his vocation.

She was at once deeply ashamed of the thought, and swiftly put it away from her. May God forgive me, she chided herself.

'I must go,' Kieran said. ' 'Twould look bad to be late on my first day.'

He was stepping out of the house when, away at the top of the street, just rounding the corner, he saw him. Turning back into the house he called:

'He's here! Dada's here!'

Molly rushed to the door, followed immediately by Breda, then Moira. The twins lagged behind just long enough to scrape their plates.

Molly took one look at her husband as he walked towards them, though he was still a way off. Her heart lifted. 'Praise be to God!' she murmured. She could tell at once from his jaunty walk, his head high, his shoulders back, that things had gone well. She knew the shape of him. But even if they had not, the sight of him, *any* sight of him, would have filled the longing she always had when he was away for more than a few hours.

Breda rushed up the street to meet him. Moira hesitated, wondering whether it was quite the thing to do at her age, then decided it was, and followed after, though more sedately. The rest of them stayed in the doorway, waiting. When he drew nearer they saw the wide smile on his face, and met it with welcoming smiles of their own. As he reached the door, a daughter on each arm, Molly stepped back into the house, else he would embrace her right there, in front of the whole street, and though she would be proud, it was simply not done. They would be a talking point.

'So all went well?' she asked quietly.

'Well enough,' James said. 'Not a fortune, but well enough.'

'Have you brought us presents, Dada?' Moira asked eagerly.

'What are they?' Breda said.

James frowned at them with mock severity. 'So that's the way of it, is it? It is not your Dada you want home, 'tis what he has brought you! Supposing I say there is nothing, will I go away again?'

'No, Dada!' Breda said. 'I am pleased to see you, even though you did break your sacred promise to me.'

'But you forgive me?' James said seriously. 'Even if I'm empty-handed?'

Breda took a deep breath.

'I forgive you.'

'So do I!' Moira said eagerly.

'You have nothing to forgive him for,' Breda said. 'He did not break a promise to you, so!'

'That's enough talk,' Molly interrupted. 'Your Dada will do nothing, say not a word more, until he has had his dinner.'

She took a piled-high plate from the oven and set it on the table.

'Get that inside you,' she said to her husband.

'I can't stay,' Kieran said. 'I have to be back at the shop.'

'Can we go out again now?' the twins asked in unison. They were not bothered about gifts or homecomings. As always, they were contented with each other, following their own ploys. Even when they fought, which was not infrequently, it was their own private fight; they remained close in spirit as well as in flesh.

'And you, Breda, *and* you, Moira, are not to sit there staring at Dada while he eats his dinner,' Molly said. 'You can clear the rest of the table and start to wash the dishes.'

All the same, she was as curious as the girls about what he might have brought them all; but fair was fair and a man must be fed. She looked for some small gift, but hoped that he would not have been too extravagant. What she needed most of all was money. She was trying desperately to save towards the new shoes they would all need to go back to school at the end of the long summer holiday. None of their present ones could be repaired any more, and she would never, unlike some mothers in Kilbally, allow her children to go to school barefoot, though in the holidays it was less important.

James scraped up the last of his dinner, patted his stomach, sighed with satisfaction, then pushed the plate away.

'Come here!' he ordered Molly.

She sprang to obey him, and he rose to meet her.

'You have not given me a kiss,' he complained. 'Does a man not get a kiss at his homecoming?'

The corners of her mouth turned up in a smile, but before she could speak he had pulled her into his arms and was kissing her with passion. Her hands stole around the back of his neck, and she was returning his kisses.

'Other mothers and fathers do not kiss all the time,' Breda said sternly. It was so time-wasting when there were other matters of importance to come.

'Then more fool they!' James said, releasing Molly. 'Now, *dote*, would you be waiting for something? Is that it? And what can it be?'

'Oh Dada, you *know*!' Breda said.

'Yes, you know!' Moira echoed.

'Don't tease them any further,' Molly begged.

'Or you?' James said. 'Aren't you just dying to know? Tell the truth, now!'

He began to feel through his pockets as if he had forgotten exactly where he had put the gifts, pockets large and small, inside and outside his jacket. Breda stood close, jigging up and down in a flurry of impatience.

'Why do you need so many pockets, Dada?' she enquired impatiently.

'Don't they all have their uses?' James said. 'Now where in the world . . . ? I could have sworn . . . !' He started the search again.

'James!' Molly implored.

'Ah! Here we are then!' he said, fumbling. 'Now who should this be for?'

Breda stood on tiptoe, trying to see into the pocket.

'No, not for you, Breda,' he said. ' 'Tis for Moira. Yes, I distinctly remember buying this for Moira!'

From the large pocket inside his jacket he drew out a small hand-mirror. It was oval, with a handle, and pink-backed. Moira flushed with pleasure at the sight of it.

'Isn't it exactly the right thing?' Molly said.

She'll be able to put her lipstick on properly. The words rose to Breda's lips, but she bit them back. This was no time to be ungracious, and perhaps Dada had also bought *her* a mirror, only a different colour. Blue would be nice. The thoughts flew round in her head while James's hand strayed to another pocket.

'Ah! 'Tis here,' he said.

Then it couldn't be a hand-mirror, Breda thought. That pocket was too small.

It was a hair slide, in the shape of a butterfly. Green with a design on it in blue. She drew in her breath sharply at the sight of it. It was entirely beautiful.

'Oh, Dada,' Breda said, 'it is wonderful! It is just what I wanted!' She hadn't known that before she had set eyes on it, but now she was quite certain.

'I knew it the minute I saw it,' James said. 'And now what are you going to give me?'

'A big kiss!' Breda said.

She raised her arms and he swung her up so that she was level with him. When she kissed him his face was rough and itchy on hers, like a scrubbing brush, and the breath of him was strong and sweet. Like cough mixture, she thought. Oh, he was the best of fathers, even though he *had* broken his sacred promise, for which she now totally forgave him, and God would too.

James put Breda down again, and bent so that Moira could kiss him also. She was getting too big, too much of a young lady, to be swung through the air. He hoped his little bright one would be a while yet before she grew up.

'Thank you, Dada,' Moira said. 'It is just right. It will be very useful.'

'Sure, you're very welcome,' James said.

Then he sat down, and stopped searching in his pockets, as if it was all over. Breda looked at him in dismay.

'Mammy!' she said. 'What about Mammy?'

'Oh!' he said, straight-faced. 'Was I supposed to bring something for Mammy? Oh, dear me!'

'You forgot!' Breda said in horror.

She turned to Molly.

'Then you can share my hair slide, Mammy,' she said. 'We can wear it in turn.'

'And you can look in my mirror any time you want to,' Moira offered.

'You are good girls, both of you,' Molly said, 'but I'm sure Dada is teasing us again.'

'Mammy knows I would never be forgetting her,' James said.

He fished inside his waistcoat pocket and brought out a small, dark blue, cardboard box, which he handed to Molly.

'It's a lovely box,' she said.

'Never mind the box. Open it up!' he ordered.

Inside, against dark blue velvet, lay a pair of earrings; tiny crosses, not more than half an inch long. Molly gasped.

'Oh! They're beautiful!'

'Nine carat gold,' James said proudly. 'You're to wear them all the time. You are not to keep them just for feast days. All the time, mind you!'

While Moira held up her mirror, Molly fixed the earrings. Hadn't she always wanted some just like this?

'But too fine for me!' she said.

'Nothing is too fine for you, sweetheart!' James said. 'So there you are! Everybody pleased! It was worth the money, all of which I spent, except for a few coppers to give to the boys. Oh, and a shilling left over, which is all yours, my Molly.'

With a flourish he handed her the coin. She struggled not to show her disappointment. Oh, the earrings were lovely, and wasn't it true that they were what she had always wanted, but she did so need the money. A shilling would go nowhere. Still and all, he meant to be generous. His heart was in the right place, even if his head was not. She had best go down to O'Reilly's now, not wait until tomorrow, but spend it before James asked to borrow it back to go out with his mates.

'And how is Mrs O'Reilly?' Molly asked.

'Not well. Not well at all. She is a sorely tried woman.'

He weighed out a pound of sugar (to the last grain, Molly thought) and tipped it into a blue bag. And wasn't he a sorely tried man, Luke O'Reilly asked himself? A man with a grocer's shop to run and a wife who was always ailing, so that he had everything to do, in the house as well as in the shop.

'I'm sorry to hear that,' Molly sympathized. 'And what would seem to be the present trouble?'

She said 'present trouble' because Mary O'Reilly seemed to have been poorly on and off ever since Luke had brought her back from Dublin as his bride, more than a dozen years ago. There were those who said serve him right for not choosing a woman from the county when there were plenty who would have been willing to step into a nice little business, and serve him well, and have his children, which Mary O'Reilly had failed to do. Also, she had Dublin ways, she set herself above the people of the west, she did not stand and chat to anyone after Mass. That last was true, though the bit about Dublin ways was usually said by those who had never been there, nor ever would.

'You may ask,' Luke O'Reilly said. 'But indeed 'twould be hard to tell you. Isn't Dr O'Halloran entirely mystified?'

And no wonder at that, for one time it was her head and another time her back, or her legs, and all the times in between those mysterious things which went on in women's bodies.

'Dear me!' Molly said. 'Well, give her my best wishes. And I'll take two ounces of tea, please.'

'Ceylon?'

She hesitated. It cost more, but it made a better cup, which was important if you were going to use it twice over.

'Yes,' she said. 'Ceylon it is.'

'Ah!' Luke O'Reilly said, 'You know what's best, Mrs O'Connor.'

'It's one thing knowing, another affording,' Molly observed. 'I hope Kieran is being a help to you?' She looked around the shop for a sight of her son.

'He's doing well enough,' the grocer said. 'Inexperienced, of course.'

'He'll learn quickly,' Molly said with confidence. 'He's a willing worker.'

'I'll give him that. He's out at the back, unpacking goods. Would you be wanting him, then?'

'Oh no!' Molly said quickly. 'I'll not take him from his work!' She would let Luke O'Reilly know that she would not be an interfering mother.

'Will there be anything else, then?'

'No. Nothing else.'

In fact, the shop was full of things with which she would like to have filled her basket: tinned peaches, chocolate biscuits, ox tongues, apricot jam. She averted her eyes from the well-filled shelves, picked up her purchases and left.

Luke O'Reilly, having no other customers to distract him, moved to the open doorway and watched her walk down the street, noting the free swing of her hips, her slender ankles, the way she held her head so upright on her shoulders, as if she *was* somebody. She was a fine woman, none finer in Kilbally. Why would a woman like her fall for a man like James O'Connor? She was wasted on him; he was not fit to tie her shoelaces.

It could have been different, he thought. Hadn't he had his eye on her when she was sixteen? He'd been thirty then, already the owner of his own shop. He'd waited until she should be a little older, not wishing to frighten her off, but he'd waited too long. While he was busy, occupied in building up his business, she'd met James O'Connor, and that had been that.

He watched until she was out of sight, then turned back to answer a petulant call from his wife, who now appeared in the doorway at the back, which led into the parlour.

'I'm parched!' she said. 'My head's throbbing and I shouldn't wonder if I have a fever. Wouldn't you be making a cup of tea?'

'Just coming!' Luke O'Reilly said. 'Just coming!'

Molly continued down the road. It was hot, the sun still high in the sky, but she liked it that way. She loved the long school holiday, the children all at home, under her feet. Except Kathleen, she thought bleakly. As well as shoes, she was trying to save enough money to travel to Dublin to visit Kathleen, even if she might only be allowed to see her for a short time.

44

A few weeks only and the others would all be back at school, Kieran cycling fifteen miles each day to school on a bicycle which was long past its best. He should be a boarder, but it couldn't be afforded. Secretly, though she knew it was selfish, she was glad.

She put on a spurt now, remembering that she had left the bread to prove and it would likely be brimming over the top of the bowl.

Only Breda was in the house.

'Where's Dada?' Molly asked.

'Gone down to the harbour,' Breda said. 'He has to arrange about a fishing trip, he said.'

'Is that it?' Molly said. She had not thought he would want to go fishing, not his first night home. Perhaps it would be tomorrow night. It wouldn't put much money in his pocket, but at least they'd get a change of diet.

'Can I help you to make the bread?' Breda asked.

'Of course!'

Between them they shaped the loaves. Molly cut the cross in the top of one, and allowed Breda to do the other.

'Why do you cut the cross?' Breda enquired.

'Why, to let out the Devil of course!' Molly answered.

Three

'Drat! It's doing it again!'

Molly slowed down the sewing machine to a stop, raised the foot, took out the garment she was making – a dress for Moira – and turned the material over to inspect the back of the seam. As she expected, instead of a straight, even stitch like that on the front, there was a row of twirls and curls of thread, rapidly getting tighter as the seam went on.

Kieran, sitting at the other side of the table, raised his head from his books and looked at her.

'I'm sorry,' Molly apologized. 'Take no notice – I didn't mean to disturb you. It's the tension gone again. I'll get it right, sure I will, but 'tis a nuisance. I'll have to unpick the whole seam and do it again.'

'Can I do anything?' Kieran asked.

'Not really. You'd be worse than I am!'

She spoke kindly. It was not a rebuke but he was the least mechanically minded person in the family, possibly in all Kilbally. And why not? Did he not have other gifts?

'I'll see to it,' she said. 'I'll be twiddling a few knobs, turning a few screws, and 'twill come right in the end. It usually does.'

Patrick and Colum were the ones she needed now. Either of them would know exactly what to do. Even James might. But at the moment all except herself and Kieran were out of the house; the twins and Moira at work, Breda gone with her father, who was helping Farmer O'Farrell with the hay.

What she *actually* needed was a new sewing machine. Her mother had given her this one, having decided, the minute the last of her family left home, that she had done all the sewing she ever intended to do, not to mention that she couldn't see very well.

'It's all yours, with my blessing,' she'd said as she'd bequeathed the machine to Molly, 'and if ever I need the odd seam stitching, sure, I know you'll do it for me!'

The blessing had worked more like a curse, Molly thought, unpicking the stitches. The plain truth was that the machine was so old, she wondered it didn't lie down and die. One day it surely would.

Kieran, absolved, returned to his books. He had left the Christian Brothers at the end of last term. They had been both sorry and pleased to see him go; sorry because he was well liked, pleased because of the life which lay in front of him. His own emotions had been much the same. In September he would go to the seminary in Dublin to start his long training for the priesthood, but in the meantime there was so much to do: books to read, notes to make, things to learn. He couldn't afford to waste any time, though in any case it absorbed him. He could think of nothing else he would rather be doing.

Wasn't it a miracle, Molly asked herself, that he could concentrate at all, what with the rattle and vibration of the sewing machine, with her own remarks when she forgot for a moment to be silent, and with people constantly passing to and fro in front of the window? They *had* to share the table; there was nowhere else where he could spread his books or she her sewing.

She tightened one more knob, checked that the shuttle wasn't all jammed up with thread, then set to work again.

After a few inches, she eased the material out and inspected the back of the seam. It was all right, thanks be to God! Was there a special saint for sewing machines? Saint Dorcas? She crossed herself quickly, reinserted the material, then began to turn the wheel with her right hand while skilfully guiding the material with her left.

For the next half-hour she machined away while Kieran read and wrote, both of them in silence. She was aware of a deep but simple happiness. She completed the side seams, the shoulders and the sleeve seams. She would wait until Moira came in from her work before setting in the sleeves, so that she could pin it up on her. It was a tricky bit of the operation; she hadn't much confidence and Moira was so fussy.

'There!' she said, breaking the silence 'That's as far as I can go! Will I make a cup of tea, then?'

' 'Twould be very welcome,' Kieran said. 'Have you much more to do?'

'On Moira's dress, not a lot. But then don't I have to start on Breda's? 'Tis a great pity there was nothing in Aunt Cassie's last parcel suitable for the occasion.'

They were going to Dublin, going to visit Kathleen for the first time; she and Kieran, Moira and Breda. Since there wasn't enough money for all of them to go it was just as well that Patrick and Colum couldn't get time off their work, and James said he'd have to be at home to look after them. That last fact did not ring true. They were old enough to be left, but James said there was no telling what they'd get up to, and who would there be to stop them?

He didn't have to spell it out. She could sense that James didn't want to go. It wasn't that he didn't want to see Kathleen, though there had always been a little distance between them. His relationship with each of his children was different. Molly knew, without anything being said,

48

that he didn't fancy too much time spent in the convent. He did his religious duty, went to Mass, but he shied away from anything too holy. Molly let it lie. In any case, there just wasn't enough money.

'Are you having a new outfit for yourself, Mammy?' Kieran asked.

'Indeed I am!'

She stirred the low fire under the big black kettle which hung there, ready filled, most of the day. It would take but a minute to come to the boil.

'A new dress, at least,' she said. 'I have my eye on the material at Kitty Shelley's. She's promised to put a length by.'

She had been saving for at least three years for this event, a penny here, threepence there; whatever and whenever she could, not always telling James. From time to time there had been extra work at the Big House, especially in the summer and at Christmas when the family came, and she had taken every scrap of extra work she could get. Then, of course, for almost a year now, Patrick and Colum had been in jobs, and though the money was small, and hardly kept them in food and clothes, it all helped.

The twins, leaving the National School, had gone on to the technical school at Molly's insistence. She wanted them to get on in the world. So far, the opportunities in Kilbally being what they were, they had not gone far, and it seemed uncertain that they ever would.

Patrick had taken the job which she had hoped Kieran might have had. Indeed, after two years of holiday work Luke O'Reilly had offered it to Kieran.

'You'd do well,' Luke said. 'I'd teach you all I know.'

But Kieran had politely refused. He could not be deflected. It had been Molly herself who had asked Luke O'Reilly to take on one of the twins.

49

'Either of them would serve you well,' she said. 'I'd see to that.'

She would too, Luke thought. She was a woman who had her family well in hand. She was also exceedingly pretty, more so in his eyes than any of her daughters.

'Well, I suppose I could give one of them a try. Is it to be Patrick or Colum?' he'd said. 'Who would be best?'

'That's for you to choose,' Molly said. 'And I'm very grateful to you! I'll send them both along tomorrow.'

What a pity, she thought, that his business wasn't big enough to take on both of them. She knew they would hate to be separated, but there was no help for it. There wasn't a concern anywhere which would hire the two at once.

Luke O'Reilly, after an interview in which he found it impossible to make a choice, left it to them.

'One of you turn up at eight o'clock sharp on Monday morning,' he said. 'I'll give whoever it is a month's trial.'

He wondered if he would be able to tell which one it was. They were like two peas in a pod.

In the end, back at home, neither of them enamoured by the thought of the job but knowing it was needed, they tossed a coin, heads to take it, tails to look elsewhere. It fell to Patrick.

'And what will you do?' Molly asked Colum.

He shrugged. 'Whatever I can!'

In the end he got a job with Eddie Murphy, blacksmith-cum-garage-owner. In the last few years Eddie had diversified into car repairs and the sale of petrol. Horses didn't attract Colum, but the prospect of messing about with cars appealed to him. One day, he was sure, he would have a car of his own.

'You do realize, don't you,' Kieran warned his younger brother, 'that there are going to be precious few cars around? You'll be back to nothing but horses in no time at all.'

He had been proved right. The war in Europe – which in neutral Ireland was known as 'the Emergency' – had brought rationing, and not only of foodstuffs. There was almost no petrol, and by the time Colum had been in his job a few months most cars were off the road, on blocks in barns and sheds for the duration.

What worried Molly about the twins was that one or other of them would get fed up and bored with his job and would be tempted to cross the water and join the British army. If either of them did this, the other would follow as night follows day. They would never let themselves be split between two countries.

Colum would be the one to start it, she thought. His job was marginally less to his liking than Patrick's to his. There were fewer people in and out of Murphy's all day long.

'In any case, it's my opinion he's afraid of horses!' James said when Molly confided her fears to him. 'I reckon they both are.'

He was good-naturedly contemptuous of this fear in them. It made for a distance between him and the twins. Horses were part of his life, together with fishing, shooting when he could get it and, truth to tell, a bit of poaching on the side. And, of course, a pint or two of Guinness whenever he could afford it. It was something the two didn't appreciate. They were a bit young, but hadn't he, at their age, already had the taste?

The only sport in which they would ever join him was the sea-fishing, though not because it was sport to them, but to make up a crew and earn a shilling or two. But James, even if he could not have made any money from it, would have done it for love. There was nothing he enjoyed more than a night's fishing, no matter what the weather or the state of the sea. He was good at it too, worth his weight in any crew. His own father had taken him out fishing when he'd been a small boy, born and bred in Galway.

Right up to the time he'd left home to marry he had felt that Galway Bay was his. It would always come first with him, though the coast here, with its rocks and its great cliffs, was not to be despised. Far from it. The sea here was changeable, unpredictable, to be treated with respect.

'We can't all be alike,' Molly defended the twins. 'They're good lads, all the same.'

'Did I ever say they were not?' James answered.

'Too good for the Army,' she said.

'Sure, there is nothing that's wrong with the Army,' James said. ' 'Tis a man's life.'

'And there speaks a man!' Molly retorted. 'Would you ever be hearing a woman talk so?'

'Here is your tea, then,' Molly said now to Kieran. 'And a scone with it.' She cleared a space beside his books. 'I shall buy you a new white shirt to go to Dublin, and a tie if it will run to it. I dare say I could make a tie if I found the right material. It can't be too difficult.'

Kieran bit into the thick, fluffy scone. No-one made them like Mammy.

'There is no need for new clothes for me,' he said through a mouthful.

'There is so!' Molly was firm about it. 'We have to be a credit to Kathleen. Isn't it a new suit I'd be buying you as well, if I could afford it?'

'Can I have another scone?' Kieran asked. 'Will you send me a tin of them when I'm in the seminary. And your soda bread?'

She turned away quickly, made heavy weather of splitting another scone and buttering it, not wanting him to see her face. She wished he hadn't spoken so. She wanted, for the

52

few weeks left, to pretend that he wasn't going. There was so little time, she couldn't do enough for him. It was her way of getting through it, of stifling her resentment at the feeling that he was being taken from her. Her feelings had been bitter, so much so that they had troubled her, and she had taken them to Father Curran.

'You have it the wrong way round, my child,' he'd said. 'He's not being taken. You have given him. You have given him to God!'

'Does it count as that,' Molly asked, 'if I don't want to give him? If I do it all unwillingly? And I would stop him if I could?'

'It counts even more, child,' Father Curran said. 'It counts double. God sees your sacrifice. You will be blessed.'

She had yet to feel that, she thought, handing Kieran the second scone.

'I will send you whatever I'm allowed to,' she told him. 'You know that. But I daresay you'll be amply fed there. And now I must clear my things away, and so must you before long. They'll all be in for tea.'

So, she would put everything except the present moment out of her mind.

While he drank his tea and ate his scones, Kieran watched his mother. She was forty years old, he knew that, and it was middle-aged, but she looked exactly the same to him as she always had.

Her hair, thick, straight, as black as night and with no hint of grey, swung in her face as she bent over the table. She raised an arm to put it back and anchor it behind her ear. The flesh of her arm was firm and creamy, her face glowed with health, the skin tight over cheekbones and jaw. Only a fine line or two at the corners of her mouth, and smudgy shadows beneath her clear eyes, hinted that she was no longer a girl. Otherwise, and in every way that mattered, she was ageless.

He wanted to stretch out and stroke her face with his finger, as he might have done when he was a small boy; but now he was too old.

He knew she hated the thought of his leaving. So often he watched her trying – and failing – to hide her feelings about it. But did she know that, though he was set on what he was doing, with part of him he hated the thought of leaving her? He would not say so; it would make matters worse.

Molly, had she known, could have told him he was wrong about that, that such an admission would give her comfort.

He took refuge now in talking of everyday matters. She was folding Moira's half-completed dress, looking critically at it.

'The colour will suit Moira,' Kieran said.

'I hope so,' Molly said. 'I'm doubtful that bright red is the right colour for a visit to a convent, but you know Moira! 'Twould break her heart, she declared, if she had to choose differently.' She had given in over the colour – she knew that Moira would look good in it – but she intended to be quite firm about the neckline.

'And yours and Breda's?' Kieran enquired.

'Light blue for Breda,' Molly said. 'Blue is good with red hair, much more subtle than green – though if I manage to buy the material, I shall have green. It has a small, white spot in it. Very smart!'

She put away her sewing in the sideboard cupboard.

'I'll move the sewing machine,' Kieran said. He picked it up as if it weighed no more than two ounces and carried it to its shelf in the corner.

'You'll have to put your books away before long,' Molly repeated. 'They'll be home soon.'

Moira was home first. She usually was, never working a minute longer than she had to. For Moira, life started when the day's work was over and she was free, though never free enough. She longed for the day she would be free to leave Kilbally, which was the most boring place on earth. Failing that, and until that day arrived, she longed for the chance to get away just for the evenings. She had several friends of both sexes. If her parents – well, it was her mother really – were not so strict, so stick-in-the-mud, she could go with her friends to Ennis. There was dancing in Ennis; dancing and singing, and far more exciting people.

'Hello there!' Molly said. 'Is it a good day you've had, then?' She spoke cheerfully, trying to set the mood.

Moira flung herself down in the armchair. 'Would you call washing people's dirty hair, sweeping the floor, cleaning the basins, a good day?'

At fourteen, there had seemed no point whatever in Moira going on to the technical school. She wasn't interested in anything school had to offer, and when she wasn't interested she wouldn't work, not at lessons, not at anything. Molly didn't want any of her children to stop learning at fourteen. She did her best to persuade Moira otherwise, but James thought that that was a waste of time.

' 'Tis certain sure that not another thing is going to go into her head at school,' he said. 'Won't that one do most of her learning out in the world?'

He grinned at Moira when he said it. It was his own philosophy. And anyway you only had to look at her to know that she'd be married before you could turn round. If there was to be a couple of years when she could earn a few shillings before that happened, then why not?

Moira had smiled back at him. He was on her side, so he was. Inwardly she asked herself how anyone could describe

Kilbally as being 'out in the world'? Outside the world, more like. But she was glad to be leaving the National School and she hated the thought of technical school. 'I'd rather sweep floors than go there!' she said passionately.

In fact, when the chance of working in Glenda's Hairdressing Salon came up it had not sounded so bad though, as Miss Glenda said, she could not expect to be earning more than pocket money because wasn't she being taught a trade? Moira had seen herself creating wonderful hair styles, far too good for Kilbally, as the first step to being sought out and whisked away to a career as a top hairdresser in Dublin. She had not expected to be cleaning floors, sweeping up the clippings every time a customer had a cut. She had tried, when she thought Miss Glenda was too busy to notice, letting the hair lie where it fell. It didn't work. The door would open, a gust of wind would enter and the hair would blow all over the place, including in her mouth and up her nose.

' 'Tis all part of the learning,' Molly said. 'Everyone has to start at the bottom!'

'Why?' Moira demanded. 'Why do I have to sweep floors and clean basins? 'Tis not something I'll ever do once I've got away from it.'

'Will I wet the tea again?' Molly said soothingly. The child did look tired. Hadn't she been on her feet all day? ' 'Twill take a drop more water. Take off your shoes in the meanwhile.'

She gave Moira a cup of tea and a scone.

'And now I'll have to get on with the meal,' she said. 'It will never do not to have it ready when Dada comes in. I'm all behind because I've been sewing your dress.'

Moira's face showed a flicker of interest. 'Is it finished, then?'

'Not quite,' Molly admitted. 'Not a lot to do, though.'

'Where is it? Can I see it?'

'No,' Molly said firmly. 'When the meal's over and we've cleared away, I'll fit it on you.'

'But I want to go out this evening!' Moira protested.

'Take your choice,' Molly said. 'Have your dress fitted or go out. Either way I'm starting on Breda's tomorrow. Where are you going, anyway? Who with?'

She was aware that at fifteen years old Moira couldn't be kept on a leash. Would it were so! She didn't feel safe with her gone so much as beyond the end of the road.

'For a walk,' Moira said briefly.

'I asked who with.'

'Friends. I don't know, do I? It depends who turns up.'

The argument was interrupted by Patrick and Colum who came in at the door like a tidal wave. They were so big, so full of life. How is it that my sons are huge and my daughters small, Molly wondered.

The twins, though they worked in different places, left home at the same time and somehow always managed to arrive home together.

'Tea not ready?' Colum demanded. 'I'm starving!'

' 'Twill not be more than a few minutes,' Molly said. 'Moira, lay the table.'

'Why me?' Moira complained. 'Haven't I been working all day?'

'That's true,' Molly said. 'And if Breda was here I'd be asking her, but since they're haymaking she and Dada might be a bit late. Would you all want to be waiting for your tea until they came home?'

'No!' Patrick and Colum chorused.

'Then why shouldn't *they* lay the table?' Moira demanded.

She had a point, Molly thought, though not a very good one. There were things women and girls did, other things men and boys did.

57

'Because that's the way it is,' she answered. 'Do I ever ask you girls to bring in the water, or mend a chair or put up a shelf? No, I do not! So get on with it. What sort of a wife will you make if you're not willing to lay a table?'

The meal itself would take no time at all to make. It was, as always, fresh soda bread with jam, except that today, as a treat, there were eggs; only four amongst seven of them, but she would scramble them, adding a drop of milk to make them go further. Earlier in the year, in the spring when the hens were laying prolifically, there was nothing she liked better than to serve every one of her family with a new-laid egg, boiled to perfection, with two for James, of course. But the hens were not laying so well now.

The difficulty was in dividing seven into four with people coming in at different times. In the end she decided on two for the four children already present and the other two between James, Breda and herself. She would wait until they came in. That way James would have almost a whole egg to himself. Haymaking was hard work.

'Mr O'Reilly sent you this,' Patrick said.

It was a small sample packet of assorted biscuits.

'The traveller left a few for Mr O'Reilly to give to his best customers,' Patrick said. 'This is the only one I've seen him give out.'

'You couldn't call *me* a best customer,' Molly said. 'Though I'd like to be.'

Patrick laughed.

'I think he's sweet on you, Mammy!'

'Then it is not reciprocated,' Molly said. 'Though you must never tell him so. He's nice enough, poor man, and I'm sorry for him with that wife of his. Just tell him thank you kindly.'

She vaguely wondered if Patrick could be right. Luke O'Reilly frequently sent her small things from the shop, though usually samples which he himself had been given. Well, he was on the road to nowhere there. Why would anyone with a man like James O'Connor coming home to her give a sideways glance at anyone else, even if it was not a sin in a married woman, which it was, though not one *she'd* be likely to have to go to Confession for.

The smell of the scrambled eggs was tantalizing in her nostrils. She could have sat down there and then and eaten the lot. She hoped Breda and James wouldn't be too long.

She had hardly finished serving when Breda came in, on her own. 'Dada said we were not to wait for him because he will go to the Golden Harp with the others. Didn't he have a terrible thirst on him, he said. I would have liked a dandelion and burdock but he said I was too young to go into such a place.'

'Indeed you are!' Molly said. 'I'd be very cross if that were to happen. Did he say how long he would be?'

'No, Mammy.'

He wouldn't. There was no telling, especially as he would have some money on him, for Farmer O'Farrell paid his casual men daily. He might be home in an hour or it might be bedtime before he rolled in.

'Oh well!' she said. 'I'll scramble the one egg for you and me right away. Are you hungry?'

'Starving!' Breda said. 'Though Mrs O'Farrell gave us some tea and bread earlier on.'

'As soon as I've finished I'll start again on your dress,' Molly said to Moira.

For modesty's sake, since the boys were around, Molly and Moira went to the bedroom to fit the dress. Molly slipped it over her daughter's head and stepped back to judge the result. Not bad, she thought. Not bad at all. Now for fitting the sleeves.

'The neck's wrong!' Moira said.

'Wrong?'

'Oh, Mammy, it's not at all what I wanted! Did I not say I wanted a sweetheart neckline? You'll have to cut it lower.'

'I will do no such thing!' Molly said. 'Stand still, and hold out your arm while I fit the sleeve.'

'But Mammy, I can't possibly have this high, round neck!' Moira wailed. 'It's childish.'

'You *are* a child.' Molly spoke through a mouthful of pins. She had known what would happen. She was well aware of Moira's wishes.

'I am not! I am fifteen!' Moira cried. 'I want a sweetheart neckline!'

'So you are fifteen,' Molly said. And well developed, she thought, with a high, round bust, not at all the figure for a low neck. 'It is not grown-up, and you will not have a low neck! Do you want to make an exhibition of yourself?'

She probably did. Her pretty daughter liked to be noticed. What she didn't realize was that it didn't need low necks for her beauty to be appreciated. To display herself in the way she desired was to invite the wrong kind of attention. Moira had to be protected from herself.

'I don't care if I do!' Moira said.

'Well I do,' Molly said. 'And do you want to embarrass Kathleen in front of the sisters? You will have a round neckline, not too high, not too low, with a white collar which will look good against the red.'

It would also show off Moira's elegant neck, Molly thought, but there was no need to say so. Wasn't the child vain enough already? She fervently hoped she would have none of this trouble over Breda's dress. She hated dressmaking, it was the least of her womanly skills. Only

60

the lack of money prevented her going into Ennis and buying ready-made dresses for the three of them.

In the end, Moira was called for by her best-friend-of-the-moment, Brigid Duffy. The twins had already set out on their own pursuits.

Molly was uneasy about Moira's choice of friend. She reckoned that Brigid was fast, a bit wild; not the sort of companion for Moira, who needed a restraining hand rather than encouragement. But you couldn't blame Brigid, she reasoned. The Duffys were not up to much all round: friendly and cheerful, but slatternly, not over-scrupulous, and frequently in trouble with the Garda.

'Don't be late back,' she cautioned Moira. 'Not a minute after half-past nine!'

'Oh, Mammy, that's too early!' Moira protested. 'It's a summer's evening. It doesn't get dark for ages. Brigid never has to be in by any special time.'

I can well believe that, Molly thought.

'You just don't trust me,' Moira grumbled. 'You've forgotten what it's like to be young!'

It was the sad truth, Molly admitted to herself, that, at bottom, she never quite trusted Moira. It was an awful thing to think about your own flesh and blood.

'Quarter to ten, then,' she said. 'And if you are a minute later you'll not go out for the rest of the week!'

She had not, however, forgotten what it was like to be Moira's age. She remembered it all, though it did seem a long time ago. And had she ever, at fifteen, envisaged how it would all turn out? In fact, she thought, she had always accepted that either she would marry an Irishman and raise a family or, if no man asked for her, she would emigrate, make her way in the world.

But wasn't raising a family the highest calling a woman could have? Didn't Father Curran preach it all the time?

Didn't he say that mothers were raised high, were precious in God's eyes, and that in heaven a special place would be reserved for them?

She hoped he was right. It didn't always feel like that.

'Will you start my dress tonight?' Breda asked when Moira had flounced out.

'Not tonight. I don't want to clutter up the place when Dada's coming for his supper.'

'Why don't you like sewing, Mammy?' Breda enquired.

'I don't know. I never have, nor my mother before me. There'll be no sewing in heaven for me!'

'What will there be?' Breda was curious. It was the kind of conversation she loved, and Mammy never dodged it.

'We don't know, do we? But in *my* heaven there'll be running water, hot and cold, scented soap, and bathrooms like they have at the Big House, only warmer.'

'What else?'

'Well, let me see now! Sure, there'd be plenty of food, all kinds, but not too many potatoes. And someone else would have cooked it, which is why I don't care what kind of ovens they have. Of course, just now and then I might feel like making a batch of soda bread. And as for clothes, they'd all be off-the-peg, perfectly fitting, and in beautiful colours!

'I'm afraid it's very domestic, my heaven!' She glanced across at Kieran as she apologized, but his head was in a book, he hadn't heard her.

'So what about you?' she asked Breda.

'It would be like Kilbally,' Breda answered. 'With the beach and the sea and the cliffs. And I'd have a dog. And nobody would have to cross the water if they didn't want to, just to earn money. We'd all be together. And there'd be free sweets: toffees, chocolate, fudge. You could eat as

62

much as you liked without feeling sick, and not a penny to pay. Can I stay up until Dada comes in?'

'Not unless he's home before nine,' Molly said. 'That's your latest. You're a growing girl.'

She doubted now that he would be home before then, and it turned out she was right. All the family, except herself, were in bed before James came home, Moira sneaking in at ten o'clock, charging through the living room and into the bedroom, eyes down, looking neither to right nor to left.

James was not quite precise in his movements or in his speech. He had clearly had a lot, but he couldn't quite be called drunk. But in any case, Molly thought, even when he *was* drunk he was never loud-mouthed or violent. On the contrary, he was mellow and amorous, as he proved now, taking her in his arms, holding her close, kissing her with passion.

She succumbed to his embrace with pleasure, while at the back of her mind wondering how much of the day's earnings had gone to the landlord of the Harp.

'I'm as hungry as a hunter,' James said, releasing her. 'And Farmer O'Farrell gave me some rashers. I could eat a couple.'

'I'll put them on,' Moira said. 'And I saved you an egg, which will go nicely with them.'

Four

It seemed to Breda that the trip to Dublin would never happen, so long was the waiting. In reality it was little more than a week from the time her dress had been completed – as it happened, to her utter delight – but each day seemed at least the length of two. In the evenings she went to bed early, hoping that the night hours would pass more quickly than those of the day, but it didn't work. The August evenings were bright, the sun still in the sky, so that she couldn't get to sleep.

She was still awake this evening when Moira came to bed – indeed she usually was – and she couldn't refrain from starting a conversation with her sister.

'What will it be like?' she asked.

'You've asked me a hundred times!' Moira protested. 'I've told you, I *don't know*! At least it'll be better than Kilbally.' She spoke with deep disgust.

'I *like* Kilbally,' Breda said. 'But Dublin will be different, won't it?'

'How am I supposed to know?' Moira asked impatiently. 'I've never been, any more than you have. None of us have been except Kathleen, and she never writes a word about the city.'

She was peering into her hand-mirror, a worried frown on her face. She had a spot just starting, bang in the middle of her chin, and she could tell by the look of it that it was going to get worse before it got better. As she stroked it it felt like a large, round hillock under her finger. Should she squeeze it, she wondered anxiously? Or perhaps bathe it with hot water? How could she face Dublin with an angry spot on her chin? All those people looking at her. It was too humiliating for words.

'I don't suppose Kathleen sees the city,' Breda said.

In her mind she saw Kathleen shut away behind the high walls of a fortress, rather like the convent along the coast from Kilbally, which looked, with its towers and its windows set high from the ground, like her idea of a prison.

'What's the point of being in Dublin if you never see it?' Moira said. 'You could be anywhere!'

'I wish we were going tomorrow,' Breda said. 'I wish when we woke in the morning we could just set off!'

She turned over and buried her face in the pillow, trying to summon sleep.

'I don't!' Moira said. She sighed, and put down the mirror. The three days which lay between them and the start of their journey were not enough for the spot to come to fruition, then fade and die. It was too much to hope for.

'I'll pray for your spot.'

Breda's voice came muffled but kindly from her pillow. A minute later she was asleep. When the twins came to bed a little later she didn't hear them.

Now that the children were getting older, the boys close to manhood, Molly had fixed a curtain across the room to divide it. The girls were in the farthest end so that the boys, coming to bed later, didn't have to walk through their area. In many families, when the children reached their teens, the mother would share the girls' room and the father the boys', but James would have none of that.

'You're my wife,' he said to Molly. 'We share the same bed. Isn't that what marriage is about?'

Molly was happy to agree with him.

But the day came at last, and with it, almost unbelievably, the disappearance of Moira's spot.

'Just look, Mammy,' she cried, rushing into the living room. 'It's gone! It's magic!'

'It is not magic,' Breda contradicted. ' 'Tis a miracle, no less! Didn't I say I would pray – and so I did!'

But she was awestruck herself. Did this mean that she could actually work miracles – with God's help, of course. Might she become quite famous?

' 'Twill be a miracle if we catch the train,' Molly said. 'Get your breakfast both of you. Kieran finished his ages ago.'

The twins had already left for work and James, who had been out all night with the fishing boats, had not yet returned. Molly hoped he would do so before they left. She always wanted to see him back safe and sound after a night's fishing, though there was no real worry on this occasion. Wasn't the sea as smooth as glass?

'I don't want any breakfast,' Breda said. 'I couldn't eat a bite.'

'Then you'll not be going to Dublin,' Molly threatened. 'Not without good food inside you. And that goes for you, Moira!'

'I'm quite hungry,' Moira said. 'I don't know why Breda's fussing so.'

Spotless of face, she could now afford to be calm. It was childish to show too much enthusiasm.

When they were ready to go Molly lined them up at the door for inspection. Yes, she thought, I can be quite proud of them. They are a credit to me. The girls' dresses, and her own, had turned out well, and she had

66

managed to buy new cotton gloves. Kieran's shirt was immaculate, as dazzling white as driven snow, and he had, after all, a nice shop-bought tie, navy with red stripes.

'You'll do,' she said. 'It's a pity Dada isn't here to see you all looking decent.'

But as they left the house, carrying the bags which contained their night things and cardigans in case it should turn cold, as well as a new loaf of soda bread baked that morning and a tin of scones, gifts for Kathleen, James was walking towards them up the street.

'Well, well!' he said, feigning surprise. 'And where might you lot be going, all dressed up to kill?'

'Oh Dada, you *know* where we're going!' Breda said. 'We're going to Dublin! You're teasing us.'

'Dublin, is it? Well then, in that case I'll turn right around and walk to the station with you, make sure you get on the right train.'

'There's only the one train we *can* get on,' Molly said. 'But we'll be glad of your company. 'Tis a pity you're not going the whole way with us.'

James spun around, took Molly's holdall from her, and started to walk with them.

'We can't all go gallivanting off when the mood takes us,' he said. 'Some of us have to stay and look after things. I suppose I'll just have to manage.'

'I've left plenty of food, as you well know, James O'Connor,' Molly retorted. 'All you have to do is heat it up.'

'Sure, it wasn't only the food I was thinking of.' He winked at her, and she blushed.

'We'll be back tomorrow night,' she reminded him. 'Will I give Kathleen your love?'

'Of course.'

In spite of Molly's fears, they were in plenty of time for the train, which was a local one. Further down the line they would have to change on to the Dublin line.

'Quick, children!' Molly said. 'Get in! This compartment will do.'

'There's no hurry at all, at all,' James said. 'They've got stuff to unload and things to take on. Will you look around, you're the only one in a rush!'

It was true. The engine driver had jumped down and was having a smoke. The platform was strewn with things waiting to be loaded while a porter, and they all knew him to be Terry Fenton, was leisurely offloading some of the contents of the guard's van. Boxes, hens in crates, a mewing cat in a basket, several wooden boxes labelled for Luke O'Reilly's shop, followed by a roll of linoleum, a tin trunk, a sack of letters and various parcels all had to be lifted onto the platform before Terry Fenton could think of dealing with the items waiting to go on.

'This is awful,' Moira complained. 'How much longer must we wait?'

They were seated in the compartment now, James standing by the open door.

'What's the rush?' he said. 'Dublin won't go away before you get there. Anyway, Kilbally's only one station. You'll go through all this at the other stations.'

'Dada knows,' Breda said. 'Didn't he once go to Dublin?'

'And right now,' he said, 'I'm going home to get some sleep. Mind you look after Mammy and the girls, Kieran.'

'Sure I will,' Kieran promised.

It was true what James had said. At almost every station they had the same delays, but it didn't seem to matter now. They were on their way and everything was part of the excitement. Breda, from her seat by the window, and sitting opposite to her mother, watched the landscape change from the cliffs and dramatic coastline of Kilbally to the low-lying plain of the middle of Ireland, with its emerald green grassland, its horses, its lakes and, in parts, its acres and acres of dark brown peatland.

'When I was at school,' Molly said, 'wasn't I taught that Ireland was shaped like a saucer, high around the outside and low and flat in the centre, and because of that, wet in the middle? That's why it's so green.'

'Oh, they still teach that stuff!' Moira said.

The first thing they did on leaving the train in Dublin was to look carefully around the station in the hope of seeing Kathleen. It would be so much easier to find the convent if she was there to guide them. It was a forlorn hope; she had told them that more than likely she wouldn't be able to come, and certainly there was no sign of her.

'Oh dear!' Molly said. 'I did so hope—'

'It's all right, Mammy,' Kieran broke in. 'She sent us the map, and clear instructions. I'll have no difficulty in finding the way.'

'Well, I'm glad you're with us, Kieran,' Molly said. 'I can't follow maps. I'd be lost in no time at all.' She took hold tightly of Breda and Moira on either hand and prepared to follow him.

What struck them with force when they emerged from the station onto the street was the vast number of people on the pavement and the amount of traffic on the wide road; buses, trucks, horse-drawn vehicles, cars, though anyone who knew Dublin would have vouched for it that there weren't as many cars these days. Petrol rationing had seen to that. Everything and everybody moved faster than they had ever before seen anything move. They stood there, gazing around them in bewilderment.

'It's far worse than Ennis on market day!' Molly said.

'Oh Mammy, of *course* it is!' Moira said impatiently. 'This is Dublin, not the back of beyond.'

'I'll thank you not to call Ennis the back of beyond,' Molly said.

Kieran was studying the map, and Kathleen's instructions.

'She says we're to start by crossing the road,' he said. 'And then we make for the river.'

'Cross the road!' Molly was horrified. 'However will we do that? Just look at the traffic!'

'We'll do it all right,' Kieran assured her. 'If 'twill make you feel better we'll cross with a crowd of other people.'

'Well, hold on to me tight, girls,' Molly said nervously. 'Don't let go of my hands whatever you do!'

Since the convent was no more than a mile and a half from the station, Kathleen had suggested they should walk rather than take a bus.

'If Kieran knows where we're going I'd much rather walk,' Breda said. 'We might not know where to get off the bus.'

'Of course I know!' Kieran assured her. 'Here, you take my hand and you and I will walk in front, so. Mammy and Moira can stay close behind us.' He shortened his long stride to fit in with her small one.

Kathleen's instructions couldn't have been more clear, he thought. Really, he had no need of the map. He was slightly disappointed at this; he'd looked forward to working it out, facing the challenge of the city. They walked east until they came to a bridge over the Liffey.

'This is where we cross over,' he said.

In the middle of the bridge they stopped, and stood looking at the river, turning from one side of the bridge to the other to see it in both directions.

It was wide, black, murky, with seemingly little flow to it; not nearly as good as the sparkling rivers of their own

70

county and not at all to be compared with the beautiful Shannon.

'But at least we've seen it,' Molly said. 'When we read about the Liffey, we can remember we've seen it.'

They crossed to the north side of the city, where the convent was situated.

Breda, clutching her brother's hand, walked the streets with her head permanently tilted back. So many buildings, all of them so high, and of pale stone with fancy doorways and huge windows. 'Mammy, look at the windows!' she called out. 'They're so big!'

'Don't I know it,' Molly said enviously. 'Aren't I thinking how light it will be inside those rooms!'

They were at the convent almost before they knew it. A plate on the big gate – 'Convent of Our Lady of Lourdes' – confirmed it.

'There you are!' Kieran said. 'I told you I wouldn't lose you!'

Kieran tugged on the bell at the gate. It was quickly answered by a young nun who led them across the flagged forecourt and into the house.

'Sister Teresa is expecting you,' she told them. 'I'll let her know you've arrived.'

They waited in the wide, handsome hall, with its wood-panelled walls.

'And will you look at that cciling, Mammy?' Breda whispered. It was not a place where you raised your voice.

They were all four of them craning their necks to admire it, so high, so elaborately scrolled and moulded, that they didn't hear the nun's soft tread as she came back to them.

'And is it not beautiful?' she said. 'Sister Teresa will see you now.'

Sister Teresa came forward from behind her desk to greet them. She would have seemed imposing in any garb, but her long, grey habit, tied around her ample waist with the Francisan cord, the black veil and high, white collar (like a baby's bib at the front, Breda thought), all added to what would have been an awesome severity had it not been for her ruddy cheeks, like polished apples, her blue eyes glinting behind round, steel-framed spectacles, and the welcoming smile on her face.

'Reverend Mother is sorry she can't greet you herself,' she said. 'She's busy with the Bishop. Catherine will be with us in a few minutes. 'Twill be herself who will show you to your rooms.'

'Catherine?' Molly said.

'Your daughter. We call her Catherine. Did she not tell you in her letters?'

'No,' Molly said. 'How is she? Is she . . . satisfactory? Doing well?'

'Oh yes!' Sister Teresa assured her. 'Isn't it early days and she has a long way to go, but she'll be all right. God has blessed her. She has a true vocation, which we must nurture.'

A quiet knock interrupted her.

'Come in!' she called.

Kathleen – I can't think of her as Catherine, Molly told herself – stood before them. Her simple habit was less voluminous than Sister Teresa's and her white veil hid every vestige of her beautiful hair, but otherwise she was the same Kathleen, with the same pert face, the same merry eyes, so exactly like her father's. I haven't lost her, Molly thought. Isn't she still our Kathleen?

'Take your family to the guest house,' Sister Teresa said. 'When they're settled in, say in half an hour's time, you can take them to tea. You must return after that, but Reverend Mother has said 'twill be all right for you to spend most of the day tomorrow with your family.'

Their rooms in the guest house were plainly furnished, but comfortable. Kieran was delighted to have a room to himself. It would be the first time since they were very small that he had not had to share a bed with his brothers.

In the short time before tea Kathleen showed them the garden. With its high walls, its lawn, its riot of summer flowers, it was an oasis in the city.

'There's one thing I'm after knowing,' Molly said as she walked with Kathleen. 'Are you happy? Are you truly happy?'

Did she ever need to ask, she wondered. Wasn't it all there in her daughter's face, in her eyes, in the set of her mouth. But she needed to hear it spoken.

'Oh Mammy, of course I'm happy! I was never so happy in my life! Oh, I miss you, I miss you all, but I think about you and pray for you often.'

'That's all right then. You seem to have made the right choice.'

But there was a long way to go yet, a lifetime ahead of her daughter.

'Do not forget, 'tis not too late to change your mind,' she added.

'I know that,' Kathleen said. 'But I won't.'

The next day, after early Mass, and breakfast, they all set out with Kathleen to explore the city: its squares, its gardens, churches, buildings; its rivers, its shops. It was the buildings, the magnificence the like of which she had never seen and could not have imagined, which impressed Breda most. They were so high, so big, with carvings and pillars and statues everywhere.

'Even the post office is fit to be a palace,' she said.

Kathleen had taken them to the post office in O'Connell Street because Molly had bought a picture postcard which she must send to her mother.

73

'Why are you sending a card when we'll be home tomorrow and you'll see her?'

'Because it will please your grandmother,' Molly said. 'I shall send love from all of us.'

It was the shops which interested Moira most of all. She could have spent a week just gazing in the windows, and so, for that matter, could Molly. It was Kathleen who reminded them that there wasn't the time.

'There's so much still to see,' she said.

They ate the sandwiches with which the convent had provided them in a park, and drank from a water fountain, then all too soon, it was time to return to the convent, to pick up their bags and make their farewells.

'And are you happy about your daughter, Mrs O'Connor?' Sister Teresa asked.

'I am so,' Molly answered. Happier, she thought, but would she ever be reconciled? If she were a good Catholic she would be. Perhaps in time it might happen.

'You can come again,' Sister Teresa reminded her.

Did she have any idea, Molly wondered, the difficulty she'd had to afford this trip? But of course she would do it again, somehow, sometime.

'And what about you, child?' Sister asked Moira, with a smile. 'Will you not follow in your sister's footsteps, in the footsteps of our Lord?'

Moira said nothing. She could think of few things she would like to do less than live here forever.

Molly was amused by the look on Moira's face. There, at any rate, was one child she'd never have to give up to the Church!

All the same, Moira was thinking, one day, and that day not too far ahead, she *would* be back in Dublin. She was determined on it. It was her belief that you could get most things if you wanted them hard enough.

In the train on the way home, they were most of the time silent, partly because they were tired, but also because they were absorbed in their own thoughts.

Kieran was happy that he had seen Kathleen's contentment in her new life. They had not talked much, but what they had said to each other, and even more the sight of her, had strengthened him in his own vocation. He looked forward more than ever now to starting his training. Less than four weeks to go.

Moira was engrossed in planning how she would get back to Dublin, how soon. Would she get a job? What sort of job? Could she serve in a shop? Or a café? She didn't mind what it was, just as long as she could earn enough money to live there. But how would she find out these things?

Molly leaned her head back and closed her eyes. She was glad to have seen Kathleen. She'd been pleased to have seen Dublin, though she could never live there. Too dirty, too noisy. Not the convent, of course, that was different. Though she dreaded the short time which must elapse before Kieran left home, she was glad to be returning, looking forward now to seeing James and the twins.

It was Breda who broke the silence, taking from her pocket and examining once again the small medal of Saint Francis which Sister Teresa had given her.

' 'Twas lovely, wasn't it? Everything was lovely. I like seeing places, but Kilbally is best of all!'

It was dark by the time they reached Kilbally. The journey back had been every bit as slow as the outward one, just as many loadings and unloadings and, because of that, because of all the banging and shouting, even though most of it was good-natured, Molly had found it too noisy to sleep, though the girls had slept and Kieran had dropped off for a short time.

Molly watched them and thought, guiltily, how lucky she was; these three here, Kathleen settled in Dublin, and her two lovely, rascally twins at home. Not to mention her lovely James. It was wicked to feel unhappy. She must not allow it.

Kieran had been awake for some time when they reached Kilbally station, but the girls had to be roused, Breda to be shaken because she threatened to fall off to sleep again immediately. Neither James nor the twins were at the station to meet them but Molly wasn't surprised. James was almost certainly out with the boats again and the boys had their own pursuits.

'Oh, I'm so tired!' Breda yawned. 'Give me a piggy-back, Kieran.'

'Wouldn't you be too old for that?' Kieran teased.

'I am not. And I am not very big for my age,' Breda said. 'Isn't everyone always telling me that?'

'All right then,' he said. 'Jump up!'

'What about me? Aren't I tired too?' Moira demanded.

'Then you must just put your best foot forward,' Molly said briskly. 'It won't take long.'

As they neared the house she could see that the lamp was lit, which meant Patrick and Colum must be home. If James had not gone on the boat he would be down at the Harp. There was no way he would waste an evening on his own.

In fact, as they approached the house the door opened and James stood there, silhouetted in the light from the lamp. So he had not gone fishing after all, Molly thought. She was too pleased to see him to give more than a passing thought as to why. Her face widened in a smile.

'Did you hear us coming? Were we so noisy?' she asked.

'I was listening out for you.'

It was his voice which alerted her. She expected his usual exuberance, and a welcome; but his tone was flat, a nervous note in it.

'What is it?' she asked. 'Are you not well? Is that why you haven't gone on the boat?'

'I'm well enough,' he said. ' 'Tis not that. Will you come into the house?'

They followed him in. Kieran loosened Breda from around his neck and deposited her on the hearthrug. Molly stared at James. He was white-faced, his eyes sharp with anxiety.

'What is it? Whatever is it? What has happened to you?'

'Nothing has happened to me . . . '

Suddenly, her strength drained away and she collapsed onto the nearest chair.

'Patrick! Colum! An accident! Which of them is it? It's not both. Tell me it's not both of them!'

'It is not an accident,' James said. 'But yes, it is both.'

She jumped up again and grabbed at his jacket. 'What are you talking about, James O'Connor?' She was shouting now. 'For God's sake make yourself plain.'

'They've gone. They have both gone.'

'Where have they gone, Dada?' Kieran broke in. 'Please tell us!'

'Isn't that what I'm trying to do?' James said desperately. 'They have left home. They have gone to England to join the British army. There is a letter . . . '

'Give it to me!' Molly cried. 'At once!'

He took the letter from behind the clock on the mantelpiece and she snatched it from him. Her hands shook so that she could hardly unfold it. She peered at it, then handed it to Kieran.

'I can't see it properly. Read it out loud.'

' "Dear Mammy and Dada," ' Kieran read, ' "By the time you get this we shall be in Liverpool. We are going to join up together. Don't worry about us, we shall be all right and we will write to you when we get digs and we will send you money every week once we are in the Army. Love and God bless, Patrick and Colum.

' "PS Please let Mr O'Reilly know and Mr Murphy." '

No-one spoke. Kieran handed the letter back to Molly. She folded it carefully and put it in her pocket.

'Which of them wrote it?' Breda asked.

'I don't know,' Kieran said. ' 'Tis impossible to tell their handwriting apart.'

Molly stared in front of her. It was also impossible to believe. Of course it happened one way or another all the time, but it happened to other people, not to her. Until now.

'They're too young.' Her voice was dull, as if the strength had gone out of her. 'They're under age. They're only boys!'

'They'll pass easily enough for eighteen,' James said. 'Older, in fact. They will have no trouble in enlisting.'

Molly came back to life, turning on him, suddenly and fiercely. 'Why did you let them go? Why didn't you stop them? You said you had to stay behind to look after them. So why didn't you?'

'When I left you at the station,' James said patiently, 'I came home to bed. Hadn't I been on the boat all night? They'd gone to work as far as I knew. I slept until three in the afternoon. The note was here when I got up. They must have come home at dinner time and then left straight afterwards.'

'And they must have been planning it,' Molly said. She turned to Kieran. 'Did you know nothing of this?' she asked angrily.

'Nothing at all, Mammy. You know they always had secrets between themselves.'

James put his arms around her but she pushed him off. 'Try to look on the bright side,' he said. 'They're young and strong. The Army is a good life, a man's life. They could do worse.' Inside himself he felt a new respect for them, felt closer than he ever had before.

'The Army,' Molly snapped, 'is where you get killed!'

Breda broke into loud sobs. 'I don't want my brothers to get killed!'

'And they won't,' Kieran said firmly. 'I am certain of it. Do not think about such a thing. Before we know where we are there will be a letter from them.' He hoped he sounded more convinced than he felt.

'Will you look at the time?' he went on. 'You and Moira should be in bed and asleep. Go wash your hands and faces and get into bed and I will bring you a cup of milk and a piece of soda bread.'

'I had the kettle on the boil,' James said to Molly. 'Will I wet the tea?' He clutched at the idea of something to do.

He poured the tea, added a generous amount of sugar, and handed it to her.

'How did you get on in Dublin?' he asked Molly.

'Do not ask me about Dublin,' Molly said. 'If I had not gone to Dublin this would not have happened.'

'Not today, perhaps,' James said gently. 'But it would have happened sooner or later. We both know that. We both know they would not have stayed in Kilbally all their lives. And it is better than crossing the water to America. It is not so far.'

'They are going into the Army,' Molly said. 'The Army might take them to the ends of the earth!' And might not bring them back, she thought.

Eventually they went to bed. James took Molly in his arms, holding her close but she would have none of it, and turned away from him. She lay there on her back in the darkness until James's heavy breathing told her he had fallen asleep, then she got up and went back to the living room. There, at last, she gave way to her grief, buried her face in her hands and sobbed.

Kieran lay wide awake in his bed. Was it only last night he had been so pleased to have a bed to himself? Now he desperately missed his brothers' presence; he would have been glad of the discomfort.

He heard his mother crying, wondered what he should do. Would she want to be left alone? In the end he couldn't bear it and went into her.

'Oh Mammy,' he said. 'I'm so sorry. Please try not to fret. I'm sure they'll be all right.'

'Kathleen gone,' she sobbed. 'And now my twins. And soon, so very soon, you! Oh Kieran, don't leave us! Promise me you won't go!'

She knew she should not ask such a thing. It was wrong; she was taking advantage of his love for her. But she couldn't help it.

Kieran was silent.

'Wouldn't you have a good life here?' she persisted. 'Marry a Kilbally girl – even an Ennis girl. Have children. You can serve God in Kilbally.'

He met the pleading in her eyes, and could hardly bear it.

'And do you think I would not be liking any of that?' he cried. 'But you know it is not for me. There are other things I must do, and we both know that.'

He had never felt so terrible about leaving, but, strangely, never more certain.

'Please go to bed, Mammy,' he begged. 'You will be so tired in the morning and there'll be a lot to do. As for me,

I'll go and see Mr Murphy and then Luke O'Reilly. I'll offer to take Patrick's place in the shop for as long as I'm here.'

She looked at him. His young face was white with fatigue, his eyes clouded with worry. She was stabbed by contrition.

'Very well,' she said. 'I will so. And you must go to bed also.'

She got up from the chair and left him.

Five

Moira burst into the house, not stopping to close the door, throwing her handbag on the nearest chair. She was white-faced and agitated, and when Molly looked up – she was scrubbing the table top – she saw at once that her daughter had been crying. Indeed, her eyes were still brimming with tears which threatened to fall.

'Oh, Moira love, whatever is the matter?' Molly cried. 'And why would you be coming home in the middle of the morning?' It was not yet half-past ten. 'Are you ill? Is that it?'

Or had she been sacked, Molly wondered? She prayed fervently that that wasn't the case, but with Moira it was always on the cards that either she would be dismissed from her job or that she would walk out on it in a fit of temper. Relations between Moira and her employer were always on a knife edge.

It would be dreadful if either of those things had happened. Quite the wrong time. Things were really bad, with James getting little work, and the twins no longer sending money home. (Though wasn't that my own fault, Molly thought. Wasn't I too independent?) Though it had increased a little on her eighteenth birthday, when she became a stylist, Moira's wage was small – and even smaller when she'd been given back what she said she must have for clothes and pocket money if she was to be halfway decent – but it was important, it made a difference. And it was regular.

All these thoughts flashed through Molly's mind with the speed of light, while at the same time she dried off the table top.

'What is it?' she repeated. 'Has something happened at work? Have you quarrelled with Miss Glenda?'

The tears spilled over now, like drops of crystal from a fountain. Moira's eyes also held a bright spark of anger as she returned her mother's look. Trust Mammy to think that it was to do with work! As if that could possibly make her feel so terrible! And naturally to imply that she was to blame! How could she be so lacking in understanding?

'No, it is not!' she sobbed.

Molly glanced at James, who had bought a newspaper and was studying the racing page. He raised his eyebrows and shook his head in perplexity. Breda moved around the table and laid her arm across her sister's shoulders.

'Then what . . . ?' Molly began.

'Oh Mammy, can't you guess?' Breda said. ' 'Tis Barry! 'Tis Barry, for sure.'

At the mention of his name Moira's sobs increased.

'For heaven's sake!' James protested. 'You're like a banshee wailing!'

'Barry, is it?' Molly said. 'Would you have quarrelled, then?' But when?

A lovers' tiff. She knew that could be painful, though she had not cast Barry Devlin, personable though he was, as her daughter's love, or at least as only one of them. True, they'd been in each other's pockets over the last fortnight, but Moira had had a dozen on a string since before she'd left school. She was skilled at playing them off one against the other, with little hurt to herself. To tell the truth, it was one of the traits she did not quite like in her daughter. But she didn't recall that she had ever seen her cry like this over any of the others.

'So what is it about Barry?' she asked.

'Has he not gone back to Dublin not an hour ago?' Moira said in a choked voice.

'But we knew he was going back this morning. Didn't you spend last evening at the *céilidh* with him?'

And not get home till after one in the morning, Molly thought, and me lying awake listening out for you? And then hadn't she heard the long, murmured farewells (though not the words, only the voices) they'd made on the doorstep, which had gone on so long that James had wakened and shouted to Moira to come in at once. 'At once, do you hear!' he'd thundered.

'I went to see him off at the station . . . ' Moira began.

'You left work to see him off?' Molly interrupted. 'You left your customers?' she said with disbelief. 'Whatever did Miss Glenda say to *that*?'

So there *had* been a row at the salon.

'I don't know and I don't care!' Moira snapped. 'I didn't go back. I don't care if I never go back again, and I'm certainly not going back today!'

'Oh yes you are, Miss!' Molly said firmly. 'I'll see to that if I have to drag you back!' Which would not be easy, since Moira was taller than she was and had the strength of youth.

'I'm too upset!' Moira said. 'Can't you see that?'

'Sure I can see it, but I cannot understand it. What did he say to you, then?'

'That's the size of it!' Moira cried. 'He didn't say anything. Nothing that mattered. I was waiting for him to say it and he didn't. He *would* have said it last night, I *know* he would, if Dada hadn't shouted at me to come in. So I went to the station this morning to give him another chance, and he didn't say it!'

'What was he going to say?' Breda asked eagerly, her eyes bright green with the excitement of it all. 'Was he going to ask you to marry him, do you think? Oh, Moira!'

She was sure that was it, quite apart from the look on Moira's face. It was so romantic, like a film! And 'twas no surprise at all that Barry Devlin should want her sister, at least to her it wasn't. She had seen the way he looked at her, and he had given her a present of a blue glass pendant; and in any case, wasn't Moira the prettiest girl in all Kilbally? In the county, even?

Moira jumped to her feet and faced her father.

'It's your fault!' she stormed. 'I hate you! If it hadn't been for you shouting me in last night I'd have been engaged to be married now. I'd have had a beautiful wedding, and gone to live in Dublin. You've ruined my life, that's what you've done. You treat me like a child, calling me in like that. And I'm not a child!'

'If I treat you like a child, it's because you act like one,' James stormed. 'I'll not have a daughter of mine standing on the doorstep with a man at one o'clock in the morning! 'Tis not decent! What will the neighbours think?'

'I don't care!' Moira shouted. 'I don't care what anyone in Kilbally thinks. Bad cess to all of them, I say!'

She ran to the bedroom, slamming the door behind her.

So that was it! Dublin! 'Twas Dublin at the bottom of it. I'm sorry Kathleen, but I wish we'd never gone to Dublin, Molly thought. Except for seeing you, no good came of it.

There was a silence, then Breda stood up as if to go to her sister.

'No, Breda,' Molly said. 'Leave her be. She'll be best on her own for a while.'

James sighed. He hated scenes.

'All the same,' he said, 'if what she says is right, I'm wishing I hadn't called her in. It's time she was married. Knowing her nature, she's best married before anything worse happens.'

'What worse could happen, Dada?' Breda asked.

Molly gave James a warning look.

'Oh, I don't know, Breda,' he said. 'I don't know what I meant by it. Nothing really!'

He means if she had a baby, Breda thought, which certainly would be awful.

In the bedroom, Moira lay face down on the bed, furiously beating the pillow with clenched fist. It was what she would have liked to have done to her father.

Now that they were the only two left at home, she and Breda had the luxury of a bed each, though at Moira's insistence they had kept the dividing curtain across. Moira liked her privacy. Breda was too inquisitive, too interested in everything, too chatty. Moira had insisted that her sister took the far side of the room so that if she herself chose to come in late there was no need for Breda to know.

What she had said to her father was the truth. He *had* ruined her life, and just when, at long last, it had taken a turn for the better, just when she'd seen all that she'd wanted within her grasp, only awaiting the few words which last night she was certain Barry had been about to utter.

She could tell. It wasn't difficult. Hadn't she had more than one proposal, and didn't she know the signs? The attention, the gifts, the invitations to meet the family (not that in Kilbally she didn't know most families anyway); and leading up to that the kisses, the mounting passion, the fumbling; the frustration when she'd allowed it so far and no further – for wasn't she a good Catholic girl, and

86

didn't she know it was a fate worse than death if she got into trouble?

So, in spite of what people thought, which was that so far she'd been lucky rather than virtuous, she had actually never succumbed, though it had not been easy.

The truth was that, apart from bed, she had met no-one so far who could offer her what she wanted. Bed was only part of it. The last thing she desired was to live a life like her mother's, right here in Kilbally. Until Barry Devlin came on the scene that was more or less what she'd been offered.

She had known Barry in earlier times. They had been at the National School at the same time, but he was three years older and therefore took no notice of her. Then, as he was about to move on to the Christian Brothers, his father had been offered a job in Dublin and the family had moved, leaving behind only Mr Devlin's mother and an aunt or two.

It was Molly who had first noticed the reappearance of Barry. Serving the tea one day she said:

'Who do you think I bumped into in Luke O'Reilly's this afternoon?'

Only Breda took her up. 'Who, Mammy?'

'Young Barry Devlin! You won't remember him, but Moira will. He was in the shop with his grandmother. He's come to pay her a summer visit.'

Moira hadn't bothered to look up – which just showed how wrong you could be – at least not until she'd heard her mother's next remark. 'My word, there is no denying he has grown into a handsome young man! And smart too; every bit the Dublin boy.'

'Why yes, I do remember him,' Moira said. 'Did they not go to live in Dublin?'

'And still live there,' Molly said. 'And the whole family doing well, according to his grandmother.'

'I suppose he will be married, then?' Moira enquired.

'Not a bit of it! But a catch for some lucky girl,' Molly said. 'I dare say there'll be one in Dublin.'

'I dare say,' Moira said nonchalantly. 'How long is he here for?'

'Two weeks, I think.'

Not for one moment had Molly been deceived by Moira's indifference. She knew her too well for that. Barry Devlin would be another string to her daughter's bow. What she did not realize was the strength of the pull which Dublin still had over her.

Returning in the train after visiting Kathleen it had all seemed so easy, so certain, to Moira. She knew she would have to wait a little while, perhaps even a year, but she was confident that she would work it out. Without a doubt she would get there.

Three years had passed since then, and she was no nearer. She was more skilled in her job now and had her own customers, but she had never managed to save enough money to keep her in Dublin until she found work. Sometimes, when she was at a low ebb, she thought she might just leave home, turn up on the doorstep of Our Lady of Lourdes. Would they help her? She rather thought not. More than likely they would send her back home on the next train. She became more and more afraid that one day soon she would find herself obliged to marry a Kilbally boy, and that was a future which filled her with despair.

But with her mother's words hope sprang afresh in her. Barry Devlin probably had a girl in Dublin – what could be more likely? – but he wasn't in Dublin now, he was right here in Kilbally, and would be for two whole weeks!

The first thing she did, next morning, was to tell Miss Glenda that she wanted to take the week's holiday which was due to her. She wanted to take it at once; she hadn't been feeling well for some time and she needed a change.

'But that's highly inconvenient!' Miss Glenda protested. 'You have appointments, bookings. What am I to tell them?'

'I'm sorry,' Moira said wanly. 'I just don't feel up to it.'

'I don't know how you can afford to take a holiday,' Miss Glenda said. 'I know I never can.'

Moira was aware that she wouldn't get paid. She would just have to manage without it and so would her mother. And for a second week if necessary, for if things went well she had no intention of going back to work while Barry Devlin was in the neighbourhood.

Everything did go well, from the moment she knocked on Grandma Devlin's door, saying she was just out for a nice walk and hadn't a nail sprung up suddenly in her shoe so that it was crippling her, and could she borrow a hammer and she'd knock it down, so? And – surprise, surprise – wasn't Barry himself in the house and not knowing what to do with himself because everyone was at work, and Moira would be doing them all a favour, his grandmother said, if, when he had knocked the nail down, Moira would take him with her on her long walk.

He found it difficult to locate the nail, but whatever he had done with the hammer, Moira said, he had worked the magic. Her shoe had never felt so comfortable.

Have I done the right thing, Nora Devlin wondered, watching them set off. Didn't everyone know that Moira O'Connor was a fast piece, in spite of the fact that her mother was the nicest woman you could meet in a day's march? But there were no flies on Barry, she comforted herself. He was a city man, wasn't he, a match for any country girl, even Moira O'Connor.

Moira had never walked so much as in that first week, which then, as she had expected, extended to a fortnight.

'You could lose your job!' her mother protested.

I shan't need it, Moira thought.

They went to the beaches, to the nearby villages where, greatly daring, she went into bars with him, drinking lemonade and sipping his Guinness. They pottered around the harbours, they walked along the cliffs and looked out over the Atlantic Ocean.

But it was not all walking. There was always somewhere to sit; on the short grass along the cliff tops, in a field or, when the rain came, in a handy barn. Anywhere.

They sat or lay close, their bodies touching. It was never long before their lips met in kisses the like of which even Moira had not known before. Barry was clearly experienced. He did things to her which set her body on fire, which made her long to give in to the demands he more and more made on her. If only she could be quite, quite sure of him! But until she was, she would never let him go the whole way.

' 'Tis not that I don't want to,' she told him.

'Well then . . . ?'

'There are some things I would only give to the man I marry,' she said softly.

It was not easy for her. She wanted him as much as he wanted her. Also she wondered if her refusal might put him off altogether, but that was a gamble she had to take. There were only two days left.

In fact, it seemed that her virtue had made her even more desirable. He talked to her about his family, his home, his job as an under-manager in a bookshop.

'You'd like Dublin,' he said.

'Oh, I've been there,' Moira replied. 'Sure, I loved every minute of it. All I want in the world is to go again!'

'And so you shall,' Barry promised. 'But this time with me to guide you. The theatre, restaurants, cinemas!'

'There is a film show tomorrow in Kilbally, in the town hall,' Moira said.

Barry laughed.

'I remember those when I was a kid!' he said. 'Stools at the front, ninepence, chairs at the back, one and fourpence! Nothing like Dublin.'

'It's David Niven,' she said. 'Would you be surprised if I said you were rather like David Niven?'

He stroked his moustache with his first finger.

'It has been said before,' he admitted modestly.

On his last day he took her to Ennis in the afternoon. There were two jewellers' shops in Ennis and he made no bones about it when she slowed to a halt in front of the windows. Everyone knew that when you started gazing at rings in jewellers' windows an engagement was close.

And then at the *céilidh* that evening, hadn't he acted all the time as though she belonged to him? Everyone could see they were a couple. She knew, oh she just *knew*, that when he walked her home afterwards he would say the words.

And now . . . if it had not been for her father . . . !

'I hate you! I hate you!' She shouted it out loud. He couldn't fail to hear.

A small, internal voice told her that Barry could have said something at the station this morning. There was nothing against proposing in the middle of the morning. Then she told herself that Barry was romantic, he wanted the time and the place to be perfect, and the station platform, with only five minutes to go before the train left, and other people standing around, was not for him. He was sensitive.

But hadn't he taken her in his arms and kissed her, in front of everyone, before he'd boarded the train? And hadn't he leaned out of the window, blowing kisses, as it pulled out?

She rose from the bed now, and dried her eyes. She must pull herself together. All was not over, but there was no time to be lost. She would write to him, and at once, so that he would get it before he was caught up in his Dublin life again. She would tell him how she felt about him, let it all out, hold nothing back, except, of course, that she would not dwell on Dublin. She had nothing more to lose, and how could he fail to respond?

She went back to join the others. Molly looked at her keenly.

'You'd better bathe your face before you go back to work,' she said.

'I'm not going back to work,' Moira said. 'Not today.'

'But you've just had a fortnight off!' Molly said.

'I'm not going. I am going to write to Barry and apologize for the rudeness of my family!'

'Then Breda, you must go down to the salon and tell Miss Glenda your sister's indisposed, but she'll be back in the morning. And ask if there's anything you can do to help her in the meantime.'

It would be good for Breda to have something to do. She had left school at the end of the summer term and so far she had not found herself a job, either in Ennis or Kilbally, or in any of the villages around. There were too many school leavers and not enough work.

It was at times like this that Molly wished she had not been so independent of Patrick and Colum. At first, after they'd enlisted, they'd sent money home more or less regularly. They'd settled down well in the Army, in an artillery regiment, content at being together. She had become almost reconciled to their absence – didn't many families have a son serving in the British army, even though

Ireland was neutral? – though she was fearful whenever she heard reports of the air raids in England.

Then, without warning, the two of them had turned up on a week's leave, and confessed that it was embarkation leave.

'Where are they sending you?' she demanded.

'We don't know,' Patrick said. 'It could be anywhere: Italy, Egypt – who knows?'

'But if we did know we wouldn't tell you,' Colum said. 'It's not allowed.'

'Wherever it is, we'll get a bit of money to you,' Patrick assured her. 'There are ways of doing it.'

Quite suddenly she had made up her mind that she wouldn't take it.

'I'm grateful,' she said. 'But I can manage. Save all you can, then you'll have money to set yourselves up when the war's over.' She'd been adamant, and they'd given in.

She knew by now that they'd been sent to Burma, to the Fourteenth Army; 'the Forgotten Army', they called it. But not forgotten by me, she thought. Never by me. She gathered and treasured every piece of news, little though there was.

Every so often a thin, blue airmail letter would arrive. Sometimes, after an interval, two came together. The letters were always signed by both of them and they told her little, but at least she knew they were alive. She read each letter a dozen times, then added it to the ones from Kieran in her treasure box. She wrote to the twins, and to Kieran, every week, and to Kathleen once a fortnight.

Breda was not keen to take the message to Miss Glenda. According to Moira she was a dragon.

'Can't Moira write a note, Mammy, and I'll push it through the letter box?' she asked.

'I'm not writing any note,' Moira said.

93

'In any case, an apology is best made face to face,' Molly said.

'Well then, isn't it Moira's face should be making it?' Breda objected. 'It's not my fault!'

'I know that, Breda. Just be a good girl and do it. And don't forget to ask her if there's anything you can do to help.'

'But don't expect her to pay you for it,' Moira put in. 'She's too mean to draw breath!'

Breda hesitated outside the hairdresser's shop, then pushed the door open and went in. She was met by a cloud of warm air, heavily scented with the cheap perfume of shampoos and setting lotions. How lovely, she thought, breathing deeply. Miss Glenda kept her waiting while she tied up her client in a pink hairnet and put her under the dryer, then she turned to her.

'I've come about Moira,' Breda said quickly. 'She's sorry, she can't come back today. She's . . . indisposed.'

'Indisposed, is it?' Miss Glenda said angrily. 'May I ask in what way she is indisposed?'

Breda searched her mind for the answer. 'I think she's *emotionally* indisposed,' she said.

Miss Glenda stared at her. '*Emotionally indisposed*? And what might that mean?'

'She's upset,' Breda said.

'Upset! And what about me? Isn't every bit of the work to fall on me? Why wouldn't *I* be upset? Tell me that!'

'Mammy said I should ask you would you be wanting me to lend a hand?'

Breda made the offer reluctantly and was much relieved when it was refused.

'You can tell your sister she had better be here at eight o'clock in the morning or 'twill be the worse for her!' Miss Glenda threatened.

Walking back, Breda met Moira on her way to post the letter to Barry Devlin.

'You should put "SWALK" on the back of the envelope,' Breda said. 'It means "sealed with a loving kiss".'

'I know what it means,' Moira said. 'It's childish! Aren't I a grown woman?'

She had composed a letter she felt would move a heart of stone, one which Barry would find it impossible to resist. She had been careful to make no demands, she'd simply told him how wonderful he was, how much she loved him, how already she was suffering deeply from their parting. She had so composed it that he could hardly fail to reply, but as an added insurance, before dropping it into the box, she drew her finger over it in the sign of a cross and made a short, impassioned prayer to the Holy Mother herself.

Breda gave her Miss Glenda's message.

'Haven't I more to think about than that woman?' Moira said dismissively.

Nevertheless, she would have to go back to work soon. She couldn't go on without money, not until she knew what her future was to be. She calculated how long she must wait before Barry replied. If he received the letter tomorrow, if he replied at once (and how could he not?), with luck, and if her prayers were answered, she could hear the day after that.

She did not have to wait so long.

When Molly answered the knock on the door and saw the telegram boy she almost fainted. The world went black, and spun around, so that she had to clutch at the door frame for support.

' 'Tis for Moira,' the boy said.

The words came to her from a long way off.

' 'Tis for Miss Moira O'Connor,' he repeated. ' 'Tis not for you, Mrs O'Connor.'

Molly's world slowed down as he handed her the telegram.

'I'm sorry. Thank you. She's at work. Breda will run down with it at once,' Molly said.

When Breda, out of breath, burst into the hairdresser's, Moira was shampooing a client. The woman was bent over the basin, the lather thick and creamy on her hair. Moira broke off at once, dried her hands down the front of her overall, and snatched at the telegram.

Seven words only. The sweetest, most wonderful words she had ever seen. She gave a shriek of delight.

'I love you. Will you marry me?'

She took hold of Breda and started to waltz her across the salon, towards the door.

'Where do you think you are going?' Miss Glenda yelled.

'What's happening?' the customer wailed. 'Somebody see to me! The soap's going in my eyes!'

'I'm going to the post office!' Moira called out. 'I have to send an urgent telegram.' She was out of the door by now, but turned back for a second.

'I will not be back! I will not be back at all, at all!'

Barry came on a flying visit the following weekend, bringing with him the engagement ring he had chosen for Moira in Dublin. It had two small diamonds side by side, set in gold.

'Oh, but it's quite beautiful!' Moira said. 'And it fits perfectly. Oh, you have such good taste, Barry!'

To her certain knowledge, no-one in the O'Connor family had ever had a diamond before, let alone two.

The wedding was fixed for three weeks ahead. There was no point in waiting, Barry said, and he couldn't keep travelling from Dublin to Kilbally; he was too busy in his job. They would live with his parents for a short time, only until they found a place of their own. Moira was in total agreement. Except that she wanted a proper wedding, with a long dress and a veil, she would have been glad to leave Kilbally within the hour.

'It's very short notice,' Molly said. 'I've your dress to make. We can't afford to buy one.'

'And mine!' Breda reminded her. She was to be the only bridesmaid and wear apricot taffeta, long to her ankles, and a wreath of lemon and apricot flowers in her hair.

'You will look a treat,' Molly said. 'But 'tis not a dress will be suitable for anything afterwards!'

'Perhaps someone else will want a bridesmaid,' Breda said hopefully. Couldn't she hire herself out, so to speak?

'There'll be those who will wonder why Moira wants to get married in such a hurry,' Molly said to James in the privacy of their bedroom.

'And if they jump to conclusions, won't they just be disappointed!' James retorted.

His navy suit, which he had had for years but not often worn, was taken to the dry cleaners in Ennis, and Molly went with him to buy a bowler hat.

'The father of the bride must wear a hat,' she said. 'And anyway, it suits you. You look very smart, very handsome.'

Heaven alone knew what she would wear, let alone how she would afford it, but she wanted to be a credit to Moira. And hadn't both Kieran and Kathleen been given permission to come home for their sister's wedding, and wasn't her own sister Josephine coming all the way from Yorkshire?

In the end it was her mother who went into her hidden savings and provided the money for both Molly's and Moira's outfits. It came as a tremendous relief.

'My family have always held their heads high,' Mrs Byrne said. (She would not have said as much for the

O'Connors.) 'My granddaughter shall have the best of weddings.'

It was a perfect day, warm and dry, and Kilbally had never seen a more beautiful bride or a prettier bridesmaid. Kieran served at the altar and Kathleen, in her habit, sat with her parents in the front pew. If only my lovely twins were here, Molly thought, we'd be a complete family once again.

And I *do* love Barry, Moira thought, standing by his side as they made their vows.

'With this ring I thee wed . . . ' he said, the gold band glinting in the light as he placed it on her finger. Then he pressed coins into her hand. 'Gold and silver I give thee, as a token of my worldly goods,' he said.

When they came out of the church he emptied his pockets of the money he had placed there for the purpose, and threw it to the children who were gathered around, waiting to scramble for it. It was not all copper, either. There was silver among it. 'He was always a generous boy,' his mother said.

Afterwards, in spite of rationing but because everyone had contributed – even Luke O'Reilly had sent a pound of sugar and Josephine had brought a full bottle of whiskey from Akersfield – food and drink was plentiful. And when the meal had been cleared the musicians, a fiddle and a concertina, started up for the dancing.

When he'd danced with his new bride, Barry came for Breda in the set. He was a good dancer, but when the music stopped he gave her a lingering kiss.

'I'm allowed to kiss the bridesmaid,' he said. 'And in any case, I'm your brother now.'

Not my true brother, Breda thought; and none of her own brothers had ever kissed her like that. But hadn't he whiskey on his breath, and also had he not given her a present of a very nice bracelet for being a bridesmaid?

Barry and Moira did not stay long at the dancing. They were to go in Murphy's hired car, apart from the doctor's the only one with petrol, to spend the night at the Falls Hotel in Ennistymon before leaving for Dublin next morning.

It was the early hours of the next day before Molly climbed into her bed beside James. He was asleep in seconds but she lay awake a while. It had been a good day, but now her last thoughts were to wonder just where Patrick and Colum were, what they were doing, what was happening to them in such a far country. But weren't we all under the same sky? God keep them safe and bring them back to me, she prayed.

As Molly fell asleep, Patrick and Colum, halfway through the morning of the next day, were hacking their way through the jungle. It was the third day of a long march. Every man in the platoon was sweaty, hungry and dead-beat tired but none, so far, were injured.

It was a march which could not be relieved by singing; even unnecessary conversation was forbidden. They did not know, from one minute to the next, where the Japs were, or, for that matter, quite where they were themselves.

It was semi-dark on the floor of the jungle. Tall trees, themselves reaching for the light, blotted out the sun, except for an occasional shaft which penetrated, making a pool of gold on the ground. It was difficult to say which was worse: the steamy heat and dimness, or the blazing sun and lack of protection from the enemy whenever they came to a clearing.

'How did we get into this lot?' Patrick whispered to Colum.

'God knows!' his brother said. 'I wonder what they're doing in Kilbally?'

' 'Tis the middle of the night,' Patrick reminded him. 'They'll be fast asleep.'

Six

Kathleen and Kieran were to leave together, after dinner, for Dublin.

'I will miss them both sorely. Moira too, of course,' Molly said to James as she dressed in the bedroom.

James grunted, and turned over in bed, drawing the covers over his head. It might have been a grunt of agreement but it sounded more like agony. 'Twas little doubt he had the sorest head in Kilbally this morning, and no wonder the way the drink had flowed, not to mention the beat of the dancing and the noise of the singing. There was a man who would not be up for an hour or two yet. But no matter; he had a place on the boats tonight, so he needed his rest. Let him take it while he could.

Molly didn't feel all that clever herself, but there was no way she would waste a minute of this day, the last with Kieran and Kathleen for who knew how long. They would go to Mass together, Moira's marriage and her new life their intention, but she would be praying for all her children, near and far.

Josephine, who was staying with her mother, was at Mass, and spoke with them afterwards.

'I'll not come back with you now,' she said. 'Mammy's not too bright this morning. I'll settle her, then I'll be around for my dinner, and I'll go to the station with the rest of you.'

'There's no need for anyone to see us off,' Kieran said gently.

'We want to,' Molly said. Certainly she did.

When breakfast had been cleared away Kathleen said: 'Mammy, if we're not needed for a while, Kieran and I thought we'd take a walk.'

'Can I come?' Breda asked quickly.

'Of course!'

'Where will you go?' Molly asked.

'Down to the strand,' Kieran said. 'Or perhaps along the cliffs, wherever the mood takes us.'

' 'Twill be nice to see the familiar haunts,' Kathleen said.

No-one knew how often she thought of them – even dreamt of them – these places she had known as a child. In her cell-like room in the convent she could picture the pale sands and the small pools, hear the roar of the sea on a stormy night. She missed the places almost as much as the people. And it was the same with Kieran; they had talked about it on the journey from Dublin, though they both knew it was wrong to be attached to either.

When they had left, Molly set about her chores. She intended to prepare a very special dinner; a boiling fowl, which was already in the pot, and plenty of vegetables. She would also make a piece for the two of them to take on the train. She was glad to have these jobs to do. She just wished they would occupy her mind as well as her body.

The house was too quiet. Yet when all the children were young, and around her feet, hadn't there been many a time when she'd longed for a bit of peace? Now she didn't want it.

She was thankful when Josephine arrived, well before dinner time, and broke the silence. There were fourteen years between herself and her eldest sister. In the few years they'd lived in the same house, before Josephine, at eighteen, had married Brendan Maguire and gone with him to Yorkshire where he'd got a job in the building trade, she had hardly known her. There had been all those other children in between them, so that she had thought of Josephine more as a second mother than as a sister.

It had all been so long ago, before the first war, and now half the world was in the middle of another one.

Now Josephine was in her fifties, and with grand-children. Most of them still lived in Yorkshire, but a son and a daughter had emigrated to America.

'So, how does it feel to be a mother-in-law?' she asked Molly.

'I haven't had time to feel it so far,' Molly said. 'I hardly know Barry, and will I ever? I don't suppose they will spend much time visiting Kilbally, not if Moira has anything to do with it.'

'I think the Irish have itchy feet,' Josephine said. 'It's not just that they can't get jobs where they are. Look at those two of mine. Doing perfectly well in Akersfield, and they have to go, even with young babies, to America. Now all I'll ever know of *those* grandchildren is photographs.'

'At least you *have* grandchildren. I sometimes wonder will it ever happen to me. Not that I'm in any hurry, mind you!'

'Oh it will, all right,' Josephine assured her. 'This time next year won't Moira be dandling a baby on her lap?'

Molly could not imagine Moira with a baby. In fact, she would almost pity the child. And she would not put it past this daughter of hers to defy the Church and prevent it, though she would not discuss it with her.

'We shall see,' she said. 'Must you go back on Thursday? Can you not stay longer?'

Josephine shook her head.

'No. Though 'tis not Brendan. He can manage, after a fashion. 'Tis Grandma Maguire. His own mother, but he cannot cope with her, though truth to tell, who can? She'll have little truck with any of the children. It has to be me.'

'She *is* in her eighties,' Molly said.

'And getting more awkward with every day that passes. Don't let anyone talk to me about sweet old ladies! I know better!'

'Mammy herself is no easy matter,' Molly said.

'Compared to Grandma Maguire, Mammy is a saint!'

But you are only seeing her for a few days, Molly wanted to say. She's on her best behaviour. She had watched her mother at the wedding, being all sweetness and light. It wouldn't last.

'Do you reckon this is how our own children will see us when we're old?' she asked Josephine.

'Not at all! 'Tis not possible!' Josephine spoke firmly. After more than thirty years in the West Riding she had taken on its accent, but every now and then, as now, she sounded more Irish than the Irish.

'We *shall* be sweet old ladies,' she said, smiling. 'Won't we be the exceptions that prove the rule?'

James came into the room. He looked bleary-eyed and pale, but when he'd been to the tap outside and washed himself in cold water he came in again, improved. My, but he was a handsome man, Josephine thought. No wonder Molly had fallen for him. 'Twas a pity he did not have regular work, though as far as she could tell it seemed not to bother him.

'Where are they?' he enquired.

'Gone for a walk,' Molly said. 'They should be back soon. The dinner's all but ready.'

'You'll be eating with us, Josie?' James asked Josephine.

He liked his sister-in-law. A sensible woman. Not beautiful, like his Molly. She was grey-haired and plump, her figure and face beginning to sag, but as bright-eyed as ever, and kind, he wouldn't wonder.

Josephine nodded. 'I will so. And go with you to the station to see them off.'

In the end, James did not accompany them to the station. He feared there might be tearful farewells and those he could not abide. He was wrong, though. Molly smiled and waved until the train was out of sight. Only then did she take out her handkerchief and give her nose a good blow.

Leaving the railway station, Molly's heart was heavy, though she was determined not to show it. Hadn't she much to be thankful for? She must remember that.

They took a detour and strolled by the sea. It was a balmy autumn afternoon, the sun shining gold on the water which, for once, was calm.

'Would you ever think the way it could rage?' Josephine said. 'Though I miss the sea. After all these years I still miss it, and most of all when it's stormy.'

'Don't you ever get to the sea, Aunt Josie?' Breda asked.

'Sometimes. Not often. It's sixty miles away. Sometimes we go on the train, go for the day.'

'I wouldn't like to live away from the sea,' Breda said.

'Oh well, it's a matter of where life brings us, *álainna*,' Josephine answered. 'Haven't you a far way to go yet, and who can say where 'twill bring you? Akersfield is not the worst place in the world.'

'But Kilbally is the best!' Breda's judgement was final.

'Since you've nothing better to do with yourself at the moment, you could come and visit me in Akersfield,' Josephine suggested. 'In fact, you could come back with me on Thursday, for a week or two!'

'Oh no!'

The words were out of Molly's mouth before she could stop them.

'I'm sorry. I don't mean to be rude, Josie. It's just not a good time, what with Moira and all the others away.'

'As you wish,' Josephine said. 'But you mustn't look to Breda to take the place of the rest. 'Twould be quite unfair.'

'I know,' Molly sighed. 'But just for the present . . . '

'I'll come some other time,' Breda said politely. She wasn't sure that she ever wanted to go. 'Perhaps Mammy and I will both come!'

' 'Twas not what I had in mind, but we'll see!' Josephine said.

'Spend as much time as you can with us, I mean while you're in Kilbally,' Molly said to her sister. 'I shall miss you when you've gone. It's going to be very quiet here.'

'Indeed I will,' Josephine promised. 'And while I remember it, I must call on Luke and Mary O'Reilly. I was at school with Luke. I met Mary only the once, on a visit, but we got on well. And Mammy says she's quite poorly.'

'It seems so,' Molly admitted. 'Though we're never quite sure. She gives Luke a hard time of it. Did I tell you Kieran worked for him in the school holidays? And Patrick, before the twins went into the Army.'

'You did so. Do you not think he might give Breda a job? Will I be asking him when I call tomorrow?'

Breda had left them, had run down to the beach in search of pebbles.

'She's been collecting pebbles all her life,' Molly said. 'Well, at least there'll be more room in the house for them now!'

'So what do you think? About Luke O'Reilly, I mean.'

'I had not thought of it.'

'Well, think about it now. 'Tis not good for a girl who has left school behind her to be hanging around doing nothing.'

'She can help me in the house.'

'You don't need help. A little house and only the three of you! You mustn't tie her down. 'Tis bad for you and a sight worse for Breda.'

'I'll think about it,' Molly promised. 'I will so. I'll see what Breda says.'

'Do that. I'll call in on my way down to Luke's tomorrow. And think on, isn't it what's best for Breda that counts?'

Before he left for the fishing, and when Breda was out of the house visiting Deirdre O' Farrell, Molly told James what Josephine had said. Unexpectedly, he took Josephine's side.

'She's quite right,' he said. 'In fact it would not be the worst of ideas for Breda to go back to England with her for a spell.'

'Oh no!' Molly disagreed. 'All our children gone! You and me left alone!'

He grinned at her, pulled her towards him and looked into her eyes.

'And what is so terrible about being left alone with your loving husband? No-one else to think about. Wouldn't I give you the best of times?'

'I didn't mean anything like that,' Molly said. 'It's just . . . '

'It's just that you can't let your last chick leave the nest. Isn't that the size of it? Well, you will have to, sooner or later.'

'She is only fourteen,' Molly protested.

'Old enough to be out working,' James said. 'Wasn't I doing just that by the time I was twelve, and I daresay you also. Anyway, there is no harm in asking Breda what she thinks. Now, give me a kiss. I have to be off.'

' 'Tis a calm sea,' Molly said. 'You'll have a smooth night. God go with you, James O'Connor!'

'And be with you, my Molly!'

She stood in the doorway and watched him – he had a proud walk, shoulders back, head held high – until he was out of sight. She loved this man, oh, how she loved him! And one reason she loved her children so was surely that they were part of him. He would never be rich, in her heart she doubted that he would ever be in regular work; she faced the fact that she would always have to struggle to make ends meet, to put food on the table; but it didn't matter. As she watched him walk away she knew that, all those years ago, she had made the right choice.

She was still standing in the doorway, shading her eyes against the bright rays of the setting sun, when Breda arrived.

'I've had my supper,' Breda said. 'I had it with Deirdre.'

'Good! How is Deirdre, then?'

'She has warts. Two of them, one on her finger and one on her thumb. Her mammy has rubbed them with fresh-cut potato and buried it after in the garden. Will I be getting warts, do you think?'

'I dare say not,' Molly said. 'But if you do, 'tis a well-known cure! What would you think of going to work for Luke O'Reilly?'

'Luke O'Reilly?' Breda was astonished. 'I had never thought of such a thing. Why would I want to work for Luke O'Reilly?'

'Because you must get a job as soon as you can. 'Tis not good for you to be doing nothing. Aunt Josie is going to see him tomorrow. She could ask about it.'

Breda sat down, rested her elbows on the table and cupped her chin in her hands. Her face, so framed, with locks of red hair falling over her hands, looked so young, no older than eight or nine. Her pale skin still had the same powdering of freckles, which were the bane of her life.

I wish *she* was still nine years old, Molly thought. She would gladly have lived every one of those years with Breda over again, and not only because she was the last child. Breda was the child she had enjoyed to the full. But she was not nine years old and the clock could not be put back.

'Did you think any more about Miss Glenda's?' she asked.

They had discussed whether Breda might enquire of Miss Glenda was there any hope that she could take Moira's place, though of course she would have to start at the beginning.

Breda pulled a face.

'Moira said not to do it at any price. Miss Glenda is a cow,' she said.

'Breda! That is not the way to describe *anyone*!' Molly cried.

'I didn't,' Breda said. ' 'Twas Moira said so!'

'You and Moira are two different people,' Molly said. 'I know she's my daughter, and your sister, but was she ever easy to get on with?'

'But Miss Glenda might take it out on me because of Moira,' Breda objected.

In any case she would not like sweeping the floor and washing the towels. She was not even sure that she wanted to be a stylist in the end, though it sounded glamorous enough.

'You could be right at that,' Molly admitted. 'Though there is not much choice, is there? Perhaps we had better let Aunt Josie speak to Luke O'Reilly. We don't know that he needs anyone, but we could find out.'

Breda half hoped that he would not, though she knew it was wrong of her. She must take whatever work she could get.

Didn't Mammy desperately need the money? As each of them had grown they had looked forward to earning a bit, putting something in the purse. It was the way with every family, and now it was up to her and she couldn't shirk it.

It was strange, going to bed that night. She drew the dividing curtain aside as far as it would go. She had this fear, though she knew it was stupid, of what might lurk behind it. She would ask Mammy if she could take it down for good tomorrow.

The trouble now was that the room was bigger than she had ever thought it. Two wide beds, and instead of five or six of them like sardines in a can, only herself filling less than half of one. How often she had envied Deirdre, with her very own bedroom, but now that she had it herself she didn't like it at all. She longed for a sister or a brother. Even Moira would have done.

She was still wide awake when she heard Mammy come to bed, but she would not call out, she would *not*!

She did not have to.

'Are you still awake?' Mammy whispered, coming into the room.

'I can't get to sleep, Mammy!'

'It's strange, isn't it, *dote*? I know. Don't think I don't feel the same!' She stood by the bed and looked at her daughter. What would become of this one?

'I'll tell you what,' she said. 'Since Dada's on the boats, why don't I join with you? Only for tonight, though. Anyway, we'll both feel better by tomorrow, sure we will! I won't be a minute!'

She went to her own bedroom and got into her night-dress. To undress in front of any of her children was not to be thought of. It had taken all James's persuasion to get her to do so in front of her husband.

She slipped into the bed beside Breda, then stretched out an arm and snuffed the candle. It was not quite dark in the room; a shaft of moonlight splashed the floor. She pictured it lighting up the sea, where James was. Thank God for a calm night, though James didn't mind when the sea was rough. He was in his element on the water. Of all the jobs he had, the fishing was his favourite. God keep him safe and bring him home to me, she thought.

'I was thinking,' Breda said. 'I was thinking what I would do if I didn't work for Mr O'Reilly or Miss Glenda. If I could choose.'

'And what would you do? If you could choose anything in the whole world?'

'Well . . . ' Breda considered. 'Well . . . I could be a nurse . . . '

'You would make a good nurse.'

'I'd like the uniform. And a grey cloak, lined with scarlet! Or I could be an actress, or a film star!'

'Hey! Come down to earth!' Molly cried.

'We said I could choose *anything*,' Breda reminded her. 'Or paint pictures, or write books; or a dancer. A dancer would be nice!'

'Very nice!' Molly yawned. It had been a long day.

'*Or* I would marry a rich man, very handsome, and have a big house in Kilbally, and seven children – seven is my lucky number – and you and Dada could live with us . . . and then . . . and then . . . '

'Good night, Breda,' Molly said.

But Breda was already asleep.

Only the earliest of early birds was on the wing when James walked back from the harbour next morning. There were lights in a farm two field lengths away, and as he passed the creamery there was the rattle and clanking of milk churns. Nothing more.

He let himself into the silent house, poked the fire into life, and went through to the bedroom. He could not believe it when he saw the empty bed, not slept in, the covers smooth and undisturbed. Sudden fright gripped him until he saw Molly's day clothes folded and draped over the chair, the way she left them every night. Then he slipped off his boots and tiptoed into the other bedroom.

She was there all right, Breda sprawled across most of the bed, a red head and a dark head side by side on the pillows, both of them fast asleep.

Gently, he stroked Molly's face until she opened her eyes and saw him.

'Come back to your own bed,' he whispered. 'Come back where you belong!'

She took his hand and went with him.

Breda was still in bed when Josephine called in on her way to Luke O'Reilly's.

'She should be up and doing by now,' Josephine said. 'You mustn't let her get into bad habits.'

'Oh, Josephine, surely you remember what children of this age are like!' Molly protested. 'They could sleep the clock round!'

'If you let them,' Josephine said. 'Well, she'll not be able to do that when she gets a job – which is why I am here. Will I speak to Luke O'Reilly, then?'

'Well, last night she was deciding between being a dancer and a film star, until such time as she found herself a rich husband,' Molly said. 'But I reckon this morning she'll have to settle for a job with Luke O'Reilly – if he has one, that is.'

'I'll do my best,' Josephine promised.

Little more than an hour later she was back again. Breda was peeling potatoes; James was in bed.

'Will you be taking a cup of tea?' Molly asked Josephine. 'And the soda bread is warm out of the oven.'

'I will have both,' Josephine said. 'Not a bite nor a sip did I have at the O'Reillys, but there is good reason for it. Luke is busy in the shop and 'tis clear that Mary is not fit to do a hand's turn! I never saw a woman go downhill so. You never mentioned it,' she rebuked Molly.

'What do you mean?' Molly asked. 'When I go in the shop I always ask after her. Only last week Luke said she was much as usual.'

'It's what he always says,' Breda put in.

Josephine nodded. 'In fact, that's what he said to me. I said to him would I go through and see her. I can tell you I was surprised when I did.'

'She always looks pale,' Molly said. 'And thinner than she once was. But hasn't she always enjoyed poor health, ever since he brought her here? She was delicate as a bride, all those years ago. Mary O'Reilly is a creaking gate. 'Tis Luke everyone is sorry for.'

'I am wondering how many people go and see her, or if the doctor calls,' Josephine said doubtfully. 'She looks more than a creaking gate to me.'

'The doctor not as often as he used to, I dare say,' Molly said. 'Will you stay and have your dinner with us? There's plenty, though 'tis mostly potatoes.'

'I'll get back to Mammy,' Josephine said. 'I'll come this afternoon when she takes her rest.'

She has said nothing about the job, Breda thought, cutting up the potatoes, putting them in the pan. Perhaps there isn't one. She was glad and sorry, both at the same time.

'However, 'tis an ill wind that blows nobody any good, and in this case the good is to Breda,' Josephine said. 'I persuaded Luke that Mary needed more attention than he could give her. Also that himself could do with help in the shop. The upshot is that he will take on Breda and she will do whatever and wherever the work is.'

Breda's heart plummeted. So this was it! But Josephine's next words cheered her a little.

'He will pay you ten shillings a week, which is not bad, seeing you are as green as grass, no experience at all.'

Ten shillings! She would give it all to Mammy, with the hope that she would give her back at least ninepence a week for pocket money, and perhaps the material for a new dress. The thought quite cheered her up.

'That is wonderful!' she said. 'Ten shillings!'

'He will make you work for it,' Molly said. She remembered how hard he had worked Kieran and Patrick. But then, hadn't he sent them home with two ounces of this and two ounces of that on top of the wages? And ten shillings, less what she would give Breda, was a decent sum, and regular. There would be no worry about the rent.

'You can start as soon as you like,' Josephine said. 'So why not tomorrow?'

'Does he not want to see Breda about it first, make sure she will suit?' Molly asked.

'It seems not. He said he could trust any child of Molly O'Connor's to work well.'

'And he *has* known Breda all her life,' Molly said. 'All the same, I still think you and I, Breda, should go down and thank Mr O'Reilly, tell him you are willing to start tomorrow. We want him to know that you have the backing of your family.'

All the details having been thus settled, Breda presented herself at the shop at eight o'clock the following morning. In a brown paper bag she carried a clean apron, one of her mother's which Mammy had cut down to size the previous evening, and, wrapped in a piece of paper, two thick slices of soda bread in case she was not allowed to slip home at dinner time. She hoped she would be. The shop kept open until eight in the evening, which would make it a long day.

Walking down the street she had wondered, for the hundredth time, what it would be like. She was not particularly fearful about the shop part. Sure, she could weigh out tea and sugar, peas and beans, currants and raisins if there were any to be had, which Mammy said was unlikely. And she could take the money and give the right change. Hadn't she always been good at the sums?

No, 'twas not the shop. It was Mrs O'Reilly. She had not seen her the previous day because she had been resting. She wondered how they would get on. She had never, ever spoken to her, and neither Kieran nor Patrick had ever said much about her, so that all she knew was from the few remarks her mother had let drop from time to time. Thinking of them did nothing to reassure her.

Luke O'Reilly was unlocking the door at the precise moment she arrived.

'Ah! So you're here. Well, at least you're prompt. I set great store by punctuality. Never be late, never try to skive off early!'

'Oh I won't, Mr O'Reilly,' Breda assured him.

There was no smile of welcome in him. But perhaps he did not have much to smile about, what with a poorly wife, she thought. He was not very tall. He had dark hair, with a lot of grey in it, a high forehead above thick eyebrows. His eyes were worried, as if he had too many things to think about.

Breda unwrapped her apron and tied it around her waist to show that she was ready.

'What do you want me to do first, Mr O'Reilly?' she asked.

He sighed.

' 'Twould be best if you attended to Mrs O'Reilly first. She's in bed, she doesn't get up too early. Make her breakfast and take it in. She likes strong milky tea, one slice of bread and butter and a boiled egg. Can you boil an egg?'

'Of course!' Breda said. 'How does she like it?'

'The white well set and the yolk runny,' he replied. 'Try to get it right.'

If the girl got it right, the job was hers for ever. He never could. He never wanted to boil another egg as long as he lived.

He took Breda into the bedroom and introduced her to his wife.

'Mary, this is Breda O'Connor, Josephine's niece. She has come to help out, here and in the shop. She'll be after making you a bit of breakfast now.'

'Can you boil an egg?' Mrs O'Reilly demanded. 'Himself is no good with the eggs. Are you good at it?'

'Expert, Mrs O'Reilly,' Breda said firmly.

So what was there to boiling an egg, she wondered. She had not often done it because Mammy was always there, but what could be simpler?

'You look very young!' It was an accusation.

'I'm going on fifteen,' Breda said. 'I'm just not tall for my age, but Mammy says I might shoot up any time now.'

'I must get back to the shop,' Luke said. 'Can't keep customers waiting!'

Now less than ever if he was to pay Breda O'Connor ten shillings a week. He wondered if he had been too generous – would seven and sixpence have done? – but it was Josephine who had driven the bargain.

'Why wouldn't I shake up your pillows and make you comfortable before I bring the breakfast?' Breda suggested.

Mrs O'Reilly looked very pale, with a yellowy cast to her skin and no colour in her lips. Her voice was tired, as if she had spent the night in bed without sleeping much.

She was thin, too; no visible shape beneath her flannelette nightdress.

In the kitchen Breda laid the breakfast tray, put the water to boil for the egg, cut the bread, then wet the tea. All these things must wait on the egg. She stood poised, with the egg in a tablespoon, while she waited for the water to come to the boil. When the first bubbles appeared she said 'God bless this egg!' and launched it into the water like a ship taking to the sea.

It was at that moment she realized that there was no clock in the kitchen.

'Jesus save us!' she cried.

She would have to count out the three and a half minutes! Two hundred and ten seconds! Quickly, she began to count, out loud, and hovering over the pan in case she should lose concentration.

' . . . Two hundred and eight, two hundred and nine. . . . '

She scooped the egg out of the water, set it in the egg cup, and bore the tray into the bedroom.

'Here we are!' she said brightly. 'Will I take the top of the egg off for you, Mrs O'Reilly?'

It was perfection; milky, set white, yolk like liquid gold. Breda observed the corners of Mrs O'Reilly's mouth turn up in the beginnings of a thin smile of approval. Thanks be to God and all the saints, she thought.

The rest of the day went reasonably smoothly. She helped Mrs O'Reilly to dress, settled her in the living room, then went back and tidied the bedroom. It was the only housework she'd be called upon to do, she was informed, because Flora Milligan came in twice a week to see to the rest.

'You had better go and give Himself a hand,' Mrs O'Reilly said presently. 'No need to hang around here.'

Breda spent the rest of the morning tidying shelves. Never a customer was she allowed to serve, though didn't she know most of them, and they surprised to see her there, and ready to talk?

'Will I go home for my dinner?' she asked Mr O'Reilly at midday. She would not mention that she had brought the soda bread. She wanted to get into the fresh air, go home for a spell.

Mr O'Reilly looked disappointed.

'I was hoping that you would make a bit of dinner for us. You could eat at the table,' he added kindly.

'I think Mammy expects me,' Breda said, not quite truthfully. 'I'll be back punctually.'

Aunt Josephine was there when she got back to the house. Breda took her place at the table while Mammy put food in front of her, then tried to answer their questions through mouthfuls of potato.

'You'll be needing a better way to time the eggs,' Mammy said.

'I know,' Breda agreed. 'Deirdre has a wristwatch!'

Mammy laughed.

'No chance of that! I expect Luke O'Reilly has a clock, if you ask him.'

'I know a woman who timed them by singing "Abide with Me" ' Josephine said. 'Two verses for lightly boiled, three for hardboiled. But then she was a Protestant, wasn't she?'

'You had better get back,' Mammy said. 'You mustn't be late.'

'Tell Mrs O'Reilly I'll be in to see her later,' Josephine said.

The following day it was time for Josephine to return home. She called for Molly, who was to accompany her to the station.

'Sure, I shall miss you so much,' Molly said. 'Come again soon.'

'Whenever I can,' Josephine said. 'When the war is over I hope 'twill be easier.'

'Won't it be easier for all of us?' Molly said. 'I pray for it every day.'

When they were ready to leave the house they paused to say three Hail Marys together, for safety on the journey.

On the station platform it was difficult to know what to talk about.

'Look after Mammy,' Josephine said. 'She's getting old.'

'Oh, I will,' Molly promised. 'I'll pop in and see her on the way home.'

It was time to board the train. The sisters embraced each other.

'May God hold you in the hollow of His hand,' Josephine said.

'May the roads rise with you on your journey,' Molly said. 'May the wind be ever at your back!'

'I seem to spend too much time seeing people off at the station,' Molly said to her mother a little later.

'Now you know how I have felt,' Mrs Byrne said. 'And is it not what every Irish mother knows?'

'And is that not because we have too many children, more than the land will keep?' Molly ventured.

'We have the children God sends!' Mrs Byrne's voice was sharp. 'Don't let me hear you speak otherwise, Molly Byrne! Every child is a blessing!'

'I know that,' Molly said.

Seven

When the end of the war in Europe came in May 1945 the majority of the inhabitants of Kilbally, indeed probably of the whole county, were pleased. There had always been a minority who spoke up on the side of the Germans, but they were now silent. On the other hand, there were in Kilbally none of the great goings-on of the kind which, according to Josephine's latest letter, were happening day and night in Akersfield.

'Just listen to this,' Molly said. ' "Brass bands in the parks, flags over all the buildings, the Government allowing red, white and blue bunting without coupons, if you can find it, that is. Street parties for the children, dances for the grown-ups, and church bells ringing fit to make your head burst! Such shenanigans! But it's lovely!"

'She goes on and on,' Molly said, turning the page. 'Now why don't we celebrate like that?' she asked James.

'I suppose because it's not our war.'

He said it through a mouthful of nails. He was resoling his shoes.

Molly stared at him.

'*Not our war?* Not our war? What in the world can you be meaning? Have we not two sons fighting? And are there not hundreds of Irish boys side by side with the English? How many homes have given a son or two? So how can you say it is not our war, James O'Connor?'

James spat out the nails, then lowered his head and held his hands outspread over it in mock terror, as if to ward her off physically.

'Whoa! Don't be so fussed! Not that anger does not make you the more beautiful, sparks flying from your eyes and all!'

'Never mind that! I'm serious!' she snapped.

'So am I. 'Tis a statement of fact. We are a neutral country. We have the Emergency here, but we have not been at war.'

'It certainly felt like it to me,' Molly said furiously.

'Our lads who joined up were volunteers,' James said patiently. 'You would have known the difference if it had been *our* war. All the men would have *had* to go. There is no choice in war. Why, even I might have had to go in the end!'

'Get away with you!' Molly said. 'And you about to be a grandfather!'

She was smiling now. His logic had calmed her down.

And perhaps I would have been of more use than I am here, he thought. I would have had a proper job of work. But I wouldn't have wanted to take orders. That's not my line.

'All the same,' Molly added, 'I feel like celebrating. It is the best of news.'

'It is good news,' James acknowledged. 'But the best of news will be when the war in the east is over. When the fighting stops there, when our sons come home, *then* we will celebrate.'

'Oh, indeed we will! Such celebrations as we've never known!' Molly agreed. 'And please God it will not be long now.' She could not understand why the war didn't stop everywhere at the same time. 'But when I go to Mass I shall thank God for those other mothers and sons.'

As far as she knew – and she never stopped praying or offering masses for their safety – the twins were all right. It was three weeks since the last letter, but she tried to tell herself that no news was good news.

On the other hand, over the last few months the news from Moira had been positive and welcome. She was by now five months pregnant, though many people wondered, and made no bones about asking, why was it it had taken so long for her to conceive. Would she not have been married almost two years by the time the baby came?

Father Curran had started asking before the first Christmas after the wedding, was there not yet a child on the way, and he had kept at it. Almost as if he was accusing me, Molly thought. Well, he had never been quite satisfied about her, had he?

A little girl, Moira said in her letters, was what she wanted. You could dress little girls so prettily. And now she said in her latest one, 'Didn't Barry's sister, Rose, hold a cork on a piece of string over my stomach, and weren't we quite certain from the direction it spun round that I am indeed carrying a girl?'

'She is *so* lucky!' Breda sighed when she read the letter that evening. 'Imagine having a baby of your very own! When will it ever happen to me?'

'All in good time,' Molly said. 'The husband must be found first!'

That would not be difficult, Molly reckoned. Her daughter was growing from the pretty child she had always been into an even more attractive young woman. And as she had always said would happen when Breda had despaired about her shortness, she had put on almost two inches in height and her figure, once too thin, had developed its womanly curves. And with it all, though the freckles were no fewer, she had kept her clear, creamy skin.

It was only a matter of time before the right man came along. And it is not I who am in a hurry, Molly thought. I would like to keep my daughter a little longer.

The truth was that so much of Breda's life was taken up with the O'Reillys – eight o'clock in the morning until eight at night, except for Sundays and a half-day on Wednesdays – that there was time for little else, even if she had had the energy. Molly worried that her daughter worked too hard, but there was nothing to be done about it.

'Deirdre is walking out with Paddy Murray,' Breda said. 'She says she is serious. They might get engaged at Christmas!'

'Stuff and nonsense!' Molly declared. 'She's only sixteen. Time to have half a dozen boys before that happens!'

But even as she spoke, she wondered, was it safer for a girl to have a number of boyfriends or to stick to one? Either way, wasn't it an anxious time for the mother?

'She's happy enough,' Breda said. 'He takes her to all the films, and in the best seats, no less!'

It was ages since she had been to the pictures, though she knew it was her own fault, 'twas not for the want of being asked. There were all the boys she had grown up with: Danny Quinn, Eammon O'Toole and the rest. Danny was always after her: would he meet her from O'Reilly's and they'd go for a walk? Wouldn't she go with him to the *céilidh*?

After Mass on a Sunday they would all stand on the pavement outside the church, though in two separate groups, girls in one, boys in the other, never mixed, but close enough to hear what was being said, to catch the eye, to interpret the admiring glance and decide whether to throw one back. They had been doing it since they were thirteen or so, but now they were of an age where they would soon be pairing off. A new, younger group would emerge and start the process all over again.

Breda would not be pairing off. Neither Danny nor any of the others, though they were nice enough, were what she wanted. She was not sure what she *did* want, she could not have put a description to him, except to say that she had never seen him in Kilbally. But when – and wherever – she did see him, she would recognize him at once. She was certain of that, and she was prepared to wait – well, not for ever, but at any rate a little longer.

'And how was Mrs O'Reilly today?' Molly asked. 'Was she any better?'

Breda's face clouded. She shook her head. 'She was not, Mammy. I would say she was not as well as a week ago. She hardly eats a morsel and she seems to have a lot of pain.'

'What does Mr O'Reilly say?' Molly asked.

'He says nothing. They don't seem to talk to each other, Mammy; not the way you and Dada do. Oh, I don't mean he neglects her. He sees to it she's well looked after, at least when I'm there, and I expect the rest of the time as well. 'Tis not easy to describe, but they don't seem to have any comfort for each other.'

' 'Tis sad,' Molly said. 'Isn't that what marriage is about, even when some of the other things have gone? That each comforts the other? Remember that when your turn comes.'

'Oh, I will!' Breda assured her.

Most of her working day was now spent with Mrs O'Reilly. Only two hours in the afternoon, when the sick woman managed to sleep, were spent in the shop. Although she had grown quite fond of Mrs O'Reilly over the period of getting on for two years, and did all she could to make her life more bearable, to quit the living quarters and step into the shop came as a relief, especially as by now she was no longer entirely relegated to cleaning and stacking shelves, unpacking deliveries, sweeping floors. Quite often now she served customers, and that she enjoyed. It was contact with the real world instead of the twilight world of the sickroom.

An even better contact with the world outside was that on two afternoons a week she was allowed to deliver orders to customers by bicycle. It was tricky work because the iron basket at the front of the bicycle and the panniers at the back were so filled with goods as to make the whole thing heavy and unbalanced. The outward journeys, when sometimes all she could manage was to push the bicycle up the hill, were compensated for by the return, with no more than her own weight in the saddle, so that there was nothing to stop her flying down the hill, terrifying every living thing in her path.

On the same evening that Breda and her mother were discussing the relationship between the O'Reillys, Luke, cashing up in the shop, with the doors locked and the blinds drawn, heard his wife call. 'Luke! Luke, what are you doing?'

There was a whining note to her voice which set his teeth on edge. Sometimes his life seemed bounded by that cry. It was as constant and melancholy as the wail of the seagulls which flew around all the time. He could never escape it. Nevertheless, he tried now, as always, to hide his feelings.

'Just coming!' he called out.

He left the money on the counter and went to the living room. He would have liked to have stayed in the shop until bedtime rather than spend the evening in his wife's company, but he knew where his duty lay. He would do his duty, though each day that passed it was heavier on him.

'What is it?' he asked. 'Do you want something?'

'I'm cold,' his wife said. 'Mend the fire!'

The room felt hot and stuffy to Luke. It was a summer's evening after a warm day and all the windows were tightly closed.

'It feels quite warm to me,' he said mildly.

'Well, I'm cold,' she said. 'Is it the fire you begrudge me now?'

'I begrudge you nothing,' he answered, stirring the fire, piling on more fuel.

It was true he begrudged her nothing material. Whatever she wanted or needed she could have. What he could not give her was love and understanding, though God knew he had tried.

He had grown out of such things long before she became ill, and it had been her fault, he thought, not his. Soon after he had brought her back from Dublin, a proud and happy man to have won her – for wasn't she a cut above the Kilbally girls? – he had discovered his mistake. Oh, she was good in the house, she managed the money. On the outside she was attractive, everyone acknowledged it, but there it ended. Inside her was a splinter of ice. She never touched him, and if he touched her, even if he brushed against her, she flinched. In bed it was like sleeping with a stranger.

He straightened up. 'Is that better? Shall I get you a shawl?'

'I don't want a shawl,' she said. 'What's keeping you in the shop?'

'I'm cashing up. It's been a busy day.'

At one time she would have done that. She had liked counting the money, entering it in the ledger; but not for a long time now.

'I'm always alone,' she grumbled.

'No you're not,' he said mildly. 'Hasn't Breda been gone only an hour?'

'You're my husband,' she said.

Husband, he thought bitterly! How could she say that, and what would she do with a real husband anyway? Sometimes, in his frustration and his longing, he had felt he would tear the clothes from her and take her whether she would or not, but that had been when she was fit and well. As her illness advanced he could no more touch her than she could him. The worst moment of every day came when he must climb into the bed beside her.

'I must finish the cashing up,' he said. 'I'll not be long.'

Every morning when she came to work Breda tried to think of something to say, some topic of conversation to cheer things up, to enliven the atmosphere. Mrs O'Reilly's talk varied only between her illness and complaints about this and that, though nowadays she seldom complained about Breda, as she had in the beginning.

'She knows which side her bread is buttered!' Molly had said when Breda had remarked on this improvement.

Luke O'Reilly, when in the house, seldom said a word about anything. There he was the most taciturn of men. In the shop, though, he was civil to his customers, ready to pass the time of day, to enquire about their welfare; but there was no banter in him, no jokes.

'I think my Dada is really looking forward to being a grandfather,' Breda said this morning. 'He pretends he's not, says he is too young, but he does not deceive me!'

Her remarks caused not a single ripple on the still pond of the living room. No answer. And serve me right, she chided herself. Wasn't it a tactless remark to make to a couple who had neither chick nor child? But there it was, she was not good at keeping a guard on her tongue, never had been.

And what has James O'Connor done to deserve such fortune, Luke asked himself? He has never worked hard, never been a good provider, has spent his time and money in the bars. Yet O'Connor had a brood of fine children, and now there was another generation coming along. What good thing has *he* done that I have not?

There was no need to look far for the answer. O'Connor had married Molly Byrne, while he had gone to the trouble, and made the mistake, of bringing Mary from Dublin.

He had learned early in his marriage that there were to be no children; no son to carry on the business in the way he had taken over from his father; no daughter who would brighten his life when she was young and look after him in his old age. Mary did not want children, and since she was a true daughter of the Church there was only one road for her, the road of abstinence.

'Well now, Mrs O'Reilly, I'll be seeing to your breakfast,' Breda said. 'An egg, is it?'

'I don't fancy an egg,' Mrs O'Reilly said. 'I have no hunger, none at all.'

'But you must eat something,' Breda said gently.

Luke left the room.

'I'll tell you what,' Breda said. 'I'll poach you an egg. 'Tis lighter that way, Mammy says.'

Mrs O'Reilly protested, but Breda went ahead regardless. With the shelled egg waiting in a cup, she brought the water in the saucepan to a boil, added a few drops of vinegar – she had no idea why – then vigorously stirred until the water was a swirling vortex. When it was at its fastest she neatly dropped the egg into the whirlpool and watched while it spun around and quickly solidified, the white wrapping itself in a protective cocoon around the yolk. It was over in no time at all, and she never could work out how it happened.

It was mostly in vain. Mrs O'Reilly ate a couple of teaspoonfuls, with one small finger of bread, and that was it.

Breda sighed.

'You will have to do better than that! 'Tis not enough to feed a sparrow. Will I bring you a bowl of my mother's broth tomorrow, then? That will be full of goodness.'

Mrs O'Reilly shook her head without speaking.

I will so, Breda determined. No matter what.

She washed Mrs O'Reilly every day now, knowing that left to herself she would neglect it. Once a week she gave her a bed bath, and today was the day. In a way, she disliked doing it, feeling it an intrusion into the woman's privacy, even though she bared only a little of her body at a time, drying it and covering it up again before moving on to the next bit. I would not like anyone to do it to me, Breda thought. I would be mortified. Even so, Mrs O'Reilly always seemed better after it.

But not today. Today she protested that her limbs ached, that the flannel was too hot, too cold, that she could not bear the smell of the soap, even though it was Yardley's lavender. Breda was shocked by the sight of Mrs O'Reilly's body. Even in the last week the flesh seemed to have fallen off her.

When Breda tried to brush her hair Mrs O'Reilly, with what strength she had, pushed her away.

'Leave me be!' she said. 'Go and help in the shop.'

'Only if you will definitely take a nap,' Breda said.

Mrs O'Reilly took her rosary from under her pillow, clutched at it, and closed her eyes.

'I will so,' she said.

Breda waited until the woman's breathing, and the loosening of her grip on the rosary, signified that she had fallen into a sleep, then left the room.

'Mrs O'Reilly does not seem at all well today,' she said to Luke. 'When is the doctor due?'

'Tomorrow. Are you saying I should send for him sooner?'

' 'Tis not for me to say,' Breda told him. ' 'Tis for you to decide.'

'She looks no different to me,' he said.

And isn't that because you never really look at her, Breda thought.

Yet he looked at *her*. She was always conscious, these days, of his eyes following her as she moved around the shop. Sometimes, when she turned too suddenly, she caught him at it. She knew she did not imagine it because when that did happen he would redden and move away, busying himself with something or other.

She hated the way he looked at her. Aside from hating it, it made her uncomfortable, slightly apprehensive. Though she could not have said she was afraid of him, she felt better when there were customers in the shop. But he was not unkind to her, and he was always polite. Also, as he had when Kieran and Patrick had worked for him, he gave her little extras in the way of food to take home to her mother. Dada did not like it, but Mammy did not mind. She saw it as kindness.

Today he gave her a punnet of strawberries to take home.

'Though if he'd kept them they would not have been fit to sell tomorrow,' Breda said as she handed them over.

'That is not a nice thing to say,' Molly reproved her. ' 'Twas kind of him to do it.'

'Perhaps it was,' Breda agreed. 'He is not easy to understand. Kind in some ways; not kind to his wife.'

'Perhaps he has reasons for it,' Molly said. Half of Kilbally suspected the reasons; some said they knew. It was not a subject she proposed to discuss with Breda.

'Does he ill-treat her?' she asked.

'Oh no, Mammy. Nothing like that. He's just . . . well, cold.'

He had not been cold as a young man, quite the reverse, or so Molly had heard. Of course she could not actually know, but that was what had been said.

'Well then,' she said. 'As long as he is not unkind. And I dare say he is a very worried man.'

'Could I be taking some of your broth for Mrs O'Reilly tomorrow?' Breda asked. 'It might tempt her. The flesh is falling off her.'

'Of course!'

It troubled Molly that Breda was poised between a woman as sick as Mary O'Reilly and a man she didn't like. It was not the right job for her. But what could be done about it? They needed the money. It always came down to that in the end.

'Do you think Moira will let me be a godmother?' Breda asked, changing the subject. There were times when she wanted to shake the O'Reillys out of her hair, and this was one of them.

'Who can tell?' Molly said. 'Aren't you her sister, and won't you be the baby's aunt, but who can ever tell what Moira will do?'

It would depend partly on where the child was to be baptized. Would it be in Kilbally or in Dublin? Molly knew well the dilemma for Moira and Barry. It was to court bad luck to take the baby too often or too far from its own home before it was baptized; better for it to stay within its own place, with the windows and doors signed with the sign of the cross against all evil. It might be no more than superstition, but even Moira would hesitate to take chances with her baby and Kilbally was quite a journey.

On the other hand, Great-grandmother Devlin, as she would be, was no longer fit enough to travel to Dublin. She was bent double with the rheumatics and could hardly move out of the house, and wasn't it Grandma Devlin who had the money and had declared that if she could not be present at the baptism of her first great-grandchild, perhaps the only one she would live to see, then might she not just as well give the money to the Poor Clares? For Moira and Barry it was a difficult decision all right.

'If the baptism takes place in Dublin,' Breda said, 'Moira might choose one of her fashionable friends to be godmother.'

'Though if it was in Kilbally, she could hardly fashion not to ask you,' Molly said.

'I wonder could we even afford to go to Dublin, you and me and Dada?' Breda said.

'I don't know,' Molly admitted. 'We shall have to see. After all, the child is not yet born.'

She had other things on her mind now. Every day she listened avidly to the news on the wireless about the progress of the war in the Far East. It couldn't be long before it was over, surely it must end soon.

When the news came, she was alone in the house. Her reaction was not what she had thought it would be. She had thought she would rush out of the house, shouting to the world.

She did rush out of the house, but not shouting. She ran all the way to the church, and there prostrated herself before the altar in deep and silent thanksgiving.

'How long before they'll be home?' she said to James that evening.

'It might be a long time,' he cautioned. 'They cannot get from the jungle of Burma to the shores of Kilbally in a flash. There are no magic carpets. We must be patient.'

'Now that I know they are safe,' Molly said, 'that will be less difficult than I thought, though it cannot come too quickly.'

Moira's baby came into the world on a rainy day in September, with considerable trouble to its mother, who decided quite quickly that no way could she ever go through all this again. Contrary to all predictions, it was a boy, for whom the name Peter was hastily chosen. He weighed nine and a quarter pounds, recovered quickly from his rough passage (more quickly than his mother) and cried frequently and lustily for sustenance.

'For Jesus' sake, take him away!' Moira cried to her mother-in-law, who was there most of the time.

Mrs Devlin made the sign of the cross over the baby before lifting him into her arms. Until he was baptized it would be unsafe not to do this.

'You must make sure that *everyone* does it!' she warned Moira. 'The midwife, the doctor, neighbours, *everyone*. Even Barry! Right up until he's baptized, bless his heart!'

'Superstition,' Moira said weakly.

Her mother-in-law was full of superstitions. Hadn't she sewn a coin into the baby's clothing, for luck? And when Moira's labour had proved so difficult and prolonged, hadn't she wanted to bring a seventh son into the bedroom to help things along? Moira had protested, she wanted no man in the room, but as it turned out no-one actually knew of a seventh son who could be called upon.

But I do not care what signs or incantations they make over the child, Moira thought, breathing a long sigh of relief, as long as they take him away whenever possible!

Mrs Devlin, deeply concerned about exposing the baby to the wiles of Satan before the sacrament of baptism had made him safe, was the person most exercised about where this should take place. If she kept a close watch on him here in the house in Dublin, he would be safest, but the inheritance from his great-grandmother in Kilbally was not to be sneezed at, far from it.

In the end it was her husband who made the decision. 'We shall go to Kilbally!' he said firmly. 'We all know Mammy will not change her mind. Would we not be robbing the child otherwise?

'Besides which,' he continued, in an unctuous tone, 'Mammy is frail. Who knows when the call might come?'

It was a sobering thought. It also made the inheritance seem nearer.

'You are quite right, Dada!' Barry said. 'The moment Moira is fit to travel!'

'I suppose I must agree,' Mrs Devlin said reluctantly. 'But we must take every precaution over little Peter.'

The problem then arose as to where they would stay. Grandma Devlin's cottage would not take four extra adults, plus a baby with all its accoutrements.

' 'Tis no matter at all,' Molly said when she read out the letter from Moira. 'Mr and Mrs Devlin can stay with Grandma Devlin, Moira, Barry and the baby can have the bedroom here, and you, Breda, can sleep at Grandma Byrne's.'

'Oh no!' Breda protested. 'Yes, of course they're welcome to the bedroom, but I don't want to stay with Grandma Byrne. I want to be here where the baby is. Especially now that I *am* to be the godmother!'

Wasn't the godmother almost the most important person in the whole affair – apart from the baby, of course? She had studied the service in the missal. It was awesome.

When it came to the real thing, with its solemn promises which Breda fully intended to keep, it was even more awesome, but it was happy and cheerful into the bargain. Everyone was in the best of moods. Mrs Devlin got over the nervousness she had had at the thought of the baby being out of her sight and care while staying with the O'Connors. Her husband had almost reassured her. 'Molly O'Connor is a nice, sensible woman,' he'd said. 'And in any case the baby is with his mother!' The look his wife had given him had told him what she'd thought about that last bit.

Grandma Devlin had been taken to church in Murphy's hired car.

'Peter has a distinct look of you, Grandma!' Barry said.

'Just what I was thinking,' Mr Devlin said.

'Is that so?' James O'Connor said. 'And wasn't I thinking how much he favoured the O'Connors?'

Peter had behaved perfectly, remaining calm even when Father Curran poured the water over his head.

'Aren't you the darling?' Breda enthused, taking him in her arms, which was her right, she thought, as his godmother.

Afterwards, Molly somehow managed to serve a feast to everyone. 'Though how I would have managed it without Luke O'Reilly's help, I do not know!' she whispered to Breda. Then there was talk, and some singing, and more talk. Mrs Devlin took home Grandma Devlin in Murphy's hired car, the baby was fed and put to bed. Moira followed soon after. The men went to the Harp. Molly and Breda cleared away and washed up.

At last Molly sat down, yawning.

'Go to bed, Mammy,' Breda said. 'I don't mind waiting up on my own. I can't go to bed until Dada and Barry do so.'

She was asleep in the chair when they came in, but their noisiness – they were singing – wakened her.

'Oh Dada!' she said. 'I'm waiting to go to bed!'

When they had gone she undressed quickly, bedded down on the sofa, pulled the blanket over her, and was asleep at once.

She had no idea how long afterwards it was that she suddenly wakened. She looked up, and saw Barry Devlin looking down at her. He was smiling. She stared at him.

'Sleeping Beauty!' he whispered. 'By rights you should have been wakened with a kiss. You were too quick.'

'What do you want?' Breda said. She was nervous, but trying not to show it. 'Mind you don't waken Dada. He's a very light sleeper.'

It was a lie, it would take an army on the march to waken him, especially after the drink, but it served.

'I came through for a cup of water,' Barry said.

'There's some in the jug,' Breda said.

He poured himself a cup of water and took it back to bed with him. She was a corker, his little sister-in-law, he thought. And not so little as she had been.

He stared down at Moira. It was no use waking her. She would have nothing of him since the baby's birth. Far too soon, she said.

The next morning, Breda had gone off to work before he, sleeping late, got up.

She was late for work, which was unusual. What was even more unusual was that the shop door was locked. She knocked loudly, and when there was no response she rattled the latch as hard as she could. Where was he? What could have happened? She was about to move around to the house door at the back, but as she took the first step she heard the key in the lock.

The door opened and Luke O'Reilly stood there, still in his grey flannel dressing-gown, his face as white as a sheet and his eyes staring.

'Why, Mr O'Reilly . . . !' she began.

'Run for the doctor!' he said. 'Run as fast as you can! I've done all I can!'

She ran all the way. The doctor was in, and returned with her, but it was too late. Mrs O'Reilly was dead.

A little later, when she had opened up the shop for Mr O'Reilly – he was not disposed to keep it closed – Breda asked a customer to take the news to her mother.

'Tell her I will not be home to dinner. I cannot leave here, there is so much to do. I am sorry not to see my godson before they take him back to Dublin.'

In the afternoon, when the Devlins had left, Molly went down to the shop to make sure that Breda was all right.

'Would you like to see Mary?' Luke O'Reilly invited.

'Of course,' Molly said. It was expected. It would be rude indeed to refuse.

Breda had made the fact that she could not leave the shop, Mr O'Reilly being engaged in all the paraphernalia of death, her excuse for not going in to see Mrs O'Reilly, though in the past hour a steady stream of people (far more than had ever come to see the poor woman in life, Breda thought) had stopped by to pay their respects. Now that her mother was here she would do what must be done.

'Can I go in with you, Mammy?' she asked.

'Of course, love.' Molly observed her daughter's pale face. 'There is no need to be frightened.'

'It's just that I've never seen a dead person,' Breda explained.

It was not nearly as bad as she had expected. Mrs O'Reilly looked tranquil, peaceful. The deep lines of pain which had etched her face in the last year or two had disappeared as if by magic. There is nothing to be afraid of, Breda thought.

'She looks younger,' she whispered. 'She looks almost . . . pretty!'

'Yes. She looks as she did when Luke first brought her here,' Molly said. 'She was a fine-looking young woman.'

'If there is anything at all I can do for you,' Molly said to Luke when she took her leave, 'you have only to be asking.'

Breda was busy all the rest of the day in the shop. Far more people came to buy than on an ordinary day. She was glad when eight o'clock came and she was free to go. She left Mr O'Reilly cashing up. That he would not delegate to her.

'I will see you in the morning, then,' she said as she left.

'But what will there be for me to do?' she asked Mammy later. 'Most of the time I've looked after Mrs O'Reilly. Will there be a job for me?'

The same thought had been in Molly's mind most of the day.

'I don't know,' she said soberly. 'We shall have to see what the Good Lord sends.'

Eight

For several weeks, indeed months, after Mrs O'Reilly's death Breda clung to her job, though she felt it was only by a thread. Every Friday afternoon when Mr O'Reilly paid her wages she held her breath in case at the same time he should give her a week's notice or, at best, tell her he must reduce her hours. But Christmas had come and gone and it had not happened.

It was true that she had tried hard to make herself as useful as possible, even seeking out jobs that she would not have thought of a year ago when Mrs O'Reilly's needs filled most of her day. The stockroom at the back of the shop, and the shed outside where the overflow of goods or empty crates and bottles waiting to be collected were stored, were, for instance, both as clean and tidy as new pins. Everything was to hand, in its right place, everything that could be labelled was labelled.

She enjoyed doing this. She was alone and free, and because she was out of earshot she could allow herself to sing, which she would never have done in the house, out of respect, and certainly not in the shop, even if there were no customers. It would not be fitting. So she sang away like a small, tuneful bird, all the latest songs she knew from the wireless. She could pick up a tune and remember the words in no time at all.

She was not sure that Mr O'Reilly appreciated the work she did in the back. Sometimes she wondered if he actually noticed. He seldom remarked on it.

'But if he doesn't care about it,' she said to her mother, 'why would he keep me on? He is not one to throw his money about.'

'I expect he does notice,' Molly said. 'Some people are just not good at saying thank you. Anyway, he thanks you by paying your wages.'

'The one thing he does appreciate is having his dinner made for him,' Breda said.

It was something she had started in the last few months of Mrs O'Reilly's life, when that lady was no longer up to it. She had not wanted to continue with it, and still less had she wanted to take her dinner with Mr O'Reilly, as he expected her to. She found it an uncomfortable situation, but Mammy had said that if she wanted to keep the job she couldn't afford to be choosy. She must take the rough with the smooth.

Of course she wanted to keep the job, or needed to. There were no other prospects, not even Miss Glenda, who had long ago taken on someone else.

'I expect he is also glad of your company,' Mammy said now. 'Men do not like to cook. And I don't suppose he likes to eat alone, poor man!'

Molly was sorry for Luke. He had had a poor marriage, and perhaps life as a childless widower was even worse. He had the money, of course, which put food in his mouth and clothes on his back, and would give him the best of funerals when the time came, but there was a lot of time to be passed before then, and money didn't brighten empty hours. He had never been one for spending his evenings at the Harp. Mary had seen to that.

'As a matter of fact,' Breda said, 'I do not usually get much chance to sit with him at the table. It is my job to answer the shop bell at dinner time, so am I not jumping up and down like a jack-in-the-box?'

'Then what are you complaining about?' Molly asked.

'There's another thing,' Breda said. 'He has asked me would I go through Mrs O'Reilly's things – clothes and suchlike. 'Tis months since she died and he has done nothing about it, not even made a start. I wonder would you be after helping me, Mammy? You would know better what to do with things.'

'He might not wish me to do it,' Molly said. 'I thought he might have asked Mrs Milligan.'

'That he would not hear of,' Breda said. 'But you he would not mind a bit. He likes you.'

'Very well,' Molly said. 'We will do it on Wednesday afternoon when the shop is closed, if that will suit.'

When she told James what she had promised to do he was not best pleased.

'Why should not Mrs Milligan do it?' he asked. 'She worked for his wife.'

Molly shrugged. 'I don't know. Didn't I ask Breda the very same thing? She said he would not hear of it.'

Then, as she was leaving the house after dinner on Wednesday, James said, 'What is in your basket?'

'A few scones and some soda bread.'

'Are we so rich, then, that we can give food to Luke O'Reilly, who has his pockets well lined?' he complained. 'Can't he afford to buy his own?'

'You cannot buy what is home-made,' Molly said. 'And I hope we are never so poor that we cannot give to a neighbour! It will cheer him up.'

James shook his head in mock despair, but he could never resist her for long.

'Very well then! But you are too soft. You are as soft as butter!'

Luke O'Reilly was pleased with the gifts.

'It's a month of Sundays since I tasted newly baked soda bread,' he said.

Molly was surprised. She had thought perhaps there might be a stream of widows and single ladies bringing offerings to his door. But she would not say so. He was not a man you could tease.

'Kieran always liked my scones. I used to send them to him when he first went away,' she said.

'And how is Kieran?' Luke enquired.

'He is very well. Next year he will be priested. Then there will be no happier man in all Ireland.'

And Kathleen was now professed, and happy. They had both done what was right for them, but never a day passed that she did not miss them, and her other children away from her. Christmas had come and gone with Breda the only child at home to celebrate it, though the twins, according to their last letter, were all right, and looking forward to being home very soon. Moira, to her disgust, was already pregnant again.

'Moira might be disgusted, but Father Curran will be pleased!' Molly had remarked.

'So where shall we start?' she asked Luke. 'And what do you want me to do with the clothes, or whatever else there is?'

'I don't know,' he said helplessly. 'There are clothes in the wardrobe, and other things in the chest of drawers. I just don't know what. You must tell me if anything is fit to sell, or only to give away. You would know better than I would.'

'Then leave it to me,' Molly said. 'It must be a painful task for you. But I won't decide anything without asking.'

Would it be painful, he wondered? He didn't know. Since Mary's death he never knew from day to day how he was going to feel about any of it. Some days he was grateful for the new freedom, as if heavy chains had fallen from him. At other times he felt incredibly alone, even in the presence of his customers. There were moments when he thought he heard his wife's petulant voice calling to him, and he would step halfway to answering it. Even though his loss would have been greater he would have been happier, he was sure, if they had had a good marriage. As it was, he felt guilt that they had not been in accord, and anger that it was partly her fault.

What he could not yet bring himself to do was to enter into his new state of being a widower, start a new life, as he knew he must. Even when he went to bed he could not allow himself to trespass on the half of the bed which had once been hers. He sometimes wondered would she ever leave him? Was it an illusion that he was free? Would he ever be?

He left Molly and Breda to it and went back into the shop. Once a month, on a Wednesday afternoon, he visited the wholesaler in Ennis, but this was not the week for it and aside from this monthly excursion he seldom went anywhere on his half day. He did his accounts, paid bills, made out orders, fried himself a rasher and an egg for his tea, and that was it.

'There's some good stuff here,' Molly said looking through the wardrobe. 'Good quality. Of course it's not up-to-the-minute fashion because it's a few years since Mary O'Reilly stopped going out of the house. But anyway, who is out-and-out fashionable in Kilbally?'

'I would be if I could!' Breda sighed.

Molly smiled at her.

'I know you would. Haven't I told you, you should learn to make your own clothes? You could study the pattern books. That might help.'

'Perhaps I will,' Breda said. 'Mammy, if there was anything of Mrs O'Reilly's you would like for yourself, I'm sure Mr O'Reilly would give it to you.'

'Perhaps so. And there are one or two nice things. But I wouldn't fancy them.'

She had not really liked Mary O'Reilly in life; she felt guilty that she had seldom had a good word to say about her. To wear the dead woman's garments would be hypocritical, unacceptable.

'But it would be different for you,' she said. 'You liked Mary and I think she liked you. Probably she would want you to have something and Luke has just not thought about it. You would suit this green jacket, for instance. Here, try it on.'

Hesitantly, looking around at the door in case Mr O'Reilly should enter – and what in the world would he think if he did – Breda slipped her arms into the jacket.

'I feel awkward doing this,' she said. 'But I never saw her wear it, so it doesn't *quite* feel as though it belonged to her.'

'I wonder, did she ever do so? 'Tis like new,' Molly said.

She was on her knees, sorting through the drawers now, but she broke off, sat back on her heels and appraised her daughter.

'Yes indeed, you *do* suit it. The sleeves would need shortening, but that's no trouble.'

Molly returned to the contents of the drawer.

'Good gracious!' she said. 'There are lengths of quite new material here. I wonder why she hoarded these? Well, I suppose we shall never know!'

Breda, wearing the jacket, studied her reflection, at least that part which was not blocked out by various ornaments and vases of artificial flowers, in the mirror over the sideboard.

'Yes,' she said. 'I do like it. All the same, there is no way I could ask for it. If he were to mention it, that would be different.'

She took off the jacket and draped it over a chair, the second before Luke O'Reilly came back into the room.

'We have almost finished,' Molly told him. 'We have sorted things into different lots. The clothes on the armchair you might manage to sell. They seem almost new.'

She was wondering when and where Mary could have bought them. It was a long time since she'd been as far as Ennis and there was nothing like these in Kilbally.

'She bought things by post, from Dublin,' Luke said, answering the question in Molly's face. 'She bought them and never wore them. But I didn't deny her. I never denied her anything. No-one can say I did!'

'I'm sure you didn't,' Molly said kindly.

Except what she needed most, which was love and understanding, Breda thought, with wisdom beyond her years, wisdom born of daily observation.

'You will need to take them to the second-hand clothes shop when you go to Ennis,' Molly told Luke. 'It's near to the church. They will give you something, though perhaps not what they're worth.'

'I wonder if you could . . . '

She guessed what he was going to say, and interrupted him.

'I couldn't do it for you, Luke. I'm sorry. I seldom go to Ennis.'

That was true. It cost money to travel to Ennis, and money to spend when you got there, but the real truth was that James would have a fit if she did this further thing for Luke O'Reilly.

'Anyway,' she said, 'being a man you'll no doubt get a better price than I would. Now these two piles here I think will be suitable for the church jumble sale. They'll be glad of them. And the shoes.'

There were ten pairs of shoes. In all my life I have never had more than one pair of shoes at a time, Molly thought. But never mind that, she admonished herself, haven't I been far happier than Mary O'Reilly, who never had the pleasure of buying a pair of shoes for a child of her own?

Luke gazed at the shoes.

'She had tiny feet.'

'Yes,' Molly agreed. 'Size three!'

When he had first met her, Luke thought, she had had dancing feet. 'Twinkletoes,' he had once called her. Where had all that gone? He pulled himself together.

'If there is anything you would like . . . ' he said to Molly.

'Well, since you mention it, I was looking at this green jacket,' she confessed. 'I would buy it from you if you didn't want too much.'

'It's yours,' Luke said. 'You are welcome to it. I don't want anything for it.'

'Thank you very much,' Molly said.

'You will suit it,' Luke told her.

'Oh, it is not for me! It is for Breda here!'

He was disappointed. For a moment, giving the jacket to Molly O'Connor, he had felt good. He would have seen her wearing it to church. He was not sure that he would have given it to Breda. 'Twas not that he had anything against the girl; she was pretty and pleasant, and a good worker, though by rights there was not enough for her to do, and he must think seriously about that. But he knew, though no-one else ever would, that he kept her on for the sake of her mother.

'And there are some lengths of material in the bottom drawer,' Molly said.

'Take them!' Luke said. 'Take what you want!'

When he had gone back into the shop she and Breda made their pick of the materials.

'Now is your chance,' Molly said. 'Here is a navy wool which will make you a smart skirt to go with the green jacket . . . '

'And a navy and white spot for a blouse. It's lovely fine cotton. Oh, you will make them for me, won't you, Mammy?'

'I will not!' Mammy said firmly. 'Sure, I'll buy the pattern, and I'll show you how to do it, but you will make both garments yourself. And unless you're willing to do that, we'll not take the materials.'

'Oh Mammy! Supposing I make a mess of it!'

'You won't,' Molly said. 'I'll show you every step. But it's high time you learned to make your own clothes. So what is it to be? Will you take the materials or not?'

'Then I'll take them,' Breda said.

Already she could see in her mind's eye how she would look. If there was enough material she would make the skirt in gores, flaring out to the hem, and the blouse with a neat collar, and small white buttons down the front and on the cuffs. She could see the picture, but could she ever do it?

'And since Luke said take what you like,' Molly said, 'though I don't want to be greedy I will have this nice white cotton. It will make me a Sunday blouse.'

A week later the telegram came. The delivery boy thrust it into her hands and departed quickly. He didn't like to be there when people opened telegrams. They were mostly bad news.

Molly's heart raced. While she tried to open it – her hands were trembling and clumsy – she thought of a dozen catastrophes which could have befallen her family. Kieran was seriously ill. Kathleen had been knocked down, crossing a busy Dublin street. Moira had lost the baby. It could not be the twins because, she hoped and believed, they were by now on the high seas on their way home. But Patrick could have fallen overboard and Colum jumped to save him!

All these thoughts rushed through her mind in the time it took her to open the telegram and make out the words.

It *was* from the twins. They had not fallen overboard. No calamity had befallen them. She read the words silently, and then out loud. ' "Landed in England. Expect us home Saturday. Patrick and Colum." '

She had to tell someone. She could not possibly wait until James and Breda came home from work. She wanted James, who was helping Mr O'Farrell with the harvest. She wanted Breda, who was down at the shop. She had to tell them, she just had to.

Tears were streaming down her face, and her legs were suddenly so weak that she felt they would not hold her; nevertheless she ran out of the door and away down the street, waving the telegram.

She ran in the direction of Luke O'Reilly's shop because it was closer than the farm. She ran straight past neighbours she knew, not really seeing them, not aware that they had to jump out of her way.

She burst into the shop and scattered two women patiently waiting their turn, only coming to a stop as she hit against the counter, behind which Breda was serving a customer.

'They're coming home!' she shouted. 'Patrick and Colum! They're in England. They'll be home on Saturday!'

She thrust the telegram at Breda, then she laid her head on the counter and burst into sobs. Breda ran around and eased her mother into a chair, knelt on the floor with her arms around her, and joined her tears with Molly's.

Luke rushed in from the back. 'What's happening? What's the noise about?'

He saw Molly and Breda crying in each other's arms. 'Something's wrong!' he cried. 'What is it? What's wrong?'

Luke's voice was the first to penetrate Molly's consciousness. She raised her head and faced him with a watery smile. 'Nothing's wrong, Luke. I'm sorry to cause such a commotion in your shop. It's just that I'm so happy . . . '

Her voice faltered. Luke, bewildered, thought she would burst into tears again.

'It's the twins,' Breda explained. 'They've landed in England. They'll be home on Saturday.'

'I must go and tell James,' Molly said. 'He's helping on the farm.'

'You had best have a cup of tea first,' Luke said. 'Come into the living room and Breda will make one.' It was the only thing he could think of to do for her.

'Well, thank you, I will,' Molly said. 'If it won't take too long.'

'Two shakes of a lamb's tail,' Breda promised.

'I feel very shaky,' Molly apologized.

'Then Breda can go with you to find James,' Luke said.

Molly stared at him. 'That's very generous of you, Luke. She'll come straight back afterwards.'

She rose to follow Luke to the living room, then paused and spoke to the other customers. 'I'm sorry for making such a scene,' she said. 'It was a shock.'

She became aware that she was still wearing her pinafore, and none too clean at that. It was entirely unlike her to leave the house wearing her pinafore.

'And was it not the pleasantest shock in the world?' a customer asked.

'And they are well are they, the twins?' another woman asked.

'I expect so, thank you, Mrs Fitzpatrick,' Molly said.

She drank the tea and felt better. 'I feel as though I want to go out and tell the whole of Kilbally!' she said.

'There will be no need of that,' Luke said. 'Mrs Fitzpatrick will see to that. In no time at all they will all know!'

It was all go for the next few days; scrubbing, cleaning, polishing, blackleading the range, washing the curtains.

'Why are you doing all this?' James demanded of Molly. 'Is not the house always as clean as a whistle? And in any case, will they even notice?'

'They will so!' Molly retorted. 'Won't they appreciate a clean home after all the dirty places they've been in? And good food. Who knows what they have been living on, out there in the jungle?'

She could not conceive of the jungle, other than she had occasionally seen it in films she had not particularly enjoyed; giant trees, monkeys swinging from branch to branch, wide rivers infested by crocodiles, and man-eating lions and tigers behind every bush. Her sons would certainly be glad to get back to Kilbally.

Breda would have liked to have spent every spare minute making up the material into her new skirt and blouse, so as to present a smart appearance on her brothers' homecoming. It was impossible on several counts. Her mother did not have a minute to show her anything. The table was always cluttered with baking or cooking, or with cutlery and ornaments to be cleaned. There was not enough space even to cut out a pocket handkerchief. But first and foremost, though she had chosen a pattern from the catalogue in the post office, and it had been sent for to Dublin, as yet there was no sign of it.

Though Breda longed to see her brothers, she had one big worry about their return, which as yet she had mentioned to no-one. What would happen *now* to her job? Before he went into the Army, hadn't Patrick worked very well for Mr O'Reilly, and wouldn't the latter want him back in place of herself? It would be unfair, she knew, for a man who had returned from fighting in the war to find his sister in the job which should by rights be his. Mammy had not said a word about it, but surely it must have occurred to her?

In fact, it had flitted in and out of Molly's mind like a butterfly, but never settling. All that counted was that the boys were coming home. Nothing else mattered.

On Friday evening she stood in the middle of the room and surveyed her domain. Everything sparkled and shone. The cupboards were filled with food, which would never have been possible had not her friends and neighbours in Kilbally contributed from their rations to the homecoming. Twists of tea, cups of sugar, wedges of cheese, rashers and eggs from the farm, pots of jam. There had been a procession to her door. Luke O'Reilly had sent Breda home with a basket of assorted groceries. For a little while they would want for nothing.

'Will tomorrow never come?' she said to James.

'It will be there when you wake up in the morning,' James said. 'Nothing will stop Saturday following Friday. And in the meantime, since you have nothing whatever left to do, put on your shawl and we'll take a dander down to the strand.'

'Very well,' Molly agreed.

She had not been out of the house for three days. She had a sudden panicking thought that perhaps her sons would arrive this evening instead of tomorrow, and she not be there to greet them, but she stifled it, and followed James out of the door. It was a perfect evening, cooling down refreshingly after a hot day, the sky over the sea just beginning to turn pink. She took a deep breath, filling her lungs with the clean air.

Not many married couples in Kilbally took walks. The children came quickly and there was always a baby who could not be left. After that the habit was lost. But it never had been with James and Molly. Nor had she ever shed the habit of linking her hand through his arm, for all the world as if they were still a courting couple.

James, as she had known he would, made for the sea. It drew him like a magnet, especially that area around the harbour, from which, as they neared it now, the boats were getting ready to put out for the night's fishing.

He waved, and called out to some of the men. 'Good luck go with ye! Good catch!'

'You wish you were going with them, don't you?' Molly said.

He nodded. Over the years he had grown fond of this small harbour even though, except that the same sea, part of that wild ocean, flowed or pounded, lapped or beat, according to its mood, against the shores, it was so different from the wide Galway Bay where he had spent his youth.

'Once,' he admitted, 'I wanted to have my own boat, to be in charge.' Now he was lucky to get a night's work from time to time on someone else's boat.

'Sometimes the sea frightens me,' Molly confessed, 'though not at this moment.' It was lapping gently against the harbour wall as though it was nothing more than a large lake.

'Why should it not?' James said. 'It is all-powerful, bigger than all of us. Man can do nothing against the sea when it so decides.'

They stood there watching as the whole sky turned every shade of pink and red, salmon and mauve, each band of colour reflected in the still water. Then, when the sun dipped over the horizon, they turned for home.

'They will have a fine, calm night,' James said.

As darkness fell he walked with his arm around Molly, holding her close. When they reached home, Breda had already gone to bed.

'And you and I will do the same,' James said. 'From tomorrow you will have eyes for no-one but your sons, but for now you are mine!'

'I am always yours,' Molly said quietly. 'You know that.'

'Then we will prove it,' he said, leading her into the bedroom.

For one second, when she wakened next morning, Molly forgot that this was not just a day like any other day, and then she remembered, and leapt out of bed.

James stirred in his sleep. She grabbed him by the shoulder and shook him. 'Wake up! Wake up!'

He opened his eyes slowly. 'What is it? What is the matter?'

'Nothing is the matter,' she said impatiently. 'Except that this is the day the twins arrive!'

He turned, and looked at the clock on the bedside table.

'But it's only six-thirty! They'll not be here for hours!'

'How do you know that?' Molly demanded. 'They have not given us the time, only the day. They could have crossed on the evening boat and be here any time! And me with everything to do. Fresh bread to bake. Vegetables to prepare. I must waken Breda at once!'

Breda also protested.

'I can have at least another half-hour! I don't have to be at the shop until eight o'clock.'

'I want you to fetch the milk from the creamery,' Molly said. 'We shall need a quart extra today, and we will treat ourselves with some cream to go with the fruit pie. You must get up at once, Breda. It would not do for us not to be ready when they arrive!'

She adjusted the curtain which had been reinstated to make a separate part of the bedroom for the twins. She would have liked to have bought a new curtain – this one was so shabby – but the money would not run to it.

Though a dozen times she stood in the open doorway, looking down the street, willing her sons to turn the corner at the bottom which led from the station, it was teatime before they arrived, and she did not see them until they opened the door and walked in on her, as large as life.

It was a case of who could hug her, whom she could hug, first and fiercest, so that they stood in a tight circle, arms around each other, not able at first to find words to express their delight at being together again.

'Stand back!' Molly said in the end. 'Let me take a good look at you both!'

They were her sons all right, she thought. Their smiles were as broad as ever, their voices as warm. Yet they were not the same. There was a different look in their eyes. Also though they had always been slim, now, in spite of their bulky uniforms, they were as thin as laths. Their faces, too, were hollow-cheeked, and under the sun-tan their skin was pale and yellowy.

'You need feeding up,' Molly said. 'And I shall see that you get it!' It would give her great pleasure.

'There is no need to worry about us, Mammy,' Patrick said. 'We are as fit as fleas!'

'Though we have had our moments,' Colum added.

He would not go into them, nor would Patrick. They had had countless hours of talking together over the last few years. People who hadn't been there thought that war was all action, all excitement. Well, some of it was, there were horrors of which they would never tell, but much of it had been long, boring hours of inaction, in which they had decided that, once home, the past would be past. All that would matter would be the future they had planned together, and about which they must talk to Mammy and Dada as soon as possible.

'Where is Dada?' Patrick asked.

'He has work on the farm for the moment,' Molly said. 'But he will get home as soon as he can. And Breda, as you know, is working for Luke O'Reilly. It will be after eight o'clock before she is home.'

'We'll go down and see her,' Colum said.

'Not until you have eaten,' Molly told him. 'I am making potato scones. I doubt you tasted those in the British army!

'There are a lot of people you will be wanting to see,' she went on as she turned the scones on the griddle. She hoped, though, that she would have them to herself for a little while.

'For instance,' she said to Colum, 'you will want to see Mr Murphy about your job.' She turned to Patrick. 'It is not so simple for you, because of Breda, but I'm sure it will work out. It is important for men to have jobs.'

'We will not worry about any of that just yet,' Patrick said easily. 'It will be a week or two before we are officially demobbed.'

'Of course! And there is no hurry for either of you to start work. You have earned a good rest.'

As soon as they had eaten, and drunk several cups of strong tea, it was clear that they wanted to get out of the house. Molly was disappointed, but it was a natural restlessness, she told herself. They were not used to sitting around. And wouldn't it be good for them to see old friends? Wouldn't it help them to settle down all the quicker?

It was a long time before the twins returned. In fact, Breda was home before them.

'Where can they be?' Molly wondered out loud.

'They didn't stay long with me,' Breda said. 'We were busy in the shop. They said they were going off to see Dada. I expect they're with him.'

'In that case they will be in the Harp,' Molly said. 'I hope they don't stay all evening.'

But if James had his way, and the twins had money, then that was more than likely. She was disappointed; not only because she had a meal which would be ready to lay on the table any minute now, but because she had seen so little of them since they arrived. But never mind, though. The war was over. Once they were out of the Army she would see them all the time.

In fact, they were home within the hour, all three of them, bright-eyed, slightly flushed, and full of loud talk. They must have put in some swift drinking since collecting James at the farm, Molly thought.

'I wondered where you were.'

'Now Mammy,' Patrick said. 'Would you not have known that we had gone for a pint or two of Guinness? There was not much of that in Burma, I can tell you!'

'And would I be begrudging you?' she asked. Would she begrudge them anything? 'Now sit to the table and I will serve the supper before it is completely dried up.'

She had no complaints about the way they ate, relishing every mouthful, scraping their plates clean.

'This is *real* food, Mammy!' Colum said.

'Will you have more?' she asked.

'No more!' they said in unison.

'We learned to live on small helpings,' Patrick added.

'Then Breda, you can help me to clear,' Molly said.

'Did you see Mr Murphy while you were out and about?' she asked Colum. 'He did not take on anyone in your place when you went, trade being bad because of petrol rationing, but now that things are looking up again I daresay he will be glad to have you back. When you are ready, that is.'

Colum didn't answer. That didn't matter, but Patrick and James, who had been in the middle of a noisy conversation together, instantly stopped talking. There was a sudden silence in the room, broken only by the clatter of dishes as Molly and Breda cleared the table. Molly, looking at Colum, saw him meet her eye for a moment, then turn away with an embarrassed, uncomfortable look on his face.

She stood still, a pile of plates in her hand. Something was going on and she didn't know what. She looked at James.

'Sit down, Molly,' he said. 'Leave the plates and sit down. You too, Breda.'

Neither of them thought of disobeying him. He looked unusually serious.

'The boys have something to say to you,' James said. He turned to the twins. 'Which of you will say it?'

Patrick spoke up. 'I will!' Hadn't he always been the one to take the lead? 'Mammy, we will not be taking jobs in Kilbally. We had hoped not to mention this just yet, but now we think we had better. We shall not be staying here.'

'Not stay in Kilbally? But I thought . . .'

'There is nothing for us in Kilbally, Mammy,' Colum said.

'Then Ennis . . . ?'

'No.' Patrick's voice was firm.

157

She was suddenly shot through with anger.

'Don't tell me that two more of my children are off to Dublin!' she cried. 'At this rate we might as well all go to Dublin!'

'Be quiet, Molly love,' James said. 'Let them say what they have to say.'

'It will not be Dublin,' Patrick said. 'We are going to America. Oh, Mammy, we know what this will mean to you. We've thought about it carefully, for a long time . . . '

He ran out of words at the look on his mother's face.

'You have no idea what it will mean to me,' Molly said. Her voice was dead calm, and that was because she felt dead inside, all the life sucked out.

'You have no idea,' she repeated. 'Nor will you have until you have children of your own. And even then you won't, because you are not women. You won't bear them, nurse them, bring them up. No, you have no idea.'

There was a stabbing pain in her heart. She felt she would stop breathing, and be glad to.

'Tell Mammy what you are going to do in America,' James said.

Molly clapped her hands over her ears.

'No! I don't want to hear it! I don't want to know!'

'You must listen! You have to know!' Gently, but quite firmly, he took her hands, pulled them away from her ears, and held them in his own.

'We shall go first of all to Auntie Cassie and Uncle Fergal in New York,' Patrick said. 'They will sponsor us, if we need sponsors. We shall stay with them, and find jobs, until we can set up on our own. We have quite a lot of money between us, all the pay we couldn't spend, *and* our gratuities. We shan't be going penniless.'

'And how do you know that Uncle Fergal and Auntie Cassie will have you?' Molly asked.

'We've written to them. They wrote back and agreed. We asked them not to mention it to you and Dada. We wanted to tell you ourselves.'

'Even though I am the last to know!'

'Because you and Dada are the most important,' Patrick said. 'Please, Mammy, try to understand! It will be a new life for us. We've met Americans. We liked them. There'll be opportunities there. If not in New York, then in other places.'

'And I might never see you again,' Molly said in a flat voice.

'Nonsense!' James's voice was stern now. 'Of course we will! One day we shall visit!'

'When we are set up we shall send you the fare,' Colum said.

'Will I be able to visit?'

Breda had sat silent, torn between excitement for her brothers and pity for her mother.

'Of course!' Patrick said.

'Unless, of course, you decide to take off on your own!' Molly said in a sharp voice.

'Why should I do that, Mammy?' Breda asked. 'It's different for me. I'm happy here in Kilbally.'

'And don't be forgetting that I am here,' James said. 'You do have a husband.'

Molly bit her lip, trying to keep back the tears.

'I know,' she said. 'I know.'

Nine

It was soon around the whole of Kilbally that the O'Connor twins, only just home from the war, were off to America to seek their fortune. Molly herself could not recall telling anyone, but like most news in Kilbally it was borne on the wind.

She had hoped for sympathy from her mother but in fact she got little. ' 'Tis commonplace enough,' Mrs Byrne said. 'You know that. 'Tis the history of Ireland. And in this case they are not going into the unknown. Fergal and Cassie will be there. 'Twill be home from home.'

'But did you not feel terrible when Fergal and Cassie left?' Breda asked.

There was a pause before Mrs Byrne answered, and when she did it was in a flat, calm voice. ' 'Twas a long time ago. You don't forget, but even the worst scars heal over. They no longer hurt to the touch.'

Nor did Father Curran offer her any comfort, though she should have known better, she told herself later, than to have sought it from him. And it did not help to recognize that he was right.

'We are not given our children,' he said. 'They are lent to us so that we may nurture them and bring them up in the truth. When the time comes we must let them go. Meditate, my child, on the mother of our Lord, who gave up her son even to the Cross. Patrick and Colum are only going across the water to America.'

Even James gave her no encouragement to be sorry for herself, though he was tender and loving in other ways. As for Breda, all she saw in it – though of course she would miss her brothers, but hadn't she been doing so for years now? – was the chance that one day she would visit America.

'Of course I would not *stay*, Mammy,' she said. ' 'Twould only be a visit. Perhaps a month. Or perhaps six weeks. I would like to see Auntie Cassie and Uncle Fergal, and my cousins. I have never seen any of them.'

And would I not like to see my sister, Molly thought. She had almost forgotten what Cassie looked like, though in any case she would be different now.

The twins returned to England to be demobbed, and when they came back to Kilbally their arrangements to leave Ireland began in earnest.

'We'll be wanting to go to Dublin to see Kieran and Kathleen before we leave,' Patrick said.

'And Moira and the baby,' Colum added. 'Don't forget, we are uncles now!'

They thought they would visit Dublin in a week's time and stay for two or three days, if Moira and Barry would put them up.

'Oh I wish, I do so wish I could go with you!' Breda cried. 'Don't forget, *I* am a godmother as well as an aunt.'

'And will you also remember that Moira's baby is almost due,' Molly warned. 'She might not want visitors, even though she will wish to see Patrick and Colum before they leave.'

'But isn't that the best reason for me to go?' Breda said. 'I can give Moira a hand in the house. I can look after Peter.'

She was bubbling with excitement at the prospect. Why, she might even be there when the baby was born! Then suddenly her face fell.

'But 'tis not possible. I can't go, not even if the twins were to pay my train ticket . . . '

' . . . Which you can be sure we would,' Patrick interrupted.

She shook her head.

'I can't go because I can't leave Mr O'Reilly. He could not manage without me, and that's a fact! All the same, I have not had a single day's holiday since I went to work for him. But 'tis no good. He would not allow it.'

Molly looked at Breda's disappointed face. I know how she feels, she thought. I would like to go myself. She longed to see Kieran and Kathleen, but it would not be possible for her, either. There was her job with Mrs Adare, though now it was only two mornings a week, but the money was important. And there was her mother, increasingly dependent. Every night now Molly saw her ready for bed and settled her down. But Breda was young. She didn't get many treats, and she worked so hard.

'What if I was to ask Luke if he could spare you?' she said tentatively.

Breda's face lit with excitement. 'Oh Mammy! He might, he just might, if *you* asked him!'

'Then I will do it, so I will!' Molly said.

'How would I ever get by?' Luke O'Reilly said when Molly asked him the following day. 'There is the shop, always busy. There is the dinner to be cooked, the orders to make up. If Breda were not here, then I might have to get someone else. Of course there is no shortage of people wanting jobs . . . '

'Then what about me?' Molly said impulsively. 'What about me taking Breda's place?'

How would I do it, she thought? For one thing, I would have to ask Mrs Adare to change my times. Then there was James. He would be far from pleased.

But Luke clearly *was* pleased.

'Well, if you would take Breda's place, I dare say that could be managed.'

'Thank you, Luke. I will do my best,' Molly promised.

As she had expected, James was not pleased. 'Why do you do these things for this man?' he grumbled.

'I am not doing it for Luke O'Reilly,' Molly said patiently. 'I am doing it for Breda. Surely you don't begrudge her?'

He had no answer to that.

'I must, I absolutely must, finish my new skirt and blouse,' Breda said.

The pattern had arrived and, with Molly's help, she had cut out both garments and tacked the skirt, but there was still a long way to go.

'You will help me now, won't you, Mammy?' she asked.

'Well . . . ' Molly began reluctantly, 'I will help you with the finishing off, but no more. I wanted you to do this yourself and you were doing so well. I thought you showed quite a flair for it. But in the circumstances . . . '

'Oh, Mammy, thank you!'

'There is more! I will help you to finish this outfit on condition that when you get back from Dublin, you will make my new white blouse.'

'*Make* it?' Breda sounded doubtful.

'From start to finish. Sure, I know you can. I want to see you do it. I reckon you have a talent there and who knows when it might come in handy?'

'Very well,' Breda said. She had no choice, and to tell the truth she had quite enjoyed the sewing she had done so far. How had it come about, she wondered, that she had reached the age of sixteen without having made a single garment for herself?

'You look very nice, very nice indeed!' Molly said to Breda on the morning they were setting out for Dublin. 'When you chose the pattern I thought hadn't you been ambitious for a first time, but you have brought it off!'

'I was set on it,' Breda admitted. 'It was exactly what I wanted.'

The skirt had six gores. It fitted closely over the hips, then flared out towards the hem. She had seen Ginger Rogers wearing almost the same thing as she danced with Fred Astaire.

Breda executed a few dance steps across the floor, ending in a complete spin, which gave the skirt a lovely movement but, owing to the lack of room, caused her to knock into a chair and almost lose her balance.

'For goodness sake, be careful!' Molly said. But she was laughing.

'It *is* the nicest outfit I've ever had,' Breda said. 'All the same, I never forget the dress you made me when we first went to Dublin!'

That had been five years ago. She had worn it not only until, even with the hem let down, it was too short for her, but until it fell apart at the seams.

'Now put your hat on,' Molly said.

Breda had taken an old straw hat, swathed a band of the material of her new blouse around the crown and pleated the same material on the underside of the brim. It was really quite fetching.

'You will not be ashamed of that hat even in Dublin,' Molly said.

She inspected Patrick and Colum with a proud mother's eye. 'You will do,' she said.

They were so tall and straight, so handsome, she could have hugged them on the spot. She had, however, made a sacred promise to herself that she would show no undue emotion towards them or about them for the rest of the time they were in Ireland. Time enough for that when they had gone. Too much time for everything there would be then.

Breda was deeply impressed by Moira's house. It was two-storeyed, in the middle of a row, stone-built. Never had Breda lived in a house where you went upstairs to bed. It was also well furnished, with a handsome oak table and matching chairs in the dining room, a three-piece suite in the front room and, wonder of wonders, a separate kitchen *and* a bathroom.

'Barry must be quite rich,' she said to her sister. She was being shown the best bedroom, which boasted a dressing-table, a chest of drawers, and a wardrobe with a full-length mirror in the door.

'He is doing quite well,' Moira said complacently. 'But we are not exactly *rich*. You are judging me by *your* standards. This is Dublin, not Kilbally!'

Breda let the insult to Kilbally pass, though she did not like it. But had she not determined, from the moment she had seated herself in the train, that she would not pick a quarrel with Moira? Indeed, had she not made the success of this holiday and the welfare of all her family her intention at the Mass last Sunday.

'Everything is quite lovely,' she said graciously.

'Unfortunately,' Moira said. 'We do not have a spare bedroom for you, what with the twins, and Peter also, so you will have to sleep on the sofa downstairs.'

I would happily have shared with the twins, or slept on a mattress on the floor in Peter's room, Breda thought, but she sensed that that might not be the thing in Dublin. She hoped that Barry would not think to come down in the middle of the night, though he could hardly search for a drink of water in the front room!

'Sure, I won't mind that!' she said to Moira.

'Then will we go downstairs again and I'll make the tea.'

'Let me help you,' Breda offered. 'Should you not be resting? When is the baby due?'

Her sister looked huge and ungainly. As she negotiated the narrow stairs Breda's heart was in her mouth that she would take a tumble.

' 'Tis due in ten days' time,' Moira said. 'And shan't I be glad when 'tis all over! Oh, they are all right when they are here, but the having of them is hell fire!'

Breda followed her sister into the kitchen. It was small, and with Moira's bulk there was hardly room for the two of them.

'Sit down,' Breda ordered. 'I will do it.' She sliced the soda bread Mammy had sent, and buttered it liberally.

'I would like to be having several children,' she said.

'You are welcome to it,' Moira said. 'I have told Barry that this is definitely the last!'

'What does he say to that, then?'

'He is not pleased. Being a man he would not be. But you don't know about men. You have all that to learn.'

The next day the three of them – Moira refused to go because, she said, she looked so ugly, and anyway she was tired – went to see Kathleen. The plan was that they would go on to see Kieran afterwards, but to their surprise and delight he was there at the convent to greet them.

' 'Twas so that we could all be together at one and the same time,' Kathleen explained. 'Though 'tis a pity Moira could not come.'

They spent almost two hours together in a room which had been set aside for them. Afterwards, when Mammy eagerly quizzed her about it, Breda could not remember what they had talked about. It had been everyday things: childhood memories, reminiscences about people in Kilbally, school, teachers, church, friends.

When the time came for them to leave Kathleen hugged her brothers tightly. 'God go with you!' she said. Then she put her arms around Breda and kissed her tenderly.

' 'Tis you will have to look after Mammy and Dada now,' she said. 'Do it well, Breda.'

'Oh I will, I will!' Breda promised.

On the third and last night of their stay in Dublin Breda was awakened in the early hours by Barry. As he stood by the side of the sofa she knew the moment of fear she had experienced in Kilbally, after the baptism, and now there was no father to call upon in the next room. Then almost immediately she realized she was in no danger, it was not to do with her.

'It's Moira!' he gasped. 'She's started! She's bad. I'll have to fetch the midwife and you'll have to stay with Moira until I get back!'

'Me? But what shall *I* do?' Breda said. 'I know nothing about having babies!'

'You know as much as I do,' Barry said. 'Anyway, you're a female. Won't it come naturally to you? And Moira will tell you what to do. But she can't be left and she *is* your sister.'

'Of course she is!' Breda was thoroughly awake now. 'Don't worry. I'll do whatever I can.'

She snatched up her jacket and put it on over her nightgown. She doubted if there was time to dress.

'I'll be back as quickly as I can,' Barry said.

As he hurried out of the door, Breda ran up the stairs to meet the screams coming from the bedroom. They were sounds such as she had never heard in her life before, like an animal in torment. How could she deal with this?

'Oh Mammy!' she cried out loud. 'Help me, Mammy!'

The noise had already wakened Peter, who was crying – a loud frightened cry. Patrick appeared on the landing, rubbing the sleep from his eyes.

'What is it? What in the world . . . ?'

'It's Moira! She's having her baby. One of you get Peter, take him in with you, try to quieten him. The other go downstairs and put water on to boil. The kettle, pans, anything!'

She had no idea what the boiling water was for, only that whenever a baby came in a film, the white-coated doctor said 'Quick nurse! Boiling water! And tear up some sheets!'

But the films did not show the pain and the noise. The only sound they gave was the baby's first cry, when the immaculate nurse held up an immaculate baby.

She would have given a year of her life for the sight of a white-coated doctor, or even some woman who knew what she was doing.

In a state of trepidation, fearful of what she might see, Breda went into her sister's bedroom. Moira was quiet now, lying with closed eyes, sweat pouring down her white face, clutching her stomach, her knees drawn up.

Breda closed the bedroom door. She knew now that the pain and the cries must come again, and there was no point in spreading her own fear around the house. Above all, she thought, I must not panic. That will be no good to anyone.

While she mopped the sweat from Moira's face, and stroked back her hair, she told herself that birth was natural. Didn't animals give birth on their own, without help? And if dogs and cats and horses and cows could do it, then she could surely help her sister. Except, were human beings different?

She had no time to answer her own questions. The pain and the screaming started again, and except for holding Moira's hand and wiping her face, there was nothing she could do to stop it. She felt completely helpless.

'Where's Mammy?' Moira shrieked. 'I want Mammy!'

So do I, Breda thought. More than anyone else in the whole world at this moment she wanted Mammy. She wanted her to walk in at the door and rescue her from this nightmare.

Then pains came again, and subsided again, and came again, and subsided again, but all the time the intervals between them were getting shorter and the pains longer and more fierce.

'Where is Barry?' Moira asked. Her voice was weak.

'He has gone for the midwife. She will be here very soon,' Breda said. Why weren't they here? What was keeping them?

Then the worst and fiercest pain of all gripped Moira.

'I can't wait!' she shouted. 'I can't wait!'

There was a cry like all the hounds of hell, and next moment there was the baby's head coming out, and then the whole baby, on the bed.

Breda stared in astonishment. It had happened so quickly that she had almost missed it. But now she knew what she must do. Instinct told her. She needed no instructions.

The baby was dark red, its body and face covered in mucus. There was a long, shining tube attached to its stomach. She must wipe its tiny face, clear its nose and mouth, otherwise, she thought, it would not be able to breathe. She would not touch the long tube because she didn't know what to do about that.

Gently wiping the baby's face, she didn't hear footsteps on the stairs. The midwife was in the room.

'Well, Mrs Devlin,' she said cheerfully. 'Were you not impatient, then? But 'tis a fine, healthy little girl you have now!'

Breda thankfully moved out of the way while the midwife took over. Her legs were shaking.

'You have done very well,' the midwife said to Breda.

'I didn't know what to do next,' Breda admitted. 'I told my brother to boil the water. What would you be wanting it for?'

'Well now, one of the things it is wanted for is to make the midwife a good, strong cup of tea. And yourself. You look as though you could do with one. So why don't you make it, and take a cup back to bed with you? I'll do the rest.'

'I will,' Breda said. 'Where is Barry?'

'Himself has gone to fetch his mother,' the midwife said.

She turned to Moira.

'I will have you comfortable in no time at all,' she said. 'And do you have a name for the child?'

'Teresa!' Moira mumbled. She was so tired, she could hardly keep awake.

Molly enjoyed working for Luke O'Reilly. She had been nervous at first about whether she would do it well, but after the first hour or two there was nothing to it, nothing she felt she couldn't cope with. She particularly enjoyed working in the shop, serving the customers, most of whom she knew anyway. While they stood there, waiting to be served, they gossiped amongst themselves. She could not join in, of course. Wasn't she here in a professional capacity? But she could listen and enjoy. It made for an interesting life.

At the four dinner times she was there she made good meals for herself and Luke, each day something different, for there was no shortage of ingredients: meat from the butcher, fresh fish from the harbour, tinned peaches, rice pudding. Luke enjoyed every mouthful, and for that matter so did she.

'Nothing against your Breda,' Luke said. 'She does her best. But she's not the cook her mother is!'

'And wouldn't that be because I've never taught her?' Molly said. 'I reckon the youngest child gets let off everything. 'Tis because you don't want them to grow up.'

She did not tell James how much she enjoyed the job. It would only upset him, and what was the point in that? In any case, didn't he benefit, didn't she bring home all sorts of tidbits, leftovers far too good for the pig bin? When they turned up on his plate he never queried them, never wondered where they had come from.

She was careful to pay him a lot of attention, and that she did not find difficult, perhaps because she was happy in her new-found (though temporary) freedom. Or at least as happy as she could be with the thought of Patrick and Colum at the back of her mind.

When Luke, at the end of the four days, paid her what he would have paid Breda, she decided that she would divide it between the two of them. It was not much, but Breda had so little to spend on herself.

'It belongs to you by right,' Breda said when Molly handed over the money. 'You earned it.'

'I would like to share it,' Molly insisted. ' 'Tis not a fortune, anyway!'

It was the twins who took Molly aside and told her what Breda had done when the baby was being born.

'I am proud of you, Breda,' Molly said.

'I didn't do much,' Breda said. 'Sure, there was not much I could do. But I had never known that to have a baby was so painful. It was terrible! I wonder, why does anyone ever have a baby, or have a second baby?'

'Because 'tis nature,' Molly said. 'And you forget the pain after the baby is born. It is all worth while.'

I shall never forget Moira's pain, Breda thought.

A month later, Patrick and Colum sailed from Liverpool to New York.

'I would prefer it,' Molly said, 'and if you would not take it amiss, not to go even as far as Kilbally train station with you. I would prefer to wave you off from the house where I brought you up.'

So that I can pretend, she thought, that though I see you turn the corner, you will be back in no time at all.

'We do understand,' Patrick said.

'Sure we do,' Colum added.

Why do people say they understand when they cannot possibly do so, Molly asked herself?

It was almost a month before she had their first letter. They were well, they wrote. It was early days, but they hoped to get jobs together, working as motor mechanics in a big garage. Their wartime experience would help them there. The car was everything in America, great big cars, like charabancs. The weather was cold for November, much colder than in Kilbally, and they would have to buy some warmer clothes. There were a lot of Irish in New York, so they felt at home. They would write again soon and they sent all their love.

Molly read the letter until she knew it by heart. 'It is good to hear from them,' she said to James. 'But shall we ever see them again?'

'Of course we shall!' James said.

'Do you mean that, or would you just be trying to cheer me up?'

'I mean it. Have they not promised that once they are set up they will send us the money to visit them?' He seemed so sure that she took fresh hope.

Christmas came and went; short days, long nights, rough seas, but no snow. They seldom had snow, which Breda thought was a pity but Molly was glad about. She hated the winter.

At Christmas they had had a letter and small gifts from the twins, and a sum of money to buy each of them a bigger gift, whatever they wanted. Cassie wrote also. She said how well the twins had settled in, and coming from her Molly believed it.

Best of all, the boys sent photographs of themselves, taken in Central Park. They looked fit and well, smiling happily, and in their new winter clothes – there was snow on the ground in Central Park – already very American.

Molly went to Ennis and spent every penny of her share of the gift on a silver-plated photograph frame, large enough to take two snapshots side by side. Breda went with her and bought another pattern and a length of material for a dress which would see her through the rest of the winter and into the spring. James treated his friends in the Harp.

Kieran and Kathleen wrote most regularly of all. Moira's letter, though short, said that Teresa was now doing well and that they were hoping to have a telephone installed any day now. 'You will be able to telephone us from Kilbally post office!' she said.

'What luxury to have a telephone in the house,' Molly said. 'Just imagine being able to telephone New York, or Dublin, or Josephine in Akersfield!'

'At a cost!' James said.

'Mr O'Reilly talks about having the telephone,' Breda said.

Molly thought that if she could make a wish it might be for a telephone, but even in her wildest dreams she knew it would not happen. Now that the Christmas gift money had been spent – and there she had felt an obligation to Patrick and Colum not to let it disappear into the household purse – things were at their tightest. There was no work on the land for James. All he could get now was the occasional night on the boats, and there was not much of that. He had work for the next few nights, taking the place of one of the three-man crew who was laid up with bronchitis.

Paddy Ferris, the third member of the crew of which Seamus O'Loughlin was the skipper, knocked at James's door in passing and they walked down to the harbour together. Molly saw them off. She kissed James, smiled at Paddy. 'God go with you both!' she said.

'See you in the morning,' James said.

'I am not liking the look of the weather,' Paddy said to James as they walked. 'Would you not say 'twas a sneaky wind?'

James gave an easy laugh. 'Not at all, at all! 'Tis no more than a fresh breeze!' Wasn't Paddy always a cautious man, he thought? Afraid of his own shadow.

Breda, helped by her mother, spent the evening at her dressmaking. 'I wish we had a decent sewing machine!' she said as the thread snapped for the third time.

'If wishes were horses, beggars would ride!' Molly said. 'Anyway, haven't we done enough for one evening? We'll have a cup of cocoa and go to our beds.'

It was the middle of the night, she was sound asleep, when the storm woke her, the wind howling in the chimney. She lit the lamp and looked at the clock. Two-thirty-five. She was wide awake now. How could she not be; the storm was raging, the rain lashing against the window, and behind it all she could hear the heavy thud of the waves as they broke on the strand. It was the sure sign of the highest of seas, that lying in bed here, in the shelter of the house, you could hear the thundering of the sea and the beating of the waves.

James! Where was he? How far out? Was he already on his way home?

She got out of bed, put on a coat and her slippers, and stared out of the window. There was nothing to be seen, thick blackness, no light anywhere, the rain driving in squalls, the wind thumping in fury against the house.

There would be no more sleep tonight, not while the storm raged and James was somewhere out there in the thick of it. She left the bedroom, looking in on Breda, who was fast asleep, on her way to the living room. You had to be young, Molly thought, to sleep so soundly.

She stirred the fire and filled the kettle. Her thoughts were all with the men in the boat. So small it was, and off this coast the sea so high and treacherous and the storms so sudden. But Seamus and Paddy were experienced men, she told herself. Hadn't they been on the boats since they were boys? And James himself was no fool at it.

All the same, there was no way she could go back to bed yet. She picked up Breda's sewing and began to stitch the hem, the needle jumping in her hand with the thud of the waves.

She had almost completed the full circle of the hem when she realized that the storm had subsided and the wind had dropped. The sea was now hardly audible. That was the way of it. It frightened you almost to death and then ceased on the moment. It was cruel all right. But now everything was all right again, and she was quite desperately tired.

Yawning, she went back to the bedroom – Breda had slept through it all – put out the lamp and thankfully crawled into bed.

She fell asleep at once, and knew nothing more until she heard a loud knocking at the door, for all the world as if someone had been trying to waken her, with no success. She put on her coat and ran to open the door. The garda stood there. Her heart leapt in her body with fear.

'What is it?' Her voice came out in a whisper. 'It's James, isn't it?'

'Yes,' the garda said.

She had known him all her life and now he seemed not to know how to look at her.

'He's . . . he's dead?'

'No! No, Molly!' He was full of relief at being able to contradict her.

'No! It was an accident. They've taken him to the hospital. Get dressed, and I'll go with you.'

'Step inside,' she said. 'I'll not keep you a minute. I must tell Breda.'

She was amazed, both then and afterwards, at her own calmness. It was as if someone else had taken over and everything she did and said was automatic.

Breda had already wakened. What the violence of the storm had failed to do, human voices, hardly raised, had accomplished.

'I want to go with you, Mammy,' she said when Molly gave her the news.

'No. You stay here, Breda. If I'm not back within the hour, then you can come to the hospital. Don't worry, *dote*, 'twill be all right.'

Seamus and Paddy were both at the hospital when she reached there. James lay on the bed, the sheets tidy and tight-stretched over him, his hands lying outside the covers. His eyes were closed, and except that his face was too pale he might have been asleep.

'He is deeply unconscious,' the nurse said. 'He was so when he was brought in.'

Seamus moved out of the way so that Molly could take the chair beside the bed. She took James's hand in her own and stroked it gently, murmuring his name. The nurse shook her head.

'He doesn't hear you.'

'He must! He *must*!' Molly said urgently. 'He must know I am here, even if he doesn't speak!'

'That's something we can never tell,' the nurse said. 'Sure, there is no harm in believing he does!' Even if he doesn't, she added to herself.

Molly turned her head and spoke to Seamus O'Loughlin.

'What happened?'

He shook his head.

' 'Tis not easy to know. We had turned for home, the storm was too much for us. The cleat broke loose, ripped off in the gale. The boom fell, swung round, and hit your man. At least, 'tis how it must have been. We did not see it happen. You could hardly see a thing before your eyes. The water was breaking green.'

' 'Twas I found him lying there,' Paddy Ferris said. 'And it could only have been but a moment later, or wouldn't he have been washed overboard?'

'He could have been killed, but he was alive,' Seamus said. 'Unconscious, but hardly a mark on him. The boom is smooth. It doesn't cut. We carried him into the wheelhouse and wedged him there against the storm.'

While he was speaking, Father Curran, who had been summoned by the ward sister, came into the room, closely followed by Breda.

Seamus and Paddy rose to leave.

'Do not go,' Father Curran said quietly. 'He needs the prayers of all of us.'

177

Quietly and smoothly, he administered the Last Rites.
It was not until she heard the prayers for after death that
Molly realized that James had left her for good.

> 'Eternal rest give him,
> O Lord: and let perpetual
> light shine upon him . . . '

But for me, Molly thought, it is darkness.

Ten

Afterwards, Molly had no clear memory of the twenty-four hours following James's death. She did not recall getting home from the hospital; probably Seamus or Paddy, or Breda, had brought her. She remembered nothing of how James was brought home, or who laid him out in the brown habit, in the bed where she had slept with him, made love with him, borne their children, for more than twenty-six years.

Someone must have seen to these things; have put the crucifix in his hands, placed the candles at the four corners of the bed, tied the black crêpe bow on the outside of the house door. Someone must also have sent telegrams to Dublin, to Akersfield, a cable to New York. Everything had been done that needed to be done.

Perhaps I did some of it myself, she thought. If so, she had no recollection of it. Her mind, for those hours, was a black, blank screen. She knew, though, that she had neither cried nor raged. She knew that because everything was still locked inside her like a great ball of lead.

When she began to notice things again it was to see the neighbours arriving to pay their respects. They came through the door in ones and twos. If they had brought a contribution of food or drink they placed it on the table, but at that point they did not speak to other neighbours already sitting in the room. For now they nodded silently to Molly, though some would say, ' 'Tis sorry I am for your trouble,' and make their way to the bedroom. Whenever the bedroom door was opened there was the faint clicking of rosary beads, the murmur of prayers.

On leaving the bedroom they would, as a matter of courtesy, sit and take a cup of tea with her, or a glass of whatever was going, and perhaps a slice of cake. They offered sympathy and talked about whatever was suitable to talk about in the circumstances. Most of them had known Molly all her life, and James for many years.

'He was a grand man!'

'I mind him when he came first from Galway. Wasn't he the handsomest young man you ever saw?'

'How old was he, I mean now?'

'He would have been forty-seven in the summer. But still young to me.'

People took their leave, others came. She grew tired of hearing the same phrases, answering the same questions. He was young, fit, virile. He was my husband, my friend, my support in life.

' 'Tis a gate I have been through myself,' a neighbour said. 'Himself was taken young, and me with babies. 'Twas a long time ago now, but I don't forget.'

Breda, though Molly knew she was heart-scalded, had been obliged to go back to work. Luke could not manage on his own. Indeed, Molly had encouraged her to do so, she was too young for all this and, more than any of the others, she had adored her father. I shall always have a bit of James in Breda, Molly thought. 'Tis not just that she looks like him, but she has always had his brightness. She did not wish to see that dimmed.

Kieran and Kathleen would arrive in Kilbally tomorrow, and both would stay until after the burial. Moira and Barry would come the evening before the burial and return to Dublin as soon as it was over, since they were leaving Peter and Teresa behind in the care of Mrs Devlin. Teresa was not yet six months old, but Moira had given up the task of breast-feeding her, though Mrs Devlin said wasn't that foolish since 'twas the sure way not to conceive another child, to be nursing one already. Moira knew of a more certain way, but it was not something to be said to her mother-in-law. Josephine, too, was coming from Akersfield. She had telephoned the post office to say so.

It was Breda who sorted out where they would all sleep. 'Moira and Barry at Great-grandma Devlin's; you, me and Kathleen in the big bedroom here. Auntie Josephine with Grandma Byrne and Kieran on the sofa here.'

Molly was not sure that she liked the thought of Kieran bedding down on the sofa – after all, was he not soon to be a priest? – but it was the best that could be done unless he went to a neighbour, and she wanted him under her own roof; she needed him.

By the evening before the funeral they had all arrived, including Josephine, who had had a terrible journey from Akersfield because of the weather.

'The worst in living memory!' she said. 'You never saw such snow. If I hadn't lived in Akersfield I'd never have been able to get a train. According to the wireless, everything up in the dales is at a standstill.'

'It was good of you to come,' Molly said.

'And did you ever think I would not? My own sister?'

'You have been more like a mother to me,' Molly said. More like a mother than her true one had been, she reckoned.

In the evening they followed the coffin to the church, where it would remain overnight. Molly's worst moment came when James was carried out of his home. That, she thought, was her final farewell. Goodbye, my lovely James, she said in her heart. Nothing she would have to bear the next day could be as bad as this.

And so it was. The prayers in the evening, the Requiem next day, the procession to the graveyard, in which it seemed the whole of Kilbally joined, washed over her like the waves of the sea. Wasn't it bitterly cold, they all said, with the wind from the north fit to cut you in two? She had not felt it.

She was submerged, and did not surface until, leaning on Kieran's arm, she stepped back into her own home. It was then it came to her that life from now on would be a different life, and she would have to be a different person. There was no going back to what had been. She had to start again.

Someone, she thought it must be Kathleen, had put the bedroom to rights. The candles were gone, the bed linen changed, everything dusted and polished, and the window opened in spite of the cold. Molly looked at the bed, noting that someone had replaced the usual two pillows with just one, and that in the centre. Would she ever sleep easy again in it, she wondered?

Back in the living room, she asked Kathleen: 'Did you do the bedroom?'

'Yes, Mammy. With Breda's help. We put all Dada's things on the top shelf in the closet until you felt like sorting them.'

'Thank you. It was thoughtful of you both,' Molly said.

After dinner, Moira and Barry took the train for Dublin. 'We have to get back to the children,' Moira said. 'Teresa is all right, but Peter is a handful!'

'Come and see us in Dublin, both of you,' Barry said to Molly and Breda. 'You'll be very welcome.'

'I suppose he is quite nice, really,' Breda said to her mother.

'What do you mean by that?'

'Nothing, Mammy!'

The next day Kieran and Kathleen left, but Josephine had announced her intention of staying on a day or two longer.

'I'd like to see you settled,' she said to Molly.

'Settled? Shall I ever be?'

'Of course you will! It will not be easy, but you'll do it. How will you manage for money?'

'I don't know,' Molly said. It was a worry which loomed large, and now had to be faced. 'I earn next to nothing at Mrs Adare's, barely enough to pay the rent. We shall have to rely on Breda's wage for most things. Though James never earned much – well, 'twas not his fault, there was not the work to be had – it made the difference.'

Privately, Josephine thought that James O'Connor had never rushed to meet work, even as a young man, but not for the world would she say so. And anyway, he had made her sister happy all these years. There was something in that.

'He was well liked, your James,' she said kindly. 'Just look at the number of people at his funeral, and everyone with a good word for him!'

'And remember,' she continued, 'if the worst comes to the worst, if you want to leave Kilbally, you will always be welcome in Akersfield. As welcome as the flowers in spring!'

'Oh, Josephine, however would you manage?' Molly asked.

In fact, in all her life she had never wanted to leave Kilbally, but now she wondered, would she?' 'Tis wonderful of you,' she said. 'But there is Mammy to think of.'

'I know,' Josephine admitted. 'But when and if . . . I'm sure you and Breda would both get work in Akersfield. There are more jobs there than in Kilbally.'

When Josephine returned to Yorkshire the house seemed quieter than ever.

'Your Auntie Josephine has a heart of gold,' Molly said. 'Don't I miss her sorely!'

While Josephine had been there she had, somehow, for the both of them, taken the edge off their grief, acted as a buffer between them. Now they had only each other to lean on.

'We shall have to try to balance each other,' Breda said. 'When you are down, I will try to be up, and when I'm down, you must be up.'

'For all the world like a seesaw!' Molly said. 'But you are right, and that is what we will do.'

Molly, unless she was waiting up for James, had always gone to bed early, and Breda always a little before her. Now, as the days went by, Breda noticed that her mother was reluctant to go to bed at all. She would stay up until midnight or later. The reason why was not far to seek, and Breda decided she must stay and keep her mother company.

It was not easy. She had always needed a long night's sleep, and also she had to be up early in the morning to get to work. They would sew together, or read, or sometimes to pass the time they would play a game of cards, but always by ten o'clock Breda's eyes were closing.

'Go to bed,' Molly would say. 'I'll not be long. I'll just finish this chapter.'

They both knew that that was not true. Molly knew that she would not move until she was so tired that she could hope to fall asleep quickly, not lie in the dark, her mind full of worried thoughts.

Breda was well aware that after she had gone to bed Mammy would as like as not start to do something in the house; clean out a cupboard which did not need it, or even rake the fire under the oven and bake a cake. What she did not know was that one of the things her mother did most frequently was to try to work out just how they were going to manage.

On an evening six weeks after James's death, Molly knew she would have to pull herself together. Breda was looking pale and weary, her brightness was dimmed. And it is not only that she is missing her father, Molly chided herself. Some of it is my fault. I am taking too much from her. But she too was fatigued, and that also was her fault because she would not go to bed. Also, their finances were at the lowest possible ebb. If it had not been that Luke O'Reilly gave them things from time to time – things he couldn't sell, Breda insisted, but that didn't matter in the least to Molly – it would have been even worse than it was.

Well, she told herself briskly, there were small things to be done which would help all three problems.

They were playing cards.

'Another hand, Mammy?' Breda said, trying not to yawn.

'No!' Molly said firmly. She gathered up the cards and put them back in the box.

'We are going to change our ways,' she announced. 'From now on, we go to bed in decent time. Ten o'clock at the very latest. You look whacked, and you have for weeks!'

'I am quite all right, Mammy,' Breda said.

Molly shook her head. 'No, you are not – and neither am I. And there is something else. Here we sit, night after night, the lamp lit, the fire burning. Isn't it just like burning money, and doing us no good into the bargain? And have you not noticed that when we stay up late, we get hungry again? So things must change, and we can start by going to bed this minute!'

'If you say so, Mammy!'

With great relief Breda rose to her feet, kissed her mother and was in bed and asleep in ten minutes flat. Not so Molly, though she went at once to bed. But as she lay awake she had the comfort that at least she was no longer harming her daughter. The savings on the fuel would be small, but every penny helped and somehow they would manage. And at any rate their financial situation could not get worse.

A week later, she was proved wrong.

When she went to Adare House for her morning's work she was met with the news that Mrs Adare was leaving; selling up everything and going to live with her daughter in Waterford. She would go at the end of the month. The house would be put on the market, but who knew if it would sell, or how long it would take?

And will the new owner, if any, want me? And how will I pay my rent until then, Molly asked herself? It was the regular money she earned at Adare House which kept the roof over her head and Breda's. She was trembling from top to toe with the shock, so much so that Mrs Hanratty made her sit down and gave her a cup of tea there and then.

'And what will you do, Mrs Hanratty?' Molly asked presently. ' 'Tis a blow for you also.'

'Sure and it is,' Mrs Hanratty said. 'Have I not worked here forty years? Well, I could go to my son in Derry. He would be glad of it, and so would the grandchildren. Or I wondered, would I ask Luke O'Reilly if he wanted a housekeeper? 'Tis my belief he could do with one. He only has Mrs Milligan doing the rough, and she was never much good.'

Molly's heart did a double somersault in her breast! Luke O'Reilly! She could do it! If he wanted someone, she could do it. And they had always got on well. Why had she never thought of it?

'Do you know that Luke O'Reilly wants a housekeeper?' she asked cautiously.

'No,' Mrs Hanratty admitted. 'But if 'twas put to him he might decide that he did.'

And if he did, and if I got it, would I not be doing Mrs Hanratty out of a job, Molly asked herself? – though she has her son in Derry and she might prefer to go to him in any case. But if she gets to Luke O'Reilly first I might lose the only chance I can see in front of me.

It was Wednesday, so when she reached home soon after dinner Breda was already there.

'Is it Luke's week to go to Ennis?' she asked quickly.

'No. He went last week.'

'Thank heaven for that!' Molly said.

'Why, Mammy? What do you mean?'

'I need to see him. This very afternoon.'

She explained the situation to Breda. For some reason or other, Breda was immediately against the idea, but as Molly reasonably asked, what other choice was there?

'He might not want anyone,' she said. 'But I have to find out.'

'Is there *nothing* else?' Breda asked. 'I don't like the thought of it.'

'Why ever not?' Molly said. 'And can you think of anything better? For I cannot. I have to try.'

She washed her hands and face, combed her hair and changed into a clean blouse.

'Do you want me to go with you?' Breda asked.

'I think not.' If Breda showed her reluctance, or Luke sensed it, it would go against her.

The shop was closed. She rang the house doorbell and waited, her knees knocking. She had no idea how she would begin. Never before in her life had she had to beg for work.

When Luke opened the door and saw her standing there he looked surprised and concerned. 'What's the trouble?' he asked.

'Trouble? Oh no, no trouble!'

'I thought perhaps Breda . . . '

'Breda is fine. 'Tis with yourself I wanted a word, if I might step inside.'

He stood aside to let her enter, then preceded her along the passage and into the living room.

'So what is it, Molly?' He was mystified. All the same, he was pleased to see her. 'Sit yourself down,' he said. 'I was doing the accounts.'

She perched on the edge of a chair. 'I'm sorry to interrupt.'

'Not at all,' he said politely, waiting for her to begin.

'I was wondering . . . ' she said. 'That is, now that I am . . . now that James . . . '

'I am sorry about your husband,' he said.

'Yes, well . . . now that I am not so busy, I was wondering if . . . '

'Yes?'

'I was wondering if you needed help in the house – oh, I know you have Mrs Milligan but Breda said you were never very happy with her, but in any case I don't mean a charwoman, though of course I would do whatever was asked . . . '

Stop babbling she told herself! Get to the point!

'To put it plainly,' she said. 'Would you be wanting a housekeeper, and if so, would I do?'

There, she had said it!

Luke's mouth dropped open. 'A housekeeper?'

'There is nothing in a house I can't do! Clean, bake, do the laundry – I'm very good at ironing shirts. Cook the meals, darn the socks . . . '

'I'm no good at darning,' Luke said.

' 'Tis woman's work,' Molly said. 'Why should you be? And who cooks for you at the weekends? Who gets your breakfast?'

A vision arose in Luke's mind of Molly serving him with two rashers, a fried egg, new-baked soda bread and Irish butter on the table, a pot of tea on the side.

' . . . And I could be here in time to cook your breakfast, and would stay until I had prepared your supper,' she was saying.

He came to with a start. 'Oh! I thought a housekeeper would live in!'

'I had not thought that,' Molly said swiftly. 'There is Breda to think of. I could not leave Breda on her own. And besides . . . ' She hesitated, 'would it be proper? I mean . . . '

She didn't know how to continue. She sounded so foolish. She was sure Luke O'Reilly never had an improper idea in his head.

'I would expect Breda to live in too,' Luke said. 'I had not considered otherwise.'

But what would Breda think to that, Molly asked herself? Not much!

'And there is Kieran, and Kathleen,' Molly said. 'It would not happen often, but what if they wanted to visit me?'

Luke shrugged. 'We would manage that. Or they might stay with your mother, who knows? But as you say, 'twould not happen often.'

'That is very kind. And also you do know that Breda needs to keep on her job in the shop,' she said.

She felt for someone who desperately needed the job she was laying down too many conditions, but it had to be done. She had wondered whether Luke, if he took her on as housekeeper, might expect her to do the shop part also.

'I know that,' Luke assured her.

'Then . . . then do you need a housekeeper, would you like one?'

'In fact,' Luke admitted, 'hasn't it entered my head more than once? 'Tis not easy for a man on his own, with a business to run. But I will still have to think about it. Sleep on it.'

Molly tried to cover her disappointment with a boldness which was not natural to her.

'Of course! But I would take it kindly if you would let me know soon. In case something else comes up!'

'Indeed I will.'

He was smiling at her now. He knew, and he knew that *she* knew, that nothing else was likely to come up. Didn't they both know there wasn't another soul in Kilbally wanting a housekeeper, who could also afford one?

'Well then!' Molly said. 'I'll be off. Unless you would like me to scald a pot of tea for you?'

'I would take that kindly,' Luke said.

'If I had thought,' Molly said artlessly, 'I could have brought you some of my fresh soda bread to go with it.'

'I *think*,' she said to Breda, an hour or so later. 'I *think* he might decide on it. I believe that if I agreed to live in, the job would be mine. He is lonely, poor man. I'm beginning to know how that feels.'

Breda was shocked. 'But you have me, Mammy! We have each other.'

'I know. And where would I be without you?'

But for how long, she asked herself? One day she will fly the nest. 'Twas only natural, and not too far ahead at that. And above everything, she must never let Breda feel tied, obliged to stay with her when she wanted to fly.

'How could we possibly leave this house?' Breda persisted. 'I have lived here all my life! I was born here!'

'Do I not know that? And *I* came here as a bride. *All* my children were born here. But we still have to pay the rent.

'However, we will look on the bright side,' she continued. 'Perhaps tomorrow Luke will offer me a job as a daily housekeeper, in which case the problem will be solved. When you go in to work in the morning, tell him I will call to see him after dinner.'

When Molly entered the shop early the next afternoon, Breda was serving a customer and Luke was hovering near. She could tell by the expression on Breda's face that she was anxious to speak to her, but there was no chance. The moment Luke spotted her, he broke off what he was doing. 'Come through!'

She followed him to the living room.

'So, I have decided I do want a housekeeper,' he said at once. 'And to come straight to the point, I think you would fill the bill.'

Relief surged through her.

'The only thing is,' he went on before Molly could speak, 'Mrs Hanratty has been to see me. Did you know that Mrs Adare was leaving?'

'Indeed I did,' Molly confessed.

'So you see, Mrs Hanratty is also looking for a job, and as we both know she is very experienced. She has been housekeeper to the Adares for years.'

' 'Tis true,' Molly agreed. 'But I had thought she meant to retire, go to live with her son in Derry.'

'She did not mention that to me,' Luke said. 'So you see, I have to make a choice.'

There was not the slightest doubt in his mind where his choice lay. Who would pass over a woman like Molly O'Connor in favour of Mrs Hanratty, experience or no experience? But he had another card to play. 'The

191

difference is,' he said, 'that Mrs Hanratty is agreeable to being a resident housekeeper, indeed she would prefer it. And there is no denying it would be much better for me.'

'But I would look after you just as well, coming by the day,' Molly insisted. 'You would not be neglected.'

'It would not be quite the same.'

'I have Breda to think of,' Molly said.

'And as I told you, Breda would be very welcome here. We are not short of space; you would each have your own room. You would have your own leisure time, when you could come and go as you wished. You would be comfortably housed, *and* paid a wage.'

'How much would that be?' Molly asked.

He named a sum which, though not extravagant, was reasonable. She had always thought him to be a fair man, and so he was.

'In addition you would be fed,' he said. 'Both of you, well fed.'

'I must think it over,' Molly said. 'I must consult Breda.'

'Then let me know tomorrow,' Luke said. 'Mrs Hanratty is anxious for an answer. I don't want to keep her waiting.'

When she left, Luke showed her out of the house door, so it was evening before she saw Breda – not that she could have tackled her in the shop.

'I had the feeling you wanted to tell me something on my way in,' Molly said.

'I did so. 'Twas that Mrs Hanratty had been. But perhaps it made no difference.'

For herself, she would prefer Mrs Hanratty to be given the post, but she felt obliged to think also of her mother.

'It made all the difference in the world,' Molly said.

She told Breda of Luke's ultimatum, for ultimatum it was, there was no doubt of it.

'Oh, Mammy,' Breda cried. 'I don't want to go! I don't want to live with Luke O'Reilly!'

'I'm not sure that I want to go,' Molly said. She felt in a turmoil. 'But we would not be living with him, only living in his house.'

'I don't see the difference, Mammy!'

'There is a big difference.' She was not thinking of the property now. If Mrs Hanratty, a woman on her own, considered it proper, then it must certainly be so for a woman who would be accompanied by her daughter. 'The difference is that we would always be free to leave. If a better chance came, we would be free to take it.'

For the life of her she could not think what that other chance might be, but there was always the hope.

'How can we leave this house?' Breda pressed her. 'Oh, Mammy, how can we?'

But this house will never be the same to me, without James, Molly thought. Every inch of it spoke of him, was a constant reminder, yet without him in it, it was, and never would be again, any more than four walls and a roof; an empty shell, though how could she expect Breda to feel that?

'Shouldn't you ask Kieran, or Kathleen, for advice?' Breda said. She was clutching at straws.

'Even if there were time,' Molly replied, 'which there isn't, what advice could either of them give me? I know the situation, they don't.'

'But to leave here would be like leaving Dada!' Breda cried. 'How can we leave Dada?'

She slumped into the nearest chair and burst into noisy tears. Molly drew her to her feet and took her in her arms.

'I know, sweetheart! I know! But Dada is not here, not any longer. He has left us, but can we not take him with us wherever we go?'

She could not tell Breda about the moments of fierce and inexplicable anger which welled up inside her at the thought of James's death; anger against James, as if he was somehow to blame for leaving her, though she knew he was not. Anger against God for allowing it. Breda would not understand that. She could not understand it herself.

She stroked Breda's hair, took out a handkerchief and dried her eyes, as if she was a small child.

'We should both go to bed,' she said gently. 'Sleep on it. Pray that we'll both feel better in the morning.'

When she wakened next morning she did not feel better, but she knew what she must do.

'I shall take the job,' she said to Breda. 'I *must*! I'm sure it's for the best and I'm sure it will work out. And we'll be together.'

Eleven

Breda sat at the dressing-table in her bedroom. She had never before had a dressing-table. This one was, in fact, no more than a wooden top, coloured with a walnut stain, with shelves fixed to the wall underneath; but from around the top ran a valance, gathered full, in a pretty flowered cretonne. It hung to the floor, completely hiding the shelves and all the bits and pieces with which she had filled them. The mats on top, one large oval, two small round ones, were of the same material as the valance, but edged with lace which her mother had come across in one of Mary O'Reilly's workboxes, and Luke had said she might have.

'Take anything of that nature,' he had said. 'Sure, what would I be wanting with it?'

'You are very generous,' Molly had replied.

That much was true, Breda conceded, studying her appearance now in the large oval mirror on the wall over the dressing-table, confirming that the shorter haircut her mother had given her looked really quite stylish and that what she had thought might turn out to be a nasty spot on her chin had not, after all, come to fruition. Also, at seventeen, she had left behind her brief period of puppy fat and, in spite of demolishing all the good food her mother put before her, was once again as slim as a wand.

Parts of her bedroom were also reflected in the mirror: the pale blue distemper of the walls; the curtains at the window, which matched the dressing-table and the bedspread; the fringed lampshade. Even though she had made all these things herself, and had distempered the walls, it *was* Luke's house and he *had* allowed her to do it. So why, after a year of living here, could she still not take to him?

Her mother had settled in quickly. There was a lot to be done. The house had been neglected for years, except for Flora Milligan's weekly lick-and-a-promise, and she had given in her notice soon after Molly's appearance on the scene. Now whatever was to be done, cleaning, cooking, sewing, baking, Molly got on with, was immersed in. Sometimes Breda thought her mother had forgotten all about their previous life. How could she? Had she forgotten Dada so soon?

On a day when she was downcast – it was Luke's Wednesday for Ennis so he was out of the house – Breda put the question to her mother.

'Mammy, you haven't forgotten Dada, have you?'

Molly looked up from her ironing in astonishment, but when she saw the look on Breda's face, pity welled in her. She put the iron down on its stand.

'Forgotten Dada? No, sweetheart, I have not forgotten Dada, nor will I ever be forgetting him. What makes you ask?'

Breda hesitated. 'It's just . . . well, is it not that you seem so settled here, as if we had never had another life?'

Molly shook her head.

'It is not like that, *dote*. I will not forget that other life. Did it not give me you, and all my other children? But it is over, and that is not of my choosing. I have to make the best of things, and so have you. It worries me that you do not like Luke. I know he is not Dada, but . . . '

'He is *nothing* like Dada!'

'I know that. He is himself. He is honest, he is hard-working, and he is kind. You cannot say that he is not kind, and to you as well as to me. Look at what he has let us do in the house to make it comfortable. Only think about the sewing machine! What a kindness that was.'

He had seen Breda struggling to make curtains, watched Molly turning sheets side to middle to save him the cost of new ones, with the old machine they had brought with them, the thread constantly snapping, the tension slipping.

'Would it not be nice, now, to have new curtains in the living room?' Molly had said. The present ones were a dull, dark green, and had seen better days. 'Not to mention a chair cover or two. But there is no way I can be making them on this old thing!'

She had truly not thought that anything could be done about it and it came as a great and wonderful surprise when, on his next trip to Ennis, Luke brought back a new sewing machine in the back of his van. Not new, exactly. It was second-hand, but in good working order.

'Sure, I admit he is kind,' Breda said. Though hadn't he in the end, she thought, what with the new curtains, tablecloths and the like, felt the benefit as much as anyone?

'Then try to remember that,' Molly said. ' 'Twould be easier all round if you got on with Luke.'

How could she tell Breda that Luke had asked her to marry him? It had happened several weeks ago. She had, of course, refused him. James had not been dead a year then; she was not ready for marriage. It was not in her plans. What would people say?

But he would ask her again, she felt certain of it. He would not give up. And when he did ask her she was not at all sure what her answer would be, not convinced that it would still be 'no'.

I am forty-six, she thought. If the Lord so decides, I might well live another forty years. It was no longer entirely a question of security, she was sure she would have the job with Luke for his lifetime, but wasn't he coming up to his sixtieth birthday, though as hale and hearty as any man in Kilbally? But no, it was truthfully not just the security. She was a woman who needed marriage. She recognized that in herself. She needed its closeness and its intimacy. She needed to belong. And she liked Luke; hadn't she always?

He loved her. He had declared it. It was possible, she supposed, that she could come to love him. She longed for love, for a man's love.

'Why is it that you do not take to Luke?' she said to Breda. 'Why will you not try?'

'I do try,' Breda said.

It seemed to her that she was no longer as close to her mother as she had once been. She missed the conversations – carefree, lighthearted – they used to have before Dada died. There was not so much laughter now. This she put down to the fact that, until quite recently, almost every evening had been spent in the company of both her mother *and* Luke, and however kind he was, no-one could call Luke O'Reilly a jolly person, and her mother seemed to be settling into his ways.

Or perhaps her mother was just growing old. After all, she was forty-six, no longer young!

'Then try a little harder,' Molly said. 'To please me!'

But now life had taken on a new shine, and it was entirely due to Rory Nolan. He had come from Dublin, all of a sudden it seemed, and for an unspecified period of time which might even be permanent, to help his uncle, Dermot Brady, who owned the pharmacy in Kilbally. Yet no-one remembered Rory visiting his uncle as a small boy.

'Why do you think Rory did not come to Kilbally sooner?' Breda asked.

The question was seemingly out of the blue. Weren't they talking about Breda's attitude to Luke? However, these days, Molly thought, Breda could bring the name of Rory Nolan into any conversation.

' 'Tis not certain why,' Molly answered. 'Though his mother quarrelled with her brother Dermot when she went off and married in Dublin. I don't remember that she ever brought Rory here as a child.'

The other question was, why had he come to Kilbally now, at the age of twenty-three? The reason given was that Dermot Brady, who had never married and therefore had neither chick nor child, needed help in the pharmacy and fancied his own kith and kin over a stranger. But since Rory had been a stranger all these years, it did not wash with Molly.

And what does Rory Nolan get out of it, Molly asked herself? What compensates a young man for leaving the bright lights of Dublin for a place like Kilbally?

Well, at the moment one compensation was certainly Breda. He was doing a line on her all right, and how could she not fall for it? He was tall, dark haired, fine-featured, broad-shouldered, well dressed, and with a wide smile and a gift of the gab. Business had never been so brisk in the pharmacy, with half the mothers and daughters of Kilbally queuing up to be served with headache powders, face creams, cough mixtures and babies' dummies. It was as if a star, straight from Hollywood, had shot into their midst.

Nor, as Molly reluctantly reminded herself, was there a single thing to hold against him. He was unfailingly polite to one and all, chucked small babies under the chin, and was regularly at Mass. There he sat a little in front and to the side of Breda, so that she enjoyed the pleasure of his perfect profile, yet was conveniently placed when, from time to time, he turned around and looked straight at her, turning her knees to jelly.

On the Sunday following her conversation with Breda about Luke, Molly, sitting beside her daughter, caught Rory at it, but when he knew himself caught he at once turned his warm gaze, with the hint of a conspiratorial twitch at the corners of his mouth, upon the mother. Molly looked away quickly, as if it was she who had been caught.

He was out of church well before them, Breda champing at the bit because her mother *would* stop and ask how someone was, and was the new baby thriving, and draw Breda into the conversation. Was anything more certain, she asked herself, since half the unmarried girls in Kilbally had their sights on him, that one of them would carry him off before she even got out of the building?

When they did emerge he *was* in the centre of a group, but he left them at once and came over to Breda and Molly.

'Good morning to you both,' he said in his deep voice, raising the smart fawn trilby he wore to church. 'Now would you be giving me the pleasure of escorting you two beautiful ladies back to your home, since we all walk in the same direction?'

' 'Tis not necessary . . . ' Molly began, and thought how rude she sounded. 'But very well, then,' she ended.

Her reward from him was a radiant smile, with a flash of perfect teeth. They set off, he taking the edge of the pavement and manoeuvring Breda into the space between himself and Molly. The pavement was narrow. They could not avoid walking close together, bumping into each other from time to time.

He walked all the way to Luke O'Reilly's shop with them, though it meant passing the pharmacy. He had been in the shop several times in the past week or two, on behalf, he explained, of his uncle. Now he lingered on the pavement outside the door, but if he was expecting to be invited in, Molly thought, he was due for disappointment. Also, it was not her place to be inviting people into Luke's home.

'I was wondering, so I was, if I might take Breda for a walk this afternoon?'

Rory made his request to Molly. Molly glanced at Breda, who looked as though she had had a light turned on inside her. If only the child would not be so transparent, always showing her feelings, good or bad! And I am thinking of her as a child again, she thought, and she is so no longer. She is seventeen. I was married at eighteen.

'You must ask Breda,' she said.

But it had been polite of him to ask her first – polite, or quite clever. She wished she did not have these double-edged feelings about the young man. There was no good reason for it; it was unfair.

'I would enjoy it,' Breda said. ' 'Tis a fine spring day!' She would have enjoyed it even if it had been a cold November fog.

'Then I will be calling for you at three o'clock?' Rory said.

He raised his hat once again, and left them.

No matter how much her mother urged her, Breda could not eat her Sunday dinner, which was a pity because it was always the best meal of the week, and today there was a piece of beef, pink and succulent. She swallowed a mouthful of meat, pecked at a potato, pushed the cabbage aside, refused the rice pudding, and escaped to her room.

The time crawled towards three o'clock. She changed her dress twice, and then went back to the first one. She brushed her hair until it shone. She put on her blue beads, then took them off and settled for the pink. But at least Rory was not late. When his knock came at five minutes to three, she rushed to the door. She had been watching out for him for more than half an hour. She had no intention of inviting him in; she did not want time being wasted in polite conversation with her mother and Luke.

'I wondered, would we walk along the cliffs?' Rory asked as they set off.

'I would like that fine,' Breda said.

It was a favourite walk for Kilbally people, as well as for visitors who came by bicycle, or these days once again by car, leaving their transport along the sides of the lane before climbing the steep slope to the top of the cliffs.

It being a fine Sunday afternoon, there were plenty of people about. Although Breda would have liked nothing so much as to be on a desert island alone with Rory she was, on the other hand, delighted to be seen walking with him, especially by several people who knew her. To be one of a group of young people taking the walk was one thing, she had done it often – though she hoped that if they met with such a clique Rory would not wish to join them – but to be linking arms, which Rory had done the minute they were out of the main street, just the two of them together, was quite different. She knew it would not go unremarked.

This high, the air was as clear as crystal, so fresh as almost to tingle on the tongue. The sea, far below them, was a deep, dark, almost navy, blue, with the crests of the waves turning to green at the moment before they hit against the cliff face in an explosion of white foam and spray. Further out the water was calm, but in the small bays and gullies which cut into the cliffs there was strong movement and incessant sound, added to by the whirling and dipping and crying of the gulls.

'I like the feeling of being above the birds,' Breda said. 'Of looking down on them as they fly. And I like to see the ones riding on the water, letting the waves take them wherever they will!'

'And I would like it if you would not stand so close to the edge,' Rory warned. 'I don't want to lose you. I've only just found you.'

He tightened his grip on her arm and held her close in to him. She was flooded with pleasure, her whole body trembling. Surely he must feel her shaking? She knew that what she wanted most of all now was to be alone with him. She wanted everyone else to disappear, leave the two of them with only the cliffs, the short, springing grass, the sounds of the birds and the sea for company. Minutes ago she had been pleased that there were people around to see them; now she wanted no-one but Rory.

As if he read her thoughts, he said, 'Are there not far too many people around? Why would they not go away and leave the place to you and me?'

It happened almost immediately. The rain came, as it frequently did in Kilbally, with the suddenness of someone up there, behind the clouds, turning on a tap; warmish rain, and gentle, but persistent and plentiful. In no time at all the cliff top was cleared of people. Only Breda and Rory remained, and while he held her close Breda was oblivious of the weather.

Rory was more practical. 'If we climb just a little way down, over there,' he said, pointing, 'there's a rock overhanging. Sure, we could get shelter for a wee while, until it eases off.'

He began to lead her, cautioning her to be careful. The grass was slippery, but bit by bit they inched forward and

203

made it to the place, a shelf about four feet wide, overhung by a rock.

'Why, it's quite dry here!' Breda said. 'Why did no-one else see it, I wonder?'

'We may as well sit down until the rain is over,' Rory said.

It would stop as suddenly as it had started, Breda knew that. It was the way it was on this coast.

He sat down, and pulled her down beside him, and then he was kissing her, gently at first, then harder, and holding her closer. It was not the first time in her life she had been kissed; hadn't they all larked about on the way home from a dance? But it had not been like this, it had been nothing like this. It was as if his kisses entered her parted lips and coursed through her body, to her fingertips and the ends of her toes. And all the time she wanted him to do more than kiss her, though she was not sure what.

Then suddenly he stopped kissing her and held her away from him. 'The rain has stopped, so it has, and we are both quite wet. I must take you home or your mother will not let you come out with me again!'

Breda wondered how he could change so quickly. She was still trembling inside, still half in another world where it didn't matter what the weather did, but she didn't protest as he pulled her to her feet. Whatever he did, whatever he said, was right, and she would follow him.

I am in love, she thought. I am really and truly in love! This is what it is like, and it is wonderful!

On the Wednesday he took her to the film show – Cary Grant it was, and he was not one whit more handsome than Rory Nolan, who, she was sure, could himself have been on the films if only he had wanted to. On Saturday night he accompanied her to the *céilidh*, where he spent most of his time with her, and on Sunday he again walked her and her mother home after Mass. She was, Breda could tell, the envy of all her friends in Kilbally.

And so it went on as spring gave way to summer: films, walks, dances; once a trip to Ennis; once they cycled all the way along the coast to Ballyvaughan and picnicked on the Burren. He was interested in everything about her, what she was, what she did.

'I want to know all that's ever happened to you!' he said.

'And that will not take long,' Breda told him. 'Not much happens in Kilbally.'

She told him about her family, about Kieran, about the twins in New York. She spoke to him of her father, and of how she came to be living in Luke O'Reilly's house, and why she was not altogether happy there.

'But you do not tell me anything about *your* life,' she said.

They were walking along the edge of the hayfield. A path ran along the side of the field and when the hay was ready to be cropped, as now, Breda knew they were supposed to keep to the path, not tread down the grass; but Rory ignored that, forging a path several yards in the field, then firmly taking her in his arms and pulling her to the ground. They were completely hidden now, in a world of their own, closed in by the sweet-smelling grasses.

'And isn't that because my life only started when I came to Kilbally,' he said.

She thought they were the most romantic, wonderful words she had ever heard.

And then there were better things to do than talk. He was on top of her, and she loved the weight of him, as if he was all hers and she was all his. His hands were everywhere, now caressing her neck, now undoing the buttons of her blouse, but when his hands moved downwards and he lifted her skirt and began to stroke her thighs, she pushed him away, and sat upright.

'What is it?' he murmured. 'You needn't be afraid, sweetheart. I won't hurt you!'

How could she explain that she would not mind being hurt by him, and she was not afraid in the way he meant it? It was just that she knew they must not go any further, she knew that this was what led to a baby. For a girl in Kilbally, a good Catholic girl, to have a baby when she was not married was a mortal sin and a fate worse than death; a disgrace for which she would be sent away, indeed worse. Had it not been Kitty Shane, and only last year, who had gone with a man from the summer fair and he had left her with a child inside her, and hadn't she drowned herself in the lough?

' 'Tis not that,' she said hesitantly. ' 'Tis just that . . . well . . . only if I was married. Only then.'

Perhaps he would ask her to marry him, she thought! Oh, how wonderful that would be, to be married forever to Rory Nolan, to live with him, no matter whether it was Kilbally or Dublin, to be made love to, to have his children! She was suddenly full of hope. Had he not called her 'sweetheart'? It must be what he had in mind. 'Twas only that he had not got around to saying it.

'What a little prude you are!' he said, though he was still smiling.

' 'Tis just that . . . '

'Don't explain,' he said. 'I understand.'

'And we will still be . . . friends?'

'Friends, is it? Well, why not?'

'Will I make a pot of tea?' Molly asked Luke. 'I had thought Breda might be back, but since she isn't there is no reason why we should wait.'

'She seems set on this Rory Nolan,' Luke observed. 'Dermot is right enough, but what do we know of his nephew?'

'Perhaps there is nothing *to* know,' Molly said. She spoke without conviction. She was never totally easy in her mind about Rory and she wished once again that Breda was not so besotted with him, or at least did not let him see it so plainly.

'Well then, never mind about Rory Nolan or Breda,' Luke said. 'There is something I want to say to you, Molly.'

'Oh?' She tried to sound surprised, for the sake of politeness, though she knew at once what it must be, and she had not yet made up her mind either way.

'You can guess what it is and I will not beat about the bush. Will you marry me, Molly?'

'I am not—'

He ignored her interruption. 'I love you, Molly. I don't think there was ever a time when I didn't love you, but it never worked out. I would do everything in the world to make you happy.'

'I am not sure—'

'I am not getting any younger, and one day everything would be yours.'

'Oh Luke!' Molly cried. 'That would not be why I would marry you! Not at all.'

'I would not expect you to love me, not at first. But you do like me, don't you?'

'Oh I do!' Molly assured him. 'I have always liked you, Luke. Always!' It was true. She could not remember a time when she had not liked and respected Luke O'Reilly.

'Then if I love you, and you like me, what is to stop us? There's many people happy on far less.'

'I know.'

'So what is it to be? Will you marry me?'

She looked at him directly. He was not handsome, as James had been. There was no bright twinkle in his eye, but there was great kindness there, and honesty. His hair, though still abundant, was grey, but didn't she find grey hairs among her own black ones these days? And what did the colour of his hair matter? He was utterly reliable and trustworthy and he would never let her down. Surely these alone were qualities for which she could learn to love him.

She took a deep breath. 'I will be honoured to marry you, Luke O'Reilly,' she said.

She was sitting in the chair. He took her hands and pulled her to her feet, then he drew her into his arms and kissed her.

'We will go into Ennis and buy a ring,' he said. 'You shall have whatever takes your fancy. How soon can we be married?'

'As soon as you like,' Molly said. 'Will I wet the tea now?'

'No,' Luke replied. 'I will open a bottle of sherry. We will drink to the future, yours and mine.'

From the corner cupboard he took two of the best glasses; delicately-cut Waterford they were, which Mary had brought with her when she first came to Kilbally. Molly had never seen them used before.

Rory walked with Breda as far as Luke's house. I will ask him in for tea, she thought. Why not? Surely no-one will mind? But when she did so, he refused.

'I have to get back,' he excused himself. 'Uncle Dermot is getting ready for stocktaking and I promised to help. But I will see you during the week, sweetheart!' He gave her a squeeze of the hand, and was gone.

When she went into the house she was met by the unusual sight of the sherry bottle on the table, and Luke and her mother, who was slightly flushed, with her hair uncharacteristically untidy, drinking from the best glasses.

'Let me pour you a glass, Breda,' Luke offered quickly.

'Why? What are you . . . ?'

'We have news for you,' Molly broke in.

She glanced nervously at Luke, then back again to Breda. She was not sure how to break it, but in the circumstances there seemed only one way.

'Luke and I are going to be married!'

Wide-eyed with horror, Breda stared at her mother. Molly looked back at her steadily. No-one would know that beneath her calm exterior she felt afraid, her heart pounding in her chest. She was not afraid of her future with Luke. From the moment she had accepted him she knew that that was going to be all right. Breda was another matter.

Luke fetched another glass, half-filled it, and placed it on the table in front of Breda.

'We want you to drink to our future,' he said. He raised his own glass.

'*Sláinte!*'

Without even looking at him, her eyes fixed on her mother, Breda picked up the glass and flung the contents full in Molly's face.

'Never!' she shouted. 'Never, ever! How *could* you!'

Then she threw the glass across the room, where it splintered into a hundred pieces against the stone hearth.

Twelve

While it seemed that Breda's words still hung on the air, in the same moment that the sherry glass splintered, thrown with such force that shards flew in all directions, embedding themselves in the hearthrug, one fragment cutting into Molly's ankle – though she was too stunned to notice it until later – Breda observed the sherry running in golden-brown rivulets down her mother's horrified face, smelled the strong, sweet reek of it in the room, saw the anger on Luke's face as he moved swiftly towards Molly.

For that moment, which was short, but seemed to go on for ever, she was rooted, unable to move, shocked by the announcement her mother had made, and by the enormity of what she herself had just done. Then, suddenly, life came back to her and she turned and ran out of the room. She had no idea where she was going. All she knew was that she had to get out of the house as fast as she could.

She slammed the house door behind her, and continued to run, passing two women she knew well – they were customers of Luke's – without so much as a word. They turned and stared after her as she shot up the street. Out of sight of Luke's house, she slowed down to a walk. She wanted no-one asking was there something the matter.

But where was she bound for, where would she go? She had fled without an idea in her head except to escape.

Would she go down to the strand? Would she sit on the cliff top above the beach where, as a child, she had so often gone to work off a temper? But this was more than a temper. This time there was nothing she could do to cool the boiling rage inside her. Nothing could change the awful prospect of her mother marrying Luke O'Reilly.

Or would she make for the church? Would she speak with Father Curran? But what would she say to him? He would disapprove of her anger, and she wanted comfort, not a lecture.

Then, halfway along the road, she realized she was on the way to the pharmacy. Of course! Where else would she go other than to Rory? Who else would give her the understanding and sympathy she deserved and craved?

She began to walk more quickly, then broke into a run, so that when she reached the shop door she was out of breath.

The door was locked and the shop blinds drawn down. She had overlooked the fact that it was past closing time. She banged on the door, rattled the latch, desperate now to be admitted.

'I'm coming! I'm coming!' It was Dermot Brady's voice, not Rory's.

She waited impatiently – it seemed an age – while he drew back the bolts, turned the key in the lock, then opened the door a few inches and peered out.

'Oh, it's Breda! Has your mother been taken ill, then? What can I do?'

If it was as serious as the look on her face, then why hadn't she run for the doctor? People came to him because he was cheaper, but an emergency was an emergency.

'Mammy is not ill . . . ' Breda began.

'Then Luke, is it? Has he had an accident?'

'No, Mr Brady. It is not Luke . . . at least . . . What I want is to see Rory. Will you be letting me in?'

Dermot opened the door, and she entered. Rory is it, he thought? And what has he been up to? The girl was in a fine old state.

'He has not been home many minutes,' he said, 'though he was supposed to help me with the stocktaking. I will give him a call, so.'

He opened the door at the back of the shop and shouted through. 'Rory, will you come here this minute, then?'

Deliberately, he gave no reason. Rory would take it that he was impatient to get on with the stocktaking, and so he was, but more than that, if there was trouble afoot he did not want to give the lad time to think up some fancy excuse. He had discovered quite soon after Rory had arrived in Kilbally that his charming nephew could wriggle out of most things.

A minute later Rory came into the shop wearing his white coat, ready to start work. He was speaking as he entered. 'I'm sorry I am late, Uncle. I was delayed. You know how 'tis when you cannot get away from someone!'

The words were out of his mouth before he saw Breda, but fortunately she seemed not to have heard them, full as she was of her own trouble.

'Oh Rory!' she cried. 'I had to see you! 'Tis the most awful thing, you'll not believe it!'

Dermot gave his nephew a sharp look. 'What would this be about, then?' he asked him.

He was apprehensive. *Not* Breda O'Connor, he prayed.

'I'm afraid I don't know, Uncle!'

He raised his dark eyebrows in two question marks. He was genuinely puzzled, but his conscience was clear, though it might not have been had she not turned out to be such a prude. He had misjudged her there all right, and it *was* disappointing because she was lovely and desirable, the pick of the locality, there was no denying that. Also, she was in love with him. But like the small-town girl she was, she had her sights on marriage, and that was not for him. Still, there were plenty of fish in the sea, especially along this coast.

So why was she in a state and, more to the point, what could it have to do with him?

'Could I be seeing Rory alone?' Breda pleaded with Dermot.

'Why?' Dermot asked bluntly. Then he turned to his nephew and repeated the question. 'Why?'

Rory shook his head. 'I don't know why at all.' He turned to Breda. 'There's nothing which can't be said in front of Uncle Dermot, is there?'

In fact, he thought, wouldn't he just as soon have his uncle there? He didn't know what she was up to.

Breda hesitated only briefly. She had hoped that Rory would lead her off into the back room, take her in his arms and kiss and comfort her, but there was something in his voice which made her uncertain. In any case, Mr Brady would have to know. There was no keeping it secret. Wasn't it something the whole of Kilbally would know in no time at all?

'It *is* Mammy,' she confessed. 'And it is Luke, but not the way you mean. The awful thing is, they are going to be married! 'Tis the most terrible thing that ever happened, except when Dada died. And if he had not, 'twould not have happened at all, and that's the truth of it! I cannot possibly be living in the same house as them, though I should not have thrown the glass, not at all, nor the sherry at Mammy!'

Tears ran down her face like drops of bright summer rain. Dermot and Rory glanced at each other. There was relief in the hearts of both of them.

'Is that it?' Dermot said in a kindly manner. 'But 'tis surely not all bad? Your Mammy and Luke O'Reilly have known each other since they were children, and now they have both lost their partners in life. They will be comfort for each other. It is entirely natural. I would say it is good.'

213

Breda scarcely listened. It was not what she wanted to hear. 'I don't like him,' she persisted. 'I never have.'

'Plenty do,' Dermot said. 'Luke is a good man. Though 'tis unfortunate that you do not like him, 'tis of no real importance.'

'No importance?' She heard that all right. She stared at him in astonishment. What did he mean?

'Not really.' He spoke calmly, as if they were discussing the weather; would it rain before morning. 'Not really. The important thing is that your Mammy likes him. 'Tis she who will be marrying him, when all is said and done!'

'How *can* she?' Breda implored. 'How can she do it? He is *nothing* like Dada!'

'Which is just as well, especially for Luke. Who would want to go through life with a woman, being compared all the time with her first husband? No, Breda, 'tis better the way it is. And you will get used to it.'

'I will not, so!' Breda said vehemently. 'I will never get used to it. And I cannot possibly live there!'

'Then perhaps you will go to your Grandmother Byrne,' Dermot said reasonably. 'She is an old woman. She might be glad of your company.'

He knew what he was saying. Sure, wasn't Mrs Byrne the most awkward old woman in the whole of Kilbally? No-one would want to live with her.

'I could not possibly do that,' Breda said. 'We are like chalk and cheese!'

A thought struck her. 'Could I not come here, and look after you both? I would do it very well, and charge nothing except my keep.' She would also see Rory every day.

Asking the question of Dermot, she did not see the alarm on Rory's face.

' 'Twould not be possible,' Dermot said firmly. ' 'Twould not be right. Two single men in the house, and you a beautiful young lady!'

Breda looked from Dermot to Rory, who so far had not spoken.

'I agree with Uncle Dermot,' he said. ' 'Twould not be fitting.'

'So it seems either you go to Grandmother Byrne, or you go back to your Mammy and Luke,' Dermot said. 'There is nothing else for it. So what was it you said about the sherry glass a minute ago? I didn't understand that.'

Breda told them what she had done. Dermot gave a long whistle; Rory opened his eyes wide. She had more spirit than he'd reckoned.

'So how can I possibly go back?' she asked.

'Oh, I am sure they will both forgive you!' Dermot said easily. 'Though I think it might be a good idea if I were to go back with you; to congratulate them, you understand. Perhaps I will take Luke to the Harp for a celebration, while you make your peace with your Mammy.'

'Luke does not go to the Harp,' Breda said.

'Sure, I might persuade him!' Dermot sounded confident.

He took off his white coat, lifted his hat from the peg behind the door, and was ready to accompany Breda.

'I might be an hour or two,' he said to Rory. It was quite a while since he had been in the Harp. 'There's plenty of work you can get on with.'

'Speaking of work,' he said to Breda as they set off, 'would it not be rather awkward for you to work for Luke, as you do, if you were to cut yourself off?'

'So 'twould,' Breda agreed miserably. 'I had not considered that.'

In fact, she had considered nothing in her desire to escape, and though she was not the least bit happy about her mother and Luke, and never would be – the whole idea was abhorrent to her – Dermot's words made her think. Apart from her job, where else would she live, if not in Luke's house? Grandma Byrne was not to be thought of, and who else was there?

'Would you rather I did not go home with you? Would you rather do it alone?' Dermot asked.

Breda pictured herself stepping into the house, walking into the living room with them both sitting there; finding the right words to say to them. She could not face it.

'Oh no, Mr Brady! 'Twould be much easier if you were there. The only thing is . . . ' She hesitated.

'What?'

'What will Mammy be saying when she finds out I ran to you?'

In fact, she had run to Rory, but Dermot Brady had taken charge. Rory had had surprisingly little to say.

'I dare say she will not hear of it, unless you choose to tell her. Why would you not have met me in the street and given me the news? But in any case, that is not what she will be thinking about. There are matters more important to your Mammy.'

'You mean like the sherry, and the glass?'

Dermot suppressed a smile.

'I was not thinking of that, though it was a foolish thing to do. Really, more the action of a child than that of a young woman.'

How could she tell him – she did not know him all that well – that she felt like a child, and a frightened one at that? She almost wished she was, so that everyone would pet her and comfort her, the way they once had.

They were at Luke's house now, so there was no time for Dermot to say more. 'Cheer up!' he whispered as she opened the door and he followed her in. 'They won't eat you!'

He pushed past her and stepped into the living room first.

'Hasn't Breda been telling me your good news?' he said cheerfully. 'I couldn't but call in and give you both my heartiest congratulations.'

Luke and Molly both rose to their feet as Dermot crossed the room and shook each of them heartily by the hand. They smiled, pleased to see him.

'Will you be having a glass of something?' Luke asked.

'Oh no! No, I was on my way to the Harp. Such a long time since I've been there. Perhaps you'd come with me for an hour, Luke – if Molly can spare you, of course?'

'Why certainly I can,' Molly agreed. 'Off you go, Luke. 'Twill do you good!'

Breda had not spoken. There had been no need. She had ascertained with a quick glance that there was no broken glass around. There was no sign of the sherry bottle; everything looked back to normal except that on her mother's left ankle there was now a plaster. She felt herself redden when she looked at it.

The two men left quickly, Luke hardly glancing at Breda as he passed her.

'Come and sit down for a minute,' Molly said to Breda when the men had left.

'I think I will go to bed,' Breda said.

'You will not just yet,' Molly said. 'There are things to be said.'

She indicated the chair opposite her own and, like the child she had been wishing she was, Breda obeyed, and sat down.

She pointed to the plaster on her mother's ankle.

'I'm sorry for that, Mammy!'

'It is no matter,' Molly said. 'It did not go deep, and 'twill heal soon enough. There are other matters which will take more healing. I would rather you were sorry for those.'

Breda opened her mouth to say something but Molly put up a hand to stop her.

'Wait! I will have my say first, and you had better listen to it before you have yours.

The first thing I want to say is that I fully intend to marry Luke, and that no number of tantrums, no amount of opposition from you will make me change my mind. I know how you feel, and I am *not* putting Luke in Dada's place. Dada will always have his own place in my heart, and Luke will have his place too, though a different one.'

'It's just that I can't—' Breda began.

'I haven't finished,' Molly said. 'The next thing is that while you live in his house I will not countenance your rudeness to him. Do you think he has no feelings? Do you think you are the only one who feels? Then let me tell you, you are wrong! He feels deeply about many things which you have never managed to see. So do I, for that matter, but I am talking about Luke now. I will not ask you to like him – though you could try – but I insist that you treat him properly, and give him the respect he deserves. Is that clear?'

She was trembling with the effort of what she had just said, and from the emotion of what had led up to it. She doubted whether her words had had the slightest effect on Breda, who sat there white-faced and rebellious.

'Quite clear,' Breda said. 'Can I go to my room now?'

'In a minute. I have to tell you that Luke and I plan to be married in a month's time. We see no reason to wait. But you will be breaking my heart – and hurting him – if you will not be there, will not wish us well, will not try to live in harmony.'

It was too much. She broke into tears, then held out her arms to Breda, who went into them.

'Oh Breda, I couldn't bear to lose your love! I couldn't bear it!'

'Mammy, I'll always love you! You know that,' Breda said. 'And I will try to be good. Truly I will!'

She still felt like a child, but now like one in the luxury of being comforted; and then less like a child, because wasn't she comforting her mother? She was a child and a woman all in one, and the woman in her knew it was not going to be easy, and that nothing could be quite the same again.

A little later, she went to bed. Luke was not yet back and Breda had offered to stay with her mother, but Molly refused the offer. It was seldom indeed that Luke went out drinking but, Molly thought, he had had enough to drive a man to it. She was not quite sure how he would be when he came in and, all things considered, it would be better for Breda not to be there.

Lying in bed, Breda also thought about Luke. Why did she not like him? He was always nice to her, when she let him be. He had long ago stopped following her around the shop with his eyes. All that had ceased before they came to live with him, and if his look followed anyone these days it was Molly, though not in any unpleasant way. It was obvious, though Breda hated the thought, that he adored Molly.

Am I jealous, Breda asked herself? But she refused to accept that. It was impossible.

She deliberately put Luke O'Reilly and the whole situation out of her mind, turned over on to her other side, and gave up her thoughts to Rory Nolan. She had been disappointed in him this evening. He had not sprung to her rescue like the knight in shining armour she knew him to be. But, she thought, giving him the benefit of the small seed of doubt in her mind, perhaps that was because Dermot Brady had taken control right from the outset.

Rory had had no chance to do anything. Perhaps, being dependent on his uncle, he was a little in awe of him. She had not made any plan to see Rory tomorrow, but she was quite sure he would come into the shop and fix something. Perhaps he would take her to see the film. Or for a walk. It didn't matter what. When would he tell her he loved her, as she did him? Soon, now, she was sure.

On the point of falling asleep she thought she heard Luke come into the house.

'Where is she?' Luke demanded.

'Gone to bed this hour past,' Molly answered.

He grunted. She scrutinized him. He was flushed in the face, and she could smell the drink on him, but no more than that. His voice had been harsh when he'd asked about Breda, but was that any wonder? All the same, she was thankful Breda had gone to bed.

'Did she give you a hard time, then?' he wanted to know.

'I didn't give her the chance. I told her what was what. It's really not you, you know. It's to do with her Dada. She took it so badly when he died.'

Luke shook his head, not quite believing her. 'She never really liked me,' he said. 'I always knew that. Did you tell her we were getting married in a month's time?'

'I did. And I said nothing would stop us!'

He knelt on the floor beside her armchair and took both her hands in his, covering them with kisses. 'I wish it was now,' he said. 'I wish I was taking you to bed this minute!'

For a brief moment, desire stirred in her – and was gone again.

'It won't be long now,' she said. 'And don't worry about Breda. She'll come round.'

'Once you are mine, I will not be giving a toss,' he said.

'Will I make you some cocoa?' she asked him.

'No. I have enough liquid on board!'

'Then I'll be off to my bed.'

His eyes followed her with longing as she left the room. But wasn't he the luckiest man in the whole of Ireland?

The next morning was surprisingly good. The sun shone from the moment dawn broke. Breda rose with the firm intention of being as civil, if not downright nice, to Luke as she possibly could. She saw no solution to the problem of the marriage but she would try, for one day at the very least, to put it out of her mind.

She was pleasant to Luke over breakfast, and was rewarded, as she got up from the table to go to her work in the shop, with her mother's grateful smile. It was a morning also, quite by coincidence, of her favourite customers. The only shadow over it all, as the time went by, was that Rory did not appear, and she had been so sure he would.

But then, she asked herself, did he not have to work? He was not a free agent. Of course he did, she answered herself, but didn't he practically always find a way of calling in, usually when he was on his way to or from delivering a prescription? Weren't there always ways? He had said it himself, more than once.

Had she done anything to offend him? Was he displeased, and blaming her, that his uncle had taken the initiative last evening, and made him stay behind to get on with the stocktaking? Or was he immersed in the stocktaking? In case that was it, she would go along to the pharmacy herself just to say hello. She would not keep him from his work.

At dinnertime she said to Luke, 'Can I take twenty minutes to go out? I will not spend any time at all on my dinner. Sure, I am not the least bit hungry!'

'As you wish,' he said. He was not in the mood to deny her. She had been more than reasonable all morning.

Molly tut-tutted when Breda went out instead of coming to the table. ' 'Tis that Rory Nolan, I'll be bound,' she grumbled to Luke. 'And him not worth missing one mouthful of food over!'

At the pharmacy, Breda stood waiting while Rory finished serving a customer. Dermot was nowhere to be seen. As the customer left and Breda stepped forward, the door behind the counter, which led to the living quarters, opened, and a young woman stepped out. She had golden blonde hair cascading to her shoulders, and a pert, pretty face, with a mouth like a ripe cherry. As if she had not even seen Breda, she spoke to Rory.

'Rory, me darlin' boy, will you please be coming in for your dinner,' she said persuasively. 'Or 'twill spoil. 'Twill not be fit to eat!'

There was no mistaking the proprietary air with which she laid her hand on his arm. And on the third finger of her hand she wore a wide gold band, as bright as her hair. But there was more. Her waist was thick, and below that her belly was swollen. She was several months pregnant.

Breda looked at Rory. His face was ashen. 'I can explain . . . ' he began.

'You'll get your dinner first!' the young woman said. She turned him around and gave him a playful push through the door.

'There!' she said, turning to Breda. 'A firm hand my husband needs, and I have one! Is there something I can be serving you with?'

'No! Yes! I mean . . . I will take a small packet of aspirins, please!'

'You don't seem a bit well,' the woman said, looking intently at Breda.

'I'm . . . It's just . . . ' Breda began.

The woman's gaze met hers head on. 'I do hope my husband hasn't been a naughty boy!' she said. 'He's like all men, no worse for watching!'

Breda took a deep breath. 'Why no!' she said firmly. 'I hardly know him!'

Afterwards, she couldn't remember how she had got home, whom she had passed, not seeing, on the way. When she reached home, she was sick.

' 'Tis that Rory, I know it!' Molly said. 'Whatever happened, *alainna*?'

Breda nodded, but she could tell them nothing. The words would not come.

Dermot Brady came around that evening. 'I had not known that Rory was involved with Breda, or with anyone in Kilbally, or I would have spoken out,' he said. 'He came to me because he was in trouble in Dublin, just until it blew over. His wife thought he had been away too long, and she was getting big with the baby, so she came after him.'

If you didn't know about Rory and Breda, Molly thought, you must be the only person in Kilbally who didn't. She found it hard to believe.

'I would like to get my hands on him!' Luke said fiercely.

'That you cannot do,' Dermot said. 'They took the afternoon train back to Dublin. But I have no doubt his wife will sort him out!'

It was soon around Kilbally, it took no more than a few hours, that that charmer, Rory Nolan, was after all a married man, and what was more, with his wife expecting, seven months gone. And hadn't she come from Dublin and dragged him back, practically by the hair of his head?

No-one quite knew how the news got out. Dermot said nothing more to his lady customers who enquired after Rory, than that he had returned to Dublin. Luke and Molly kept quiet. As for Breda, she would have died rather than utter a word. Someone, Molly said to Luke in private, must have seen him being borne off to the railway station by a pregnant woman. That was quite enough for Kilbally to make up the rest of the story, which in this case happened to be true.

She was deeply sorry for Breda, who appeared at breakfast with red-rimmed eyes, swollen into mere slits from crying all night. She ate nothing, but sipped at a cup of tea.

'Would you like me to take your place in the shop today?' Molly asked. 'I'm sure Luke wouldn't mind. You could take the day off.'

'No thank you,' Breda said thickly. 'I have to face it some time. Best do it right away.'

She remembered with what pride she had walked arm in arm with Rory, pleased to be seen by so many friends and acquaintances. What would they have to say now?

'You are well rid of him,' Molly said. 'In any case, didn't I know he was not fit to black your boots!'

'I would rather not talk about him, Mammy,' Breda said. 'Now or ever.'

Unexpectedly, not a single customer in the shop that day made any mention of Rory, though she knew very well that they noticed her swollen eyes and her out-of-character sad face, for she found it impossible to smile.

'It was very nice of them,' she said to Molly later. 'Even Mrs Fitzpatrick kept quiet.'

'And the Lord knows what an effort that would be,' Molly said. 'But that's Kilbally for you. They are quick to gossip, but they defend their own against any outsider.'

On the following Wednesday Luke, for the first time ever, took the whole day off to take Molly into Ennis to choose an engagement ring and a wedding ring. Breda was left in charge of the shop for the morning. When the happy couple returned Molly, having moved James's wedding ring to her right hand – which Breda immediately noticed and was deeply hurt by – proudly displayed a ring set with two small diamonds and a garnet.

'The diamonds,' Luke had told her as they sat in the train on the way home, 'are no brighter than your eyes!'

Four weeks later they would be married. Dermot Brady, with whom Luke had struck up something of a friendship since their evening together in the Harp, had agreed to act as best man and Breda, with a reluctance she tried hard not to show, as her mother's attendant. Though the rest of Molly's family had been informed about the wedding, no invitations had been issued. Both Molly and Luke wanted it to be a quiet affair. Luke had no relatives.

Kieran – Father Kieran now – sent a loving letter, as did Kathleen. Moira sent a card. It was too soon to have heard from the twins, though Molly knew she would. Josephine wrote with congratulations and approval and asked what they would like for a wedding present.

'I wish she would bring herself over for a visit,' Molly said to Luke. 'That would be the best present ever!'

Though Breda was aware of all the planning, the activity – how could she not be, it was the chief topic of conversation? – she gave little heed to it. Rory's departure, and the humiliation surrounding it, filled her mind to the exclusion of all else. She went through the motions of each day as if in a dream; working in the shop, eating (though very little), dressing and undressing, going to bed and getting up, all mechanically, like a wound-up toy. She felt nothing which did not include Rory, and everything which did stabbed her to the heart. She would never recover, *never*.

Only in the last week before the wedding, with which Molly was now totally preoccupied, did Breda begin to emerge, for short periods, from her shattered dreams of Rory, and then she found herself plunged into the nightmare of her mother's arrangements.

Two days before the wedding Molly was putting the finishing touches to the dress she was to be married in. It was a navy and white floral, smart but not fussy, and with it she would wear a navy hat and white shoes and handbag.

'Do you really think I will look all right?' she asked Breda anxiously.

'You will look fine, Mammy!' Breda said. She tried to sound enthusiastic, and failed. Molly gave her a worried look.

'I know how you feel, *dote*,' she said. 'But try to be happy, for my sake!'

'You do *not* know how I feel,' Breda contradicted. 'And I *am* trying to be happy for you.'

It was not easy; she was deeply unhappy on her own account, and as the wedding drew nearer, the thought of it grew worse. And then at last it was there. All she wanted to do when she wakened was to put her head back under the bedclothes, and stay there for ever.

Somehow she got through it, managing to say the right things, not upsetting either Luke or her mother – though it was doubtful if anything, even she, could have upset them. They seemed so happy with each other.

She was glad of the presence of Dermot Brady. Even though he was a constant reminder of Rory, about whom they kept a silence, she felt he understood her feelings about her mother. Wasn't it Dermot she had confided in in the first place?

To her relief, the newly-weds had decided to leave for Galway immediately after the ceremony, stopping only to visit Grandma Byrne, who was not well enough to be at the ceremony and was being looked after by a neighbour. They would stay in Galway two nights, returning home on the Monday. She could not have borne it if they had spent the first two nights of their honeymoon in their own house.

Together with the rest of the small wedding party, she saw them off at the station.

'Shall you be all right on your own, Breda?' Molly asked for the twentieth time. 'Are you sure?' It would be the first time ever.

'I shall, so,' Breda assured her.

What she really dreaded, though it could not be said out loud, was their return.

When the train left she hurried back home.

'I had thought you might have a meal with me,' Dermot said. 'I am a fair cook!'

' 'Tis very kind of you,' Breda said, 'but I promised Luke I would open the shop for a couple of hours. It has been closed all day.'

When she finally closed the shop and went through into the house she felt incredibly lonely, and at the same time glad to be on her own at last. It had been a long day.

What would she do with the rest of her life, she asked herself? It stretched out bleakly before her; a life without Rory, a life with her mother married to Luke O'Reilly.

At Mass on Sunday morning she prayed earnestly, though she hardly knew what to ask. Nothing would bring Rory back; he belonged to someone else. Nothing would change things between her mother and Luke. Sometimes, she thought, even God was powerless.

After Mass, she walked back with Dermot Brady and, out of the fullness of her heart, she confided in him once again.

'The only way I see it,' he said gently when he had listened, 'since, as you say, those circumstances cannot change, is that 'tis you who will have to do so!'

It was not at all the reply she had expected, or hoped for.

Back at home, she fried herself a rasher and an egg for her dinner, then took out her bicycle and cycled along the narrow, winding road which ran beside the coast. She had the place almost to herself. Though the visitors had started to return once the Emergency was over, there were not many around today. The summer was almost over and the weather was not reliable.

After a mile or two she left her bicycle in the ditch, scrambled over the low wall and climbed up the hillside. Sitting on an outcrop of rock, she looked out to sea.

'What will I do with myself?' She said the words out loud, as if the birds of the air could answer her.

I cannot stay in Kilbally, she thought. All her life she had wanted nothing more than to stay here. No matter what anyone else did, she had never even contemplated leaving. Now she thought she *must* leave. Kilbally had nothing more to offer her.

She gazed at the sea; all dark blues and greens today, with two currachs, those small boats, riding the waves like corks. The air was clear. She could see, in the distance, the Aran Islands and the hills of Connemara. How could she abandon this? Where would she go that was like it?

At the other side of this same ocean, where the sea ended, there was New York, there were Patrick and Colum.

Should she go to them? Living in Luke's house, earning a small but regular wage, she now had some savings, but she doubted if they were enough to take her to America. She would have to save for at least another year, and she did not fancy waiting so long.

She could go to Dublin. She could get a job there and stay with Moira, who would be pleased to have her, she thought, if only to help with the children. But would she want to be with Moira and Barry? She would have to think about that.

The weather changed suddenly. It came on to rain, a few large drops which quickly turned into a heavy shower. She ran back down the hill, rescued her bicycle and pedalled home.

As she rode, she thought about Dermot Brady's advice. Change yourself, he had said. Could she do that? If she tried really hard, could she learn to like Luke O'Reilly? Could she learn to live with the newly married couple in some sort of harmony? Nothing could ease her pain about Rory, but was it possible she could get on with Luke and her mother?

By the time she reached home, soaking wet, and the rain still pouring down, she had decided. She would do her very best to cope with the new arrangement. What was more, she would start from the very moment Mammy and Luke arrived back tomorrow. If she should fail, 'twould not be for the want of trying.

Yet she did fail. Or was it not, she thought, that her mother failed her? From the moment Luke and Molly arrived back in Kilbally, Breda noticed a change in her mother. Whereas before she had looked up to Luke O'Reilly, respected him, liked him, now she had, over two days, become incredibly close to him; and he to her, also. It was as if she had found something quite undreamt of in her new husband, as indeed she had. Who would have thought that the middle-aged, rather staid, reserved Luke O'Reilly could have turned out to be such a wonderful lover? Molly felt, once again, like a woman fulfilled.

They were open about it too. They would touch each other as they passed; Luke would bend to kiss the back of his wife's neck, Molly would sit beside him on the sofa, holding his hand.

It was nauseating, Breda thought. And most embarrassing of all was the way they went early to bed, as if they couldn't wait another minute. In her own room she stuffed her fingers in her ears, buried her head under the bedclothes, to shut out the sounds which came nightly from the next bedroom.

She *did* try, but she knew it wasn't working. She became silent, she had little to say, and when she did speak it was often to snap. She was aware of it and couldn't help herself.

'Whatever is the matter with you?' Molly asked her after one outburst.

'Sure, 'tis not me! 'Tis you!' Breda said. 'Haven't you changed completely?'

'No, I have not!' Molly defended herself. 'I am just the same with you as I always was.'

'You have changed towards Luke,' Breda said. 'You are quite different there. You shut me out, the two of you. There is no place for me!' She felt the tears pricking at her eyes, and blinked hard to keep them back.

'Oh, Breda love, that is not so!' Molly protested. 'You always have a place with me. You are my daughter!'

'You can't deny you have changed about Luke,' Breda said. 'Why is that?'

A flush crept over Molly from her neck to the roots of her hair.

'It is true,' she admitted. 'I have fallen in love with him! I never thought it would happen, but it has. It will happen to you one day, and then you will understand.'

Breda flounced out of the room. Had her mother totally forgotten about Rory? But that was different, or could have been. She and Rory were young: her mother and Luke were old.

The next day Breda said to Molly: 'I want to talk to you. On your own.'

'Then why not now,' Molly said. 'What is all this about?'

'I can't stay here. I'm leaving Kilbally. I've thought about it, and I have made up my mind, so don't be trying to change it.'

'I will not do that, except to say that I do not want you to go,' Molly said.

But it was not unexpected, she had seen it coming, and in her heart she knew it was for the best.

'Where will you go, love?' she asked.

Breda felt suddenly and terribly alone and unsure. 'I don't know,' she admitted. 'I could go to Moira, I suppose.'

Molly shook her head. *That* would never work. 'Why do you not go to Aunt Josephine in Akersfield? You could go for a visit, see how you liked it.'

Her daughter would be safe with Josephine. She would be well looked after. She knew in her heart that wherever Breda went, it would not be for a visit. She was saying goodbye to her.

'That might be a good idea,' Breda said. 'I will think about it.'

Molly opened her arms wide, and Breda went into them.

'Oh, Mammy!'

It was all she could say.

PART TWO

Thirteen

The train shuddered to a halt outside the station, waiting for the signal which would allow it to proceed. Breda, sitting by the window, facing forward, studied the view.

The journey had been long and depressing, right from the moment she had walked up the rickety gangway onto the boat which, even in the harbour, moved and groaned alarmingly under her feet. The Irish Sea had been horrendous, but mercifully her sickness had stopped the moment when, with legs trembling from exhaustion, she had thankfully stepped onto dry land. All the same, this moment of looking out of the train window was amongst the worst so far. The turbulent sea could be consigned to memory; what she saw now was what she would have to live with for who knew how long.

Streets of mean-looking houses ran down towards the railway line. Factories, warehouses, a church, a school, crowded together, no space anywhere. A forest of house chimneys and, rising high above them, great mill chimneys, all belched smoke against what could be seen of a grey sky.

What held the scene together into one coherent whole, silhouetted, was that everything was black. The stone of the buildings was black; the clouds of smoke were black, fading to grey only as they thinned at the distant edges. The school playground was black asphalt, and on the murky canal, which ran close to the railway line, a barge was heaped with shining black coal. Occasional stunted trees had presumably started out green, but now their leaves were black-edged. The woman sitting opposite to Breda was clad in black from head to foot.

The train gave a couple of jerks, then crept forward into the station.

'You're here, love!' the woman said. 'This is Akersfield!' She sounded pleased, as if she was introducing a well-known beauty spot.

'I'll give you a hand with your luggage,' she offered. 'And when we get out of the station I'll show you your bus stop. Unless of course you're thinking of taking a taxi?'

From the look of the girl's luggage – a large, cardboard suitcase and a couple of straw bags – she didn't look the sort to be taking a taxi, but you could never tell these days, not since the war. Now the most unlikely looking people would jump into a cab, seemingly thinking nothing of it.

'Indeed no,' Breda assured her. 'I'll be taking the bus. My aunt sent me the directions.'

'A pity she'll not be here to meet you, your auntie.'

' 'Twas not possible. I was not knowing the exact time I would arrive. But I'll be all right.'

She took her ticket out of her handbag. A single ticket, she thought. No going back. Then as she gathered together her luggage, the woman picked up the large suitcase.

'My word!' she said. 'What have you got in this, then? Gold bricks?'

'Don't I just wish it was!' Breda replied. She was worried by how little was left of her savings once she had paid for the journey and bought a few essentials: new shoes, underwear, stockings. She wondered just how long her money would last, and how she would set about earning more. She couldn't sponge on Aunt Josephine.

The two of them emerged from the station into a fine, grey drizzle which cast a curtain of mist over everything. Breda, giving a quick look around, assumed that this must

236

be the centre of the town. A long rectangle was dominated at one end by a high, Victorian Gothic building with a clock tower, and at the other end by a large church.

'Yon's the town hall,' the woman said, nodding in the direction of the clock tower. 'We're very proud of our town hall. The church is St Saviour's.'

'They're most impressive,' Breda said. 'Tell me, why are all the buildings black?'

'Black?' The woman sounded puzzled. 'I'd not noticed they were.' She looked around. 'Yes, you're right! They are. I suppose it's the colour of the stone.'

Funny, she thought, she'd been born and bred in Akersfield, never lived anywhere else, and she'd always thought that stone was black, came out of the ground like that. But come to think of it, in the last year they'd put up half a dozen houses on the edge of town, built of local stone they said, and it was almost golden.

The traffic was dense and noisy: cars, buses, lorries, vans, bicycles. Not as many horses as in Ennis, Breda thought, or even as in Dublin.

'That's your bus stop, over the other side,' the woman said. 'Number forty-two. I'll go with you. You take your life in your hands, crossing these roads, and I dare say you're not used to it.'

'I've been to Dublin,' Breda boasted.

She did not mention that she had made only three brief visits in the whole of her life, without ever mastering the traffic there. And this place, where she was attempting to cross the road, was a far cry from Kilbally.

'Thank you,' she said when they were safely across and the woman had deposited her at the bus stop. ' 'Tis exceedingly kind of you. Would you be telling me your name, now?'

'Mrs Mabel Proctor.'

'I am Breda O'Connor.'

'Well then, Miss O'Connor, I hope you settle well in Akersfield. It's not always as gloomy as this. And here's your bus!'

She watched while the bus bore Breda away. Pretty little thing, she thought, and such a soft, Irish voice, a pleasure to listen to. Well, she'd not be without her own kind in Akersfield. There were lots of Irish, though they were mostly townspeople by now, not countrified like this girl. They'd been coming for the last hundred years, seeking a living. They weren't liked by everyone. A bit unruly they were, especially with the drink in them on a Saturday night, and they did have very large families. Still, speak as you find, and personally she'd found nothing wrong with them. Live and let live, she believed.

Almost as soon as the bus had left the town centre it started to climb. Breda was soon to discover that every road out of Akersfield ran uphill, and most of the smaller streets ran uphill again from the roads. The bus chugged along, frequently in low gear, stopping and starting to accommodate passengers, with jerks which threatened to bring on the sickness Breda thought she had left behind on the boat. She took a deep breath and willed herself to overcome it. Only fifteen minutes on the bus, Aunt Josephine had said. Stay on until the terminus. Surely she could manage that? She would look out of the window, think of other things. There was plenty to occupy her mind.

The rain was heavier now, splashing against the windows, mixing with the dust to form grey splodges which interrupted the view; but since the view was mainly of people huddled under umbrellas, picking their way around the puddles on the glistening wet pavement, there wasn't much to spoil. She had not thought to bring an umbrella, but even if she had, she wouldn't have had a spare hand to hold it. Aunt Josephine's house, she knew, was five minutes from the bus stop. Just long enough to get soaked to the skin.

She was used to rain. There was plenty of it in Kilbally, but it was a different kind of rain there: clean, bright, soft. Nor did she usually walk out in it carrying a heavy suitcase, two large straw holdalls and a handbag.

The bus gradually emptied until, looking around, she saw she was the only passenger left on the lower deck. When it stopped for the last time, the conductor called out to her, 'This is as far as we go, love!'

He helped her off with her case, deposited it on the pavement, then climbed back and took out a flask of tea. The rain was heavier than ever. Breda looked at her suitcase in despair. How was she going to manage it? And in which direction was Waterloo Terrace? She would have to ask a passer-by, except that there didn't appear to be any.

Why did I ever leave Kilbally, she asked herself? Why would I not have stuck it out with Luke and Mammy for another year or so? She could have been married in that time to some nice Kilbally fellow, and have a home of her own. Sure, she hadn't thought much of the local talent when she'd been there, she was always looking for something superior, but looking back, there were some decent fellows: Eamonn Finch, or Bernard O'Laughton. If either one of them, she thought, was to come up to her this very minute and propose marriage she'd accept at once, and take the next boat back to Ireland.

Well, 'twas not likely to happen and she had better make a move to get out of the rain, not that she could ever get any wetter than she was now!

Not seeing the man walking towards her, she bent down to pick up the suitcase. When she stood up again he was standing in front of her, in Army uniform, one stripe in his sleeve.

'Could you be telling me where Waterloo Terrace is?' she asked.

'Ah! Then if it's Waterloo Terrace you're wanting, you must be Breda O'Connor! There can't be many Irish girls with this amount of luggage looking for Waterloo Terrace on this very afternoon.'

'I am so, Breda O'Connor,' she said. 'And you are . . . ?'

'I'm your cousin Tony, Tony Maguire. Hand over that case.'

' 'Tis more than pleased I am to do so, *and* to meet you,' Breda said. 'Though I would not have recognized you, since the only photograph I have seen of you, you were a small boy in short pants!' And rather fat, she thought.

'That was years ago,' he said. 'And the only one I have seen of you, you were in your first Communion dress.'

'Which was ten years ago,' Breda said. 'Sure, haven't we both changed? And I did not know you were a soldier.'

There was nothing of the round-faced, dumpy little boy about this man, not that she could see much of him because of the rain. He was tall and, underneath his uniform, broad-shouldered. There was an air of strength about him which was emphasized in the easy way he swung the suitcase, and then took one of the straw bags from her. From underneath his uniform cap his black hair fell wetly over his forehead. His eyes, meeting Breda's, were of so dark a blue as to be almost navy.

'We'd better get a move on,' he said. 'There's no point in getting wetter than ever.'

He set off at a smart pace. It was not easy to keep up with his long strides. Every so often she had to do a skip and a jump so as not to fall behind. Also, the rain was running down her face and, even worse, in cold trickles down the back of her neck and inside her collar. In quantity, it was the equal of any rain she had seen in Kilbally.

'How did you know when to meet me?' she gasped. 'I did not say.'

'I didn't know. It just happened I'm home on leave and Ma said I might as well go down to the bus terminus, just in case. She reckoned you must be due about now.'

'Well, I'm glad you did. I don't know how I'd have managed,' Breda said. She didn't tell him how much she had wanted to turn around, and go right back home.

As they reached the corner of Waterloo Terrace the rain began to ease off, then stopped, and from behind the grey clouds the sun put out a few weak rays. Wasn't that surely a good omen, Breda asked herself?

Waterloo Terrace, when it was built more than a hundred years ago, had been a place of genteel importance, its houses occupied by mill managers, head teachers, even a doctor or two, and a solicitor. Servants in uniform had scrubbed the front steps and polished the brass knockers; nursery maids had emerged, pushing smart perambulators to the nearby park. But these were past glories. Waterloo Terrace had long since come down in the world. Where the steps were scrubbed, and edged with white scouring stone, it was now done by the lady of the house herself (or more likely by the eldest child). The only thing which remained the same was that the houses still sheltered large families, though now it was those who couldn't afford something more up-to-date and convenient.

All the same, to Breda's eyes, used to the single-storey, whitewashed cottages of Kilbally, the whole terrace was splendid, and in a way she was right. The general air of shabbiness – peeling paint, broken paving stones on the front paths – could not hide its excellent proportions, the large sash windows and solid front doors.

'What nice houses!' she said to her cousin.

'Yes,' he said. 'Though they've never looked the same since the Government took away the iron railings and ornamental gates to turn them into planes or tanks. Elegant, those gates were, and whether they were actually used, or left lying around in gigantic scrap heaps, who knows?'

Number 52 was near the far end. It stood out from its neighbours on either side by the whiteness of its net curtains and the neatness of its small front garden, with a square of grass surrounded by narrow borders filled with dahlias and Michaelmas daisies.

As they drew close, the curtains twitched. 'Ma's been looking out for you for hours!' Tony said.

Josephine had seen them. As they walked up the path, the front door opened and she stood there on the top step, a beaming smile on her round face, her arms open wide.

'Welcome, our Breda!' she cried. 'Welcome to Akersfield! And have you noticed, the sun's come out for you?'

She led the way into the hall. The tiled floor, intricately patterned, was chipped and cracked but shining clean. A wide staircase led up on the left, and on the right-hand side doors gave, presumably, on to rooms. As Breda followed her aunt into the first of the rooms, seven heads turned in her direction, seven pairs of eyes fixed themselves on her.

'Here we are, then,' Josephine said. 'Cousin Breda, all the way from Kilbally in Ireland!'

Four of those looking at her were children, quite small, two of them no more than toddlers, sitting on the floor. There were two young women, who gave her a welcoming smile and, in the best chair, close to the fire, sat a very old woman. There was no smile from her. She stared hard at Breda, scrutinizing her from top to toe. Breda had no doubt who she was: Granny Maguire, about whom Josephine had only ever spoken in despair.

'This is Grandma,' Josephine said. 'My mother-in-law, Mrs Maguire.'

'Mrs Maguire *senior*,' the old woman emphasized.

'Pleased to meet you!' Breda was about to add 'I've heard a lot about you', but she realized that none of it had been good, so she smiled and bit back the words.

'You're very young.' It was an accusation.

'I'm seventeen, going on eighteen,' Breda said.

'When I was eighteen I was married with one child, and another one on the way!' the old woman said.

One of the young women rolled her eyes at Breda.

'I'm Kate Cormack,' she said. 'And this is my sister, Maureen Denton, though we're both Maguires . . .'

'And the two boys are mine. John is five, and Larry's just two,' the younger woman said.

'And the two girls are mine,' Kate said. 'Kitty and Peggy. We've each got two more at home . . .'

'And as you can see, I'm expecting again,' Maureen added.

Breda nodded at everyone in turn.

'I hope you'll excuse me if I don't get all the children's names right, just at first.'

'Don't let it worry you, love.' Kate had a strong, comforting voice. It was good to see she was Josephine's daughter. She had the same easy way with her. 'We don't always get them right, do we, Maureen?'

'Mine learn to answer to anything!' Maureen said.

'And that's not the end of it,' Kate said. 'There's Michael's brood, two so far, and if Betty has anything to do with it, which she usually does, more to follow.'

'Why are we sitting in the front room?' Grandma Maguire demanded suddenly. 'We don't usually sit in here. I prefer the kitchen. This place never gets properly warmed up.'

'You know why we're in here. It's because it seemed a nicer way to welcome Breda,' Josephine said patiently. 'But if you want to go back in the kitchen, that's all right.'

'Not on my own! I haven't reached my eighty-fourth year to be shunted off on my own, though I dare say that's what you'd like.'

'Wouldn't we just!' Maureen spoke quietly, through clenched teeth.

'What's that you said? Speak up!' Grandma Maguire ordered.

'I said I'll have to be going,' Maureen said. 'If I'm not there when Peter gets home for his tea, there'll be ructions. Though he'll be a bit late because there's a meeting after school.'

'Peter teaches history at the local secondary school,' Josephine explained.

Then she took another look at Breda.

'Good heavens, child! What am I thinking of? You're wet through! I'll take you upstairs to your room and you can get changed. Mind you strip right down to your skin. I don't want you catching your death of cold the minute you get here. What would Molly say?'

Tony came back into the room.

'I've taken Breda's case up,' he said. He smiled across at the old woman. 'Hello, Grandma! All right, are you?'

Her thin mouth turned up fractionally at the corners, her face creased into the vestige of a smile. It was clear who her favourite was.

'I would be,' she grumbled, 'if they'd let me sit in the kitchen instead of in this place. It's too cold in here! Anyway, give your old Grandma a kiss.'

She tilted her head and he planted a kiss on her cheek.

'Grandma Josie said you *could* go in the kitchen,' Kitty said in her clear, five-year-old voice. 'I heard her say it!'

Mrs Maguire senior turned swiftly on her great-granddaughter.

'You're a rude little girl! You're too cheeky by half! Children should be seen and not heard!'

Kitty turned to her mother. 'Why doesn't she want to hear me? She's always saying "speak up", so I did.'

'Come along, Breda,' Josephine said.

Breda realized, suddenly, how wet she was, and she was beginning to feel cold. She followed her aunt up the stairs. The first flight, as far as the landing, was wide and shallow, with a handsome banister rail and balusters, but from the landing to the attic, which was where her aunt now led her, the stairs were narrow and steep, covered in oilcloth, and with no rail. Except on her visits to Moira, she had never lived in a house with stairs.

Josephine opened a door at the top. 'This is your room. I'm afraid it's a bit small,' she apologized, 'but at least you have it to yourself. To put you on the floor below you'd have had to share with Grandma.'

'It's very nice,' Breda assured her. It was certainly small; a narrow bed, a small chest of drawers, a chair, and a curtained-off corner to serve as a wardrobe, completely filled it. But she would have slept in a broom cupboard rather than share with that awful old woman. She shuddered at the thought.

'There now! You're shivering! And it's all my fault.'

'I'm not really, Auntie Josephine. I'm all right.'

'Call me Auntie Josie! It's friendlier. Now mind you change right down to the skin. There's a clean towel on the bed, give yourself a brisk rub down, then come downstairs and I'll have tea ready. Oh, I do hope you're going to be happy here, love!'

'I will be, Auntie Josie,' Breda promised.

She was not as sure as she sounded. There were so many of them, and all strangers, however well-meaning. Not a single person in Kilbally had been a stranger to her. 'Had been', she thought. No longer 'is', because she had left Kilbally. 'Had been', wasn't it now?

Longing for Kilbally pierced her like a sword: longing for Mammy, for the customers she might at this very moment have been serving in Luke O'Reilly's shop, for any familiar face she had known all her life, even that of Father Curran. The pain of loss ran through her body. What had she done? But it *was* done. She must turn around and face the future, whatever it might turn out to be.

She stripped off her clothes as if she was stripping off her old life, then rubbed herself down with the towel, and put on dry ones. She tried to make something of her hair but the rain had twisted it into tight curls, which she loathed, and all the brushing in the world would not smooth them out. Oh, how she longed for straight hair!

She shaped her mouth with the lipstick Moira had given her in Dublin. 'You'd look a different person with a bit of make-up on,' Moira had said. And indeed wasn't that what she wanted half the time, to be different?

She was ready now, as ready as she ever would be. She battled with her reluctance to go downstairs and join the others. It was all too much, she was tired from the travelling. Why wouldn't she allow herself five minutes more before going down?

There was a window in her room, small and high up, so that the only way to see out of it would be to stand on the chair. She lifted the chair into position and climbed onto it. It was rickety, but no matter. If she fell, 'twas not far to the floor.

The wideness of the view from the window came as a surprise. Waterloo Terrace must be quite high. In the near vicinity was a park, with wide avenues, a bandstand, glimpses of a lake through trees which were beginning to take on their autumn tints. Beyond the park was the main road along which, she reckoned, she had travelled on the bus.

At the far side of the road the land dropped sharply away to the valley, then climbed almost as steeply up the hill on the other side. Buildings crowded against each other: houses, factories, churches, with small patches of green and a few trees interspersed here and there. Over the lowest part of the valley there was the same haze of smoke she had seen in the centre of the town, but at the top of the far hill, stretching the whole width of the horizon, the buildings gave way to a strip of purple and mauve, brilliant in the late sun, which met the sky then merged into it. She was contemplating this, wondering about it, when a knock came at the door.

'It's me, Maureen! Can I come in?'

She was in the room before Breda could answer, or climb down from the chair.

'I have to leave,' Maureen said. 'I'll see you some time tomorrow. I drop in on Mam most days. What are you looking at?'

'The view,' Breda answered. 'It's interesting. There's a band of purple on the horizon just where the sky begins. What would that be?'

'Oh, that's the moors,' Maureen explained. 'I dare say the heather isn't quite over. When it is, the moor will be brown, and then in the spring it'll be fresh green again.

247

Once you get out of the centre you can see the moors from most parts of Akersfield.'

'Shall I be able to go there?' Breda asked.

'Of course! Why not? One of us will take you. Are you a good walker?'

'Not bad,' Breda said.

Perhaps Tony would take her if he was still on leave. On the other hand, he probably had a girlfriend, or even a fiancée, who wouldn't let him out of her sight.

'Why not come downstairs now?' Maureen suggested. 'Tea's nearly ready, and I hope you're hungry because Mam's prepared a feast – as far as rations allow.'

'I am famished,' Breda admitted, getting down from the chair.

'And by the way,' Maureen said, 'don't let Grandma Maguire upset you, though she'll try it on. Best ignore her. She's a cross we all have to bear, poor Mam most of all. I don't know how she stands it. I'd murder the old witch!'

Breda followed Maureen downstairs, this time into the large kitchen. The table was set for tea, and at first glance it was crowded with food, but a second look showed the food to be spread out, more than one plate of the same dish, so as to fill the space and hide the lack of variety, to give the appearance of plenty. Even so, Breda thought, there *was* plenty. There were savoury sandwiches with a filling of sardines which had been mashed up with breadcrumbs to make them go further, fresh baked bread and teacakes, two dishes of home-made plum jam – the plum harvest had been good all over the country – and a cake. And who would know to look at that, Josephine thought, that it contained vinegar in place of an egg?

'Come and sit down, Breda love!' She indicated a place beside her own.

'Are you going to sit to the table, Grandma?' she asked her mother-in-law. 'Or will I be giving you a tray?'

Grandma Maguire cast an eye over the table. 'I'll not bother to sit to, if this is all it is. You can give me a bit on a tray. A bit of everything. I like ham and eggs for my tea, not this airy-fairy stuff.'

'Don't we all,' Josephine said. She would have given a back tooth, if she'd had one left, for a plate of ham, cut thick, fried and served with two eggs. She was sick of eking out the rations and even more sick of hearing her mother-in-law's grumbles about food.

'Two years after the war,' Grandma Maguire said, coming in on cue. 'And there's less food than ever! Why?'

'I've explained,' Josephine said. 'I've explained a dozen times. We have people in other countries to feed now. You wouldn't want them to starve, would you?'

'Serve 'em right,' the old lady spoke savagely through a mouthful of teacake. 'Bloody Germans! They're the enemy, aren't they?'

'The war's over, Grandma!' Kate said. She had stayed on to tea with Kitty and Peggy.

'Take no notice and make a good tea,' she whispered to Breda. 'There's plenty. Mam does wonders.'

'I've brought some butter with me from Kilbally,' Breda said. 'I will get it after tea, unless you want it now. And Luke O'Reilly sent some tea and some biscuits.'

Tony, coming into the room as Breda was speaking, slid into the chair opposite to her. 'Ah! So it was food in your case; I thought it was lead-lined,' he said.

'I enjoy a nice biscuit,' Grandma Maguire said. 'What we get are like sawdust! Or else they're so hard they break my dentures.'

'You shall have one of Breda's with your bed-time drink, old lady,' Tony promised her, winking at Breda.

He really was an attractive man, and not just to look at, not only because he was enhanced by his uniform, Breda thought. When he entered the room he brought an air of liveliness with him.

Brendan Maguire came in from work. He was quite different to look at from his son: short, stocky, his greying hair receding to give him a high forehead. When his wife introduced Breda he gave her a nod, then took his place at the table.

'I hope you don't mind we didn't wait for you, love,' Josephine said anxiously. 'Breda hadn't eaten for hours. In fact I expected you earlier, with it raining.'

She poured him a cup of tea, put in a spoonful of sugar and stirred it for him. 'There you are, love!'

'We've been working inside,' Brendan said. He was a builder who could turn his hand to most jobs with a certain degree of competence, though he was not a master craftsman at any one of them. Indeed, he was completely self-taught.

He tucked into his food with serious dedication, not attempting any conversation. Breda ate heartily. She was so hungry that a plate of dry bread would have been acceptable, and Auntie Josie's offering was a mile above that.

'Have another piece of cake, love,' her aunt urged. 'Don't hang back. Eat your fill! You're a growing girl.'

'She's grown-up,' Kitty said. '*I'm* a growing girl. She's growed!'

'Thank you. I really couldn't eat another thing,' Breda said.

Then suddenly she was uncommonly tired. All she wanted now was to go to bed and sleep until morning.

'Would you like to go for a walk?' Tony offered. 'The rain's stopped.'

He wouldn't mind dropping in at the Cow and Calf, showing off his new cousin. She was a good looker and no mistake!

Wouldn't he just ask me when I'm ready to drop, Breda thought? Could she possibly raise the energy?

'Breda's too tired, on her first evening here,' Josephine interrupted. 'She needs an early night. Leave it until tomorrow!'

'I really would like to go tomorrow,' Breda said. 'I'd look forward to it. But Auntie Josie's right about this evening. Also, I have to write to Mammy. I promised I'd do that as soon as I got here.'

'As you wish!' Tony said. He sounded quite good-natured about it. 'Tomorrow it is!' In any case he had half fixed a date with Joyce Denton. She'd be mad if he didn't show up.

'And don't forget when you do go, you can't take her in the Cow and Calf,' his mother said. 'She's only seventeen!'

In her young days, she thought, respectable young women didn't go into public houses, not even with a man they knew. But her day had been a long time ago. She had come from Ireland before the First World War, the war to end all wars, only it hadn't. King Edward had been on the throne then; there was an air of fun and lightness, but it was still respectable, at least in her class, though they did say there were some fine goings on in the aristocracy. It had all been different then. At this distance, with two wars in between, it seemed another life.

An hour later, though it was still daylight, Breda sat up in bed writing to her mother. She was so tired that she had been tempted to leave it until next morning, but to do it now would bring Mammy closer.

It was difficult to know what to say and what to leave out. Her heart was full of longings, misgivings, regrets, but she would not put any of these on paper, she would mention only the pleasant things. So she wrote of how she liked her room, though it was small; of her welcome from the family and a word or two about each of them; of how Tony had met her at the bus stop and carried her case. She said that Uncle Brendan was rather quiet but perhaps he had had a hard day. She did, however, permit herself one outburst.

'Grandma Maguire is a dragon, an ogre. I am sure she does not like me and I shall keep well out of her way. I miss you, Mammy. Lots of love.'

It was dark by the time she had finished. She folded the letter and put it in the envelope, then turned out the light. In the darkness two tears rolled down her cheeks but before she could cry herself to sleep she *was* asleep.

She slept the sleep of the young and very tired, hearing nothing of her aunt putting a protesting Grandma Maguire to bed, then of her uncle and aunt arguing in the bedroom. Nor did she hear Tony coming into the house much later, noisily singing.

Fourteen

The thought which came immediately to Breda when she wakened in the morning was that she didn't know where she was. This was not her bedroom in Luke's house, nothing like it. Her second thought, when she had remembered, was that the house was totally silent. Where was everyone?

She looked at the small gilt clock on the chest of drawers, Mammy's parting gift. Horrors! Half-past nine! She jumped out of bed, put on her dressing-gown, shuffled into her slippers and hurried downstairs.

Auntie Josie was in the kitchen, peeling potatoes. 'There you are!' she said pleasantly. 'I hope you slept well.'

'Like a log,' Breda said. 'I'm sorry to be so late down. Where is everyone?'

'Brendan goes off early. Tony is still asleep. Goodness knows when he'll surface. As for Grandma, she's still in bed and hopefully asleep. I like to get a few jobs done before she starts nagging.'

'So what can I do?' Breda asked.

'Well, for a start you can make a fresh pot of tea for you and me, since you've brought tea with you from Kilbally. And get yourself some bread and plum jam. You'll find everything you need on the dresser there. I hope bread and jam will suit. If I have eggs, or a rasher or two, I tend to give them to the menfolk.'

'Bread and jam is what I have at home,' Breda said. 'Sometimes cereal because of Luke having the shop.'

'So how is Luke? And how is your Mammy?'

Josephine put the question cautiously. She knew the situation only insofar as Molly had told her in letters, and that didn't include much of Breda's side of it. She didn't even know whether the girl had wanted to come to Akersfield – or even to leave Ireland. Molly had made all the arrangements, and perhaps that had been as well to start with. She didn't want to have to take sides.

'Oh, they're both well, thank you.'

'And are they happy together?'

Breda wished her aunt had not asked that question. 'They seem to be,' she said grudgingly.

'Then that's good, isn't it?'

All right for them, Breda thought.

'Now, can I ask you a question, love?' Without waiting for permission Josephine did so. 'Did you want to come here to Akersfield? In fact, did you want to leave Kilbally? Tell me the truth, then we'll both know where we are. You won't hurt my feelings if you say you didn't want to come, you were just sent.'

Like a parcel, Breda thought. And indeed hadn't there been times when she'd felt like one?

'I wouldn't ever have wanted to leave Kilbally if Mammy hadn't married Luke O'Reilly. How could she do that? He's not a bit like Dada.'

Which was just as well, Josephine reckoned. Married to James O'Connor, Molly would have been a poverty-stricken slave for the rest of her life. Luke O'Reilly – and hadn't she after all known him longer than Molly had? – was a far better prospect as a husband. But young people didn't see it like that. They looked for romance, and never mind reality.

'He's no worse for that,' she said. 'I know you thought a lot of your Dada, and so did your Mammy, but Luke's another person. He's his own man.'

254

'I wasn't needed,' Breda said. 'Mammy had always needed me, then suddenly she didn't.'

I warned Molly, didn't I warn her, Josephine thought! Hadn't she always kept Breda too close to her side, right from being a little one? She wouldn't ever let her go because she was the youngest and the last.

It was a feeling she understood. She didn't want Tony to go. She'd had him when she thought she'd never have another child. In fact, though she hadn't told anyone, she'd been pregnant with him when her two eldest had left for America. He was the apple of her eye and she wanted to keep him, but she knew it was a feeling which had to be watched. Brendan often accused her of spoiling him, of being too lenient with him. He reckoned three years in the Army would do him the world of good.

'Nobody needs me, actually *needs* me,' Breda said. It was a strange feeling.

Josephine smiled at her niece. 'Nay love, you mustn't think like that. You're a pleasure to those who know you. And you're young yet. There's plenty time. But you mustn't feel sorry for yourself. That's no way to be.'

'You're right,' Breda said. 'I'll try not to be.'

'And you haven't answered my question,' Josephine said. 'Did you choose to come to Akersfield?'

'Oh, indeed I did,' Breda assured her. 'If I can't be in Kilbally I'd rather be with you than with anyone else.'

She was not too sure about the rest of the family. Grandma didn't like her, and there was something about Brendan. Did he resent her? Tony was all right, though.

'What did Tony do? I mean, before he went into the Army?' she asked.

'He was a gardener,' Josephine said. 'He worked in Sutherland Park. You can see it from the back of the house. He wanted to be head gardener, and he reckoned he had a good chance in a year or two, but the man who had the job before he was called up has come back, and got his job back. Which is only right of course, though it means our Tony can't ever be head gardener there. So he joined up. But he'll not stick fast. He'll make something of himself, Tony will. He's ambitious.'

'Does he have a girl-friend?'

Josephine looked at her keenly. 'He has a dozen on a string, love!'

She was quite pleased by that. Safety in numbers. 'I don't know that he favours one over the others,' she added.

She drank the last of her tea, then twirled the cup around and peered into its depths.

'Oh, Auntie Josie!' Breda exclaimed. 'I'd forgotten you read the tea leaves. Will you read mine?'

'I shouldn't do it at all,' Josephine admitted. 'A good Catholic doesn't believe in such things, as I'm sure you know. But there you are, I only do it for fun!'

That was not strictly true. Sometimes she saw amazing things in the bottom of teacups, though mostly other people's, seldom her own.

'Oh please!' Breda begged.

'Go on then,' Josephine said. 'Give it here.'

Breda twirled her cup, poured the dregs of tea into the saucer, then handed the cup to her aunt. Josephine studied the tea leaves, turning the cup this way and that, frowning in concentration.

'It's a busy scene,' she said at last. 'A lot of people and you're in the middle of them. I don't recognize anybody – except – wait a minute – there's a woman here. She looks important. I don't think I know her . . . '

'Then it can't be Mammy,' Breda said.

'Don't interrupt, Breda love,' Josephine said. 'I can't concentrate if you interrupt . . . '

'I'm sorry!'

'There! It's gone! The woman's the last to go, though. Can you think who she could be?'

'I can't,' Breda confessed. Truth to tell, she was disappointed. She had hoped her aunt would see a handsome man and lots of riches.

'I'd best get back to peeling the potatoes,' Josephine said. 'You can wash these cups if you've a mind to. So did you enjoy yourself in Dublin?'

After leaving Kilbally, Breda had gone to visit her family in Dublin before taking the boat for England.

'I did so,' she said. 'I was able to see Kathleen, though not Kieran because he was in retreat, and I stayed the night with Moira and Barry.'

'And how are the children?' Josephine asked. 'Still only the two?'

'That's right. And they're lovely. I wonder, how long will it be before I see my godson again?'

'Well now, doesn't that depend on how long you decide to stay here?'

Nothing had *really* been said about that, whether she was there for a short or long visit, or for ever. They would have to see how it worked out. It was not plain sailing.

I could never have stayed with Moira, Breda thought, and certainly not with Barry. Every time he came near her he ran his hands down her back or across her shoulders, or stroked the back of her neck. She would never feel comfortable with Barry in the house.

A loud knock on the ceiling interrupted her thoughts. Josephine raised her eyes to heaven.

'There she goes! That's the gracious way Grandma informs me she's ready for her breakfast. Still, I like it better that way, me taking it up instead of her coming down. It gives me a few more minutes on my own, and I don't get many of those, I can tell you!'

The knocking began again. Josephine went to the bottom of the stairs and shouted, 'I'll be up in two minutes.'

'When she's finished her breakfast I help her to the bathroom,' she told Breda. 'Though it's my opinion she can do it perfectly well herself. But I'm all for a quiet life. You can have plenty of arguments without looking for them. And you'd best go into the bathroom while you've got a chance. Once Grandma takes over she's there for ever and a day. Anyway, when I've seen to her and got her downstairs you and me are going into the town. We need to go to the Food Office to see about a ration book for you.'

'I'd like to do that,' Breda said. She would feel more comfortable not eating other people's rations, though such a thought, living in Luke's household with all the benefits of a shop full of food, had never entered her head before.

'Can you leave Grandma?' she asked.

'Oh yes,' Josephine replied. 'She's not as helpless as she makes out. In any case I have to. I'd go mad if I didn't get out now and again.'

Breda was quite impressed by the centre of Akersfield, though the traffic was horrendous. There were scores of shops which she hoped in due time she would visit. There were two cinemas, outside which she paused, entranced to read the programmes; at one of them Bob Hope, at the other, Bing Crosby and Ingrid Bergman in *Bells of St Mary's*. She had seen neither. You could wait nearly for ever in Kilbally.

'You like the pictures, do you?' Josephine asked.

'Oh yes! Didn't I see every film that I ever could?'

Would Auntie Josie let her come into town to go to a cinema on her own? Or perhaps Tony would take her if he was on leave long enough. 'When does Tony go back?' she asked.

'Tomorrow afternoon,' Josephine said. She would miss him badly. She didn't like to think of him in the heathen South – Sussex it was. And as well as that, young men should be getting on with their careers, not playing at soldiers; which was all they were doing, because the war was over.

'We shall have to get back,' she said when they'd been to the Food Office. 'It's more than my life's worth not to be back to make Grandma's dinner. Thank goodness Brendan doesn't come home in the middle of the day. He's content to take a sandwich and have a proper meal at teatime.'

Back at Waterloo Terrace Grandma Maguire was at the front window, watching out for them. When she saw them nearing the gate she retreated to her armchair.

'You've been a long time gone!' she called out the minute they set foot in the door. 'I don't hold with all this traipsing around town, spending money.'

'As it happens,' Josephine said, 'the only money we've spent, apart from our bus fares, was a little treat for you. I bought you a custard tart from Clark's. And what are you doing sitting in the front room? I thought you didn't like it in here.'

'If other people are fine enough to sit in the front room, then so am I!' Grandma Maguire gave Breda a baleful look.

'Suit yourself,' Josephine said evenly. 'Though you'll have to come into the kitchen when your dinner's ready. I'm not serving meals in here.'

'You could light a bit of a fire in here,' Grandma said. 'You know I feel the cold.'

'No I couldn't,' Josephine replied. 'We don't have the coal.'

She went into the kitchen, followed by Breda.

'She's always on about spending money,' she said. 'I wouldn't care, only she keeps every penny of her pension, not a sausage goes into the housekeeping purse. She reckons Brendan should be pleased to keep her for nothing to repay her for bringing him into the world.'

'What does Uncle Brendan say?' Breda asked.

'Not much. But then he doesn't have to keep house, does he? He has no idea what things cost, and he doesn't want to know neither.'

'I want to talk to you about that,' Breda said. 'I've got a little bit of money I've saved, so I'll be able to give you some, and then I'll find a job and pay you regularly. I don't want to sponge on you.'

'Good heavens!' Josephine exclaimed. 'Who's talking about sponging? Can't I give my niece a few weeks' hospitality without taking money for it? Of course, if you're planning on staying, you'll want to get a job. You'd go mad hanging around here all day long, listening to Grandma. But there's no hurry, love. You can take your time.'

Breda shook her head. 'I intend to look for a job right away. I just want a bit of advice on how to go about it.'

Josephine turned the gas out under the soup she was heating. 'We'll talk about it later,' she said. 'For now you could go and fetch Grandma in while I cut some bread.'

'Does she need help?'

'It depends what mood she's in. Either she'll be a frail old lady who can't walk a step on her own or she'll bark at you for suggesting she's not capable of crossing a room. Either way, you can't win.'

Although her aunt's words were sharp her tone was mild, tolerant, as if she had learned to take it all for granted, to live with it.

With some trepidation Breda returned to the front room. 'Dinner's ready, Grandma! Can I be giving you a hand?'

The old lady gave her an icy stare. 'I'm not *your* grandmother, young lady! I have a name!'

Though who uses my name nowadays, she thought. It was Grandma this and Grandma that, not just from the family, but from their friends, from the neighbours. Everyone. She doubted if there was anyone left who knew her first name was Rose, let alone called her by it. And a pretty name it was. And hadn't she once been as pretty as this girl standing in front of her. Indeed, wasn't there something about the child which brought back long-forgotten memories?

'I'm sorry, Mrs Maguire. Can I help you?'

'I don't need help, thank you all the same,' she said a trifle more graciously. 'Just pass me my stick and leave me to move in my own time. I can't do with being rushed.'

Breda went back into the kitchen. Josephine, ladling the soup, glanced up at her.

'So it's one of those days, is it? Well, you'll not be able to do right for doing wrong.'

'She wasn't too bad,' Breda said. 'She's just not used to me. She'd rather have you.'

Josephine shook her head. It was always the same. They all wanted her full attention on themselves. If it wasn't Grandma, it was Brendan, or it was Maureen or Michael. Some days she felt she was being chopped into little bits. Yet hadn't she brought it on herself? Hadn't she, truth to tell, wanted to be the centre of their worlds? And now, occasionally, it was too much.

Mrs Maguire shuffled into the room and took her place at the table. Josephine placed a plate of soup in front of her. Her mother-in-law poked it about with her spoon. 'What's this, then?'

'Vegetable soup,' Josephine said patiently. What else could it be? But whatever it was, it would be either too hot or too cold. She was certain of that.

Mrs Maguire spooned the soup to her mouth. There was nothing she could do to stop the slight tremor in her hand, which today was more than slight. She didn't quite know whether she could target her mouth, and indeed, when she felt the small dribble of soup down her chin she knew she had failed. It was humiliating. She loathed her infirmities. But at least neither Josephine nor the sharp-eyed girl gave any sign of having noticed.

'It's very hot, this soup,' she said.

'It will soon cool down,' Josephine told her. 'Have you seen anything of Tony?' Surely he couldn't still be in bed.

'He went out. Gone to the Cow and Calf. Hair of the dog, I reckon. I heard him come in last night, singing his head off. *And* I heard you and Brendan having a barney. I don't sleep much,' she added in a pathetic voice. 'The slightest thing disturbs me and then I can't get off again.'

Josephine's colour rose at the mention of her quarrel with Brendan. Breda caught her eye and realized that her aunt was embarrassed because of her.

'I didn't hear a thing!' she said firmly. 'I must have been fast asleep.'

'You can when you're young,' Mrs Maguire said. 'But just you wait!'

You had it all your way when you were young. These days the world revolved around the young, what they wanted, what they thought about everything. When you were old, nobody wanted your opinions. They wanted you to sit in a corner, keep quiet and be docile. Well that wasn't her. If she wanted to stand up and sing 'Rose of Tralee' she'd do it. Let them try to stop her!

How would she have managed if she hadn't fought for her place? Her husband had been killed in the Boer War, leaving her with Brendan, their only child. It hadn't been easy; nothing was in Ireland if you were poor, but she'd come through, brought up her son, though only to have him cross the water to England.

'Eat up your soup, Grandma,' Josephine said.

Mrs Maguire put down her spoon. She had had enough. 'I never wanted to leave Ireland,' she said.

Josephine looked at her keenly. Where had she been? She was always taking journeys in her mind.

'I know you didn't, Grandma.' Her voice was gentle. 'But Brendan thought you'd be better here, where he could keep an eye on you.'

'I left Ireland,' Mrs Maguire said. 'But Ireland never left me.'

'Isn't it just the same with me?' Josephine said.

Tony came in, lightening the atmosphere like a rushing wind. He put his hands on his grandmother's shoulders and gave her a squeeze.

'So where were you two this morning?' he asked his mother.

'We went into town, to the Food Office. There's soup in the pan. Help yourself.'

He brought his dish to the table and sat down. 'And what did you think of Akersfield?' he asked Breda.

'Sure, it was nice,' she said. 'Lots of shops, and *two* cinemas!'

'You like going to the pictures, do you? In that case we'll go this evening, as it's my last and Ma won't let me take you to the pub. Which one do you want to see?'

'Wouldn't that be wonderful!' Breda said. She felt herself suffused with pleasure. ' 'Twould be a treat to see either.'

'You have to choose,' Tony said.

'Then Bing Crosby and Ingrid Bergman,' she said.

Why would he be making such a fuss of her, Grandma Maguire wondered? But it meant nothing, it was his way. He got on with everyone. And wasn't he the only person who didn't treat her as if she was an old lady? It was as if he recognized what she already knew, that inside her old body, which was a burden to her, and constantly let her down, there lurked a younger spirit. People thought you aged inside, but you didn't, well not much. She remembered perfectly well what it was like to be young. She'd been fond of the dancing, and if only her body would allow her she'd still get up and do it with as much zest as the best of them.

In the afternoon, both Maureen and Kate came with the youngest children. Breda liked both sisters, but Kate especially. Then at half-past five Brendan came in from work, unsmiling, not in the best of tempers. 'So you've been out looking for a job, then?' he asked Breda.

She flinched at the sharpness of his voice. 'Not yet, Uncle Brendan. But I mean to do so tomorrow. I shall go to the Labour Exchange.'

'You'd be better looking in the local paper,' Josephine said. 'The *Akersfield Record* or the *Leasfield Courier*. Though I'm sure I don't know what the rush is.'

She gave her husband a warning glance. She guessed he had been bricklaying today and, oddly, this always made him bad-tempered. She couldn't understand it, it looked simple enough. And hadn't Winston Churchill laid bricks, built a whole brick wall, as a relaxation from running the war? Tony reckoned it was because his father didn't have a straight eye, but Brendan would have none of that.

'I do *want* to get a job, Uncle Brendan; and as soon as possible,' Breda said.

'I'm glad to hear it,' Brendan said. 'And your aunt's quite right. The newspaper's the best. If you nip out now they'll happen have one left at the corner shop. No time like the present!'

Breda stood up. 'I'll go at once!'

'I'll go with you, show you where it is,' Kate offered.

'There's something I'd like to ask you, Kate,' Breda said as they walked to the shop.

Kate looked at her keenly. She could guess what it was, which was why she had offered to accompany her.

'Why does Uncle Brendan dislike me?' Breda asked. 'Have I done something wrong? I would ask Auntie Josie, only she looks uncomfortable when he snaps at me.'

'Bless you, love,' Kate said. 'You've done nothing wrong at all. In a way, it's not really you he's getting at, it's Mam. You see, he dotes on her. I think all he's ever wanted is Mam. But nine months after they were married, I arrived – and then all the rest. And there was his mother. He's a dutiful son and, in fact, he's always been a good father, but he's never had Mam to himself. I think that's why he was pleased when Tony joined the Army. He was the last one living at home.'

'And now I've landed on him,' Breda said. 'Why did Auntie Josie let me?'

'Because she has a heart as big as a house. She has enough love for the whole world,' Kate said. 'I'm sure it never occurred to her not to have you – and please don't think you're not welcome, because you are.'

'Except to Uncle Brendan.'

'Don't worry. He'll come round. And if you know what it's about, you'll understand him better. He's a good man, really. He'd help anyone who needed it.'

The *Record* had sold out but there was a copy of the *Leasfield Courier* left. Outside the shop again, Breda opened it, searching for Situations Vacant.

'Unless there's one for a shop assistant, I don't know what I'll do,' she said to Kate. 'It's the only job I know anything about.'

Kate looked over her shoulder, scanning the column.

'How about that?' she said. 'Third sales required. Fabrics department. Apply in person. Opal's, Leasfield.'

'Where's Leasfield? What's Opal's?' Breda asked. 'But at least I know a bit about fabrics, though not about selling them.'

They folded the paper and started to walk back.

'Leasfield is about three miles away,' Kate said. 'There's a bus every twenty minutes from the bottom of the road. It's as convenient as Akersfield, really, though not as big.'

'Opal's is the best store in these parts,' Josephine said when Breda showed her the advertisement. 'Some say the best in the West Riding, and I'd not be the one to contradict that. And to think she started with a little house shop, selling sweets and reels of cotton! And she's younger than me. I reckon she can't be fifty yet. You'd be lucky if you got a job with Opal's.'

'Then I shall go first thing in the morning,' Breda said.

'In the meantime,' Tony broke in, 'we're going to the pictures, you and me. We'd best get off if we don't want to miss the beginning.'

Quite apart from the fact that it took her mind off the next day's search for a job, the thought of which terrified her, the evening was wonderful from start to finish. Before they went into the cinema Tony bought her a box of chocolates, hard centres which were her favourites, at the shop next door. Then, inside the cinema, where a wide, luxuriously carpeted staircase led up to the balcony, they sat in the best seats: tip-up seats, covered in crimson plush, with broad arms – except that they sat in a double seat with no arm in the middle.

The minute they were settled Tony took her hand in his, and by the time they had sat through the newsreel and the coming attractions for next week his arm was around her, holding her close. Of course it was not the first time she had sat in the picture with a boy, and him with his arms around her and his hands straying where they shouldn't, but never in a posh place like this and with a man as handsome as Tony.

He was, in fact, better looking than Bing Crosby, now gliding across the screen in his clerical garb, though the latter was nicer than any Catholic priest *she* had ever known, and a thousand miles from Father Curran. Tony, she thought dreamily, was more like Gregory Peck. 'Twas a pity, in a way, that he was her cousin, yet if he hadn't been, would she ever have met him? She leaned happily against his shoulder and his arm tightened around her.

When it was over they took the bus home. They walked up Waterloo Terrace hand in hand, and when they reached the gate of number 52 he took her in his arms, and kissed her on the lips. It was a long, lingering kiss. It took the breath from her body and she thought she must swoon with ecstasy. When his lips left hers she recovered her breath, and held up her face again to his.

He smiled, took her firmly by the shoulders, turned her around so that she was facing the house door.

'Off you go!' he said. 'Tell Ma I'll not be late, but no need for anyone to wait up for me. I'm going off to the Cow and Calf for a pint. Should just get one in before closing time.'

He patted her on the bottom, and was gone.

She walked up the short path to the door, torn by conflicting emotions: deep pleasure at the memory of the evening, and his kiss; more than a slight disappointment at his abrupt departure. Perhaps, she thought, he had to tear himself away or he would have gone too far!

Auntie Josephine had heard her footsteps on the path and was at the door before Breda had time to ring the bell. She showed no surprise when Breda explained Tony's absence. 'Did you have a nice time, then?' she asked.

'Wonderful!'

'I've saved you a bit of supper,' Josephine said.

'I'm not the least bit hungry,' Breda sighed. 'I think I might go straight to bed. Get a good night's sleep before the morning.'

Not that she thought she would sleep a wink.

Opal's store was easy to find. The bus stopped right outside the door and the conductor called out the name. Most of the women on the bus got off at the same stop.

It was an imposing building. As good, she thought, feeling disloyal, as any store she had seen in Dublin. A commissionaire in a splendid uniform, with sergeant's stripes on his arms and gold epaulettes on his shoulders, stood at the entrance. She went up to him.

'I've come about a job,' she said.

'Then it's the staff entrance you want, Miss,' he said. 'Round the corner.'

The staff entrance was much less grand than the customer entrance; dark and chilly, the walls covered by slots with cards in them, everything dominated by a large clock. She was directed to climb a flight of stone stairs to the enquiries desk, behind which a bored-looking woman eventually broke off a conversation with her colleague and turned to Breda.

'Yes?'

'I've come about the vacancy,' Breda said.

'And what vacancy would that be?'

What an idiot I am, Breda thought! As if it would be the only one. 'In the Fabrics department.' She fished in her handbag and brought out the advertisement she had cut out from yesterday's newspaper. 'Third sales,' she added. She would have liked to ask the woman what that meant, but she looked far too fierce.

'Take a seat,' the woman said. 'I'll find out if someone can see you.' She finished her conversation with her colleague, then picked up the telephone.

'Miss Bainbridge will see you now,' she said to Breda. 'Since you're going in that direction, will you show her where it is?' she asked her colleague.

Breda followed the woman along a maze of narrow corridors. She wanted to ask her who Miss Bainbridge was, if she was frightening, what it was like working at Opal's. There were a dozen questions she'd have liked to have put but the woman was too intimidating. Also she walked too fast, keeping well ahead of Breda.

Miss Bainbridge was not at all frightening. Breda gave silent thanks at the sight of her: plump, grey haired, rosy cheeked, wearing a pink cardigan.

'Tell me something about yourself,' she invited.

What is there to tell, Breda asked herself? But whatever there was, Miss Bainbridge had it all out of her in no time at all without ever seeming to probe.

'And do you think you'll be staying in Akersfield, Miss O'Connor?' she asked. 'It won't be just a few weeks, then on your way?'

'Oh no! 'Twill be permanent,' Breda assured her.

'And is there anything you'd like to ask me?' Miss Bainbridge said.

'I think you've explained everything,' Breda said. 'Except . . . '

'Yes?'

'I was wondering. What *is* a third sales?'

Obviously not something you had in your stepfather's shop, Miss Bainbridge thought!

'Well, there's a chain of command in each department. The Buyer is the head. The first sales comes next, then the second, then the third. Last of all the junior. We usually promote the junior but the girl on Fabrics isn't quite ready for it. Each saleswoman has her duties, part of her training. The Buyer says what they are. And now, if you're interested in the job I'd like the Buyer, Mr Stokesly, to see you. Miss Opal insists that buyers meet prospective staff before they're engaged.'

'Does that mean I've got the job?' Breda asked. She could hardly believe it.

Miss Bainbridge smiled. 'Not exactly. I have more interviews to do. But you'll have an equal chance with the others. Now I'll go and find Mr Stokesly and bring him back with me. He'll want to ask you a few questions. In the meantime, there's a house magazine on the table there. It will tell you something about Opal's.'

'You'll like this one,' Miss Bainbridge said to John Stokesly a few minutes later.

'Is she pretty?' he asked.

'She's pretty. She's also bright and pleasant. She doesn't have much experience. Anyway, come and see for yourself!'

Breda's knees knocked when Mr Stokesly came back into the office with Miss Bainbridge. It was not until long afterwards that she learned that he warmed to her from the first; that after she'd left he said to Miss Bainbridge: 'She's the one! There's something about her. She'll be an asset to my department!'

Now he asked her a few questions, to which she hoped she gave the right answers, then he shook her by the hand and left.

'Is your aunt on the telephone?' Miss Bainbridge asked.

'She is, so,' Breda said. 'Will I write down her number for you?'

'Do that, please. We'll get in touch with you.'

Breda did not have long to wait. At nine-thirty next morning, her aunt answered the telephone.

'It's for you, Breda.'

Breda listened, said 'Yes' several times, then put down the receiver and screamed.

'I did it! I did it! I've got the job!'

Her one regret was that she couldn't tell Tony, since he had already left. But never mind, she would write to him. And she would be here when he came home on his next leave.

Fifteen

'It's as well your uncle leaves early,' Josephine said as Breda came into the kitchen. 'Otherwise there'd be a fight for the bathroom every day. I don't know how either of you manages to spend so much time in there!'

She said it without the least rancour. It was impossible to take offence at Auntie Josie, Breda thought. She was a person who constantly oiled the wheels for the smooth running of the lives of everyone else in the household. It would still be easy, though, to get on the wrong side of Uncle Brendan, even though she now understood more about him. She was glad that their timings meant that she seldom saw him before he left the house in the morning. Her best plan, she thought, was to keep out of his way as much as she could. Usually she waited until she heard the door slam, as she had done this morning, before going down to her breakfast.

'I have to look my best,' Breda said. 'Miss Opal insists on everyone being properly turned out.'

She had not actually heard Miss Opal say this, but the great lady was constantly quoted and her edicts followed. On Breda's first day in the store, before she was even allowed to start work, she had been treated to a string of them. All new staff were required to attend a short induction course taken, to Breda's relief, by Miss Bainbridge. She liked Miss Bainbridge, felt comfortable in her presence. But even coming from Miss Bainbridge, the list of rules, of 'dos' and 'do nots', sounded alarming.

It was very different from Luke O'Reilly's shop. She wondered if she would ever remember them all and what would happen to her if she didn't.

'First of all,' Miss Bainbridge said. 'Staff must clock in no later than eight-thirty and be on the floor by twenty to nine, ready for opening at nine o'clock. You'll find that there's quite a lot to do on the department before you're ready for the first customer. And ready you must be.'

Which was why, now, Breda ate a piece of bread and jam and swallowed a cup of tea while standing. The bus left the bottom of the road at 8.15 sharp and deposited her at Opal's just in time to punch her clocking-in card before 8.30.

'If you would get up just ten minutes earlier,' Josephine said, not for the first time, 'you would be able to sit down to a bit more breakfast.

'So what does Miss Opal mean by being well turned out?' she added.

On that first day, Miss Bainbridge had told them exactly what it meant. Smart, but never fancy, black dress, long sleeved, white collar permissible, no jewellery. Hair tidy, shoes polished, finger nails clean. Make-up allowed, but it must be inconspicuous. 'And make sure your shoes are comfortable as well as polished,' she'd advised. 'You'll be on your feet most of the day.'

'Oh, all the usual,' Breda told her aunt. 'Some of the girls say it's worse than when they were in the forces!'

The only thing which had put her out, but not for long, so grateful was she to have been given the job, was that she did not have a black dress. She had had to buy material, giving up coupons for it, and spend the entire weekend before her first Monday making the dress. It was a success though. It fitted well, looked stylish yet simple, and was well sewn.

273

'I didn't know you were so good with a needle,' her aunt said.

'But it's not all bad,' Miss Bainbridge had said. 'All members of staff are allowed a penny in the shilling discount on all purchases in the store except food, and you may have twenty minutes' shopping every morning, as long as two people are left on the department – never leave only one person – and you're back at your post by ten o'clock.'

There were lots more instructions – it took two hours to go through them before they were each ready to go to their department.

Fabrics was on the ground floor, down a few steps from the store's side entrance from which, when the wind was in the east, which it usually was, a sharp draught blew around one's feet. We should have been advised to wear snow boots, Breda thought before the first day was over.

Mr Stokesly had seemed quite pleased to see her. 'Welcome to Fabrics!' he said, all smiles. 'And now let me introduce you to the rest of the staff.'

She looks so bright, he thought, from the top of her curly red head to the toes of her gleaming shoes. But the brightest of all was her face, with its country complexion, cheeks like polished apples, her blue-green eyes alight with intelligence.

'This is Miss Craven,' he said. 'Our invaluable First Sales. She's been at Opal's longer than I have. She came when the store was first opened. Isn't that so, Miss Craven?'

'Indeed it is, Mr Stokesly!' She spoke in a slow voice with a refined Edinburgh accent, which surprised Breda though she didn't know why, and gave a condescending nod in Breda's direction.

'And Miss Wilmot is our Second Sales. Miss Wilmot is engaged to be married to some lucky man.'

274

'Jewellery is not encouraged,' Miss Bainbridge had said, 'but an engagement ring is different.' And sure enough a small diamond flanked by two smaller sapphires gleamed from the third finger of Miss Wilmot's left hand.

'And last but not least, Miss Betty Hartley, our Junior,' Mr Stokesly said.

Betty Hartley was pale and pinched and, Breda thought later, must have been sickening for something at the very moment of introduction, since that very same day, and before Breda had had a chance to get to know her, she went down with a bad case of tonsilitis, thus leaving the Junior duties to Breda, to be added to her own.

'Which goes to show that Miss Opal is right!' Miss Craven said as Betty Hartley thankfully obeyed Mr Stokesly's order to get off home and go to bed.

'What about?' Breda enquired.

'Miss Opal always says that anyone who has a cold or flu, or anything infectious, should stay at home at once. No point in spreading it around the whole store. Not,' she added in a warning voice, 'that one should stay at home for a little-finger ache. I'm sure you agree with that, Miss O'Connor?'

'Oh yes! Yes of course!'

Would she always be addressed as Miss O'Connor? It sounded strange in her ears. Until she came here it had never happened to her.

I don't suppose she'll stay, Hetty Craven thought. She's young. She's quite attractive in a countrified sort of way. She'll either get married or move on to something new, neither of which things will ever happen to me. She had no illusions left about that. She was forty-eight and plain. Her Scottish refinement was all that set her slightly apart from some other members of staff. She cherished it. And now – nature was so unkind – she was in the middle of the change of life and subject to frequent and humiliating hot flushes which she could hide from no-one. She hated bodily manifestations. Until this thing had come upon her she was pleased to say she had never perspired.

'We have an hour for lunch,' she informed Breda. 'And we take it in turns. You and I will go first, then Miss Wilmot and the Junior, when we have one, second. Mr Stokesly, being the Buyer, goes when it suits him, but usually late.'

'Do we all use the same canteen?' Breda asked.

'We do. Miss Opal won't allow separate canteens for different grades of staff.' Her tone of voice made it clear that she did not agree with her employer.

'But in fact,' she added, 'you'll find that most people sit with their equals, buyers with buyers, first sales with first sales, and so on.' And all getting as close as possible to their immediate superiors, she could have added.

I shan't know who to sit with, Breda thought. How could you spot a third sales on sight? On the other hand, she didn't particularly want to spend her dinner time with Miss Craven even if the privilege was allowed her.

That first day had seemed twice as long as any day since, perhaps because it was a Monday and there weren't many customers, perhaps because she had known so little of the department that she couldn't find odd jobs to fill her time. She had just stood and stood, and stood again on the crowded bus back to Waterloo Terrace.

She walked into the kitchen and sank into the first chair to hand.

'I am *knackered*!' she said.

'Then what you'd be like if you'd done a real day's work, I can't imagine,' Brendan said. 'If you'd been shovelling sand, carrying bricks.'

'I *have* worked in a shop before,' Breda said. 'This just seemed harder.'

'You've been spoilt,' he said. 'I dare say Luke O'Reilly's was easy stuff.'

'Well, it was easier,' she admitted.

She thought with longing of the days she had made the deliveries for Luke, scorching down the hill on her bicycle, the wind blowing through her hair. 'Though I dare say I shall get used to this quite soon,' she said.

And she had. It was three weeks now since that first day. She had learned a lot about many things and, in addition, her body had adapted to the physical regime. She was still tired at the end of the day's work, but not so tired that after she had had her tea and a wash she couldn't have gone out and enjoyed herself.

She had not had the chance to do that. There was no-one to go with. This evening Brendan sat in his chair, reading the newspaper as he did most evenings.

Josephine was knitting. 'This is for Maureen's next,' she said, holding up a small white garment. 'I like knitting baby clothes. You soon get through them.'

'I need a new cardigan,' Grandma Maguire said. 'I'm sick of this one. I'd like a nice bright colour; red, or green. I suppose you'll tell me I don't have the coupons!'

'I've told you, you can use mine,' Brendan said.

'Why aren't you out enjoying yourself?' Grandma Maguire demanded of Breda. 'When I was your age, they couldn't keep me in! Here there and everywhere!'

'I'd like to,' Breda said. 'So far I don't know anyone to go with.'

She turned to her aunt. 'Would it be all right if I went to the pictures on my own, one evening?' she asked. 'To Akersfield. It's Vivien Leigh in *Caesar and Cleopatra*. Or would you like to come with me?'

Josephine looked uneasily from Brendan to Grandma Maguire and back again.

'Well, love, I'm not sure about that. I'm not one for the pictures, really – though me and Kate did go to see *Gone With The Wind*. It was very long. We took some sandwiches and a flask of tea.'

It was easy to read between the lines. Her glances gave it away. She just couldn't escape her mother-in-law and Brendan wasn't going to help her to do so. Breda wondered how in the world she had managed to visit Kilbally. Probably only because it was for a wedding or a funeral. Even Brendan couldn't refuse that.

'I'll tell you what,' Josephine said. 'I dare say Maureen would like to go, if she can get someone to sit with the children. She doesn't get out much. It would do her good as well as you. Shall I ask her when she calls in in the morning?'

'Yes please,' Breda said.

'I'm going over to the Cow and Calf for an hour,' Brendan said.

'I think I'll go to bed,' Breda said. 'Take my book, have an early night!'

She didn't in the least want an early night. She would like to stay out until the small hours, dancing her feet off. Instead, she had joined the local library and now got through three books a week.

'Reading in bed again?' Brendan said, getting to his feet. 'I don't suppose you had these luxuries in Kilbally. I don't suppose you realize electricity costs money.'

'I'm willing to pay extra,' Breda offered. 'Or to read by candlelight.' Hadn't she done that most of her life?

'You'll do no such thing!' Josephine said indignantly. 'You'll do neither of those things. I'm sure it hardly makes a penn'orth of difference, and I should know. I pay the bill!'

'With my money,' Brendan muttered.

'And wouldn't I like to go out to work and earn my own money?' she retorted. 'And with the children off my hands what stops me? Ask yourself that, will you?'

If only Tony was here, Breda thought. If only he'd write to me! She had sent him three letters, with never a word in return. Had he entirely forgotten her?

'Have you heard from Tony?' she asked her aunt.

'He doesn't write to me,' Josephine said. 'Not unless he wants something. But that's men all over, isn't it?'

'I don't know, Auntie.'

And at this rate, she didn't see much hope of finding out. She decided that in any case she was not a good picker of men. Look at Rory. The thought of him brought a flush of shame to her face. Well, she'd not make the same mistake twice. She would give Tony one more chance. If he didn't reply to the letter she intended posting tomorrow then she would write him off. In fact, she might write off all men. The only one who'd been any good was Dada.

The proposed outing with Maureen was not to be. When Breda arrived home next day her aunt said: 'Maureen would have, but little John has gone down with chicken-pox. That's kids for you. Now I expect they'll get it in turn.'

'I'm sorry,' Breda said. 'And it doesn't matter about the pictures. I'll go down to the library and get some more books.'

She wished she had just one friend, someone with whom she could go places on her half day, or even for a walk with in the evening. She had never found it difficult to make friends in Kilbally and she had thought it would be easy in her new job, but in fact she seldom talked to anyone.

Miss Craven was too old. Miss Wilmot was only twenty, but every minute of her spare time seemed to be spent with her fiancé, just as all her talk was of him and of the wedding they planned, though it was at least a year away. Miss Wilmot's passion was collecting items for her bottom drawer. Her shopping spree around the store each morning, which she never failed to take, always ended in her bringing back something to add to the collection – a wooden spoon, a tea towel, a lemon squeezer. The drawer must be full to overflowing, Breda thought, but with what dull things!

'I wonder, what would *I* choose?' she said to Doreen Wilmot. 'I mean if I was filling my bottom drawer.' She thought for a minute. 'Well, for a start, I would have a beautiful cut-glass crystal vase, as big as an umbrella stand. Then, wouldn't I have a lamp in white alabaster with a red silk shade? And then peach-coloured satin sheets. That's what I'd choose to begin with.'

'You're not being practical,' Doreen Wilmot protested. 'You have to be practical.'

'I do not,' Breda contradicted. 'The way I'm going, will I ever need even a wooden spoon or a potato peeler?'

Miss Craven glided down from the other end of the counter as if on wheels. 'Move apart,' she said. 'Ye know pairfectly well that sales assistants must never stand together, gossiping. Ye have to look busy, but ready to sairve at once if required. After me of course. What would Miss Opal say if she were to walk by and see you idly chatting?'

She glided back to her end of the counter, the end farthest away from the draught.

Miss Opal walked by at least once a day. She walked around the whole store, usually accompanied by Mr Soames, the General Manager, but so far Breda had not seen her stop to speak to anyone on Fabrics.

'You can't go by that,' Miss Craven said. 'She'll appear to see nothing, and half an hour later there'll be a note down from the office to say that the counter is untidy, or the Second Sales has a button undone.' She gave Miss Wilmot a nasty look. 'And who takes the blame? I do!'

So Breda more or less stood to attention and held her breath when she saw Miss Opal in the offing.

And there she was now, advancing towards them. She was a small lady, slim, upright, her dark hair greying at the sides. She was probably about Miss Craven's age, Breda reckoned, but there all resemblance ended. She walked past Doreen Wilmot and Breda without a glance, moving towards where Miss Craven stood.

Miss Craven was in the middle of a particularly severe hot flush. She felt the sweat running down her face and trickling down her back and she was sure she looked like a boiled beetroot. There was nothing she could do. Now was not the time to start dabbing at herself with a handkerchief.

Miss Opal slowed down, caught Miss Craven's eye, hesitated, then quickened her pace again and walked on. Fifteen minutes later a note was delivered to Miss Craven. 'Will you please come and see me in my office as soon as it is convenient?'

'Miss Opal wants to see me,' she said, turning to Doreen Wilmot. 'I'll not be long.'

'Whatever can *that* be about?' Breda wondered out loud.

'Well, if it's anything we've done, she'll tell us,' Miss Wilmot said. 'You can be sure of that!'

Miss Craven mopped her face, then knocked on Miss Opal's door.

'Come in,' Miss Opal called. 'Please sit down, Miss Craven. When does Mr Stokesly return from Manchester?' He was away buying.

'Tomorrow morning, Miss Opal.'

Opal looked at her thoughtfully. She had known her as long as anyone in the store. She was a touchy woman, you had to be careful how you put things, but Opal often felt sorry for her.

'Excuse me, Miss Craven,' she said. 'But I couldn't help noticing when I walked past Fabrics a few minutes ago that you didn't look well.'

'It's nothing, Miss Opal, nothing at all!' Miss Craven insisted. And she must keep calm for fear it happened again, right now. She never knew the time nor the place.

'I understand well enough what it is,' Miss Opal said. 'You and I are about the same age, only I seem to have been let off more lightly than you. Have you seen your doctor?'

'I don't quite like . . . well, it's rather embarrassing . . . '

It was exactly as Opal had thought. Silly woman! 'Then you'll be glad at my bit of news,' she said. 'I've reappointed a store doctor. A woman. About our age. She'll spend one day a fortnight in the store, more if we need her, and anyone who wishes to consult her can do so. I feel sure she'll be able to help you.'

'Thank you, Miss Opal. You're very kind.'

'Shall I have my secretary make an appointment for you?'

'Thank you, yes.' As long as she didn't have to tell Mr Stokesly what it was about.

'How is your father these days?' Miss Opal asked.

'Quite frail. He's not able to do much.'

'It must be difficult for you,' Miss Opal sympathized. She knew that for years Miss Craven had been holding down a full-time job while caring for a semi-invalid father.

'And how is the new girl in the department?' she enquired. 'What pretty red hair she has!'

'She's quite satisfactory,' Miss Craven admitted. 'Raw, of course. And since the Junior has tonsilitis she is doing her own job and the Junior's for the moment.'

'That won't do her any harm,' Miss Opal said. 'She'll be all the better for being kept busy.'

Almost more than anything in those first few weeks, Breda hated going into the canteen for her dinner. It was true there was no compulsion to do so: staff were allowed to leave the store as long as they clocked out and in again, but they were also expected to have a meal, and since the canteen food was infinitely cheaper than anything which could be obtained outside, most people availed themselves of it. Breda felt compelled to do so. It saved a meal at Auntie Josie's; not only the cost of it, but the rations.

She would have been happy enough if she had had someone to go with, or even if she had known exactly where she might sit without breaking the unwritten rules about which Miss Craven had warned her. It was easy enough to spot the buyers. They were all older, and had a collective air of importance, but the rest of the staff seemed much of a muchness. The one thing they seemed to have in common was that they knew each other.

What Breda did, whenever she could, and if there was one, was to sit at an empty table. That way, if a mistake was to be made someone else would make it. But too often she remained the only person sitting there. No-one joined her. She pretended to be immersed in her book, while at the same time noticing the crowded tables, people chattering to each other, laughing, sometimes she thought, glancing in her direction.

The surprise came one dinner time when she was, as usual, alone at the table.

'Excuse me,' a man's voice said. 'Are these seats taken? May I join you?'

For a start, the voice was unexpected: educated, musical, and definitely not north-country. She thought afterwards that she had fallen for his voice before she even looked up and saw his person. If he had been small and insignificant it wouldn't have mattered. His voice would have made up for it.

In fact, his appearance needed no compensation. He was tall – she had to tip her head back in order to meet his eyes – deep blue, smiling. His fair hair flopped over his forehead. He wore a dark suit, which was par for the course, a snow white shirt, a discreetly striped tie.

All this she took in at a glance, yet none of it registered. All she knew, and she knew for certain, was that this was the most important moment of her life so far.

'May I sit here?' he repeated.

'Oh, please do! Certainly!'

He had noticed her as soon as he had walked into the room, perhaps because of her glorious hair, but not entirely. He had walked straight across to her table, not for a moment considering sitting anywhere else.

Seen close to, she was even more attractive than from a distance. It was not just that she was good to look at – which she was – but there was an air of vitality, a vibrancy about her which transcended her beauty. He asked himself how a woman, sitting alone and still at a table, eating a dish of pudding, reading a book, could exude such vibrancy. Whatever the answer was, she certainly did.

Breda didn't remember having seen him before. She was conscious that she was staring at him, and at once turned her attention to her pudding and her book. She always read at the table to show the world that she didn't mind being alone. She pushed the pudding around her plate. She had lost interest in it.

'Are you not enjoying your dessert?'

She pushed it away from her. ' 'Tis all right, I suppose, but I was never one for bread-and-butter pudding, still less for semolina, which was the only other choice. I should have made do with a cup of tea.'

She had the most delightful Irish voice, he thought. He wanted to hear more of it.

What a drab conversation, Breda thought, for a girl who feels as though she's riding through the heavens on a star! On the other hand, it was the first conversation she'd ever had in the canteen, and for that she was grateful.

It seemed as though that might be the extent of it. He fell to his shepherd's pie with gusto. Breda renewed her attack on her pudding. It would be silly to leave the table just yet.

He stood up.

'Don't go away,' he said. 'Promise!'

'I promise.'

Five minutes later he returned, carrying two cups of tea.

'I thought I'd give the pudding a miss,' he said. 'I took the liberty of bringing you a cup of tea as well.'

'Thank you very much,' Breda said. 'I shall have to drink it quickly because I'm almost due back on the department.'

'Please tell me which department that is,' the man said. 'This is my first day here. I could be searching the whole store for you! And what's your name?'

'Breda O'Connor. I'm on Fabrics. So why would you be searching for me?'

'Because I don't want to lose you,' he said. 'And my name's Graham Prince.'

The perfect name, Breda thought. Wasn't he exactly like Lieutenant Philip Mountbatten, who was due to marry Princess Elizabeth next month, and would perhaps be a prince one day? And was there a girl in the whole country who wasn't in love with Philip?

'And where are *you* to be found?' she asked. She had to know, for if he didn't seek her out she would surely seek him.

'Almost everywhere,' he said. 'I could be in Packing and Despatch, or Menswear, or in the office or in the Food Hall.'

'I don't understand that,' Breda said. 'So what's your job?'

'I don't really have one, not like you. My father sent me here to train for at least a year. I'm to go through every department in turn.'

'Why? What for?' Breda asked.

He seemed slightly uncomfortable at her question.

'My family has a store in London,' he said. 'My father didn't want me to train there, which is why I'm here. He has a great respect for Miss Opal. So has everyone in the retail store trade. She's a legend.'

'Ah!' Breda said. 'Then in that case I have to say I think you're sitting at the wrong table.'

'What do you mean?'

'Well, you'll discover that we sit according to rank. I expect you should be with the buyers, or even the top management. Certainly not with a third sales assistant.'

He smiled, showing even white teeth. 'It's not at all like that. I shan't have much truck with top management, and I'm not to be shown any favours. Strict instructions from my Pa to Miss Opal. And she'll see they're carried out.'

'I have to go,' Breda said, though she wanted never to have to move. 'There'll be trouble if I'm late back. I don't suppose that will apply to you.'

'Oh yes it will,' he contradicted her. 'Do you always come to lunch at this time?'

'Yes,' Breda said. 'Except that I call it dinner.'

'Then I'll see you tomorrow?'

'I'll be here,' Breda said.

'I thought you were never coming,' Doreen Wilmot said on Breda's breathless arrival in the department. 'Good thing for you Miss Craven is late or you'd catch it.'

I wouldn't care if I did, Breda thought. She hadn't felt so happy since the minute she'd set foot in the store; or in Akersfield or anywhere else for that matter.

The accident happened in the middle of the afternoon. Miss Wilmot, serving a customer, climbed up the small stepladder to get a roll of cloth from the top shelf. There was no telling how she did it, but suddenly, with a shriek which could be heard from one end of the floor to the other, she fell off the ladder and lay on the floor behind the counter with the roll of cloth on top of her.

It was clear there was no way she could get up, and also that she was in pain. Mr Stokesly was summoned from his dinner and Miss Craven alerted the nurse from the staff sickroom.

'In the meantime,' Miss Craven commanded, 'do *not* move her!' She had done her first aid at the beginning of the war, and although she had never had occasion to use it and remembered little, she did recall that you practically never moved anyone. You left them where they fell, and covered them up, which she now did with a roll of best-quality heavy wool cloth, at four coupons a yard.

'I'm quite sure it's a fracture, though whether her ankle or her leg I can't be certain,' the nurse said. 'Either way, she'll have to go to hospital.'

Mr Stokesly telephoned for an ambulance. By the time it arrived a small crowd had gathered to watch a deathly pale Miss Wilmot being gently lifted onto a stretcher and borne away. There was an almost pleasurable air of excitement. It was not often that anything untoward happened in Opal's well-run store.

'What in the world are we going to do?' Miss Craven demanded. 'No Junior, no Second Sales!'

Sixteen

Luckily, three days after Doreen Wilmot's unfortunate accident Betty Hartley's mother called in the store to report that her daughter's tonsilitis, which had been really bad, had taken the turn and was coming along nicely and she expected to be back at work on the following Monday. 'All being well,' she added darkly. 'Though you don't seem to be having much luck on this department, do you? Not since Miss O'Connor joined you, though I expect that's just a coincidence.'

She was not at all sure about that. She disliked the Irish. Weren't they a bit fey, a bit psychic? The girl could well be the bringer of bad luck.

'Come now, Mrs Hartley,' Mr Stokesly said jovially. 'It can hardly be anyone's fault that Miss Wilmot fell off the stepladder! And your Betty must have been sickening for tonsilitis before Miss O'Connor set foot here. But I'm pleased your daughter is improving and we look forward to seeing her on Monday morning.'

'All being well,' Mrs Hartley repeated.

It had been a hectic three days in the department since Doreen Wilmot's departure. They were now two short out of four staff, and since a particularly nasty head cold was going around the store with the rapidity of a forest fire, no substitutes could be found from other departments. Mr Stokesly could not be expected to serve behind the counter. It was not his job; he had more important things to do. Besides, he would have been stealing Miss Craven's thunder, not to mention her commission, which was more important.

'And aren't I the one who suffers?' Breda demanded dramatically. 'Doesn't it all fall on me?'

She was relating events to her family in Waterloo Terrace. Josephine, in particular, liked to hear every detail of Breda's days in Opal's. It was as if she experienced through her niece all the drama, and what she saw as glamour, of the store. Grandma Maguire, though she expressed indifference, never, Breda noticed, failed to listen avidly.

'There are still all the Junior's jobs to be done,' Breda said. 'Covers taken off in the morning, put on again at nights. Errands to run, shelves to tidy, everything to dust.'

'Doesn't Miss Craven lend a hand?' Josephine asked.

'Good heavens, Auntie Josie!' Breda said. 'Miss Craven is First Sales. I don't suppose she's handled a duster since before the war!'

'It'll do you no harm,' Grandma Maguire said.

'Oh, I know!' Breda agreed.

'Satan finds mischief for idle hands to do!'

'Then he'll not find much for me,' Breda said. 'When I'm not sweeping and dusting, I'm being temporary Second Sales. I field the customers Miss Craven is too busy to attend to.'

She didn't mind any of this. It kept her from ever being bored. The time flew by. She learned a lot about materials: how to measure them accurately, keeping an eye out for flaws and giving the customer a suitable allowance should one be found; how to roll the cloth up neatly and pin the ends so that it wouldn't disgorge itself every time it was moved from a shelf.

'I enjoy serving the customers,' she said. 'I like working out how much material they'll need for a dress or a skirt. They never seem to have the faintest idea.'

What she liked least was adding up the cost. She admitted to Miss Craven that arithmetic was not her strong point. 'I don't know how you do it,' she said. 'Three and seven-eighths yards at three and eleven a yard is beyond me.'

Miss Craven could do all these sums like lightning: any length, any price. She could also advise on how many reels of thread, how many yards of binding tape, and which zip fastener was most suitable.

'There is a ready-reckoner under the counter,' Miss Craven said. 'You'd better use it, though it won't look good to the customers.'

Nothing to do with Opal's store could depress Breda these days. It was a pleasure to come to work in the morning and, however tired she was, she was never in a rush to hurry home at the end of the afternoon. And what lightened all her days was the existence of Graham Prince. Since that first occasion he had eaten every single day at her table. Sometimes he was there before her, sometimes he was late in joining her, but he always appeared.

'You had better go to dinner,' Miss Craven said now. 'Don't be long!'

Graham was already at the table when Breda walked into the canteen. Her heart lifted at the sight of him. 'I'm in a hurry today,' she said as she joined him. 'I'm on a forty.'

'A forty?'

'Ah! Not being sales staff you wouldn't know about that, would you? I'm only allowed forty minutes instead of an hour, but I get my dinner free. It's just when we're very busy, or in an emergency. Miss Opal doesn't like staff hurrying meals. You can't get away with it just to have your dinner paid for.'

'So what are you doing today?' she asked, attacking her macaroni cheese.

'I'm on a very exalted job today,' Graham said. 'I'm working on deliveries: unpacking, checking them off, delivering them to departments, taking them to the stockroom. It's heady work, I can tell you! The stuff of management. And, Miss Breda O'Connor, I shall be visiting Fabrics this afternoon. There's something your Buyer is waiting for.

'I'll look out for you,' Breda promised.

'You can't miss me,' he told her. 'I'll be wearing a natty brown alpaca coat.'

Both she and Miss Craven were serving when he came. He was happy to wait, watching Breda at her work. She was conscious of being watched and, though she was glad to see him, it made her nervous. She was pleased when the sale was over and her customer departed.

'You tie a very nifty parcel,' Graham said. 'I suppose I shall have to learn to do that. Perhaps you could teach me.'

'Miss Craven could teach you far better than I could,' Breda said smoothly. 'She's an expert. I'm sure she'd be pleased to!'

He pulled a face.

Miss Craven despatched her customer and moved towards them.

'Now, Mr Prince,' she said pleasantly, 'what can I do for you?'

'He wants to learn how to make up a parcel,' Breda said.

'Oh no, not today,' Graham said hastily. 'I'm sure you're much too busy. I've just brought a delivery.'

'Put it behind the counter,' Miss Craven said. 'Miss O'Connor, you can start to unpack it.'

'Shall I give you a hand?' Graham offered.

'No thank you. Miss O'Connor can manage quite well and it is not your job. Thank you very much, Mr Prince. Good afternoon.' Miss Craven spoke politely but firmly.

'Good afternoon, Miss Craven. Good afternoon, Miss O'Connor,' Graham replied.

'I can see I must have a word with you, Miss O'Connor,' Miss Craven said. 'For your own good.'

It was Breda's experience that when someone said 'for your own good' what followed would not be pleasant.

'You *do* know who that young man is?' Miss Craven demanded. 'I can't imagine you don't, since you seem to share a table every day. Oh, don't think it's gone unnoticed! And don't think it will do you any good, a third sales hobnobbing with the bosses! People don't like it.'

'I'm not hobnobbing with him,' Breda said defensively. 'We just sit at the same table. We're both strangers here and it's nice to have someone to talk to. Anyway, he's not one of the bosses. He's working in Deliveries at the moment, which is an even lower form of life than mine!'

'That is as may be, for the moment. But his family is Prince, of Prince and Harper, a well-known store in London of which his father is Managing Director. Perhaps you did not know that, Miss O'Connor, but now that you do it behoves you not to get above yourself – out of your class, in fact.' Miss Craven's voice was heavy with warning.

Breda opened her mouth to protest, then closed it again. The poor old thing was jealous. She could see it in the tightness of her mouth and the hardness of her eyes.

But she would not, no matter what anyone said, stop seeing Graham at dinner time, unless he made it plain he didn't want it, and he showed not the slightest sign of that. He seemed as happy in her company as she was in his. And that, at least up to now, was as far as it went, though she made no attempt to stifle the spring of hope in her heart.

In any case, other people were free to sit at the table, and often now they did.

'It's probably because they want to get to know you,' she'd said to Graham.

'Nonsense!' he'd contradicted. 'All these fellows wanting to join me? It's you they're after. But don't forget I saw you first!'

Miss Craven moved away to attend to a customer. Breda busied herself cleaning the counter.

Was Miss Craven right, she wondered? Or at least partly right? Was she getting too fond of Graham? He was a bird of passage. When his year's training was up, wouldn't he go back to London and she'd never see him again? Wouldn't he forget all about her? She felt tears prick at her eyes at the very thought of it. For a moment she hated Miss Craven.

All the same, she had to be sure that she'd be able to forget him, and the way she felt now she never would, not if she lived to be a hundred, which was a long time ahead since she was just about to be eighteen. But hadn't two men already let her down? She had not had a word from Tony. Could she bear it a third time?

So when Graham, next day, asked her if she would like to go to the pictures one evening, she immediately said no. She was still not rid of the mood Miss Craven had pitched her into the previous day.

Graham was astonished by her refusal. 'I thought you would enjoy the pictures,' he said. 'I thought going to the pictures was what everyone around here did in the evenings.'

She flared up at once. 'Don't be so patronizing! People *do* go to the pictures, but it's not the only thing. They go to dances, concerts; they go to night school; they do all sorts of things. They're not nearly as dull as you make out. Of course I suppose in London it's all very different. Theatres, night-clubs – that sort of thing!'

She realized, to her horror, that she was quarrelling with him. How *could* she? How could she do it? She was stung by the bewilderment on his face.

'As a matter of fact,' he said, 'I've never been to a night-club in my life. As a matter of fact, *I* like going to the pictures. I wasn't being the least bit patronizing. I don't know what's got into you, Breda, but why don't you get off your high horse and say you'll come with me? It's Gregory Peck, *Duel in the Sun*.'

Not only was she ashamed of herself, she was tempted. Wasn't Gregory Peck her first favourite in the whole world?

'But if you'd rather go to night school and learn to speak Chinese, then I'll go with you,' Graham said.

Her black mood vanished. Let the future take care of itself! 'You are an idiot,' she said. 'But yes, I'd like to go to the pictures. And I'm sorry.'

'Right,' he said. 'We'll go tomorrow. I'll call for you at seven o'clock.'

'I'll meet you in the foyer,' Breda said quickly.

'Oh no you won't,' he said. 'I shall call for you, in the proper manner.'

She was ready long before seven o'clock. She had changed into a green skirt and jacket and a cream blouse, all of which she had made before she'd left Kilbally. Graham, she thought, had never seen her in anything other than her plain black work dress with its demure white collar. She pinned up her hair on the top of her head in a sophisticated style and, as a final touch, added a pair of silver-coloured earrings in the shape of fishes. Do I look all right, she asked herself, studying herself in the mirror, or do I look tarty?

Either way, it was too late to do anything about it, because wasn't that a ring at the door, and who else could it be but Graham? He had no business to be early. She had planned to answer the door herself, and to leave with him on the same instant, not even asking him in. Now, by the time she had re-powdered her nose and added a touch more lipstick, Auntie Josie had already answered the door and ushered Graham into the kitchen where everyone, Maureen and Kate included, was waiting to set eyes on him.

'I'm sorry to keep you waiting,' Breda said, joining them.

'You haven't,' Graham said. 'I'm early.'

They were unashamedly inspecting him; Kate, Maureen and Josephine with smiling approval, Brendan with caution and Grandma Maguire with suspicion.

'It's nice to meet you,' Josephine said. 'Breda has told us a lot about you.'

Was that a fact, Breda asked herself. Sure, she had hardly mentioned him. Auntie Josie was making it up just to be polite.

'You come from London,' Grandma Maguire said. 'I went to London once, on a day trip. Nasty. Noisy place!'

'You're quite right, Mrs Maguire,' Graham said agreeably. 'You stick to Akersfield!'

'I think we should leave,' Breda said, 'if we're not to miss the beginning of the film.'

They went to the same cinema, sat in almost identical seats as when she had gone with Tony, and there was no question that Graham was pleasant, yet from start to finish it was quite different, disappointingly so.

Tony had been especially attentive, had bought her chocolates, held her hand, put his arm around her. There was nothing like that this evening. Even though she sat very close to Graham in the double seat, and practically everyone around them was concentrating on something other than the drama on the screen, Graham did not even hold her hand. Is it all different in London, she wondered? Do they have different rules?

'That was great,' Graham said as he saw her home. 'I won't come in,' he said when they reached the house.

She hadn't thought of asking him in, far from it, so why did she mind his words? Worse, he made not the slightest attempt to kiss her, simply squeezed her hand briefly, said 'See you tomorrow', and was gone.

She walked slowly up the path and fitted her key in the lock.

Perhaps he had made a deliberate decision to play it cool, she thought. Well, if that was his idea it was all right by her; she had no wish to be involved where she wasn't wanted.

She had enjoyed the film – Gregory Peck would never let you down. The evening had been a great improvement on listening to Grandma Maguire's moans and groans or sitting through her uncle's heavy silences. That was all there was to it.

'Well!' said Josephine the minute Breda walked through the door. 'He seems very nice, your young man. We all thought so. Quite the gentleman!'

Too much the gentleman, Breda thought!

'Oh, Auntie Josie, he's not my young man,' she said loftily. 'Whatever made you think that? He's simply a friend, someone I work with. Nothing more than that.'

It hurt her to say the words, but facts were facts.

'Well, you know what I mean,' Josephine said. 'And you can't deny he's taken a shine to you!'

She was pleased Breda had found a friend, especially a young man. She had worried that the girl had been lonely, also that she'd fretted too much about Tony. She could have told her that that would come to nothing. Tony wasn't to be tied down, he was too fond of a good time. In any case they were first cousins. It wouldn't have done at all.

Breda knew quite well what her aunt meant. Auntie Josie saw the whole thing as romantic. Graham Prince was the son of a rich father, he was way above them, and in addition he was handsome and charming. It was just like one of the stories in the magazine she bought every Thursday.

But Auntie Josie was wrong, Breda thought. She and Graham Prince were simply good friends, not even close friends, not friends of long standing. Ships that passed in the night. She was not his sort and he was not hers, and wasn't that the size of it?

But she knew, as the matter-of-fact words ran through her head, that it wasn't true. It wasn't what her heart said.

'I didn't say I liked him,' Grandma Maguire said suddenly. 'And I didn't say I didn't! I thought he was a bit posh. Not our sort, if you ask me. All the same, *I* wouldn't mind going to the pictures with him!'

Perhaps Grandma sees further than the rest of us, Breda thought as she went to bed, but not, for a long time, to sleep. Not our sort. She would put him out of her mind. She was making too much of it.

She wondered, next morning, whether she would ask Miss Craven if it would be possible to change her dinner hour so that she'd have an excuse for avoiding Graham. She even got as far as asking, but to her relief – and she was annoyed with herself that she should feel relieved – Miss Craven refused. 'Since there are only the two of us at the present time, and we have to go opposite each other, it would mean *me* changing *my* time. I'm afraid I couldn't consider that.'

Without a doubt, Miss Craven thought, the young man had changed his dinner hour and she didn't want to miss him. Too bad!

So when Breda walked into the canteen there Graham was, sitting at the table. It would make too much of the whole thing not to join him.

'Did you enjoy the film?' he asked, looking up from his corned beef fritters.

'Very much, thank you. Didn't I say so?' She was aware she sounded cool. She couldn't help it.

'I just wondered,' he said. 'These fritters aren't half bad.'

'Very nice.' In fact they were choking her.

'I also wondered if you'd like to come for a walk on Sunday morning,' he said. 'If you're a good enough walker we could go over the moors to Hebghyll. I've been told it's a popular outing.'

'I'm a perfectly good walker,' Breda said. 'We do it all the time in Ireland. But I couldn't manage Sunday morning. I go to church.'

'I'm sorry about that,' Graham said. 'I really hoped you would. It would have been nice.'

So it would, Breda thought. Very nice. Heaven! 'I could go in the afternoon,' she offered.

'But I couldn't,' Graham said. 'I have a date. Can't break it.'

'Well, in that case . . . And how nice to be so popular!'

There was an edge to her voice. With whom, she thought? Where? Why? But especially with whom.

Graham looked at her thoughtfully. 'I do believe', he said, 'you're jealous! I'm flattered.'

'You needn't be,' Breda said. 'Me, jealous? Sure, you must be out of your mind.'

'But I wish you were! So, would you like to know with whom?' he asked. He was smiling and she could have killed him for that.

'I could not care less,' she lied. ' 'Tis no affair of mine.'

'I'll tell you all the same,' he said. 'I have a date with Miss Opal. I'm summoned to take tea. A command performance. I think my father must have asked for a progress report.'

A wide smile, which she could not keep back, lit up Breda's face. It was like the sun coming from behind the clouds, Graham thought.

'Well,' Breda said quickly, 'if you *really* want to go for a walk . . . '

'Didn't I say so? Didn't I ask you?'

'I suppose I could go to early Mass. I could meet you at half-past nine . . . '

If she'd been a nail biter, wouldn't her nails have been bitten down to the quick in the next forty-eight hours, wondering would it keep fine, what would she wear, and were her shoes up to it?

They met by the main gates of Sutherland Park. Breda had firmly squashed Graham's suggestion that he should call for her. The thought of him impinging on the Sunday morning scene at 52 Waterloo Terrace, with Auntie Josie getting a recalcitrant mother-in-law ready to be taken to church while Brendan sat in his shirt sleeves reading the *News of the World* was not to be borne.

The weather had all the greyness of early November, but at least it wasn't raining, and with luck it wouldn't. There had been a slight frost early on, which had left the air crisp.

'I've checked out the way,' Graham said. 'A bus here which will take us within a few minutes of the moor road. From there it's about seven miles, mostly on footpaths, over the moor to Hebghyll. We shall have to get the train back from Hebghyll to Akersfield so that I can be in time to spruce myself up for Miss Opal. A pity we can't make a whole day of it, but we will some other time.'

It was a stiff climb from the spot where the bus deposited them to the top of the moor. At the summit they stopped for a minute to regain their breath. Breda gasped at the width of the view, which spread before them in every direction. 'Holy smoke!' she cried. 'Would you just be looking at that! Isn't it like standing on top of the world?'

Graham nodded. 'It's like nothing I've ever seen before,' he said. 'Is it what you expected?'

'Not at all. I suppose I'd wondered, would it be anything like Ireland,' she confessed.

'And is it?'

'Not at all. At any rate, nothing like Kilbally.'

After a minute, they took the footpath ahead. The ground was rough, strewn with rocks, patched with bracken which at this time of the year had turned brown. Breda was a little disappointed that the heather, which she had glimpsed from her attic window on that first day in Akersfield, was no longer in bloom, though as they walked they found, in a few sheltered places protected by larger rocks, a few small pockets of purple.

'Tell me what Kilbally's like,' Graham said.

Breda was silent for a moment. There were times, and this was one of them, when it was almost impossible to talk about Kilbally, so much did she miss it.

'For a start,' she said, 'it's on the coast. You walk along the cliffs and you look out over the sea. Three thousand miles of ocean, my Dada said. Nothing between us and America. In one way that's like this place here. So much space, and so much sky. But the land is green there. Oh, I can't begin to tell you how green. And the houses are small and white, and the people mostly poor.'

'I would like to see it,' Graham said quietly. 'I'd like to see the place where you grew up.'

'And I would like you to,' Breda said. 'But tell me about where you grew up. I don't know anything about you, or your family – except that your father has a large store. I suppose he must be rich,' she added ruefully. She would much rather he wasn't.

'It's a family business, not just my father, though he's the head,' Graham said. 'There are two uncles, four children between them, and I have two brothers.'

'You never said!' Breda accused him. 'Why did I think you were an only child?'

'Perhaps because I'm the youngest.'

Not only that, Breda thought. He had an air of . . . loneliness, wasn't it, sometimes, and at other times a sufficiency, as if he was used to managing on his own.

'I grew up in Surrey about twenty miles from London,' he said. 'We still live there, in the house I was born in. I only ever saw it in the holidays. I was sent away to school when I was eight.'

Breda's eyes widened in horror. 'Sent away from home at eight years old! That's terrible.'

'It was the thing to do,' Graham said. 'All my parents' friends did the same thing. But yes, it was awful. I wouldn't do it to a child of mine.'

'Nor me!' Breda said. 'So are your brothers in the business?'

'Yes, and two of my cousins. As a matter of fact . . . ' he paused.

'Yes?'

'Well, to tell you the truth, I didn't want to go into the business. It's not my choice.'

They had reached the edge of the high plateau, which ended in a rocky escarpment. Down in the valley, clustered along the side of the river, lay the moorland town of Hebghyll.

Graham spread his raincoat on the flat rock.

'Let's sit down and take in the view,' he suggested. 'According to the map, that's the River Wharfe.'

'Tell me something else,' Breda said, sitting down. 'If you didn't want to go into your father's business, what are you doing in Opal's? And what else would you rather have done?'

'Don't laugh!' Graham said. 'I wanted to be a painter. Still do, I suppose.'

'A painter!'

'I knew you'd laugh.'

'I'm not laughing,' Breda said.

'My father thought I'd gone off my rocker. He's a great one for security. He never had faith in me succeeding as an artist. All he could see was me as a failure, starving in a garret.'

'So why are you in Opal's?' Breda repeated.

'We reached a compromise, Father and I. I'd do my training with Opal, then I'd do a spell in the family business. After that I'd be free to make my own choice.'

'Does Miss Opal know?'

'No-one here knows except you,' he said.

'But you seem to like it here – the store, I mean,' Breda said.

'The best way to cope with something you don't like, but have to do,' Graham said, 'is to act as though you like it!'

'And if you act it long enough, you might actually get to like it.'

Graham stood up, held out a hand, and pulled Breda to her feet.

'We'd better get going,' he said. 'Hebghyll looks close enough from here, but I suspect it's a long walk. Anyway, I've talked enough about myself.'

'I'm glad you did.' She felt she knew him so much better.

He tucked her arm through his as they walked. 'And I've learned almost nothing about you,' he said.

'Another time,' Breda said.

In the town they found a café which gave them a Sunday dinner at a moderate cost.

'I would like to take you to the best hotel,' Graham said, 'but my father keeps me on short commons. He wants me to have no more than the people I'm working alongside.'

'I've never been to a smart hotel,' Breda said. 'I wouldn't know what to do.'

'Oh yes you would,' Graham said. 'You'd know what to do wherever you landed! You could mix with anyone!'

She could always do that because she was natural, she was always herself, open and friendly.

'Well, I like it here,' she said.

After the meal they walked down to the river, and then it was time to take the train back.

'Have you enjoyed yourself?' Graham asked when he left her at the bottom of Waterloo Terrace.

'Oh, Graham, every minute!' It was true.

'And you'll come again?'

'Whenever I'm asked.'

When she left him Breda ran up the steep slope of Waterloo Terrace as if she was floating on the air. Oh, it had been a wonderful day! How could she possibly have misjudged him, just because he didn't behave like Rory or Tony, or probably most other men. He was different.

'No need to ask if you've had a good time,' Josephine said when Breda went in. 'You look like a cat that's been at the cream.'

'It's been quite wonderful.'

'Could you come down to earth for a cup of tea?' Josephine asked.

The day of Princess Elizabeth's wedding to Lieutenant Mountbatten drew near. There was some talk, and not a

303

few grumbles, about the fact that she had been allowed 300 coupons for her wedding outfit, but most people were so pleased to have something exciting to look forward to after the drab years of the war that they managed not to mind too much. Miss Opal, with one of her flashes of inspiration, announced that on the day, though the store would remain open for business as usual, staff would be excused from wearing their workaday clothes, or in the case of the men their dark suits, and might choose something more celebratory. Just so long, she said, as it was suitable and decent.

'I shall wear my best grey marocain and my cameo brooch,' Miss Craven confided to Breda.

She was also the proud possessor of a short necklace of seed pearls, left to her by an aunt, but would that be too much, she wondered? But why not? It was a very special occasion.

Breda was torn with anxiety about what she would wear. She wanted to look her absolute best, not for Princess Elizabeth, though she wished her all the luck in the world, but because she wanted Graham to see her in something special.

Then Mr Stokesly and Miss Craven came back from a senior staff meeting with the news that every department was to do something special in the form of a display. A small amount of money was to be allowed to buy materials – coloured paper, balloons and the like – and an outside person of importance, perhaps even the Mayor himself, would judge the entries and present prizes.

Miss Craven was not happy. 'I make no pretence to artistic talent,' she said with uncharacteristic modesty. 'It is not in my line, possibly because I have never had the time. I have always left such matters of display, which are fortunately not much needed on Fabrics, to Miss Wilmot.

And where is she now? Sitting with her foot in plaster, no doubt reading a novel!'

'Would you like me to try to think of something?' Breda offered. She didn't have an idea in her head, but it might be fun to try.

Miss Craven pursed her lips, shook her head in doubt. 'But if you'd rather do it yourself . . . '

'I suppose you could have a go,' Miss Craven said. 'In any case, I'm far too busy!'

Breda spent the next morning's shopping time searching around the store for ideas, and the means to carry them out. It seemed as though everyone else had the same mission. In no time at all there wasn't another scrap of red, white or blue paper to be had, and only a few balloons, mostly in the wrong colours.

It was while she was looking for suitable materials for the department that she came across the ribbon. It was stiff grosgrain, four inches wide, in a deep, sea-green colour. There were several rolls of it, part of a purchase of bankrupt stock from a wholesaler. Miss Opal often bought such things. And no sooner did Breda set eyes on it than she knew that here was what she wanted, not for the department, but for her new dress.

She knew exactly how she would do it, she could see the finished garment as if it was right there in front of her eyes. The ribbon would run vertically from shoulder to hem, each piece narrowed at the waistline and flaring out again on the skirt. The pieces would be joined by an openwork stitch in embroidery cotton – black, she thought. She would have a square neckline and full sleeves, the ribbon here going horizontally. She stood there in a daze, designing the whole thing on the spot. And the beauty of it was the ribbon needed no coupons.

'Did you want something?' the assistant asked.

'Is this ribbon expensive?' Breda asked.

'No. It's dirt cheap. Our Buyer can't think how we'll get rid of it.'

'Will you lend me a pencil and paper so that I can work something out?' Breda asked.

A few minutes later she said, 'I would need three whole rolls. Do you think I'd get a special price for quantity?'

It came amazingly cheaply. By now she realized she had no more than five minutes left to find something for the department's display. She discovered a few flowers on millinery, reels of white thread and hanks of blue embroidery cotton on haberdashery and a packet of red paper napkins. It was a pathetic collection. She hoped that Miss Craven would allow her the use of some suitable fabrics, providing she didn't actually cut into them.

'Is this the best you could do?' Miss Craven said. 'I must say, it doesn't look much!'

'Wait until it's finished,' Breda said cheerfully. 'You'll be surprised!' So will I, she thought. She hadn't an idea in her head, except for the dress, but about that she was quite certain.

It took an age to make: the strips of ribbon shaped, and tacked flat onto newspaper before being linked by the fagotting; every stitch in the dress put in by hand. Night after night she worked at it until her eyes felt as though they would drop out. But when she stepped into it on the day of the wedding even Princess Elizabeth herself, in her white satin gown, could not have felt better turned out.

Graham, wearing grey flannels and a well-cut sports jacket in Prince-of-Wales check, was at the Fabrics counter before nine o'clock, with no excuse except to see what had kept Breda so occupied for the last ten days that she had had almost no time at all for him.

'It's magnificent!' he cried. 'You look wonderful!'

'Thank you,' Breda said. 'I'm glad you like it.'

'Like it?' he lowered his voice. 'I could eat you!'

Miss Craven sidled up to them. 'Most ingenious, I must admit,' she said.

'And you too, Miss Craven,' Graham said. 'You look splendid. Very smart indeed!'

'Thank you, Mr Prince!'

She had, after all, worn both the cameo brooch *and* the seed pearls. In honour of the Princess.

'And your hair, Miss Craven,' Graham said. 'I can see you've paid a very early visit to a good hairdresser.'

Miss Craven gave him her most brilliant smile. Though she could not condone the way he chased after Miss O'Connor, it was impossible not to like him. Breeding will out, she thought. He was clearly a cut above the usual. No doubt Miss O'Connor egged him on.

'Not quite right!' she said archly. 'All my own work!'

She would say nothing of the almost sleepless night she had spent, due to a head full of metal curling pins digging into her scalp. Gentlemen did not wish to know such things.

'I mustn't stop to talk,' Breda said. 'I have to do the display. It's all to be in place before eleven o'clock. The Mayor is judging at twelve noon.'

In spite of Miss Craven's demurs, Mr Stokesly had said Breda might use any of the fabrics on the department, so long as she did not actually take the scissors to them, so she was able to mount a reasonable display, swathing and swagging the materials around the shelves and along the front of the counter, crumpling and twisting the finer fabrics and florals into exotic-looking flowers.

'They'll all have to be ironed out again,' Miss Craven warned.

'I know. I'll do it,' Breda said.

The Mayor, accompanied by Miss Opal and Mr Soames, paused a long time on the department. Even so, when the results were announced, they had not won a prize, but they were highly commended.

That same afternoon Miss Opal sent for Breda. 'I usually have a word with staff after their first six weeks in the store,' she said. 'You are just coming up to that. How are you getting on? Do you feel settled?'

'Yes thank you, Miss Opal,' Breda replied. 'I like it here.'

'And have you made friends?'

Opal knew the answer to that. She was more aware of what went on than most people gave her credit for. And, no doubt without meaning to, young Prince had given himself away when she'd had him to tea. But she couldn't totally encourage that. She had Henry Prince to answer to for his son.

'One or two,' Breda said.

'That's good. But if you're wise, you'll spread your friendships, for your own sake. Join one or two of our clubs. The Rambling Club, the Dramatic Society.'

'I'll think about it,' Breda promised.

'And now the display,' Miss Opal said. 'Though you didn't win a prize, I was quite impressed. Did you have a theme behind it?'

'Only that I wanted to show what could be done with fabrics; not just colours, but textures. Contrasts.'

'Have you ever thought you would like to do display work?' Miss Opal asked.

'I've never thought about it,' Breda said.

'And your pretty dress? You didn't buy that in the store, did you?'

'I bought the ribbon here,' Breda told her. 'I designed and made the dress myself.'

'It's quite clever. I wonder . . . ?' She hesitated. The girl was quite clearly talented, but there were other considerations; the department, Miss Craven, the fact that Miss O'Connor had only been with them six weeks. One step at a time.

'I wonder,' she continued. 'Would you lend us the dress so that we could display it in one of our windows? I'd like to show what can be done with coupon-free ribbon and a little ingenuity.'

'Why yes, Miss Opal,' Breda said. 'I'd be pleased to.'

'You've been a long time,' Miss Craven said when Breda returned. 'What was all that about?'

'Just the interview Miss Opal says she always does when someone's been here six weeks,' Breda answered.

This was not the time to tell Miss Craven about the dress, or what Miss Opal had said about the display. Her benign mood of the morning had vanished. She was hot, flustered and bad-tempered.

'Be sure you're here extra early in the morning to take this lot down.' Miss Craven waved a disparaging hand at the display. 'We can't have it cluttering up the department yet another day.'

A week later, an uneventful week, an anticlimax to the excitement of the royal wedding day, Breda was on her own in the department. It was totally forbidden, but in this instance quite unavoidable. Mr Stokesly was at a buyers' meeting, Betty Hartley had been sent on an errand by Miss Craven and Miss Wilmot was still in plaster at home. Miss Craven had suddenly been seized by stomach cramps of so violent a nature that she clutched the counter, gripping it for dear life, while the colour drained from her face.

'I'll have to go!' she gasped. 'Excuse me . . . !' And she was gone.

It had been a busy day, customers following fast one after the other, but now, fifteen minutes from closing time, the rush had died down. Breda would be glad when 5.30 came because she was going out with Graham.

She had been unrolling the ends of material from the long cardboard tubes around which they were wrapped, ready to fold the short ends into remnants for the sales table. Now she couldn't continue with it because it needed Miss Craven's authority to price remnants, so she stood where she was, at the end of the counter, behind the till. It was heaven to do absolutely nothing for a minute or two.

Without turning her head, she knew that someone had come in by the side entrance. There was no mistaking the draught, which all day had been like a miniature gale. She stood there, wondering what she would wear this evening. Graham's father had sent him a totally unexpected, magnificent ten pounds with which he was taking her to a meal *and* the theatre.

She supposed she must have heard the footsteps because she was aware that they had stopped, right by her counter.

She raised her head and looked straight into the chalk-white face of a man. His eyes were as black and shining as coals. Frightening eyes, they were. Glittering. She dropped her gaze and immediately found herself staring into the dark barrel of a gun, which protruded from the long woollen scarf he wore around his neck and draped over his head.

'If you make one sound I'll fire it!' he said quietly.

'Just hand over what's in the till. Just the notes. You can keep the change. If you do as you're told you'll not get hurt. If you try any tricks you'll end up a nasty mess on the floor.'

His voice was quite even, as if he might be asking for three yards of cotton lining.

Seventeen

For a second, which seemed like an hour, Breda stared at the man, unable to move, mesmerized, paralysed by fear.

'Get a move on,' he said quietly. 'I don't have all day. Neither do you!'

His voice jerked her back to reality.

Without taking her eyes from him – she daren't do that – her right hand moved towards the till. She pressed the 'No Sale' key and the drawer opened.

'Just the notes,' the man repeated. 'As I said, you can keep the change.'

It was as she took the notes from under the spring clips that a fierce and sudden anger hit her and, she thought afterwards, common sense deserted her. How dare he? He wasn't going to get away with this. She would stop him, though she had as yet no idea how.

Slowly, deliberately, her head a whirl of thoughts which she somehow had to get in order, she transferred the pound and ten-shilling notes to her left hand. There was a thick wad of them. It had been a busy day.

'Hurry up!' the man hissed. There was an edge to his voice.

In that moment she knew what she would do. It was there, staring her in the face. She gave no thought to the danger. Anger, and the absolute necessity of not showing it, of keeping calm, drove fear from her mind. The only thing she could not control was the thudding of her heart and the trembling of her hand as she held out the money towards him.

Then, at the same time as he moved to take the wad of notes from her she quickly grasped the long, stiff cardboard tube which lay at her right hand on the counter, and thrust it sharply towards him.

Her aim was good. The tube caught him unawares, hit him on the wrist. She saw the flash of panic in his eyes. The gun dropped to the floor and went off with a deafening report. Then the man started to run, the notes still clasped in his hand.

He made for the door, and she ran after him, but since she had to get out from the other side of the counter he was ahead of her. It was the steps, the short flight of steps which led to the street door, which were, literally, his downfall. He tripped and fell, sprawled against them.

Breda had found her voice, and the revolver shot had brought people running, running and screaming.

'Stop him! Stop him!' she shouted above the noise.

The man was getting to his feet. She was almost on him, but an assistant from Menswear was there before her. He grabbed the man who, halfway to his feet was unbalanced, and pinned his arms behind his back.

The notes lay scattered on the floor. Breda instinctively stooped to pick them up – and as she did so everything and everybody faded in front of her. The last thing she knew was that Mr Stokesly was there, and that it was all right and he would take care of everything.

'She's coming to!'

The voice came to Breda from a far way off, then moved nearer and became merged with its owner, the store nurse. Behind the nurse stood Mr Stokesly and Miss Opal, both looking anxious. At first Breda understood nothing of this. She thought perhaps she was dreaming. Then suddenly she remembered, and what she remembered was the noise of the shot. She sat up quickly, clapping her hands over her ears.

'What happened? Was someone hurt?'

'Miraculously, no,' Miss Opal said. Her voice was grim.

'The bullet went into the front of the counter,' Mr Stokesly said. 'No real harm done.'

'And there is nothing for you to worry about,' Miss Opal said. 'The man has already been taken to the police station and, thanks to you, all the money has been recovered. If *you* are all right, then everything is all right.'

'Oh, I am,' Breda said. 'I'm sure I am!'

'I'm glad to hear it,' Miss Opal said. She could hardly say the same for herself. She felt shattered at the thought of what the consequences might have been.

'I shall send you home in my car,' she said. 'And unless you are totally fit you are to take the day off tomorrow. But if you *are* well enough to come in, then the doctor will be here and I should like her to take a look at you.'

Mr Stokesly, with Miss Opal's firm backing, insisted on accompanying Breda home, though she told him she would be quite happy just to sit beside the chauffeur. He stayed there only long enough to tell her aunt what had happened.

Josephine listened with horror. 'Oh, Breda love, I can't believe it! In Leasfield! In Opal's! What's the world coming to?'

Even Brendan was shocked. 'Are you sure you're all right, love?' he asked Breda.

He called me 'love', she thought. Everyone called everyone love in the West Riding, but Brendan had never before used the word to her, not once.

'I'm quite all right thank you, Uncle Brendan,' she said.

'Breda was extremely brave,' Mr Stokesly said. 'Foolish, without a doubt, but very brave.'

'He must be a madman,' Brendan said. His voice was rough with indignation. 'If I had him here . . . He should be locked up!'

'He is now,' Mr Stokesly said. 'And I don't doubt will be for a long time. But I'll not stay any longer. I'll leave you in peace.'

'I'll see you tomorrow,' Breda said. 'I'm sure I'll be back at work.'

'Wait and see,' Mr Stokesly cautioned.

'Well!' Josephine said when Mr Stokesly had left. 'What a terrible thing! You'll not feel like going out tonight, will you, love? A bite to eat and early bed I'd say.'

Only then did Breda remember that this was the evening she was to go to a meal and to the theatre with Graham.

'Oh but I do!' she said at once. 'Just a cup of tea, then I'll get changed. I feel fine, honestly I do.'

It was not strictly true. She felt shaky – but wild horses wouldn't make her miss the evening. Wasn't the table booked at the restaurant and the tickets for the theatre? And she would be wearing her ribbon dress.

Halfway through her cup of tea – she had just put it down on the table – Graham, who had neither knocked at the door nor paused on his way through the hall, burst into the kitchen. He bounded towards her, pulled her to her feet, took her in his arms and held her as if he would never let her go. And in front of everyone.

'Oh Breda!' he cried. 'Oh Breda my love, you could have been killed.'

'Well she wasn't, was she?' Grandma Maguire said in flat calm. 'As far as I can see she hasn't a mark on her.'

No-one took any notice of her. There were more interesting things going on.

'You must *never*, *ever* do anything like that again,' Graham said fiercely. 'You must promise me.'

'Sure I will promise you,' Breda said. 'I'm not thinking it will happen to me again. Not twice in a lifetime.'

It was not easy to get the words out, for he was still squeezing the life out of her, but it was wonderful all the same.

'Shouldn't you go to bed?' Graham asked anxiously.

'That's what I've been telling her,' Josephine said.

'Are you trying to avoid taking me out for the evening, then? Is that the way of it, Graham Prince?'

'Of course it isn't, Breda love. You know that.'

'Then there's no way I'll go to bed. And if we don't get a move on we'll be late for everything. Give me fifteen minutes to get ready. You can wait right here.'

'Well, maybe an evening out will take your mind off things,' Josephine said doubtfully.

'What sort of gun was it?' Brendan asked when Breda had gone upstairs.

'I don't know,' Graham said. 'I don't know any of the details. I rushed here the minute I heard.'

By the time Breda came downstairs Graham had ordered a taxi to take them to the restaurant. 'No travelling on buses for you this evening, my girl,' he said.

The restaurant was something the like of which Breda had never seen, not that she had seen many: lighted candles on pink-clothed tables, shining silver, waiters immaculately attired. She was pleased she had dressed up, and sorry for Graham because he had had no time to go home and change out of his work suit.

'I don't care two hoots about that,' he said. 'It's enough to be here with you, safe and sound.'

If the food, when it appeared, lacked anything because of rationing, that was compensated for by its presentation, though in fact Breda would gladly have settled for baked beans on toast. She was floating on a cloud as pink as the

315

tablecloths, and it had nothing to do with the excitement of the afternoon and everything to do with Graham.

There was no longer any doubt in her mind about his feelings for her. Hadn't he made them as plain as plain, and in front of everyone? And that being so there was surely no longer any need to hold back her own.

They ate through the meal, not talking much. Breda scarcely tasted the food, which was a pity because it looked very expensive. That and the theatre would take every penny of Graham's ten pounds.

When they had finished eating and were waiting for coffee, Graham leaned across the table and took Breda's hand in his, stroking it gently.

'Oh Breda!' he said. 'What would I have done if . . .' He faltered.

'If what?'

'If anything had happened to you. Just as I've found you.'

'But it didn't,' Breda said gently. 'Grandma Maguire was right about that. I'm here, all in one piece and as good as new!'

'Breda,' he said, 'I love you. I didn't know how much until I nearly lost you.'

Her head was filled with light and music. 'Oh Graham!'

'I love you,' he repeated.

Neither of them noticed the waiter place the coffee on the table.

'And I love you,' she said. 'Oh, I do love you. But I think I always knew it, right from the first minute. Right from the bread-and-butter pudding. I shall never hate bread-and-butter pudding again!'

'What shall we do?' he asked.

'What do you mean, what shall we do?'

'I want to tell the world,' Graham said. 'I want to stand up on my chair right now and tell everyone in the restaurant "I love Breda O'Connor and she loves me!" '

'You're daft!' Breda said happily.

'I know. I want to shout it in the streets. I want to tell everyone in the store . . .'

The smile left his face. 'But we can't,' he said. 'We can't tell anyone, not even our families.'

'I think my family might have guessed,' Breda said. 'I mean, the way you behaved. So why can't we tell anyone?'

She didn't particularly want, as he did, to shout it to the world, but of one thing she was certain: she wanted to tell her family, the people she loved. She wanted to write to Mammy and tell her everything.

'I want us to be engaged,' Graham said. 'Oh Breda, I want us to be married, but that's impossible, perhaps for a long time.'

'I understand that,' Breda said. 'But we could be engaged.'

'And we will be,' he said. 'But we shall have to keep it secret.'

'Why?'

It was not that she particularly minded the secrecy, at least for a little while. She was happy to hug the knowledge to herself, to share it only with Graham, to glory in the warmth of it. But how could that last? It would surely leak out, especially if Graham behaved as he had in her aunt's kitchen earlier this evening.

'If anyone in the store knew, then Miss Opal would find out. I've already realized she gets to know everything in the end,' Graham said. 'Then she'd feel obliged to tell my father and the odds are he'd whisk me back to London.'

'Oh Graham! Oh no, I couldn't bear it,' Breda cried. 'Why would he do that?'

'Apart from all the stuff about us being too young – you not eighteen until next month, me not yet twenty-one –

I'm here to learn a job. Nose to the grindstone for the next year. He'd not allow anything to interfere with that. If it came to it he'd simply send me somewhere else. And I'm dependent on him, Breda, at least for the time being. Please say you understand, my darling!'

'I . . . I think I do.' A few minutes ago it had all seemed so simple. Now it no longer was.

'But I want us to be engaged,' he said. 'Breda, will you promise to marry me, even though we have to wait? But for now it will have to be a secret from everyone – and I do mean everyone. Could you bear that?'

She was being appealed to by the man she loved, and only she could answer his appeal. She felt a sudden surge of power, confidence, and with it the strength to do whatever he asked.

'I could and I would,' she answered. 'As long as we love each other, nothing else matters.'

'And you'd wait? As soon as I'm independent and have my own job we'll be married, I promise you.'

'Oh Graham,' Breda said. 'Sure, I'd wait for you! What else would I be doing?'

'You couldn't wear a ring,' Graham said. 'But I shall give you something to show we're engaged. I shall give you—' He thought for a moment. 'I shall give you a fine gold chain to wear round your neck. It wouldn't be seen by the rest of the world, but *we* would know. It would be special to us.'

I would like to show the rest of the world, Breda thought. I would be so proud. But if it wasn't possible . . . and wasn't there after all something special and exciting about holding such a wonderful secret?

'Yes, I'd like a gold chain,' she said.

'Then we'll choose one in Akersfield on our next half-day,' Graham promised. 'Oh Breda, I do love you. Don't ever forget that.'

'And don't forget that I love you,' Breda said.

He looked at his watch. 'We'll have to leave,' he said, 'or we'll miss the theatre.'

Afterwards, when she looked back over the evening, Breda could remember nothing of the play they had seen, except that they had enjoyed it and Graham had laughed a lot. Her own mind had been on all the things Graham had said to her in the restaurant; that he loved her, wanted to marry her, that they were engaged, however secretly.

In the taxi home he took her in his arms and kissed her lovingly. At number 52 he paid off the cab and stood with Breda in the gateway, then embraced her again.

'Oh Graham,' she said. 'How can I not tell Auntie Josie and the others? They'll only have to look at me!'

'We can't,' he said firmly. 'Not your family, not mine, not yet. But as soon as my training year is over, then I shall take you to meet my parents. I know they'll love you.'

But in the store next morning Breda was quickly made aware that people were looking at her for a reason which had nothing to do with the secret she carried. She was a heroine!

Even Miss Craven was not grudging in her praise, though it mostly took the form of self-recrimination. 'I blame myself *entirely*,' she said. 'If I had not left you in the lurch . . . '

'But you didn't,' Breda argued. 'You left me for a perfectly good reason. How were you to know what would happen?'

'Supposing the worst had occurred,' Miss Craven said. 'Just supposing . . . But no! It's too awful to contemplate. But if it had it would have been entirely my fault.'

'It would *not*,' Breda assured her. 'And in any case, it didn't. I'm hale and hearty, not one bit the worse for it.'

Miss Craven preferred not to be reassured. There was no stopping her. To everyone who visited the department – and there was a constant stream of people from every part of the store, all wanting to hear the tale at first hand and to see the site of the bullet – she said the same things.

'You would think she was the heroine of the story', Betty Hartley said, 'instead of you. Oh, you were so brave, Breda!'

Miss Craven's behaviour didn't worry Breda. She was so deeply happy inside herself that nothing else could possibly matter. *Her* only difficulty was in keeping her happiness hidden.

Halfway through the morning Miss Opal sent for her. 'Are you quite sure you feel well enough to be here?' she asked.

'Absolutely,' Breda said.

'Then first of all I wish to thank you for what you did,' Miss Opal said. 'You were resourceful and courageous. And secondly, I have to tell you that you must never, ever, attempt such a thing again. You were not only resourceful and courageous, you were extremely foolish and stupid. While I expect loyalty from my staff I do *not* expect, nor do I want, them to risk their lives for Opal's store. Do I make myself quite clear?'

'Quite clear, Miss Opal. I'm very sorry.'

Why should she be apologizing to me, Opal asked herself? And yet the reprimand had been in order.

'Then we'll go on to other matters,' she said. 'In the first place both the *Leasfield Courier* and the *Akersfield Record* have been on to me. They telephoned me at my home last night. They would like to interview you. I told them what I knew, but they want your side of the story, a first-hand account. Now you needn't do this if you don't want to, there's no compulsion, but if you do agree to it I suggest you see them here in my office.'

With great restraint she forbore to say that a column in the local papers would be better advertisement for Opal's

320

store than anything money could buy. She truly didn't want to put pressure on the girl.

'I don't mind at all,' Breda said.

She thought how wonderful it would be if she could, at the same time, announce her engagement – then swiftly put the thought from her.

'The next thing is that I am thinking of moving you from Fabrics,' Miss Opal said. 'Perhaps only temporarily. We shall see about that later.'

'Moving me? Have I not . . . ?'

'You have done well enough there, but it's coming up to Christmas. Fabrics will not be quite so busy from now until the January sales, but Display are desperate for help. There's the Christmas Grotto which must be opened on Saturday and is only half finished. There are Christmas displays to be mounted all over the store, not to mention the windows. You showed some flair in the matter of the royal wedding and I think you might be useful to Mr Sutcliffe.'

It might also help the girl to put yesterday's episode right out of her mind, Miss Opal had said, when broaching the subject to Mr Stokesly earlier, if she were to be physically distant from Fabrics. And wasn't that also, she thought privately, a good way of presenting it to Miss Craven, who would not like the move.

'So what do you think, Miss O'Connor?' she asked.

'I would like that very much,' Breda said. 'When . . . ?'

'Today. You're needed as soon as possible. We'll get the newspaper interview over, then I want you to see the doctor just to check that you're all right. After that I'll hand you over to Mr Sutcliffe.'

Everything moved with speed. Breda returned to Fabrics, wondering how to tell Miss Craven that she was to be moved on, only to find that Mr Stokesly had already done it. In any case, Miss Craven was still occupied in relating her version of the story.

The reporters came, wrote down Breda's statement, then took a photograph of her standing beside the till and a second one with her hand outstretched to indicate the bullet hole. The doctor saw her and pronounced her fit but foolish. Never, in so short a time, had she been called foolish so often!

She had a quick dinner of sausage and mash with Graham, but this time every seat at their table was taken, so there was no chance of conversation, other than to give him the news of her transfer.

Breda's first sight of Jim Sutcliffe was of him at the top of a ladder which leaned against the wall in the drab corridor which was to be transformed into the Magic Christmas Grotto. A second man held on to the foot of the ladder while a third, close by, hammered nails into sheets of plywood. Wood, cardboard, coloured paper, string, pots of paint and brushes were everywhere, in what appeared to be a glorious muddle.

'I'm looking for Mr Sutcliffe,' Breda told the young man at the foot of the ladder.

'Then look up,' the man said. 'That's him, up aloft! Young lady to see you, Jim!' he called out.

'Is she pretty?' Jim said, not turning his head.

The young man looked directly at Breda. 'Very!'

'Then I'll be right down!'

Back on the ground, Jim Sutcliffe was revealed as a short, round man with bright blue eyes and a balding head. What hair he still retained was as red as Breda's own.

'I'm Breda O'Connor. Miss Opal told me to report to you.'

He held out his hand. 'So you're the young heroine, then? We've never had a heroine working with us before, have we, lads? Come to that, we've never had a young lady. So no rough talk, no swearing. We shall have to mind our p's and q's!'

'Indeed you will not,' Breda said. 'Haven't I been brought up with three brothers, and not one of them minding what they said in front of me?'

'Well, that's a relief,' Jim Sutcliffe said. 'And I hope you're a hard worker as well as a heroine. There's a lot to be done in no time at all.'

'I'm more of a hard worker than a heroine,' Breda said. 'So if you'd like to tell me what to do, Mr Sutcliffe . . . '

'Well, for a start you can call me Jim – and this is Bill and that's Martin.' He waved a hand at the other men. 'We don't stand on ceremony here. We leave all that fancy stuff to the sales staff. Any road, you can start by sorting things out, getting a bit of order into this mess.'

'How do you want me to do it?' Breda asked.

'Nay lass, that's up to you,' Jim said. 'Just sort it out so that we can find what we want, *when* we want it, and no time wasted.'

It took all afternoon, but by the end she had reduced chaos to order. Paint pots were ranged together, like colours against like; fabrics and papers were separated and folded, cardboard stacked against a wall. Everything was visible and to hand.

Towards the end of the afternoon Graham came into the corridor, carrying two newspapers.

'May I speak to Miss O'Connor?' he asked Jim Sutcliffe.

'Make it sharp,' Jim said. 'She's busy.'

'I just wanted to show her the local papers,' Graham explained. 'I'll leave them with her.'

'Why don't we all have a look-see?' Jim suggested.

He took the newspapers from Graham and read out the headlines.

' "Shopgirl Heroine Foils Gunman!" And what does the *Courier* say? "Brave Breda Halts Hold-up!" Yes, that sounds like the *Courier*.' He handed the papers to Breda, then turned to Graham.

'Thank you, young man,' he said dismissively.

'Is he a friend of yours?' he asked Breda when Graham had left.

She hesitated. 'Yes. Yes, he is.' And so much more, she thought.

'You do know who he is – rather, who his father is?'

'Yes,' she admitted. 'Yes I do.'

'You want to be careful,' advised Jim. 'Mind what you say in front of the bosses.'

'But he's not a boss,' Breda objected.

'He's on the way,' Jim said. 'He's the boss class.'

'I'll be careful,' she promised. 'But I'm sure he's harmless. He seems quite nice.'

'He's not one of us, that's all,' Jim said. 'Now if you've finished the rest you can just sweep that bit of floor and we'll call it a day. You've done very well.'

'The only thing is,' Breda said to Josephine that evening, 'I hope he isn't going to use me just as a dogsbody, clearing up after the men. I'm sure that's not what Miss Opal intended.'

'You have to learn to walk before you can run,' Grandma Maguire said.

'I don't expect he will,' Josephine said. 'It's early days yet.'

'Not really,' Breda said. 'There's a mountain of work to get through before the Christmas rush starts.' But if he didn't let her take a real share, she thought, she would have to have it out with him. Politely, of course.

As it happened, she did not need to do that. The very next day he set her on to what she thought of as real work, though not before he had found her a pair of overalls and told her to change into them.

'I reckon yon black dress needn't see the light of day this side of Christmas. You'll not want to get it messed up wi' paint and glue.'

From then on it was all go, hard at it all day and sometimes late into the evenings. Following Jim's outlines, she painted designs on the walls, she draped materials, made giant cardboard flowers, blew up balloons, scattered artificial snow and silver dust. Bill and Martin constructed Father Christmas's cave, in which he supposedly dwelt with Mother Christmas, but which was in reality used to store spare light bulbs, assorted tools and the sixpenny parcels Father Christmas handed out to the children who came in droves.

Late on the Friday night before Saturday's official opening of the Grotto, at which Miss Opal herself would turn the magic key, they stood back and surveyed their finished work. It was indeed Wonderland, Breda thought. She had never seen anything like it and she felt a glow of pride and pleasure that she had had a part in it.

'Aye, it's not bad!' Jim Sutcliffe allowed. 'Not bad at all!'

Miss Opal, accompanied by George Soames, the General Manager, came to inspect it.

'You've excelled yourselves!' she said. 'I really do think it's the best we've ever had. Congratulations to all of you!'

'Shall I see you home?' Bill said to Breda when they were ready to leave. 'It's a bit late.'

'I'll be all right, thank you,' she said.

She couldn't tell him that Graham had wanted to wait to see her home, or at least meet her after she had left. It was she who had reminded Graham that if he did that kind of thing their secret would soon be out.

'Then if you're sure, I'll just see you onto the bus this end,' Bill offered.

The time flew by towards Christmas. Although the Grotto was finished, there were plenty of jobs to be done in the rest of the store: Christmas trees, fairy lights, paper chains, fancy lampshades – anything for which material could be found. The window displays were designed, and mostly carried out, by the small team of window dressers, but Breda was frequently called upon to help with the more mundane tasks: fetching and carrying, clearing up; sometimes, under supervision, cleaning and refurbishing the seasonal models – reindeer, robins, rabbits, snowmen – which were unearthed each year from the stockrooms.

In the Grotto, which drew great crowds, Joe Ackroyd, the Senior Commissionaire, made a splendid Father Christmas, and plump Miss Hargreaves, from Haberdashery, was given her usual temporary promotion to Mother Christmas, though it was well known that she and Joe Ackroyd did not get on. It was a matter of temperature as well as temperament. While he sweated under his voluminous robes and long white beard, she felt the cold.

'The draught in this place is cruel,' she complained to Breda, who had been sent to scatter fresh snow and glitter before the Grotto opened for the day. 'Don't anyone be surprised if I go down with pneumonia!'

Influenza, not pneumonia, laid her low in the last week before Christmas, at a point when the queues for the Grotto were at their longest and everyone in the store was occupied in taking money and tying up parcels.

'I shall have to have someone,' Joe Ackroyd said to Miss Opal when she made her daily visit. 'I can't be expected to sell the tickets, talk to the children, organize the parcels and hand them out.'

'Of course you can't!' Miss Opal agreed.

Thus it was that Breda found herself wearing a red robe which would have gone around her twice and a fur-trimmed red hood which constantly fell over her eyes.

Miss Opal's lips twitched when she saw Breda at work next day. 'This won't do at all, Miss O'Connor,' she said. 'Someone in the workrooms must alter it to fit, at once. Otherwise you'll trip over yourself and break a leg!'

It was a week in which Breda scarcely saw Graham. There was no time for dinner in the canteen; a snatched sandwich and a cup of tea behind the scenes was all that could be managed. In the evenings she was dead tired and, she reckoned, dull company.

Graham was to go home to his family for Christmas, travelling on the morning of Christmas Eve.

'You've got to come out with me the night before,' he said. 'Even if we only have a coffee. I shan't see you for the best part of a week!' He had permission to be away until the Monday after Christmas.

'I'll miss you so much!' Breda said.

Would he forget her in his home in Surrey, with his family, his friends, parties, outings? How could he help but compare it all to her family in Akersfield?

'I shall miss you, my love,' Graham said. 'Don't think I won't. But this time next year it will be different. Who's to say I won't be taking you home to meet my family?'

'Or me taking you to Ireland, to meet mine,' Breda said. 'Oh Graham, it seems so far ahead, such a long time.'

'It will pass,' Graham said.

Eighteen

Graham's four-day absence over Christmas seemed to Breda more like four months at times. It was not that there wasn't a great deal to be done. Christmas in Waterloo Terrace was a busy time and from the moment she arrived home from work on Christmas Eve she was bang in the middle of the activity. The entire Maguire family was expected for Christmas dinner.

'How in the world will you seat everyone?' she asked her aunt.

'Not easily,' Josephine admitted. 'But we'll manage. We've done it before and I don't doubt we'll do it again. We shall have two sittings, the children first and then the grown-ups. Now if you will get on with trimming the tree it will be a great help. I never like to do the tree before Christmas Eve. It doesn't seem right.'

'Now there I agree with you,' Grandma Maguire said. 'There are some as put the tree in the window the minute Gunpowder Plot night is over and don't take it down until nigh on Easter.'

'I'm glad we agree,' Josephine said mildly. 'I'll hang on to that over the Christmas holiday,' she whispered to Breda.

'What's that?' Grandma Maguire demanded. 'Speak up! I can't hear you!'

'I said it was going to be a nice holiday!'

'Too much fuss,' Grandma said. 'Too much spoiling of the children.' Why was it the children got all the spoiling?

'I'm sure you'll get your share of attention,' Josephine said.

At five o'clock on Christmas afternoon the telephone rang. The meal was over, the washing-up done. Those children who had not been put to sleep upstairs were playing with their new toys. Grandma was in the Land of Nod, snoring gently, and Brendan was clearly about to follow suit. Josephine went into the hall to answer the phone.

It's Graham, Breda thought at once. At the back of every activity of the day he had been in her mind. What was he doing? Who was he seeing? Was he missing her? She followed her aunt into the hall, certain that the call must be for her.

'Molly!' Josephine cried. She turned to Breda. 'It's your Mammy!'

The first slight pang of disappointment in Breda's heart was followed by a rush of pleasure. She waited impatiently while Josephine continued the conversation with her mother. It could go on for ever. She was giving the details of every member of her large family.

'Maureen's well. Looking like the side of a house and she'll be glad when the baby comes. Betty is expecting again. June she reckons. Tony couldn't get leave for Christmas.' Josephine didn't quite believe that. She reckoned he had other fish to fry, but she would never say so.

A loud sigh from Breda, standing at her shoulder, brought her back to earth. 'I'd better hand you over to Breda before she bursts!' she said to her sister.

In the next few minutes Breda caught up with the news of her own family in Ireland. Kathleen was well, and had been home for a two-day visit before Christmas. Kieran was settling into his parish in County Waterford. The twins had sent Christmas cards and presents from New York.

Moira and Barry were spending Christmas at home in Dublin, and no, there was no sign of another baby there.

'And what about you, Mammy?' Breda asked. 'And Luke?' she added. When she thought about Luke O'Reilly these days she wondered what it was she had had against him.

'We're both well,' Molly said. 'And happy. And you, *álainna*? Are you happy?'

'I am so,' Breda said. She longed with all her heart to tell Mammy about Graham but hadn't she promised Graham she would not do so, not yet? 'All the same, I miss you, Mammy.'

'And I miss you,' Molly said. It was wrong, she knew, to favour one child over another, and she would never admit to it out loud, but it was Kieran and Breda she missed the most.

Christmas Day being on a Thursday, Opal's store reopened on the Saturday. Even though it might not be a busy day for customers there was plenty for Breda to do, for wasn't the big January sale starting the following week and all the windows to change and sale tickets and banners to prepare? Miss Craven was miffed that Breda was kept on in Display.

'I thought you would have been sent back to Fabrics,' she complained. 'We shall be quite busy here in the sale. But of course once you get in with the boss class it's all very different!'

It had not occurred to Breda that she would ever go back to Fabrics, but this was not the time to say so. In any case, she was so happy at the thought of Graham's return on Monday that she felt charitable even to the Miss Cravens of the world. Poor Miss Craven, she thought. I have so much to look forward to, and what has she?

On Wednesday, New Year's Eve, she and Graham were to go into Akersfield to choose the gold chain he had promised. It had been impossible to do so before Christmas because Breda had had to work on most of her half-days. She rushed through her dinner at home, telling her aunt that she had some shopping to do in the town. She had arranged to meet Graham outside the railway station and he was waiting there when she arrived, standing on the very spot from which she had surveyed Akersfield on that first day.

'I thought it looked dreadful,' she told Graham now. 'I thought I would never settle here. Now I quite like it.'

'I know,' Graham said. 'It was the same with me. I didn't want to come. Now I shan't want to leave.'

A slight chill went through Breda at his last words. It was inevitable that he would leave. Would she go with him? Would he be forced to leave her behind? It was all so uncertain.

'What shall we do first?' he asked. 'Have something to eat, or choose the chain?'

'The chain,' Breda said. She could hardly wait.

He had obviously, and unknown to her, sought out the jewellers because he led her without hesitation to a small, but select-looking, shop in the middle of the town.

'We would like to look at some neck chains,' Graham said to the assistant.

There were several to choose from. 'What about this?' Graham suggested. He pointed to one from which hung a gold cross. 'It seems just the thing!'

'No,' Breda said. 'Not that one.'

In the end she chose a fine gold chain from which hung a small gold heart.

'It's lovely,' Graham said. 'Are you quite sure?'

'Quite sure,' Breda said. 'I love it. It's exactly what I want.'

Graham paid for it, then put the small box in his coat pocket.

They left the shop, and found a small café nearby.

'I'm starving,' Breda said as they sat down. She picked up the menu and began to read.

'Me too,' Graham agreed. 'But there's something more important before we order.'

He took the chain from its box, then came and stood behind her.

'Unbutton your coat,' he said. 'Take off your scarf. I want to put it on myself.'

With trembling and somewhat clumsy fingers, for the clasp was small and difficult to grasp, he fastened the chain. Then he placed his hands on Breda's shoulders and swiftly dropped a kiss on the nape of her neck before moving around to sit opposite to her. She put up her hand and held the chain, with the small gold heart, against her skin.

'I shall never take it off!' she said. 'Never, as long as I live.'

'I wondered why you didn't choose the one with the cross,' Graham said.

She hesitated fractionally. 'It's to do with the fact that . . . well, that I'm a Catholic and you're not. I don't even know what you are – if anything. So I didn't want anything religious. I don't want religion to come between us. We *shall* have to discuss it, but not now.'

'Nothing will come between us,' Graham promised. 'And before this time next year I shall be putting a ring on your finger for all the world to see.'

He had thought long and hard while he had been at home over Christmas, missing Breda as much as she missed him, whether he would come out into the open and tell his parents about her. It had been a difficult decision not to do so, but it had been the right one for now, he thought.

'Nineteen forty-eight will be *our* year,' he said. 'And it starts tomorrow.'

'Happy New Year, my love!' Breda said.

'Happy New Life!' he said.

'Where will we be at the end of the year?' Breda wondered out loud.

'Married, I hope,' Graham said.

'The time can't pass too quickly for me,' Breda said. 'I just wonder . . . '

'What?'

'When we're married, where will we live? Will it be in London?'

'Would you do that?'

'I'd live wherever you chose to live. In a tent in the Sahara Desert if that was it.'

Graham laughed. 'I hope it won't come to that!'

There were parts of the year which did pass quickly. These were the times when Breda and Graham managed to be alone; then, perversely, the hours flew by. But almost from the beginning of the year these times were, by mutual consent, fewer than they had been. They had made the decision that they must not be seen so much together, but when they were not together, then the time dragged.

They worked out ways they could be with each other, even though in the presence of other people, and to this end they joined several of the clubs which abounded in Opal's store. There was the Rambling Club, whose members, in almost any weather, took off every other Sunday throughout the year. With them Breda and Graham tramped, more than once, over the moors to Hebghyll – though the outings were never as sweet as that first occasion when they had done it alone. They took the train to Grassington and walked by the river, or climbed the fells in Wharfedale. They took the bus to Harrogate and rambled in Nidderdale. That first winter they also joined Opal's Dramatic Society, and in the summer they became members of the Art Club and went out sketching, or painting in water colours.

Given that they had committed themselves to doing things when other people were present, this last was the activity Graham knew he would enjoy most.

'I'm happy to tag along,' Breda said, 'but I can't paint for toffee.'

'That's not strictly true,' Graham said. 'You did some nice stuff in the Christmas Grotto.'

'Following Jim Sutcliffe's outlines! I doubt I can draw a straight line.'

'That's what people say,' Graham told her. 'But you don't have to. Anyway there are no straight lines in nature. Paint what you *see*, as *you* see it – never what you think you ought to see.'

Then standing behind him on the first occasion he had painted a water colour of the river near Bolton Abbey, Breda recognized that here was real talent. The strength and exuberance of his work took her breath away: bold lines, striking colours; nothing wishy-washy, which was rather what she'd expected of a water colour.

'It's wonderful!' she said. 'I really had no idea . . . '

'You shouldn't be so surprised,' Graham said. 'I told you it was what I wanted to do for a living – though I dare say it wouldn't be much of one.'

'Then perhaps it's what you *should* do,' Breda said thoughtfully. 'Perhaps you shouldn't be in the retail trade at all.'

What would that do to them, she wondered? Where would it leave her? It was true what he said: unless he was lucky there wouldn't be much of a living in it. Would he be able to keep a wife?

'I could always go out to work and be the breadwinner,' she offered, thinking out loud.

He shook his head. 'I wouldn't want that.'

He cleaned his brushes and packed away his gear, then he held up the painting and studied it critically. He was not satisfied, he would never be satisfied, but he was not too disappointed.

'This is for you – if you like it,' he said.

'Oh Graham! Of course I like it! But I have a better idea.'

She had decided, it had taken only seconds, that whether he was a retailer or whether he was a painter, and even if, in the latter case, she had to scrub floors to keep them both, she would stay with him, she would never let him go.

'So what's your idea? Are you thinking I could sell it?'

'Oh I dare say you could. But that's not what I have in mind. No. You must keep it, and we'll hang it on the wall in our very first home!'

It was at times like this, when he wanted to take her in his arms and kiss her there and then, that he cursed the presence of the rest of the group; but there was no-one standing very close, and he stroked her arm.

Not all their time, however, was spent with others. They reserved the right to go occasionally for walks alone, or to the cinema, or for a cheap meal, and on these occasions he insisted on calling for her at Waterloo Terrace.

Josephine was never for a moment deceived by the casualness of their manner towards each other when he came to the house.

'If ever I saw anyone in love,' she said to Brendan in the privacy of their bedroom, 'it's those two. They might hide it from others but not from me. And I worry about it.'

'Leave them be,' Brendan said. 'Let them work it out for themselves.'

'It *won't* work out,' Josephine said. 'That's just the problem.'

'Leave it be!' Brendan repeated. He had grown fond of Breda. She had become like another, much younger, daughter.

Josephine could not leave it be. It nagged at her. As the weeks went by she worried and fretted until in the end she knew she must speak to Breda. She owed that much to her sister Molly. Wasn't she, so to speak, in a mother's place?

She chose a time when Breda had just come in from an evening out with Graham, when Grandma Maguire was tucked up in bed and Brendan had gone to the Cow and Calf.

'Did you have a nice time, love?' she asked.

'Very nice, thank you. It was a good picture – and there was Ronald Colman in the newsreel. He's on a visit to England.'

'Ronald Colman!' Josephine cried. 'Oh, I should like to have seen him! He only has to speak to send shivers down my spine!'

'Auntie Josie, you are a dark horse!' Breda said, laughing. 'I never knew you had a crush on Ronald Colman!'

'We all have our dreams,' Josephine said. 'But that's as may be.' The thought of her film idol had almost, but not quite, put her off what she'd firmly intended to say. 'Though never mind that just now. I want a word with you, love, before Brendan comes barging in.'

Breda looked up at the change in her aunt's voice. 'Is something wrong? Have I done something?'

'Bless you, no!' Josephine said. 'At least . . . ' She hoped fervently that she was right about that. 'Well, I'll come straight out with it. It's about you and Graham.'

'What about us?' Breda asked. She hardly needed to ask. She could guess what was coming. She had seen it in her aunt's face on more than one occasion when Graham had

336

called for her, and had been relieved that nothing had been said.

'It's not that I've got anything against him, love. Don't think that,' Josephine said. 'He's a nice young man. We all like him. Even Grandma likes him, which is saying something.'

'But . . . ' Breda said. 'I *know* you're going to say "but".'

'Yes I am. I'm worried that you're getting too involved with him, getting to care about him a bit too much, *and* him about you.'

If only you knew, Breda thought. If only I could tell you. More than anything else she hated keeping her feelings from her aunt, being with her every day and saying nothing.

'You see, Breda love, it would never work out, not between you and Graham.'

'Why wouldn't it work out . . . I mean, just supposing there was something to work out?'

'Well, two things – and both very important. In the first place, he's not a Catholic. A good Catholic girl like you couldn't think of going outside the Church . . .'

'I would never leave the Church,' Breda interrupted.

'That's not what I mean. You know it isn't. And then there's another thing. He's not our class, love. We're good solid working class, and nothing to be ashamed of in that. He's different.'

'His grandfather built up the business from nothing,' Breda said. 'Graham told me. So did Miss Opal, come to that, and you know how much you admire her.'

'It's not the same, is it?' Josephine said. 'Graham was born into a well-off family. He's never known anything else. He's been to public school. Everything in his life has been different from yours. His whole background.'

337

'And you mean I couldn't rise to that?'

'Of course I don't! To my mind you could rise to anything. You have it in you. But also . . . well, I'm sure you know what I mean, Breda. I don't want you to make it harder for yourself. I'm not putting it very well, though I'm sure you understand.'

'I do,' Breda admitted. 'But you needn't worry, Auntie Josie. Honestly you needn't. I'm not on the point of marrying Graham, and if I were you'd be the first to know. I'll take notice of what you say, but you just don't need to worry.'

Brendan's key in the lock put an end to their conversation.

'Did Betty call?' Breda asked her aunt as her uncle walked into the kitchen. 'How was she?'

'She seemed a bit better,' Josephine said. 'She'll be glad when the day comes. It can't be long now.'

Indeed it was not. The very next week Betty had her baby, a son. Maureen's son was three months old now, and getting bigger by the minute.

'They'll grow up together,' Josephine said happily. She could never have too many grandchildren to knit for and to love.

In July Graham had his twenty-first birthday. Knowing it was coming, Breda had thought he might go home for a weekend to celebrate it with his family.

'I'm not going to do that,' Graham said. 'And my father agrees with me. He doesn't want me to break into my training.'

'Not even for a weekend?' What a stern father he must be, Breda thought.

'He thinks it would be better if we wait until I've finished here and then we can celebrate it in more style than we could in a hurried weekend.'

Breda felt a chill when Graham spoke of the end of his training, not that he had to mention it to remind her. She was aware all the time now that it was nearing the end, only two more months to go. She tried to banish it from her thoughts. She had none of Graham's certainty that things would turn out right for them. There were too many difficulties in the way.

'And what would *you* rather do?' she asked Graham.

'If my birthday signifies anything,' he said, 'I want to spend it with you. What else do you think? I wouldn't go home for it unless I could take you. As to what we might do – well, you can choose. I've been saving up, so we could do something special.'

Breda had no hesitation. 'If the money will run to it, I'd like us to go to the same restaurant we went to when you gave me my gold chain.'

'Then that's exactly what we'll do. And the theatre afterwards if there's something worth seeing.'

In the restaurant they talked about the future – their future, not the world's, which seemed to be in turmoil everywhere, just their own.

'We shall soon have waited a year,' Graham said. 'I'm not prepared to go beyond that. It's been necessary to do it, but the moment the time comes I want to be free of this hole-in-the-corner business.'

'Me too,' Breda said.

'Oh Breda, I want you to be all mine. It isn't easy going on like this. Every time I see you I want to make love to you. You understand that, don't you?'

He stretched his hand across the table and took hers, looking at her intently. She had no idea, he thought, how desirable she was, how powerful her sexuality, what she did to him. She was less conscious of her attractions than anyone he had ever met.

'Indeed I understand,' she said. 'Sure, 'tis not easy for me, either. Don't I have the same feelings and longings? Don't you believe 'tis different for women. That's not true.'

'Well then . . . ?'

Breda shook her head. 'Not before we're married, my darling. Oh, 'tis not that I'd ever try to hold you to ransom or blackmail you into marriage. 'Tis just that . . . ' She broke off.

'It's the way you've been brought up.'

'Perhaps. Or just the way I am. I'm sorry.'

'No need to be sorry,' Graham said. 'I love you for the way you are, so I'm not complaining. But we'll be married the first possible minute.'

'And proud I'll be,' Breda said.

Two weeks later Miss Opal sent for Graham.

The summons did not surprise him. He had not seen her to speak to for several weeks now, except at a distance in her perambulations around the store, but he was sure her hand was behind his moves from department to department, and now, finally, into the office with its Accounts and Personnel sections.

There had been no more invitations to tea, though he had neither expected nor wanted them. It was better, and especially since he had now made friends in the store and seemed to have overcome the earlier suspicions of him as a member of the boss class, to keep his distance from her. Since she was a wise woman she had no doubt worked this out for herself.

But some day soon, he had realized, she would want to talk to him about his future, about where he stood, and what report she would give to his father. He had no doubt that this request to be in her office at ten o'clock tomorrow morning was it.

Breda was nervous about the interview.

'You don't need to be,' Graham said. 'Isn't everything a step nearer to what *we* want, you and me? Anyway, I've made up my mind about one thing.'

'What's that?'

'I'm going to tell her about you and me – though only if you agree. But please say you do. It's the first step and I want to take it.'

'Oh Graham!' Breda said. 'I don't know! Supposing she sacks me on the spot? You said she wouldn't keep us both in the store if we were engaged, and it wouldn't be *you* she'd ask to leave.'

'Nor you,' Graham said. 'I shall give her the news in confidence. I'm not telling the world, much as I'd like to. I'm sure she'll not break that confidence. Anyway, if she did ask you to go, I'd simply walk out with you. I don't know where, but we'd find something. I just want her to know how the land lies before she starts talking to my father. And who knows, she might be on our side?'

So now Miss Opal sat behind the desk in her tower office, a room perched on the top of the Victorian building as if it were an afterthought, and Graham sat opposite her.

'I expect you know why I've asked you to come,' she said. 'I thought it was now time we had some sort of assessment of how you've done; what *you* thought of it and what *I* thought of it, where we go from here. So tell me, how have the last eleven months seemed to you?'

'I've learned a lot,' he said. 'I know I was as green as grass when I came here. All I'd ever done in Prince and Harper was to help behind the scenes a bit in the school holidays. Playing at it, really. Mostly getting in the way, I suspect.'

'And having gone through most of the departments here,' Miss Opal said, 'have you decided which bit of store life you like best?'

'I have. I think I like the behind-the-scenes stuff. The organization, the financial side, the way things work.'

'You like the broad view?'

'I suppose that's it,' Graham said.

'Well, so do I. But you have to combine that with keeping an eye on the detail. Detail is what the customers notice, and without them you'd be closed down in no time at all.'

She shuffled through a pile of papers on her desk. 'I have a report from every department you've worked in – well, you didn't suppose I wouldn't have, did you? They are all reasonably good but it seems, as you've indicated yourself, that your strengths lie on the financial side, and in organization. What I'd appreciate is a written report from you about how you found things. I want something I can show your father. It will be a help to him when he's placing you in Prince and Harper. Will you do that for me? It needn't be long.'

'I will,' Graham promised.

'Do you feel ready to go into your father's store?' Miss Opal asked.

Graham hesitated. 'I dare say my father told you I didn't want to go into the retail business. I wanted to be a painter.'

'He did tell me. It was a familiar story to me. I have a son in the same situation, except that he flatly refused to come into Opal's. And he was right, as it happens. He's earning a modest living as a painter in London and he's a very happy man, though I don't think your father would thank me for saying this! Anyway, are you still of the same mind?'

'Not quite,' Graham said. 'Things have changed in the last year.'

'Oh! In what way?'

'There's something I want to tell you, Miss Opal. I came in here determined to tell you, but it has to be in confidence.'

'I see. Or rather, I don't. I'll do my best, unless it's something I have to tell your father. In any case, whatever it is, it's best for *you* to tell him, not me.'

'I'm engaged to be married!'

She looked hard at him, trying not to show her feelings. She didn't need to ask to whom. She had observed the attraction between him and the red-haired Irish girl months ago, but since they had taken to going around with a crowd, joining in things, she had found it easier to put it out of her mind.

'You don't want to know who?' Graham asked.

'I dare say I can guess! It's Miss O'Connor, isn't it?'

'Yes.'

'Are you wise?'

'I think so. I dare say it's store policy, but I hope you won't dismiss her because we're engaged. If you do, Miss Opal, I have to say that I would go too!'

She raised her eyebrows. The beginnings of a smile caught the corners of her mouth. He looked suddenly so young, so defiant. She remembered Daniel looking exactly like this.

'No-one knows except you,' Graham said quickly. 'Nor will they, just yet.'

'Well, I hadn't got anywhere near to thinking of dismissals,' Miss Opal said. 'And I have to say that if I had to choose it wouldn't be Miss O'Connor I'd want to lose. She's far too valuable. She's done some very good work in Display, and will do more. No, Graham, if I had to lose one of you, I'm afraid it would be you!'

Graham stared at her open-mouthed, and then, suddenly, a broad smile spread over his face. 'Then that's all right!' he said.

'For the time being,' Miss Opal agreed. 'But what am I to tell your father?'

'Nothing, yet!'

'And how does this alter your attitude to going into the retail trade – if that's what you're thinking?'

'Because I have to earn some money,' Graham said. 'I can't wait to be married until I can make a living as a painter. As for my father, I intend to tell him about Breda as soon as my year here is up, as soon as I see him. I don't intend to wait after that.'

Miss Opal picked up a letter from her desk. 'Then, my dear Graham, you won't have to wait long! Your father's coming here tomorrow. He has a business meeting in Leeds. That was one of the things I had to tell you. I thought you might have heard from him yourself.'

There was a knock at the door and George Soames put his head inside the room. 'I'm sorry,' he said. 'I didn't realize you were engaged.'

'Come in,' Opal said. 'Mr Prince is just going. Have you brought me good news?'

'I reckon so,' George Soames said.

'Please excuse me,' Opal said to Graham. 'I'll speak to you later about your father's visit.'

Nineteen

When Graham reached his lodgings that evening his landlady, Mrs Hartopp, handed him a letter.

'It came not ten minutes after you'd left this morning,' she told him.

She hovered, hoping to hear who it was from and what it was about. He was a young man who didn't receive many letters, and since she scarcely had any at all it was quite an event for the postman to call.

Graham quickly put her out of her misery. 'It's from my father. He has a meeting in Leeds today, so he's coming to Opal's tomorrow morning to see me.'

'Oh, well then! That'll be nice for you,' she said.

Will it, Graham wondered? He doubted it, in the circumstances.

'So I dare say you'll not be in to your dinner?'

He almost always came home to his dinner on early closing day and she tried to give him something nice, something a bit special.

'I don't suppose I shall,' Graham agreed.

'Well it's a pity, because the butcher's promised me a nice bit of kidney and I was going to make you one of my steak-and-kidney puddings. But there you go, I expect you'll be living it up with dinner at the King's Hotel!'

If his meeting with his father went badly, Graham thought, he might not get any dinner at all. His father was capable of simply catching the next train back to London. He was not a man who liked to be crossed.

When Graham had left Miss Opal's office earlier in the day he had sought out Breda.

'Can you come for a coffee and a sandwich with me at lunch time?' he asked her. 'Not the canteen today. I want to talk to you.'

She scarcely tasted her sandwich while he described what had taken place.

'But I'm glad you told her,' she said. 'About us, I mean. I'm glad to have that bit out of the way, and pleased I'm not going to be sacked!'

'So tomorrow you'll meet my father,' Graham said.

'Oh Graham! Oh Graham, I'm so nervous! Do you think we should – just yet, I mean?'

'Of course we should. There's no point in putting it off. And you mustn't be nervous. He can't eat you. And you can hardly marry me without meeting my family, now can you?'

'I wish I could,' Breda said. 'Sure, I wish there was no-one to think about except you and me. Supposing he doesn't like me?'

'Of course he'll like you!' He spoke with more confidence than he felt, not because of Breda, but because his father was an awkward man, unpredictable.

'Well there's one thing certain,' Breda said. 'You've told Miss Opal, tomorrow aren't you going to tell your father, so I absolutely must tell Auntie Josie. Hasn't it been the most terrible thing for me, keeping it from her all this time?'

'I know. Of course you must.'

'And tonight. I'm not going to meet your father and leave Auntie Josie in the dark.'

'Shall I come with you, and we'll do it together?'

'No. I'll be best alone, so.' She knew her aunt would voice objections. She didn't want Graham to hear them.

'She can't stop you, you know,' Graham said. 'Remember that. Nobody can stop us being engaged.'

'Don't I know that? But she's been kind to me and I don't look forward to upsetting her.'

Wasn't it lucky, Breda thought, back at Waterloo Terrace, eating her tea, that for once there was only her aunt and uncle at the table, no other member of the family. Grandma Maguire had been collected to take part in a church outing to Harrogate by coach, and wouldn't be back for another hour or more.

'Have another scone, Breda love,' Josephine said. 'You're not eating much.'

'I'm not very hungry,' Breda said.

'Are you not well?' Josephine enquired. 'You usually whip right through my scones.'

' 'Tis not that. 'Tis . . . ' Breda faltered, then took a deep breath and came out with it. 'Graham and I are engaged to be married!'

Brendan all but choked on the piece of scone he had just bitten off. Josephine, raising a cup of tea to her lips, put it down again on the table. They stared at Breda. Brendan was the first to recover. 'Engaged, is it? So aren't you the dark horse, then – but congratulations, love!'

'What are you saying, Brendan?' Josephine interrupted sharply.

'I'm saying congratulations! Hasn't the girl told us she's engaged to be married? What else would I be saying?'

'If your wits hadn't deserted you for the moment you'd be telling her it was highly unsuitable. You'd be giving her some fatherly advice, as she hasn't got a father of her own to do so.'

Brendan looked at his wife in astonishment. 'Unsuitable? You like Graham! We all like the lad.'

'Of course we do. That's not the point – and our Breda knows it's not. We've discussed this before. And didn't you . . . ' She turned to Breda and spoke accusingly.

'Didn't you tell me there was nothing in it? You knew that wasn't the truth, didn't you?'

'Hold on, Josie!' Brendan remonstrated. 'Don't be so fierce with the girl. What's got into you?'

'Worry's got into me, that's what,' Josephine snapped.

'Auntie Josie, I'm sorry!' Breda said. 'I didn't mean to deceive you, I didn't want to, ever. But I couldn't tell you because of Graham's father, and he might have taken Graham away, and now he's coming tomorrow and I've got to meet him and I'm so scared, and if you're going to be cross with me I just don't know what I'm going to do except that I'll never give up Graham, nor he me, no matter what anyone says! We love each other and that's all there is to it!'

She ran out of breath. She had known it wouldn't be easy but she hadn't thought it would be quite so awful.

Josephine stretched across the table and took her hand. 'I'm sorry I was so sharp with you, love, but you're in my care. And you see, that *isn't* all there is to it. He's not a Catholic and he's not your class, nor you his. That's a lot of trouble to take on your shoulders.'

'We can take it,' Breda said firmly. 'We love each other. It won't be the first mixed marriage in the world and 'tis unlikely to be the last. We'll work it out. And I know I'm not in his class . . . '

'There's no need to let that worry you,' Brendan broke in. 'You'll manage that all right. You have it in you, and don't let your aunt or anyone else tell you otherwise. I'll say here and now, I don't agree with your aunt on any of this. I'm on your side!'

Who would have supposed, Breda thought, a few months ago, that Uncle Brendan would be on my side in anything? Or that Auntie Josie would be against me?

'We're not taking sides,' Josephine said. 'And I've said my say. You know my views, and I can't do any less than give them. That much is my duty. But in the end it's your choice, Breda, and you'll be the one who has to abide by it!'

'And I will!' Breda said. 'But please don't be against me, Auntie. I need your support. Haven't I got to meet Graham's father tomorrow?'

Sitting in the train on the short journey from Leeds to Leasfield, Henry Prince thought about the meeting he was to have with Opal Carson, and then afterwards with his son. He had known Opal a long time; she was a remarkable woman. How unusual it was that a store so far from London, so far from the centre of things, should be known and respected throughout the retail fashion trade; and even more so that its owner – who had not inherited her business as he had Prince and Harper – was a woman in a man's world? He took off his hat to her. There was no-one he would choose above Opal to train his son in the groundwork. Opal's was a model of how a store should be run.

About his son he was less sure. Graham had gone to Opal's under protest. All *he* had wanted was to go to the Slade and paint. If I'd offered to support him in that, which I could well have done, Henry Prince thought, he'd never have looked at the retail trade. He'd have been lost to me, we'd have been in two different worlds, and I don't want that.

From the railway station he walked the mile to Opal's store. He needed the exercise, but apart from that he had always made a practice of walking through the streets around his own store. You learned more that way than sitting in the back of a taxi cab. He had not been to Opal's since the beginning of the war. The buildings looked shabbier, in need of a lick of paint, some of them, but there was none of the bomb damage which had so changed the area around his own store.

He reached the main door, but before going in he walked around the windows, studying the displays. Very good, he thought. Not too far short of London standards.

Ten minutes later he was being shown into Opal's office. She came from behind her desk and held out both hands to him. He thought how attractive she looked. Her black hair was beginning to grey at the sides, but her fresh skin and her trim figure were those of a woman fifteen years younger than he knew her to be.

'My, but it's good to see you, Henry! How are you? Would you like some coffee?' He was putting on weight, she thought. But with his height, he could carry it.

'I'm very well,' he said. 'I won't have coffee just yet. I had a good north-country breakfast at the hotel.'

'And how is Miriam? It's a long time since I saw her. And the family?'

'All well. And yours?'

'Also all well. Daniel, as you know, is in London. Emmeline has just gone off to her very first Guide camp.'

'And Edgar?'

'Fine. His company is building up again. Insurance took a knock in the war, but he's picking up now.'

It had taken the threat of war to bring her husband back from Canada to her, but their relationship had quickly found itself again.

'So,' Opal said. 'Would you like Graham to join us right away?'

'No,' Henry said. 'I'd like to hear from you first. I want to know what you think of him – and you can be as frank as you like. It's no secret that he didn't want to come here.'

350

She picked up a file from her desk and took a chair next to Henry Prince. 'I have reports from all the different parts of the store he's worked in. I made sure he had as much variety as possible. There isn't one of them which doesn't speak well of him. Aside from being hard-working, which he is, he has the knack of getting on well with people.'

Henry took the file from her and began to read through it. 'Yes,' he said eventually, 'it's quite satisfactory.'

'More than satisfactory,' Opal said. 'You can be proud of him.'

'The big question is, is he going to be right for the job I have in mind for him? You know that one day he'll have to take over a big part of the running of Prince and Harper. I don't intend to work until I drop.'

'Oh, he's capable enough,' Opal said quickly. 'He's especially interested in the organization and financial side. But whether . . . ' She hesitated.

'Yes?'

'Whether he *wants* to do it is another matter. That's something you'll have to ask him yourself. I haven't done so. That's not my province.'

Nor was it her job to tell Henry Prince about his son's engagement to Breda O'Connor. That was Graham's task and she didn't envy him one bit. She liked Henry Prince, and got on well with him, but he was a hard man, a man who liked his own way. He was not a man she would like to cross. And since Graham had shown determination bordering on obstinacy in the matter of Breda, there was going to be a battle.

'But what do you think? You must have some idea!'

Opal shook her head. She was not to be drawn. 'If you've finished looking at the reports, why don't I send for Graham?'

When Graham came into the room Henry Prince rose to his feet and the two men shook hands formally. What a pity, Opal thought, that they can't get closer. If Graham were my son and I hadn't seen him for several months I'd put my arms around him. That was the difference between women and men, and the men were the losers, though she felt sure that Graham was of a warmer nature than his father.

'I'll leave you to it, then,' Opal said. 'If you want me, give my secretary a buzz. She'll know where to find me.' She was glad to be out of the way for the next half-hour.

'Unless you and Graham want to lunch alone, Henry,' she added, 'I hope you'll let me give you lunch. I won't subject you to the canteen. They do a very good meal at the King's Hotel.'

'Well now,' Henry said when Opal had left them, 'how have you been getting on?' He pointed to the file on Opal's desk. 'I've been through that. It all seems quite satisfactory. And Opal's pleased with you.'

'I'm glad,' Graham said. He had one thing only on his mind, and until he had come out with it he knew he could find no other conversation.

'So only a week or two before you finish here,' Henry said. 'Are you ready to start in Prince and Harper?'

'It's not quite so simple,' Graham said.

'Why not? It seems simple enough to me. We can discuss where you'd want to start, which department. And if you want a bit of a holiday before you begin, then that's all right. I know that's what your mother has in mind. I can't spare the time, but you could take off with her for a few days.'

He was willing to give and take a bit, but after that he wanted no shilly-shallying.

'Before we go into that, Father, there's something I have to say to you.'

Henry Prince felt a stab of annoyance, not only at Graham's words, but at the determination in his voice. They were in for another argument. He knew what the boy was going to say. He was going to tell him he still didn't want to go into the business, he still wanted to be a painter.

It was a mad idea, Henry thought, shifting in his chair. He had no time for it, but since Graham had compromised by doing the year's training, he supposed they'd have to discuss it. He sighed. He would appeal to the lad's common sense – if he had any.

'Speak up, then!' he said trying not to sound irritable. 'Get it said.'

'I'm engaged to be married!' Graham announced.

There was a silence which seemed to Graham to go on for ever. He waited for his father to speak.

'You are *WHAT*?'

'I'm engaged to be married. Her name is Breda O'Connor. I love her; she loves me. We want to be married as soon as it's possible.'

Graham watched his father's body stiffen, his face go white with anger. 'Married!' He choked over the word.

'As soon as we can,' Graham said.

'Are you telling me you're *forced* to be married? You fool! You idiot! What were you thinking of? Well, we'll soon see to that! I'm not having any son of mine trapped into marriage by a girl with an eye to the main chance! I won't—'

'SHUT UP!' Graham bellowed. 'You don't know what you're talking about. It's nothing like that, nothing at all! She's not that kind of a girl!'

'Oh indeed? And what kind of a girl is she then, to get pregnant?'

'Will you stop talking, and listen,' Graham shouted. Rage gave him the strength to say whatever he wanted to say to this bully of a man. 'She is *not* pregnant. Nothing has happened to make her pregnant. She is a lovely, decent, wonderful girl, and I mean to marry her. You can't stop me, Father. I can do what I like now.'

'And how will you keep a wife?' Henry demanded. 'Tell me that! What kind of living can an amateur painter earn to keep a wife on?'

Graham gave his father a long, hard stare. When he spoke, it was with more calm; he had himself in control now.

'You've jumped the gun there, Father,' he said. 'You've made another of your assumptions.'

'What do you mean?' Henry barked.

'I had thought that if you accepted Breda in the way I wanted her to be accepted, welcomed her in the way that's due to her, then I would go into Prince and Harper – I would work hard, I thought, and we'd make a good life. You didn't give me a chance to say any of that, did you?'

'I didn't know . . . '

'You didn't wait to find out, did you? You just bulldozed through, hurling insults right and left. Which makes me think the best thing Breda and I can do is to cut loose. Make our own way.'

'You must be mad! Tying yourself down!' Henry said.

'And before you decide that,' Graham retorted, 'you might at least have the decency to meet Breda, see for yourself. However, if that's your attitude, I'll leave you. I'll get back to work.' He started to walk towards the door.

'Wait a minute!' Henry called after him. 'Don't be so hasty!'

'You're the one who's being hasty,' Graham said.

'I haven't said I won't meet the girl,' Henry blustered. 'But there's your mother to think of. What will *she* say?'

'She'll take whatever attitude you push her into.'

354

'She'll naturally be upset. We know nothing of the girl, or her family!'

'But I do,' Graham said. 'I'm satisfied – and I'm the one who's marrying her. Anyway, you're not likely to find out!'

'I haven't said I wouldn't meet her.'

'Unless you can treat her in a decent, civilized manner, I wouldn't let her near you,' Graham said.

'There's no need for that,' Henry said, flushing. 'I know how to mind my manners. You can bring her to meet me this afternoon.'

'Not unless you promise to behave properly.'

'I've said I will, haven't I? Where we'll meet I don't know. I'll have to ask Opal.'

'Well, we certainly don't want an unseemly row in some café,' Graham said. 'And as it's early closing here the store will be closed.'

'I'll arrange something with Opal,' Henry said.

Graham, still angry – his father was insufferable – strode out of Miss Opal's office and went back to the desk he now occupied in the Accounts section. He badly wanted to see Breda and he knew she would be eagerly waiting to hear how things had gone, but until he had calmed down he would not seek her out. He opened a ledger and tried to rid his mind of everything except the columns of figures in front of him.

Henry Prince sought out Opal's secretary in the adjoining room. 'Can I do something for you, Mr Prince?' she asked. She had been intrigued by the sounds of battle coming from her boss's office. It made quite a diversion in her well-ordered routine.

'If you will,' Henry said. 'Miss Opal said you would know where to contact her. I'd like to see her as soon as it's convenient.'

He returned to Opal's office and stood by the window, looking down at the street far below. But though he looked, he saw nothing. He was angry and confused, but somewhere in the middle of it all there was a chance of keeping his son – his favourite son, though he would never have confessed that.

When Opal entered he swung around sharply. 'You knew about this!' he accused her. 'You knew all about it and you chose to say nothing.'

'Sit down, Henry! And calm down! I suppose you're referring to the fact that Graham's got himself engaged?'

'What else would I be referring to?' he snapped. 'Why did you let it happen?'

Opal took the seat behind her desk, distancing herself from him. He might bully everyone else, but she would not allow him to bully her.

'I did not let it happen,' she objected. 'Your son is a grown man. Breda O'Connor works for me, and works well. I have no jurisdiction over the private lives of either of them.'

'When you saw it happening you should have fired her! That would have put a stop to it!' He was pacing up and down the room.

'I did not know it was happening,' Opal said. 'I knew they were friendly. Did you expect your son not to make friends, even of the opposite sex, in the time he's been here? I heard of their engagement only yesterday, and in confidence, from Graham himself. He assured me he would tell you as soon as he saw you – and he has.'

'Then at least you'll fire her now?' Henry demanded. That way, Graham would forget her.

'I will do no such thing,' Opal said. 'I choose who I will fire. I don't choose to fire Breda O'Connor. She's done nothing to deserve it, and in any case, Graham is due to leave soon.'

'Which he says he won't do without this girl in tow!'

'What do you expect?' Opal asked. 'They're in love. They want to marry. Now Henry, will you for heaven's sake stop pacing up and down. If you want me to do anything at all – if indeed there's anything I can do or would do – then let's sit down and talk sensibly.'

He sat down. 'You can tell me what she's like,' he said.

'With pleasure. She's a nice, well-brought-up Irish girl. She's fairly newly over from Ireland, not well off, I imagine. Not well educated but as bright as a button. And she has character.' And however nervous she is, Opal thought, I reckon she won't let you bully her!

'Irish!' Henry said. 'So she's a Catholic? He didn't tell me that!'

'I imagine so. I don't know. That's another thing I don't interfere in, the religion of my employees. Do you, may I ask?'

'No,' Henry growled. 'But if Graham has his way, she'll be family. It won't make things easier.'

'I'm sure they'll work it out – if there's anything to be worked out. Why don't you just meet the girl instead of condemning her unseen?'

'I've said I will. This afternoon. And that's another thing. Where can we meet? Some hotel lounge, I suppose, but it doesn't seem suitable.'

'It wouldn't be,' Opal agreed. 'Especially not with you in this mood. But that's something I *can* solve. As soon as I've given you lunch I'm off to Hebghyll with my brother-in-law, George Soames. You remember meeting him? He's my General Manager. We have a bit of business in Hebghyll.'

If Henry Prince hadn't been in such a pig-headed mood she might have told him what it was, but not now.

'So the three of you can meet in my house,' she offered. 'My housekeeper will look after you, give you a meal before you go back this evening – if that's when you're leaving. George and I will drop you there on our way to Hebghyll, introduce you to Mrs Foster. Graham and Breda can join you later.'

'Very well then,' Henry agreed, though reluctantly. 'And thank you. I'll see if I can't talk some sense into the young man.'

Opal sighed. 'You're going the wrong way about it. If I were you, Henry, I'd try meeting them with an open mind. You might even think, if you let yourself get to know her, that Breda O'Connor is a very good thing to have happened to Graham. You might be quite surprised. Now shall we just let Graham know the arrangements and then I'll take you off to lunch?'

A little later Graham found Breda and told her what was to happen. 'I'll call for you at Waterloo Terrace at half-past three. We'll get the bus to Miss Opal's.'

'Oh Graham, do you think 'tis going to be all right?' Breda asked anxiously.

'The important thing is that everything is all right between you and me, and always will be. Nothing can alter that. Not my father, not anyone. The rest can be settled later.'

When the store closed at one o'clock Breda rushed home, washed and dried her hair and brushed it until it shone like red silk.

'What shall I wear?' she asked Josephine. 'Not that I have a lot of choice.'

'Well, it's a nice warm summer's day so you can wear a summer dress. Your pale blue cotton is nice.'

'But is it smart enough?'

'Of course it is. You look lovely in it. In any case, no point in trying to be something you're not. Just be yourself,

358

love. That's good enough for all the Mr Henry Princes in the world.'

When Graham came he echoed Josephine's words. 'You look gorgeous!'

'Not too much lipstick?'

'Just right, except that I'd like to kiss it off – and I will later on.'

His thoughts were not as jaunty as his words. Unless his father's mood had changed since this morning, there would be fireworks.

'Don't let my father rattle you,' he said. 'I think he'll be all right, but if he's awkward, if he upsets you, we shall just walk right out on him.'

Sitting on the bus, Breda thought how excited she would be, going to visit Miss Opal's house, if only it was in different circumstances. She had a deep curiosity about the inside of people's homes.

Mrs Foster answered the door and showed them into the large, comfortably furnished sitting room. Henry Prince rose to meet them.

'Father, let me introduce Breda O'Connor, my fiancée.'

He knew by the flash of steel in his father's eyes that he had said the wrong thing, but he had said it on purpose. He wanted everything plain from the beginning, no beating about the bush.

Henry recognized what his son was doing. He stifled his spurt of anger. It was, after all, what he himself might have done in the circumstances. Graham had more grit in him than he would once have given him credit for. His wife, he knew, would say that the son had inherited the father's stubbornness.

He held out his hand to Breda.

'Good afternoon, Miss O'Connor. Won't you sit down?' He was every inch the polite, well-mannered man of business.

359

'Good afternoon, Mr Prince,' Breda said.

She perched uncomfortably on the edge of an easy chair – there was not a single straight-backed chair to be seen – and was greatly relieved when Graham sat on the broad arm of the same chair. His nearness gave her confidence.

Henry Prince took the seat opposite. So it was to be like that, was it, he asked himself? The two of them indivisible, he thought. A united front against him.

'Well,' he said, 'we all know why we're here, don't we, so let's not beat about the bush! My son tells me, Miss O'Connor, that you and he are engaged to be married!'

Breda looked him straight in the eye. 'Indeed we are, Mr Prince.'

'Well, in my opinion you are both far too young—'

'We've gone into this before, Father,' Graham interrupted. 'I'm of age.'

'I was speaking to the young lady,' Henry said smoothly. No matter what, he wouldn't lose his temper.

'And 'tis I will answer,' Breda said. 'I'm sorry you think that, Mr Prince, but I don't agree with you. We are both very sure about each other.'

'And you realize my son could not possibly keep a wife? If he persists in his artistic dreams he will have nothing. If he goes into the family business, of course he will have a job, but he will earn very little in the first few years. I don't believe in paying for inexperience. But being in love, I don't suppose you've thought of these things?'

'I don't like to be contradicting you,' Breda said, 'but of course we have. Whatever Graham decides to do, I will stand beside him. If he wants to be a painter, then, for as long as that's necessary, I will be the one to earn the money for the two of us. 'Twill be the same if he goes into your business. I will either make do on what he earns or

I will take a job myself. I am not afraid of work. And the choice of what he does is his.'

She looked afraid of nothing, Henry thought, sitting there so upright.

'And you've thought that you might have to live in London? It's all very different.'

'I have so. I wouldn't choose it, but I've already come from Ireland. I left my home there, where I'd lived all my life. 'Twas the most difficult thing I ever did. So I suppose I could put up with a few more miles. After all, I would be with Graham, and that's what counts, not *where* I am.'

As the words came out of her, so her last remaining scrap of fear left her. She held up her hand and Graham took it in his. It was true what she had just said. Nothing mattered as long as she was with Graham. What was more, she realized that this man sitting opposite to them, no matter how important he was in his own world, could never come between them.

Henry shook his head. He felt almost bewildered, an emotion hitherto unknown to him. He could not have believed, an hour or two ago, that he would be beaten. But he was. He had not reckoned on this gutsy Irish girl, who also had enough charm to tempt the ducks off the water. She and his son made a formidable pair.

'Well,' he said, 'I admire your loyalty, young lady. Graham can count himself lucky on that score. But I still think you're far too young to be married. Marry in haste, repent at leisure. True and wise words.'

'We had not thought of marrying in haste,' Breda said. Her voice was gentler now. She knew she had won this round. 'We have not set a date.'

'But we don't want to wait too long,' Graham said.

'We will marry when we are ready to set up home together,' Breda said. 'Not before.'

361

'Well, Miss O'Connor, it's true I can't prevent you and my son being engaged, but I'd like you to promise me you won't rush into marriage.'

'Sure we'll not do that,' Bredà said. 'And could you please call me "Breda"?'

'I shall have to break the news to your mother,' Henry said to Graham. 'And I would have liked to have met your family,' he said to Breda. It was something his wife would certainly want to know about.

'If you can stay a little longer you could meet my aunt and uncle tomorrow,' Breda said. She put the thought of him encountering Grandma Maguire swiftly out of her mind.

'I'm afraid I can't do that,' Henry said. 'I have to be back.'

There was a silence.

'Well then, perhaps now would be the time to have that cup of tea Mrs Foster promised us,' Henry said.

Graham and Breda left soon after tea. Henry stood in the window and watched them walk down the drive together, arm in arm. For a moment he envied them – so sure of themselves and each other. Perhaps Opal was right. Perhaps Graham had done himself a good turn when he'd chosen this girl. And if she persuaded him to stay in the business, then he would have her to thank for that. In any case, he could not but like her, though it would take every bit of her determination and charm to cope with life in London. She was, after all, a simple Irish girl. Yet perhaps not so simple, he thought.

The two of them had been gone no more than an hour when Opal returned.

'I didn't expect you,' Henry said. 'I thought I'd have left for my train before you returned.'

'I wanted to be back,' Opal told him. 'How did it all go?'

'Well, you were right about the girl. And you were right that there's very little I can do. An obstinate pair.'

'I'd say determined rather than obstinate.'

'I don't know how she'll fit in in London,' Henry said doubtfully. 'I don't know what Miriam will say to it all.'

'I have been wondering . . . ' Opal began.

'What?'

'Would it be a good idea if Graham were to stay on longer, a few more months? There's still a lot for him to learn, plenty we could teach him before he goes back to you. And it would give Breda a chance. I think she deserves that.'

It was only part of the idea forming in her mind, but now was not the time to tell Henry Prince.

'I don't know. I shall have to think about that, see what Miriam says. She misses him.'

Twenty

Henry Prince rose from his seat in the first-class Pullman car as the train slowed down, drawing into King's Cross. He stepped off the train the second it stopped, and in an instant a porter sprang towards him and took his overnight case.

'A cab,' Henry said. 'Quick as you can! Victoria.'

If he was lucky he would catch the last train to Reigate. If he missed it he'd have to stay overnight at his club, and that he didn't want to do. He was anxious to get home. He had telephoned Miriam from Opal's so that Tompkins, his chauffeur, would be waiting for him at Reigate.

'How are you? Is Graham all right?' she'd asked. 'Is he there? May I speak to him?' She had wanted to keep him talking on the telephone but he had cut her short.

'I'll have to go or I'll miss the train,' he said. 'Don't wait up!'

I hope she won't, he told himself as his cab sped through the labyrinth of streets towards Victoria. All the way from Yorkshire he had thought about Graham, and about the girl, Breda. He should never have sent the boy to Opal's. He had good connections in the trade; there were half a dozen stores in London and the home counties which would have welcomed his son, places closer to home, where he'd have continued to mix with his own kind.

It was too late now. He still reckoned that Opal had let him down, but she hadn't agreed. 'I couldn't have done anything differently, Henry,' she'd said as he was leaving.

'You could have sacked her.'

'You don't suppose he'd have stopped seeing her? It would have had quite the opposite effect. You know better than I do how obstinate he is.' A chip off the old block, she'd thought. 'Anyway, aren't you making too much of it?' she'd asked. 'It could be worse!'

Would Miriam see it in that light, he wondered, paying off the cabby at Victoria, hurrying for the Reigate train and catching it by the skin of his teeth. He hoped once again that she would have gone to bed. One thing was certain: he wouldn't bring up the subject tonight. A good sleep was what he wanted. Time enough for the rest in the morning.

On the verge of sleep, Miriam opened bleary eyes and half-raised herself as Henry tip-toed into the bedroom. 'Was everything all right?' she asked drowsily.

'Quite all right,' Henry said firmly. 'Go back to sleep. We'll talk in the morning.'

When he came down in the morning, having slept longer than usual, Miriam was already at the breakfast table, slim and trim, her greying hair becomingly waved. She smiled at him and spoke in a cheerful voice. 'You had a good sleep, darling! Were you very tired?'

'I was.'

She poured his coffee and handed it to him.

'So! How did it go? How was Graham? When will he be home? Was Opal pleased with him?'

'Very pleased. Good reports all round.'

'That's lovely! I shall be pleased to see him back.'

'I'm afraid it's not as simple as that,' Henry said.

A piece of toast was halfway to Miriam's mouth. She put it back on the plate, and looked at her husband. He was never the most cheerful man in the world at breakfast, but now he looked unusually grim. 'What do you mean, not simple? I don't understand. Is something wrong?'

'You're not going to like this, Miriam. Graham has got himself engaged to be married!'

She stared at him, not believing her ears. '*What* did you say?'

'I said, Graham has got himself engaged to be married.'

'I don't believe it!' she said. 'How in the world has that happened?'

'I assume in the way it usually does!' Worry made him brusque. 'He said "Will you marry me?"; she said "Yes!" '

'You know that's not what I mean,' Miriam said. 'Has he . . . ? Is she . . . ?'

'She is not pregnant,' Henry said. 'And having met her, I'd say she's not that sort of a girl. No worries on that score.'

'So what sort of a girl *is* she?' Miriam demanded. 'Please, Henry! You're telling me nothing!'

'She's young – eighteen. She's pretty. She's very bright. And I'd say she's as much in love with Graham as he is with her – which is a lot.'

'But? There is a but. I can tell by the look on your face.'

'She's an unsophisticated country girl, not long from Ireland. She's an assistant in Opal's store. Although she's bright, she's not educated.'

'And her family? What about her family?'

'She's living with an aunt and uncle in Akersfield,' Henry said. 'I didn't have time to meet them. Graham says they're decent people.'

'Whatever that means!' Miriam said. 'And it probably means she won't fit in. And she's undoubtedly after him for his position and his prospects.'

'I don't somehow think so,' Henry said.

Miriam hardly listened. 'Oh, why did Graham have to be so foolish? And why didn't you bring him right back with you so that we could talk some sense into him?'

'Because he's not a child,' Henry said impatiently. 'He's a grown man. He'll come home when he chooses, and I can tell you for certain, he'll not come without Breda.'

'Breda?'

'Breda O'Connor.'

'She sounds very Irish.'

'Irish to the core.'

'I suppose we'll have to see her,' Miriam spoke with the utmost reluctance. 'I'll write to Graham.'

'Don't get the wrong idea about this,' Henry warned. 'It isn't a question of you getting her down from the North of England, inspecting her to see if you approve. If she's not welcomed as Graham's future wife, then he won't stay either.'

'But Henry, what *will* they do? For a start, what will they live on? His future is good, but he has nothing now, and we must make that plain to her.'

'Unless the girl is accepted by us, he won't go into Prince and Harper,' Henry said. 'That's for sure! And whatever he decides to do, she'll support him.' And they'll be happy together, he thought suddenly. They'll be truly happy. Nothing I can do, or his mother can do, will prevent that. He felt a swift pang of envy.

'So we must welcome her,' he said to his wife. 'We have nothing to lose if we do and a great deal to lose if we don't.'

'You can't say we've nothing to lose,' Miriam protested. 'I had such plans for Graham. There's Fiona Palmer, a lovely girl, and all her family such good friends . . .'

'It doesn't do to make plans for one's family,' Henry said. 'I've discovered that. Anyway, look on the bright side. You might actually like the girl!'

'And did you?'

'I think I did,' Henry said thoughtfully. 'Yes. In the end I did.'

'You always fell for a pretty face,' Miriam said tartly. All the same, she must meet this girl, and the sooner the better. It was surely not too late, once Graham saw her in his own environment, for him to change his mind?

While Henry Prince was in the train, speeding south, Graham and Breda were walking arm in arm in Sutherland Park.

'He doesn't like me,' Breda said. 'He doesn't approve of me.'

'I don't think that's true,' Graham assured her. 'I think he likes you at least as much as he'd like anyone else in the same circumstances. It's just that it's come as a big surprise to him. My father likes everything to go according to plan.'

'*His* plan,' Breda said.

'That's true. He's used to getting his own way. But it makes no difference. He knows we're engaged, he knows we intend to marry when we can. He can't change that, and he knows it.'

The bell sounded across the park, signifying that the gates were about to be closed before darkness fell.

'Sure, I don't want to go home yet,' Breda said. 'There's a lot we have to talk about – and besides, won't Auntie Josie be bursting to ask me a thousand questions?'

'I don't want you to go. So we can walk around the streets, or we can go to the coffee bar, or have a drink in a pub. Oh Breda,' Graham said impatiently, 'I long for the day we'll have our own home to go to!'

'And do you think I don't? Nor do I care what it's like. One room of our own, just anywhere, would be heaven. But in the meantime we'll go to a bar and I'll have a Guinness to remind me of home.'

The public house was crowded, but they found a small table in a corner. Graham watched Breda while she lifted the glass and sipped the dark liquid, the pale gold froth clinging to her upper lip.

'Did you drink Guinness in Ireland?' he asked.

'Indeed I never did, though everyone else drank it. But tonight I felt like it.'

'Does that mean you're homesick, my love? I don't want you to be homesick.'

' 'Tis only because I'm suddenly not sure of anything,' Breda said. 'But then, I was no longer sure of anything in Kilbally. Wasn't that why I left?'

He took the glass from her hand and put it on the table, then grabbed her by the wrists and held her tightly. 'Breda, you must never say that, do you hear? Never! We love each other. We're together. We're sure of each other, and beside that nothing else matters.'

'Will nothing and no-one separate us?'

'Nothing!' Graham said firmly. 'And no-one. You must believe that.'

'Then I do,' Breda said.

'And if you're really homesick, why don't we go to Kilbally for a few days? We both have some holiday to come. Besides, I want to meet your family, I want to see where you grew up. I want to know everything about you from the day you were born!'

'Sure, there's little to know,' Breda said. 'But I would like you to come to Kilbally with me.'

And she would like to do it, she thought, before she had to meet Graham's family. She wanted him to know where she had sprung from before he took her into the affluence of his own upbringing. She was not ashamed of her beginnings, not in the least, but it was essential to her that he knew them, and could accept them.

'And after that,' Graham said, 'you must meet my family, especially my mother.'

She vowed to herself that she would not tell him, now or at any time, how much she dreaded the thought of that.

'And afterwards?' she asked. 'What will happen afterwards? What will you do about a job? Where will you be? What will *I* do?'

'I don't know,' Graham said. 'But I'm not worried. We'll work it out together.'

He *was* worried, but he would never admit it. If his mother would not accept Breda, then he would not work in Prince and Harper – but in that case where *would* he find work? On the other hand it was possible that his mother would take to Breda. His darling was surely an easy person to love.

At about the time Henry Prince was at the breakfast table with his wife in Reigate, Opal was already behind her desk. From the very first day she had opened the store she had taken pleasure in being at her job early. She loved the peace of it, before the telephones began to ring, before the day's demands started. Equally, she would have admitted, she loved the moments when the staff began to arrive, when the covers came off the counters and everything was ready for the first trickle – or heavy rush if it was a sale day – of customers coming through the doors. Almost always she walked around the store at this time, inspecting, noting, asking questions, greeting the many customers who over the years had almost become friends.

This morning, however, she stayed in her office. This morning she expected George Soames early, and they had important business to discuss. And while she waited she pored over the sheaf of papers she had been given yesterday afternoon in Hebghyll. She had read them several times and she had made a list of questions to be asked, points to be discussed, when her brother-in-law arrived.

She didn't have to wait long. He was as efficient as herself, and utterly reliable, which was why, before the war, when she had returned to the store from almost a year's absence after her terrible accident and found almost everything except the restaurant, over which George Soames presided, going to rack and ruin, she had immediately pulled him out from that job and made him her General Manager. Without him she could never have rebuilt Opal's store into the highly successful business it now was.

There was a tap on the door and he entered. 'Good morning, Miss Opal!'

Though he had married her sister in 1938 and had therefore been an intimate member of the family circle for many years, in the store he still addressed her as Miss Opal.

'I caught the early train from Hebghyll,' he said. 'Good thing I did because there's trouble on the line and everything's running late.' He nodded towards the sheaf of papers. 'So what do you think, now that you've slept on it?'

'I haven't slept much,' Opal admitted. 'I was too excited! But I still think it's a good idea. I reckon we could make a go of it. Edgar thinks so too, though he was worried about me taking on more responsibility. I told him most of the responsibility would be yours. That satisfied him.'

'Good! And Mary's happy. She likes the thought of me working only ten minutes away from home instead of coming into Leasfield every day.'

It was not only the thought of her husband working closer to home which pleased Mary. Opal knew that. George had had a heart attack last year – a mild one, and he had recovered well, but Mary remained anxious, watching over him, though trying not to show it. He was the light of her life. She had met him when she had given up hope of marriage. They had no children. He was her only love.

The war years had been difficult in the store. There were shortages of everything; staff, because most of them were young, were constantly being called up into the armed forces, women as well as men, and there were coupons and rationing, and new regulations all the time. George Soames, above the age of conscription, had shouldered a great deal of the responsibility, and it had taken its toll.

'It was smart of you to spot the business,' Opal said.

She had been hankering, for almost a year now, to spread her wings, perhaps open up a branch in one of the towns within a reasonable distance of Leasfield. Harrogate, Ilkley, perhaps Skipton, had been in her mind – the store drew customers from all those areas – but it was George who had spotted the opportunity in Hebghyll.

'It helped, living on the spot,' George said. 'I'd been noticing for some months now that Fawcett's was running down. Well, you couldn't help but notice it. I think the war was too much for John Fawcett. He hadn't the reserves of Opal's.'

It had been with this in mind that Opal had approached the owner of Fawcett's store. It was easier to take over a going concern, however run-down, than to start from scratch, as she had done all those years ago in Leasfield. It was to this end that she had left Henry Prince to his own devices yesterday afternoon, and gone to Hebghyll with George.

'I must say, I was appalled by the condition of everything,' she said to George Soames now. 'I found it more run-down than you'd described, and in spirit as well as physically. Which means, of course, we'll get it for a reasonable price.'

She had been acutely reminded, looking over Fawcett's yesterday, of the day she had discovered what was now Opal's store. Fawcett's, however, was very different. It was considerably smaller, much less than a quarter of the size of Opal's, but the right size for Hebghyll. It was also old-fashioned, staid, shabby.

'There's a great deal we'd want to alter,' she said. 'And quickly, too. It needs an entirely new image.'

'If you change the name to Opal's, we're halfway there,' George said.

She pushed the pages of notes she had made across the desk. 'I've had one or two ideas. You might like to take a look at them. And you'll have your own ideas too. After all, you'll be in charge. You must feel free to follow them once we're going.'

'We've usually thought much alike,' George said. 'I don't foresee much difficulty there. Let's go through your list, shall we, and then we'll come to mine?'

It was almost noon before they paused in their discussions. Opal leaned back in her chair and pushed her hair from her face. 'It's nearly lunch time, and I'm hungry. Will it suit you if we pause for a while and have coffee and a sandwich here?

'Oh George, I'm going to miss you so much!' Opal said as they ate their sandwiches, 'Yes, I know we'll be in touch all the time, but it won't be the same. I can never really replace you. Herbert Ransome's very good, and I know you've taught him just about everything he knows, but he won't be the same.'

'Herbert will be just fine,' George said. 'And it's time he had promotion, which he never will while I'm here. Which brings me to the question of staff in Hebghyll. I wasn't over-impressed with what I saw there.'

'Nor I,' Opal agreed. 'I dare say they've gone downhill with the business.'

'That being so, I'd like to steal a few people from here,' George suggested. 'Not permanently, but until we get on a firm footing.'

Opal sighed.

'And I expect you'll want the *crème de la crème*?'

'To start with, yes.'

'I had an idea yesterday about which I haven't had time to talk to you,' Opal said. 'But it *is* only an idea and you're free to turn it down.'

'So?'

'You'll need a deputy, someone to understudy you. What would you think of Graham Prince?'

'Graham Prince?' George's mouth dropped open in surprise. 'I wouldn't have given him a thought. Besides, isn't he due to go into Prince and Harper? Why would he want to work with me?'

'For more reasons than one,' Opal said. 'But apart from that, how would *you* feel about it?'

'I'm not sure,' George admitted. 'Of course I *like* him, and he's done very well here. And there is one advantage in having someone new to the job; he could learn my ways from the beginning. I don't particularly want to take on a member of Fawcett's staff as my deputy. There might be a conflict of ideas there.'

'You're talking yourself into it,' Opal said. 'But it's up to you.'

'So why might he not go into Prince and Harper? His father said nothing of that yesterday.'

'Poor Henry doesn't know whether he's on his head or his heels,' Opal said. 'Graham has got himself engaged to be married, to Breda O'Connor!'

'The little Irish girl in Display?'

'The same. She's a nice enough girl. *I'd* be glad to have her for a daughter-in-law,' Opal said wistfully. Sometimes she thought Daniel would never marry. 'But she's not what Henry had in mind, and still less will she appeal to Miriam. Miriam Prince has big ideas. So you see the

374

difficulty. No way will Graham subject Breda permanently to the disapproval of his family.'

'That's in his favour,' George said.

'And there's another thing,' Opal pointed out. 'If you took Graham, you'd have to take Breda O'Connor. He'll not leave her behind, because the minute they can afford it they intend to marry.'

'I'd be glad to have *her*,' George said. 'From what I've seen, their display work needs brightening up.'

'And I don't want to lose her,' Opal said. 'To my mind she has great potential. But if Graham goes, I can't keep her. Anyway, think it over. But not too long, if you don't mind. It would be nice to have it settled one way or another before either Henry Prince or Graham does anything rash.

The following day Graham made an appointment to see Opal.

'I was wondering,' he said, 'if I could take a few days' holiday? I want to go to Kilbally with Breda. She's already asked her manager and he's agreeable.'

'I don't see why not,' Opal said. 'You're due for some holiday, and this isn't the busiest of months. I take it you want to meet Breda's family?'

'I do.'

'Well, it's none of my business,' Opal said. 'But did you tell your father you intended this?'

'No. Breda and I didn't decide ourselves until last night. But I'm not in his good books. He won't approve.'

'Oh well!' Opal rose to her feet. She didn't want to get further involved. 'Off you go to Ireland, and have a good time. And my advice to you is not to make any decisions in a hurry – I'm talking about work now. You can always stay on here a little longer until you decide what you want to do next. I told your father that.'

375

The following Monday Graham and Breda took the boat to Ireland and then the train to Kilbally.

'Sure we will stop off in Dublin on the way back so you can meet Moira and Barry, not to mention my godson. And we might meet Kathleen if we're lucky, but not Kieran, for isn't he away to England now?'

For the moment, she wanted it to be first stop Kilbally. She could hardly wait to get there, and, oh, how she longed to see Mammy!

There had been excited telephone calls between Akersfield and Kilbally, with the result that both Mammy and Luke were there at the station when the train arrived.

' 'Tis so good to see you, *álainna*,' Molly cried, flinging her arms around her daughter. 'And sure, you're not looking a day different! Except that you look more grown-up, and you're thinner, and your hair's shorter!'

'But otherwise I'm the same?' Breda laughed. 'Oh, Mammy!'

' 'Tis the spirit that is the same,' Molly said. But now there was more to the spirit. She had never seen her daughter happier, not since she was a small girl with her Dada, and wasn't that an entirely different kind of happiness?

'I now have a motor car, as well as the old van,' Luke said, leading them out of the station. 'There it is! 'Tis not the grandest in all Ireland, but it goes well. You will be able to get around while you are on holiday!'

He turned to Graham. 'Can you drive, then?'

'Oh, yes!' Graham replied.

I had not known that about him, Breda thought. There was so much to learn about each other, so many little things. Perhaps they would have a car one day, and if so, she also would learn to drive.

'So how is everybody?' Breda asked when they were in the car.

'Your Grandma Byrne is not at all well,' Molly said. 'She is too old to live alone and she might have to come to live with us. Luke is willing, bless his heart.'

It was really not worth bringing the car for this short distance, Breda thought. They had walked it all their lives, but she guessed Luke was proud of his possession. Hardly had they settled in before they were back at the shop.

As Breda stepped inside the familiarity of it all overwhelmed her: the same smells of tea and cheese and bacon and soap; the same canisters on the same shelves. She could have found anything blindfold. She felt choked with emotion. Her eyes, meeting her mother's, were bright and shining. Why was I so keen to leave here, she wondered? And why did I dislike Luke O'Reilly, who by any standards is a nice, kind man?

But if I had not left, she thought, I would never have met Graham, and wasn't that the answer to everything?

'The kettle is on the boil,' Molly said when they were in the living room. 'And since you will both be as hungry as hunters I will fry you some rashers and eggs. And there's soda bread not an hour old.'

'I could eat a piece of soda bread right away,' Breda said. 'Haven't I longed for your soda bread!'

'Doesn't Aunt Josephine make it?' Molly asked.

'So she does, but 'tis not like yours!'

'That's one thing I don't understand about soda bread,' Molly observed. 'Everyone uses the same ingredients and everyone's turns out different.'

'I will put your cases in your rooms,' Luke said. 'You will not want to be unpacking them before you have eaten.'

Never had a meal tasted better, Breda thought. Because of her stomach's squeamishness she had not eaten since before they had stepped on the boat. She'd been as empty as a drum.

'That was delicious, Mrs O'Reilly,' Graham said, having cleared his plate. 'I understand now why Breda goes on about your soda bread. And if you'll excuse me, I'll be off to bed now.' Breda and her mother, he knew, would have things they wanted to say to each other, and not in his presence.

'Won't I do the same?' Luke said. 'These two women will stay up half the night talking and I have an early start in the morning!'

Breda, though she was delighting in seeing her mother, would also have liked to escape. She knew what Mammy would be saying to her the minute they were alone. She was not wrong.

'Oh, Breda!' Molly said. 'He's a lovely man, he is indeed, but why did you do it? Why did you not choose a Catholic man?'

'I did not choose a Catholic and I did not choose a Protestant,' Breda said. 'I chose Graham, and he chose me. I would have chosen him if he had been a Hottentot! Can't you understand that, Mammy?'

'Sure I can,' Molly said gently. 'But you must see it's wrong. It won't work.'

'We shall make it work,' Breda said. 'Other people have.'

'Who do you know in Kilbally who has done that?' Molly asked.

'Oh, Mammy! Kilbally isn't the world! 'Twould be difficult to find anyone who *wasn't* a Catholic in Kilbally!'

'It's my world,' Molly said. 'It was yours.'

'It was,' Breda admitted. 'And I love it, and always will. But it's not my world now. My world is with Graham.'

'Father Curran will want to speak to you,' Molly warned her.

'I don't doubt he will,' Breda said. 'But he'll be wasting his breath.'

'Will you be doing me a favour?' Molly asked. 'Will you go to early Mass with me in the morning?'

'Of course I will, Mammy. It's never been in my mind to stop going to Mass. And will you do me a favour? Will you not bring up this subject again while I'm here? We have less than a week. I want Graham to get to know you. I don't want him put on trial. And you can't change me.'

'I suppose I never could,' Molly said. 'But I had to say it. Isn't it my duty?'

'Shall we go to bed?' Breda said.

Her bedroom looked exactly as she had left it, not a thing moved or out of place. The only difference was that on the other side of the thin dividing wall was Graham. It was the first time they had spent a night under the same roof. She put out her hand and touched the wall. How long before there would be no wall between them, and they would lie in the same bed?

The days flew by, each one filled with visits to places Breda wanted Graham to see, people she wanted him to meet, because they were part of her life. 'And always will be,' she said. 'Even though I don't live here, and perhaps will never do so again.'

She would have liked a future, though the details were hazy, in which she and Graham would live happily ever after in Kilbally, but she had enough sense to know that it was impossible.

'Not impossible,' Graham said. 'Not if I made a living as a painter – and heaven knows there's enough around here to keep a man painting for a lifetime! But unlikely, I grant you.'

They borrowed Luke's car only twice: once to take them along the winding coast road to Ballyvaughan, and on another day to go to Galway.

379

'My Dada came from Galway,' Breda said. 'I think he was always homesick for the sight of Galway Bay and, of course, he used to go to the races. If he won, he would bring us back presents.'

Most of the time they walked, often in the pouring rain. On the very first day she took Graham down to the strand.

'Didn't we all play here as children?' she said. 'And had picnics in the summer holidays. And when I wanted to be alone, or I was cross-tempered, I would climb the track and sit on the headland, and think furious thoughts.'

She showed him the small house where she had lived all her childhood. 'How we fitted in I can't think,' she said. 'But we were happy.'

They walked the path by the high cliffs, where Breda terrified Graham by standing too near the edge, looking down at the turbulent sea. They visited the small harbour, watched the boats going off for the fishing.

'Dada went on his last trip from this place,' Breda said.

The only fly in the healing ointment of the whole week was the short time she had spent with Father Curran, who had asked her to stay behind after Mass on that first morning. He had lectured her severely but she remained politely immovable.

'Then if I can't put the sense into your head, perhaps you'll be bringing the young man to see me?' he said.

'I will ask him,' Breda said, though in fact she didn't do so. It occurred to her, both at the time, and later, that if Father Curran had been more understanding, mixed even a little warmth with the doing of his duty, she might well have asked Graham if he would consent to meet him. As it was, she had no intention of submitting him to Father Curran's hostility, and said so, in private, to her mother.

'Sure, you have got it wrong,' Molly said. 'He is not hostile, not at all. He is concerned about you.'

'And are you still concerned about me, Mammy?' Breda asked. 'I mean, about me and Graham?'

'Less than I was,' Molly admitted. 'Graham is a good man, and he loves you. I can see that. But you know what my concern is and I shall pray for you both about that.'

On the last morning a tearful Molly saw them off on the Dublin train. 'Give my love to Moira and Barry, and the children. And Kathleen. I'm glad you'll be able to see her.'

She waved until the train was out of sight, then turned and left the station.

She wished she was going to Dublin with them. She missed her children sorely, and knew she always would. When would she see Kieran again, now that he was in a far away place called Sussex? As for Patrick and Colum, she was almost resigned to never seeing them, though Luke still promised that one day they would visit America.

Twenty-One

Opal said nothing of her plans to Graham before he and Breda left for Kilbally. He might just have a change of heart when he saw Breda in the bosom of her family. It would be a far cry from Reigate. But that was unlikely, she thought. He was intent on marrying Breda and she doubted if anything would stand in his way.

But aside from that, she must give herself more time for thought, though not about opening up in Hebghyll. She was rock-solid certain about that and could hardly wait.

'I thought of Graham on impulse,' she admitted to George Soames. 'There was a problem there, and it seemed to be the solution. Now I have to think about whether it was the right one. And it's even more important for you, George. You must be happy with the idea before I breathe a word to Graham.'

'I don't see any obstacles,' George said. 'But you're right. It bears thinking about. Anyway, we have a week before he's back from Ireland. Do you intend to speak to Henry Prince first, or to Graham?'

'Henry will expect me to put him first,' Opal said. 'But I shan't do so. It's Graham's business. It's up to him to tell his father when he's made his own decision.'

'There is one thing,' George said. 'If we agree Graham will be suitable, and if he agrees to go to Hebghyll, he must, right from the first, be seen as my deputy as well as my assistant. He must be given the authority he'll need for the job. He mustn't be seen as a trainee, even though you and I know quite well that he still has a lot to learn.'

'Certainly,' Opal agreed. 'And whatever extra training he needs, it will be up to you to give him. But now let's get down to other matters. When do you think we can open, for instance? We must fix a date and work towards it.'

Two days later Opal took a call from Henry Prince. He sounded tetchy, uncomfortable. 'I wanted to speak to Graham,' he said, 'but his landlady isn't on the telephone. Well it's Miriam, really. *I* thought, still think, that the whole thing is best left to simmer down for a bit, but Miriam won't have that. She wants him to come home for the weekend, preferably without the girl, but bringing her if he must.'

Opal kept silent in the pause which followed. For a supposedly clever man Henry, with language like that, was going the wrong way about things.

'If you can't bring him to the telephone, which I'd quite understand,' Henry went on, 'then will you tell him to call me at home, Opal?'

'I'd gladly do either of those things,' Opal said, 'except that I can't. Graham has gone to Kilbally – Breda's home. They'll be there for the rest of the week.'

She felt a stab of shame that she'd almost taken pleasure in giving Henry the news, but they were such a bombastic couple, Henry and Miriam. Such snobs.

'Didn't he tell you?' she asked.

'He did not!' Henry's voice was tight with anger. 'He tells us precious little these days. Well, just you tell him from me he's to phone home, the quicker the better! His mother's going to be very upset about this.'

'I'll pass on your message when I see him.' Opal's voice was cool. She put down the telephone. If Henry Prince thought he could give her orders, he was mistaken. Any sympathy she had had for him melted away. She now felt herself firmly on Graham's side.

It was Sunday evening before Graham and Breda were back in Akersfield. They had left Kilbally, and a tearful Molly, on Saturday morning. Molly had hovered in the bedroom while Breda packed her case.

'To think I will not be present at my daughter's wedding,' she said. ' 'Tis a terrible sadness!'

'And your own fault, Mammy.' Breda's voice was gentle, but as firm as bedrock. ' 'Tis no great journey you would be making to England. Auntie Josie has been here several times, and she that much older than you. I'm certain sure Luke would be agreeable to your coming, even if *he* couldn't leave the shop.'

'The distance is not the only reason, and you know it, Breda.'

'I do so,' Breda said. 'Why wouldn't I? Have you not told me a dozen times in this past week, even though not when Graham was present? If only I was not marrying a Protestant! Well I am, Mammy. No two ways about it. 'Twill not be the same if my own Mammy is not at my wedding, but 'twill still happen.'

Breda was glad of two things. Graham had been treated with the courtesy and politeness due to a guest, though as a guest, not as a member of the family; also, Mammy had reluctantly agreed to give her legal consent to the marriage.

It had been easier in Dublin. If either Moira or Barry had any doubts, then they didn't show them. In fact, Moira took to Graham at once. 'He's quite gorgeous!' she said. 'Isn't he like a film star – though no doubt he'll be the same as all the rest once you're married. Men are after only one thing!'

384

Which I long to give to Graham, Breda thought. She wondered if Moira still gave it to Barry, for there was no sign of more children, which was surely not natural. 'You know he is not Catholic?' she said.

Moira shrugged. 'So what?'

'If Mammy heard you say that she would have a fit,' Breda said. 'It upsets her.'

'Well, don't let it upset you,' Moira said.

Those were the nearest to kind words Moira had ever spoken to her, Breda thought. She felt an unusual rush of affection for her sister.

It was different again with Kathleen, whom Breda and Graham visited on the Sunday morning. Though Kathleen knew the circumstances which made their mother so unhappy, and to which Moira was indifferent, she gave Graham the loving welcome she would have given to a brother.

'I shall be glad when we are well and truly married,' Breda said to Graham later. They were sitting side by side on the ferry, crossing an unusually calm Irish Sea, only the smallest ripples disturbing the smooth surface of the water.

'And so shall I,' Graham said. 'And for reasons other than your mother. But don't be too hard on her, my darling. In any case it will happen in reverse with my family. Yours doesn't like it because I'm not a Catholic, mine will be against it because you *are*.'

'Graham,' Breda said, 'even if we can't be married just yet, will you come with me to see Father Delaney at St Peter's? He's the nicest of men. Auntie Josie thinks the world of him. He will tell us what we should do.'

Graham put his arms around her, drew her close. 'Of course I will. Whenever you like.'

He kissed her on the lips and she struggled to free herself. 'Everyone will be watching!' she protested.

'I don't mind in the least,' he said. 'Nor should you.'

On Monday morning Opal, with George Soames also in her office, gave the news to Graham. 'But I must caution you,' she said. 'All this is confidential. I don't want any leaks before I'm ready to announce the opening day. You do understand that?'

'Of course!'

'So what do you think?' Opal asked. 'Oh, I'm not asking you for a definite answer on the spot, you can have a day or two to decide, but obviously I'll need to know soon. There's a lot to be done, especially between you and Mr Soames here.'

'I don't need a day or two, Miss Opal,' Graham said. 'All I need is the answer to one question.'

'Which is?'

'What about Breda? Will there be a job for Breda in Hebghyll?'

Opal and George Soames exchanged smiles.

'Mr Soames and I have already thought about that,' Opal said. 'In fact we'd have been surprised had you not asked the question.'

'And . . . ?' But he knew by the expressions on their faces that the answer was the one he wanted.

'Breda O'Connor can go to Hebghyll if she wishes to,' Opal said. 'She would be part of a small display team. Of course I must interview *her* about the job, not you. I must make sure it's what *she* wants.'

'Oh, it will be!' Graham interrupted. 'She'll look forward to it as much as I do!' He was all eagerness, all enthusiasm. He felt lifted up by the news, as if he had come into a fortune. He saw his whole future, and not least because it included Breda, in the brightest of bright colours.

'Nevertheless I must speak to her directly,' Opal said. 'And I'll do it soon. Her appointment will be quite separate from yours. It means I shall be going away from the usual practice of not having engaged couples working in my store – though I've never quite believed in it. But I shall require totally professional conduct from both of you. Your personal relationship must be kept outside your work. You do understand that?'

'Of course,' Graham said. 'And may I ask one more question?'

'You may.'

'Then what is your attitude towards married couples working for you? When we're first married Breda will probably need to have a job.' Miss Opal had not offered him a princely salary in the new job, nor did he expect it.

'We'll meet that when we come to it,' Opal said. Privately, though the occasion had never arisen, most new brides seeming to be only too happy to stay at home and keep house, she had never been against married couples in her store, providing they acted professionally. And if they didn't, then she didn't want either of them.

'In the meantime,' she said, 'you should spend some time with Mr Soames. I'm sure he has a lot to discuss with you. But let me warn you again, all this is confidential.'

'Does my father know?' Graham asked.

'No. I had thought of telling him but I changed my mind. I think the most you can say to your father is that you've been offered a job here. I'd like you to do that yourself but naturally I shall speak to him, as a matter of courtesy. But not before you've done so.'

When Graham had left the room Opal turned to George Soames.

'I think I'd better see Breda O'Connor as soon as possible. Graham will burst if he can't discuss it with her!'

'Shouldn't you have a word with Jim Sutcliffe first?' George suggested.

'You're right,' Opal agreed. 'I can't go around stealing his staff from under his nose, without a word. Anyway, we shall need Jim's co-operation on several things, and he's discreet enough. He's been with me since I opened here.'

Breda was summoned to Opal's office immediately after dinner. She had not eaten her midday meal with Graham. They did so less often now that they were free to meet at other times and in other places. Now she stood just inside Miss Opal's office, close to the door, her feet sinking into the thick carpet which was that lady's one touch of luxury.

She had no idea why she had been sent for. Jim Sutcliffe, without a word of explanation, had simply told her to report to Miss Opal. 'At the double!' he'd said. It was an unusual command. Miss Opal only saw junior staff herself on more serious matters. Breda had had no contact with her since the time of the shooting.

What have I done, she asked herself, waiting for Miss Opal to finish a telephone call with her secretary. Had something gone wrong with her work during her week's absence in Kilbally?

'Don't stand in the doorway, Miss O'Connor,' Opal said. 'Please come and sit down.' She sounded brisk and businesslike but not in the least angry.

Over the next few minutes Breda found herself listening with almost total disbelief to what Miss Opal had to say. Wasn't it all quite incredible, and at the same time wasn't it the answer to all those prayers she'd said? Not that she'd ever asked for anything as specific as this. Just, 'Dear God, make it come out all right for me and Graham.' Well, wasn't this more than just all right?

'So what do you think, Miss O'Connor?'

Breda knew by the tone of Miss Opal's voice that she was repeating the question. She jerked herself back to reality from the daydreams into which the offer had propelled her.

'I'm sorry, Miss Opal! 'Tis wonderful, which is all I can find words to say. And if you're after offering me the job, then I'm accepting, and thank you very much indeed, and I'll do my very best to please. And when do I start?'

'That's not certain. It might not be until December, or even the beginning of January. There's a lot to be done. Which brings me to this: you mustn't talk about this to anyone.'

'Not Graham?' Breda's face fell.

'Of course you can discuss it with Graham, though only away from the store. And Mr Sutcliffe knows, but not many others. It might seem unnecessary to you, all this secrecy, but it's essential for several reasons. I shall announce the whole project as soon as I reasonably can, but in the meantime you are to say nothing.'

'Please, Miss Opal . . . what about my aunt and uncle? You see, I live with them.'

'I'm afraid not,' Opal said. 'I'm sure they wouldn't gossip intentionally, but rumour flies around the West Riding as swiftly as a bird in flight. And with a good deal less accuracy.'

Later that same week Graham and Breda went together to see Father Delaney. 'We want to be married as soon as possible,' Graham said the minute they were settled in the priest's study.

Father Delaney smiled. 'I'm sure you do! But in a case like yours and Breda's it's not entirely straightforward. You wouldn't expect it to be. There are obligations to consider, questions to be asked and answered, on your part as well as mine. We have to be as sure as we can, and this is for the sake of both of you and your life together, as well as for the Church.'

'We've discussed it between ourselves,' Graham said. 'We're sure of ourselves.'

'And perhaps rightly so,' Father Delaney said. 'We shall see. In the first place I want you both to come to see me every week for at least four weeks, and not until this marriage preparation is over, Graham, shall I ask you to make any of the promises which will be required of you. And remember that these promises are not just for you, they are for the future of your marriage, and for the children you will have.'

'I see,' Graham said. 'And after that?'

'After that, if you have made your promises, and the Bishop sees no other impediment, then he will grant you a dispensation. You will be married in the Catholic Church, though since you are not a Catholic, it can't take place in the Mass.'

'How long . . . ?' Graham began.

'Let's say between three and six months,' Father Delaney said. 'It sounds a long time, but it will soon pass.'

'I never dreamt it would take so long,' Graham said to Breda as they walked back to Waterloo Terrace. 'I'm ready to make the promises here and now.'

'I know,' Breda said. 'But perhaps Father Delaney was right and 'twill soon pass, especially with all the changes we'll be going through between now and then.'

'It can't pass quickly enough for me,' Graham said. 'Oh, Breda, I want you so much. I can't tell you how much.'

'You don't have to,' Breda said. 'Aren't I made of flesh and blood, the same as you?'

*   *   *

The day before Breda and Graham had gone to see Father Delaney, Graham had telephoned his father. He said nothing at all of Opal's offer. That could wait. Nor did he discuss his visit to Kilbally. What he did was to accede to his father's request that he should come home for the weekend.

'Though it depends on whether Miss Opal will let me have Saturday off – and Breda, of course. And we'll have to come back on Sunday.'

'We'd have liked you for longer,' Henry said.

Breda was dismayed at the prospect. 'It's so soon!' she objected. She had vaguely hoped that it might be put off, though she knew it would have to happen eventually.

It was late on Saturday afternoon when they reached Reigate. Tompkins was at the station to meet them. Breda had never ridden in a chauffeur-driven car in all her life, hardly ever in any car, come to that. Nevertheless she smiled at Tompkins, took a deep breath and climbed into the back as to the manner born. It was the way, she decided, she'd meet the whole weekend. She would just do her best in every situation. Less than twenty-four hours, she reminded herself, as the car sped smoothly out of the town and in a mile or two along a tree-lined country lane.

'Here we are, darling,' Graham said.

There were high gateposts, surmounted by stone pine-apples. As they turned into the short drive, the imposing house facing them, Graham held her hand tightly. 'Chin up!' he said.

As the car drew up, Henry and Miriam Prince came down from the terrace to greet them. When Tompkins sprang to open the door and Graham handed her down from the car Breda felt that this must be how royalty felt, but at the same time she wished the ground would open and swallow her up.

Henry Prince approached, hand held out to Breda. Miriam Prince kissed her son warmly on both cheeks. 'So lovely to have you home again, darling!'

'This is Breda, Mother,' Graham said.

Miriam Prince extended a manicured hand on which rings shone and sparkled like miniature suns.

'How do you do, Miss O'Connor,' she said pleasantly.

'I'm very well, thank you,' Breda replied. 'I hope you are.' And wasn't that the wrong thing to say, she asked herself? Had she not read in the magazines Auntie Josie bought that when someone said 'How do you do,' they didn't actually want to know? 'Please call me Breda,' she said.

'I suppose Breda is an Irish name?' Miriam asked. And you couldn't say she didn't say everything graciously and politely, Breda thought. Oh no, you couldn't say that!

'Sure, 'tis very common in Ireland,' she said.

'Now why don't we go in and I'll show you to your room?' Miriam said.

She accompanied Breda up the wide staircase which ran from the centre of the hall. How wonderful, Breda thought, to have a staircase on which two people could walk side by side!

Mrs Prince took her along a corridor and around a couple of corners, then showed her into a large, prettily furnished bedroom.

'I'll leave you to it, then,' she said brightly. 'I expect you'll want to wash. You have your own bathroom. Tea on the terrace. Come down when you're ready.'

Breda surveyed herself from all angles in the triple mirror over the large dressing-table. She had never seen so much of herself before. Where was Graham, she wondered? She had been whisked away while he was still talking to his father, and she doubted that he'd even seen the going of her. And now his parents would have him to themselves, which was no doubt what they wanted, and was fair enough. Well, she'd be glad to leave them be for a while, and then she'd go down if ever she could find the way.

She looked out of the window. The garden was large, immaculately kept, fringed by trees. It gave way to farmland, fields of gold and brown stubble where the corn had already been harvested, and beyond that, softly rounded green hills. There was nothing of the wildness of either Kilbally or Yorkshire. It was altogether more civilized. Also, she thought, it was where she might have ended up had Graham not been offered the job in Hebghyll. She wondered what his parents would say to *that* bit of news.

She remained there, staring out of the window, nervous about joining the others. What could she possibly have to say to Mr and Mrs Prince? She wished Graham would fetch her.

A minute later he did so. He took her in his arms and his kisses restored her. 'I thought you must be lost!' he said.

'Have I been too long? I was looking out of the window. This is a large place – but very nice,' she added quickly.

'It's much too large,' Graham said, 'now that we've all flown the nest. Which reminds me, both of my brothers and their wives will be here this evening, and a few friends my mother's invited. But don't look so worried. I'll stick to you like a leech.'

'Oh, I will not worry.' Or at least she wouldn't show it. It was only the one evening, after all. This time tomorrow it would be over. And Graham would be with her.

He took her hand and led her downstairs to where tea was laid on the terrace.

'Do come and sit down,' Mrs Prince said. 'We wondered where you'd got to, Breda.'

She poured pale golden tea from a Wedgwood teapot into exquisitely fine cups. Breda sent up a swift prayer that she wouldn't drop one.

'It's getting late in the year to be sitting outside, but I do so love tea in the garden, don't you?' Mrs Prince asked Breda.

'Oh, indeed I do,' Breda replied. 'Sure, there is nothing I like better!'

'And what do you do in Opal's? Graham hasn't told us. I've always thought it must be most amusing to work in a shop. I tell my husband he should let me have a go.'

'I'm in Display,' Breda said. 'But I used to serve behind the counter in my stepfather's store in Kilbally. That was amusing all right!'

'Your stepfather has a *store*?'

'A village store,' Breda said. 'You could get the whole of it on this terrace. But there's little he doesn't sell. Paraffin, sugar, candles, bacon, brushes . . . '

She stopped suddenly, aware that nervousness was making her talk too much.

'How very interesting,' Mrs Prince murmured.

'It's very much the way my grandfather started,' Henry Prince said. 'Only in the East End of London, not in Ireland.'

'But a *long* time ago, darling,' his wife said. 'Would you like another cup of tea, Breda?'

'No thank you, Mrs Prince.' What she craved was something to eat. There was nothing, not even a biscuit. They'd had sandwiches on the train to London, but that was ages ago.

'Has Graham told you that Hugh and David, his brothers, will be here this evening? And a few old friends of Graham's will drop in for a drink before dinner.' She turned and smiled at Graham. 'Everyone's dying to see you, darling! You've been very much missed.'

394

A chill breeze sprang up from nowhere, shaking the petals from the roses, rustling through the trees. Breda, in her thin frock, shivered.

'You're cold, Breda love,' Graham cried. 'I think we should go in.'

'Nearly time we went up and changed,' Miriam said, rising to her feet. 'Your dinner jacket is hanging in your wardrobe, Graham. I had it cleaned.'

'I'm not wearing a dinner jacket, Mother,' Graham said. 'Not for an evening at home. All that nonsense went out with the war.'

'But the war's over, darling. I do think we ought to get back to civilized standards again, don't you?'

'Not if it means wearing a dinner jacket for an evening at home,' Graham persisted.

'You're right, my boy!' Henry Prince said. 'I shan't wear mine, either.'

Miriam Prince gave a deep sigh. 'You're very tiresome, both of you! Oh well, we ladies will just have to make up for you!' She gave Breda a smile.

Thank the good Lord I packed my ribbon dress, Breda thought. It would do nicely.

Graham stood up. 'Come along, Breda. I'm going to give you a conducted tour of the house before we go up.'

'Be sure you're down at seven. Don't be late,' Miriam cautioned.

At five minutes to seven, having had a warm, scented bath, done her hair – which obligingly for once went the way she wanted it – Breda carefully applied her make-up, put on her ribbon dress, and then her precious gold chain. She took a last, critical look at herself in the mirror. Yes, she would do. She wouldn't disgrace Graham in front of his posh friends.

Waiting now for him to collect her, she looked out of the window again. The sun was low in the sky and any minute now it would sink out of sight and dusk would fall; time to draw the curtains. Darkness came earlier than in the north, and much earlier than in Kilbally.

'Come in!' she called, in answer to Graham's knock on the door. She remained standing by the window.

'I'm looking at the view,' she said. 'It's very pretty.'

'I'd rather look at you,' Graham said. 'Turn around and let me see you!'

She turned around slowly and faced him. For a moment Graham looked at her, saying nothing. It *was* only a moment, she supposed, but it seemed a long one. She was suddenly apprehensive. 'Will I do?' she asked anxiously.

'You look absolutely lovely, my darling! Oh, I wish we could just stay here, the two of us; not go down at all!'

'And don't I wish the same?' Breda said. 'Aren't I as nervous as a cat?'

'Come here, my love,' Graham said. 'I want to hold you.'

He crushed her tightly against him, kissing her with passion, his hand stroking the length of her spine, moving over the curve of her hips. She stroked the back of his neck, ran her fingers through his hair, pressed against him, desperately wanted her body to be one with his. But when he began to propel her towards the bed she suddenly resisted.

'No Graham! No! We have to go down. I'll crease my dress! Everyone will notice. They'll guess!'

By the time they went downstairs the drawing room, it seemed to Breda as she stood in the doorway clutching Graham's arm, was filled with people, all chattering like magpies. She wanted to turn and run, though she would never allow herself to do so. In any case Mrs Prince was advancing towards them. There was no escape.

The girl looked very nice, Miriam thought. She was a pleasant enough child, but not what she would have chosen to be the wife of her favourite son. 'There you are!' she said. 'Everyone's arrived. So why don't I take Breda around, Graham, and introduce her while you catch up with your friends?'

Graham felt Breda's pressure on his arm. 'Thank you, Mother,' he replied. 'I'll introduce Breda. She *is* my fiancée.' He took Breda firmly by the elbow and they moved away.

'My brother David, his wife Laura; my other brother Hugh and his wife Elaine.' Graham said, breaking into a group. 'This is my fiancée, Breda.'

There was a swift moment of silence when they first looked at her, and after that they were pleasant enough, especially Laura. Breda took to her at once. The eldest brother, Hugh, she did not care for. He was tall and supercilious, looking down at her from his great height, speaking to her, though only occasionally, in a refined drawl.

When they left his family, Graham shepherded Breda from group to group, from person to person until, it seemed to her, she must have met everyone in the room. They were nice, or not so nice, in varying degrees, though it was uncanny the way they all stopped what they were saying and gave her their rapt attention for the first moments.

Why did they do this, Breda asked herself? Why did they stare?

'Wait just here one moment,' Graham said, 'while I get us both a drink. Don't move, now!'

The minute he left, Laura Prince came up to her. 'How are you doing, Breda?' she asked. 'It's a bit of an ordeal, isn't it?'

'Sure, I've never met as many people at once in all my life, unless at a *céilidh* or a funeral. Like as not then I knew them all. But what I don't understand is why they stare at me. Have I got a smut on my face, or what?'

'No smuts,' Laura said. 'And you have a very beautiful face.'

'But not beautiful enough to stop the traffic,' Breda said. 'So what is it? Is it the way I sound? But it can't be, because up to now I've hardly said a word.'

'In the first place it's because you're the girl who's captured Graham, when some of them have been after him for ages. They've been curious to see you ever since they heard!'

Breda looked round. The young women were so smart in their little black dresses and pearl earrings, their hair expertly coiffured. Why have I been the fortunate one, she asked herself?

'And in the second place,' Laura said, 'I think simply because you're worth looking at; you're so lovely! I'm sure Graham must have told you that a hundred times! As for your Irish accent – don't apologize for it. It's most attractive, I assure you.'

Breda was suffused in one tremendous blush. 'I wasn't fishing for compliments!'

'I know,' Laura said. 'And your dress is beautiful.'

Graham reappeared, carrying two drinks. He noticed Breda's heightened colour and his eyes questioned her.

'I've been telling Breda how lovely she looks,' Laura said.

He could have hugged his sister-in-law. 'I agree with you,' he said.

A little later, people began to leave, all except family, who were staying to dinner.

'What a peculiar arrangement,' Breda whispered to Graham. 'They all come, they have two drinks, then they go home again! In Kilbally wouldn't we all be dancing 'til midnight?'

She was, all the same, thankful that there was now to be a meal. She was starving. 'My front's touching my back!' she confided to Graham. There had been dishes of cheese straws and nuts, but Graham had been so busy introducing her that she'd not had a nibble of anything. And now the second drink was going to her head and if she didn't eat something soon she'd pass out.

The meal was good. She ate every scrap on her plate, which was probably not ladylike, but she was *so* hungry. After dinner they moved into the drawing room, where Mrs Prince served strong coffee in ornate cups so small that it was difficult to take a hold of the handles.

'There!' Mrs Prince said when they were all settled down. 'Now wasn't it pleasant to catch up with your friends again, Graham?'

'Very nice,' Graham said.

'So when are you coming back to us, dear?' she asked. 'When are you going to take up your place in Prince and Harper?'

Breda put down her coffee cup on the small mahogany table beside her. She found herself gripping it so hard that she felt in danger of breaking it. This was the moment she had been dreading. She looked across at Graham, but his face was expressionless.

'So when do you think?' Miriam Prince repeated.

'In fact, Mother, I won't be working in Prince and Harper.' Graham's voice was cool and decisive.

Henry Prince sat bolt upright. 'What's that you say?'

'I said, I shan't be working in Prince and Harper.'

Breda looked around at the circle of faces. On Mrs Prince's was an expression of confused disbelief. The two brothers, Breda thought, though surprised, looked not displeased, their wives non-committal. Henry Prince was flushed with a rage he made no attempt to conceal.

'It's this painting nonsense! That's what it is, isn't it? You're all set to starve in a garret! Well, it won't work, and when it fails, don't come to me for help!'

'It's nothing to do with painting, Father,' Graham said. 'The truth is, Opal Carson has offered me a job, and I've decided to take it.'

'Opal?' Henry spluttered. 'She hasn't said a word to me! Why hasn't she consulted me?'

'I imagine because the job was for me,' Graham said. 'But she'll be in touch with you quite soon.'

'I should damned well hope so,' Henry thundered. 'So what is this job that you'll throw up a job in Prince and Harper for it?'

'I'm afraid I can't give you the details just yet,' Graham said. 'When you speak to Opal, perhaps she will.'

'But darling, you can't live in *Akersfield*!' Miriam sounded shocked to the core.

'Of course I can, Mother,' Graham said gently. 'I've never been happier than in Akersfield. And it's not the end of the world, you know. And I'm not really needed in Prince and Harper. There's quite enough family there already.' He looked at Breda. His smile was so warm, so loving, that she felt as though he had touched her, embraced her. It gave her the strength she needed.

'If you'll all excuse me,' she said. 'I'll be going to bed.'

Mrs Prince's glance implored Breda. 'Graham will never be happy in Yorkshire,' she said. 'It's not what he's used to.'

'I hope to make him happy, Mrs Prince,' Breda said. She felt surprisingly calm as she stood up and made for the door. Laura Prince caught hold of her hand as she went past. 'Good-night, Breda! I've enjoyed meeting you.'

'And haven't I enjoyed meeting you?' Breda said. 'And when we are married and have a place of our own,' she added, 'I hope you'll come up and stay with us.'

Graham had risen to his feet at the same time as Breda. 'I'll also say good-night.'

'But we have matters to discuss,' Henry protested. 'You've hardly told us anything. Why are you doing this? I'm not at all sure that I agree with it.'

'I'm sure you will when I'm able to tell you more about it,' Graham said. 'You'll realize what a good chance it is for me. So no hard feelings, Father. And now if you don't mind, I *will* go to bed. It's been a long day. I'm quite tired, and I'm sure Breda is.'

He put his arm around her and they left together.

When they reached her bedroom he went in with her and closed the door behind them.

When Graham took her in his arms, Breda lifted a troubled face to his. 'They think it's me! They think I'm taking you away. I'm not, am I?'

'Let's put it this way, sweetheart,' Graham said. 'Wherever you were, that's where I'd want to be. Yorkshire or the North Pole, it wouldn't matter!'

He pushed her onto the bed, her head against the pillows, and began to kiss and caress her. 'Shall I tell you what I'd like to do with this dress, lovely though it is? I'd like to take it off. Please, Breda!'

She offered no resistance while he undid the buttons and pulled it from her. Resistance was beyond her now, and in no time at all she was caught up, as he was, in a frenzy of passion. She had not imagined it could be as sweet as this.

Then suddenly, with no warning at all, she pushed him away from her and sat bolt upright.

'What in the world . . . ?'

He tried to push her down again but she would have none of it. 'No!' she cried. 'Not here! Not in your parents' house. Not the first time ever!'

She left the bed, took her dressing-gown from the hook behind the door and wrapped it around her.

'Oh Graham, please understand!' she begged. 'I couldn't do it here.'

He was white faced. She thought he was angry, but when he spoke his voice was gentle. 'I do understand.'

'And forgive?'

'There's nothing to forgive,' Graham said.

'I'm very tired,' Breda said. 'I'd like to go to bed. I'd like to go to bed with you, my darling. You know that. And one day I will. But not now. We must say good-night.'

He looked at her long and uncertainly. Then he said, 'You don't know how hard it is, Breda. Nevertheless, good-night.'

Breda slept fitfully, longing for Graham, and was glad when morning came. They were to leave after breakfast.

'I hope you know what you're doing, my boy,' Henry Prince said grimly.

'I think I do, Father. And I'll keep in touch.'

At the door, Miriam Prince bade a loving farewell to Graham. Her eyes were bright with tears she would not allow herself to shed. Then she turned to Breda. 'We must all keep in touch,' she said. 'Please come again. You'll be welcome.'

'Thank you,' Breda said. 'I will. And I hope you'll come to Yorkshire.'

'I will,' Miriam said.

She hesitated, as if she wanted to say something and couldn't find the words. Then she said, 'I'm sure you're going to make Graham happy.'

402

Twenty-Two

Plans for the opening of Opal's of Hebghyll under its new management moved with the speed of light. It would start with a bang on New Year's Day, with a grand clearance sale.

'A clean sweep,' Opal said to George Soames. 'Everything that's old or tatty or out of date goes in that sale. I want a fresh start, with everything clean and bright and up to date.'

She would have liked, with a few exceptions, to have made a clean sweep of the staff, but it was not on the cards. There was not enough time to recruit new staff, even if they were to be had.

'In any case, it wouldn't do,' George warned her. 'What sort of an image would you have in the town if you started off by sacking people?'

'Oh, you're quite right,' Opal agreed. 'It was never anything more than wishful thinking. Anyway, they can't all be as bad as they seem. They've just been allowed to get slack. Perhaps what they need is a good shaking up.'

A few members of staff had already decided to leave, not liking the thought of a new broom which looked ready to sweep everything thoroughly clean, and none of it under the carpet. They were mostly the older ones, some due for retirement, some already well past that age. Opal and George Soames between them had drawn up pension plans which were more than generous.

'The rest will weed themselves out without any help from me, once the retraining scheme starts,' Opal said.

In the meantime she would manage with the addition of the hand-picked team from Leasfield – although its members could only be spared for a short time – and a few new assistants she had been able to get locally. 'We shall *have* to manage,' she said firmly. 'No two ways about it. If it means we all have to work harder, so be it!'

How much harder they could all work George was not sure. The team from Leasfield was at full stretch behind the scenes, putting in evenings and weekends when the place was closed. George had also managed to recruit some of the Hebghyll staff, who were keen for the changes as well as pleased to earn extra money, to work overtime.

Within ten days of returning from the visit to his parents Graham had left Leasfield for good. He had expected to travel to and from his new job each day, but Opal had insisted that he found lodgings in Hebghyll.

'Let's face it,' she said, 'as Deputy Manager you have a lot to learn, and it's best learned by putting in the hours on the spot. It will also do you no harm to be seen around the town. Let people know who you are, what you're doing.'

For Breda it was another matter. She was sent to Hebghyll, together with Jim Sutcliffe – only the two of them could be spared, as it was coming up to Christmas – at the same time as Graham, but for the moment she must travel daily. Miss Opal paid her fares, but there was no question of her financing lodgings, which Breda would have preferred but couldn't afford.

She and Jim Sutcliffe were put to work with the two existing members of Hebghyll Display, but with Jim firmly in charge, his word to be law, his decisions, though he would listen to the others, to be the final ones. Miss Opal had made this quite plain. It was not a popular ruling with the Hebghyll faction.

'So what will it be like when you go back to Leasfield and I'm left here?' Breda asked Jim after a particularly argumentative session.

'You'll be all right,' Jim assured her. 'I'll back you to hold your own any day of the week.' He had watched her growing confidence ever since she'd started to work under him. And she was certainly talented. He'd be sorry to lose her from Leasfield.

Then, as the weeks rushed by towards the end of the year, Breda was so busy, there was so much work to be got through if the appearance of the store was to be changed to fit Miss Opal's idea – and they were not all Miss Opal's ideas; some of her own had been accepted – that she had no time to worry about dissensions and pinpricks.

Besides, wasn't Graham there? What else mattered beside that? Since the store was small, and his job took him into every part of it, she saw him often, even if only in passing. In business hours they spoke to each other only when work made it necessary, but he was there. She was aware of his presence and it lightened her life.

The only fly in the ointment was that she saw so little of him outside work – there *was* so little life outside work. Almost their only time together was when they had both finished for the day and he would walk her to the station to catch her train. The nights were cold and dark, but the darkness meant that they could walk with their arms around each other, stopping to kiss, and as for the cold, held close to Graham Breda felt nothing of it. Only when she left him, watching out of the carriage window as long as ever she could discern his shape on the dimly lit platform, did Breda begin to shiver, and feel the cold all the way until she was safely inside her aunt's house in Waterloo Terrace.

Two nights before Christmas the weather was particularly nasty, with a strong wind from the north and showers of icy rain. Josephine, hearing Breda's step on the path, opened the door to meet her.

'This is ridiculous!' she protested. 'You look perished! Come into the warm at once. I've got some cocoa ready. How long is it since you had a bite to eat?'

'I had a sandwich at tea time,' Breda said. It seemed an age ago, and she *was* hungry, but even more she was cold and tired. What she wanted above everything was to thaw her chilled body and go to bed.

'Well, I'll not have you going to bed on an empty stomach,' Josephine said. 'I've saved some potatoes and onions to fry up for you. They'll not take a minute. What I want to know is, how long is this state of affairs going to go on?'

'I suppose until we take over properly in the New Year,' Breda said. 'We might get back to normal shop hours then.' And I'd be able to see Graham in Hebghyll in the evenings, so I'd be home just as late, but it wouldn't matter then, she thought.

Josephine moved the potato mixture around in the frying pan, turning up the gas to get it crisp and brown. The savoury smell teased at Breda's nostrils and suddenly she was famished.

'Well, I never thought to hear myself say it,' Josephine remarked, 'and it's not that I want to lose you, but I do think it'd be a sight better if you could take lodgings in Hebghyll. You could still come home at the weekends.'

She thought of her house as being Breda's home. She had grown so used to her, so fond of her. She felt towards her almost as she did towards her own daughters.

She served the potatoes and onions onto a large plate and placed it in front of Breda.

'Get that down you!' she said. 'It'll do you no harm – though goodness knows it would half kill me with indigestion! But at your age I don't suppose you know what indigestion is.'

'I don't,' Breda said. 'And as for going into lodgings and coming home at weekends, I couldn't afford it. It's been hinted I'll get a raise in the New Year, so it might be possible then. I wouldn't want to leave you, Auntie Josie, but . . . '

'But you'd like to see more of Graham! Well, that's understandable, love.'

If only we could be married, Breda thought with longing. They had done everything that was required of them. There was nothing now except to wait. How much longer?

'Have patience, love,' Josephine said, reading her niece's thoughts.

On the morning of Christmas Eve Opal drove straight from her home to Hebghyll.

'I'm not staying long,' she told George Soames. 'As you know, Daniel's coming up from London to spend Christmas at home, and not for the world would I be elsewhere when he arrives. He comes north all too seldom.'

'In fact, I hardly expected to see you today,' George said.

'Oh, I told you I'd be here, but I also have to go into Leasfield. I couldn't fail to visit my own store on Christmas Eve. I just wanted to check how things were here and to have a word with a few people. Especially I want to see those who are leaving. Will you arrange for them to come in turn to my office, starting in half an hour? Give me ten minutes with each one. Tell the switchboard I don't want any interruptions.'

The short time she spent with each of the leavers seemed, to them, totally unhurried, since her whole interest was concentrated on each one in turn, enquiring about their plans, wishing them well for the future. To those who were leaving after long service she presented gifts – bracelets for the women and gold tiepins to the men. When the ten minutes were up she rose leisurely to her feet, came around to the front of her desk, and shook hands. 'I hope you'll come into the store often,' she said. 'We shall value your custom, but if not to buy, then just to look around.'

When the last one had left, George Soames returned. 'Have we time for a quick coffee?' Opal asked. 'And then I want to go around and speak to as many people as I can. I'd like you to go with me. I want to make it clear that though they'll see me from time to time, *you* are the one in charge.'

'If you hadn't suggested I accompany you,' George said, 'I'd have done it on my own. It's been a difficult time over the last few weeks, and on the whole people have been quite co-operative. I also think it would be a good idea for Graham to do his own tour. Christmas greetings and all that.'

'Fine!' Opal said. 'Are you pleased with him?'

'Very pleased. He's shaping well, learning fast. It was good thinking on your part to take him on.'

From the pleased and surprised reception the two of them received as they went around, Opal formed the opinion that such a thing had not happened before. 'That went down well,' she said to George afterwards. 'I was particularly impressed by how many names you knew! I can't hope to catch up with you on that.'

'I've still a number to learn,' George admitted.

Opal crossed to the coat cupboard and took her coat from its hanger. George held it while she slipped her arms into it. It was the pride and delight of her life, this coat; black Persian lamb with a dark mink collar. At the same time, she felt it a great extravagance to own such a coat even though she told herself she had earned it. She had worked long and hard for this luxury. She pulled it around her, snuggled into it. 'I'll be off, then,' she said. 'I think those who have to go back to Leasfield shouldn't leave it too late. The weather forecast is bad.'

'I'll see to it,' George promised.

'Right! Then we'll expect you and Mary for Christmas dinner!'

Breda snatched a word with Graham in the brief interval she took at midday to eat her sandwiches.

'Do you think we'll get away on time?' she asked anxiously. 'I don't want to be late. I promised to give Auntie Josie a hand with the Christmas preparations.'

Graham was to go home with her and stay the nights of Christmas Eve and Christmas Day. The latter was on a Saturday, but although Boxing Day was officially on Monday they had promised, along with some others, to go into work that day.

'I don't see why not, sweetheart,' Graham replied.

Breda's face creased into a smile. 'You're not supposed to call me "sweetheart" in working hours!'

'It's your dinner break,' he said. 'I can call you anything I like – sweetheart, gorgeous, beautiful, darling!'

Breda glanced around nervously. 'Stop it! Someone might hear you. Can we catch the six-thirty?'

'I expect so,' Graham said.

He had received an imploring letter from his mother, asking him to go home for Christmas. He was glad to have the excuse that, in the circumstances, he couldn't take enough time to make it worthwhile. In fact he would not have gone whatever the position in Hebghyll. He did not plan to make another visit to Reigate before he and Breda were married. Sometimes he wondered, with a degree of impatience, when that would be. He couldn't understand the delay, saw no reason for it. It all seemed quite simple to him.

Just before two o'clock the snow started to fall. It fell in great, heavy flakes, staying where it fell, except where it was blown into drifts by the sharp wind. Customers coming into the store for Christmas Eve shopping appeared like snowmen, hats and coats covered in a layer of thick flakes. By three o'clock the stream of customers had thinned to a trickle.

Graham looked out from his office window. It was coming down as fast as ever, falling onto a silent and now largely deserted street. Only an occasional car went carefully down the hill. He watched a solitary pedestrian slithering and sliding on the opposite pavement. Then he went in search of George Soames. 'Have you seen what it's like, Mr Soames?' he asked.

'I have! It doesn't look good, to say the least. I'm thinking I'll send home at least half the staff, those who live farthest away. But we can't shut the shop until closing time, half-past five.'

'I doubt we'll get anyone in, sir,' Graham said.

'Probably not. But we must stay open. Come with me and we'll go round and see who we can send home.'

By four o'clock two-thirds of the staff had been despatched and there was not a customer left in the store. Graham was ordered to make a thorough check in every department.

'There's no-one except staff,' he reported. 'The maintenance man is trying to clear a path from the pavement to the main door but as fast as he shovels, the snow comes down and covers the ground again.'

'Right!' George Soames said. 'I'll now send everyone home except one person in each department, and if no customers come in the next half-hour, that's it. We'll close.'

No-one came. Outside the warm, brightly lit store, with its stands and shelves and counters filled with gaily coloured offerings, the world was another place; strange, alien. There were no sounds at all now, everything was deserted, even the footprints and tyre marks which had shown in the snow a while ago had been obliterated, as if no-one had ever passed that way.

'We'll lock up,' George Soames decided. 'Tell everyone to leave as quickly as possible, and where they can, to go in twos and threes. And when you've done that you and Breda had better get off. Leave the rest to me.'

The station was no more than a quarter of a mile off, although the way looked impenetrable as Graham and Breda set out, arm in arm.

'You should perhaps have left earlier, with the rest of the Leasfield lot,' Graham said to Breda. 'It would have been easier for you.'

'I wouldn't have gone. Not without you, and I knew you couldn't leave. Never mind, once we get on the train we'll soon be home – though we don't know what it'll be like in Akersfield, do we?'

And they were not to know. Waterloo Terrace was not to see them for Christmas. A solitary porter emerged from the station office. 'Sorry, sir! No trains at all getting through. There's deep drifts on the line in both directions.'

They stared at him in disbelief. 'No trains?'

'That's what I said, sir. And none tomorrow, it being Christmas Day – even if they clear the line.'

'What shall we do?' Breda asked Graham.

'Only one thing *to* do,' Graham answered. 'We go back to my digs and see if Mrs Wharton can find you a bed for the night!'

'And if she can't? What then?'

Graham smiled. 'You can always share mine!'

Mrs Wharton looked doubtful when a room was requested. 'I can't honestly say there isn't an empty bed in the house, because it wouldn't be true. There is, but by rights it belongs to Miss Evans. She's a teacher and she's gone home for Christmas.'

'Do you know anywhere else I could try?' Breda pleaded.

'I don't. And it's a night not fit to turn a dog out. So I'll take it upon myself to let you have Miss Evans's room for tonight and tomorrow. She's a kind lady. I reckon she'd understand.'

With Graham following, she showed Breda to the room. It was clean and bright, but cold. 'There's an electric fire you can switch on,' Mrs Wharton said. 'But I'll ask you not to leave it on when you're out of the room. It comes a bit expensive.'

'I'll be careful,' Breda promised.

'This is very good of you, Mrs Wharton,' Graham said. 'We both appreciate it.'

'Well, if you'd like to come down in about half an hour I'll make a bite to eat, though I don't promise what it'll be. I'm up to the eyes. And in the meantime, take off your wet coats and I'll see to them drying. We don't want them dripping over the carpet, do we?'

'I'll carry them down,' Graham offered. 'And our shoes, though Breda doesn't have a change.'

Mrs Wharton looked at Breda's feet. 'I reckon you're about the same size as Miss Evans. I dare say in the circumstances she wouldn't mind if you borrowed a night-gown *and* her slippers. She's sure to have some lying around.'

She had. There was a pair of fluffy pink mules under the bed, not at all the kind of thing Breda would have chosen, but when she took off her wet shoes and stockings and thrust her cold feet into the slippers it was heaven.

Graham was back in five minutes. He came into the room and immediately took Breda into his arms. She relaxed against him, the warmth of his body seeping into hers as he held her close. He was kissing her, deep, passionate kisses, while his hands moved over her body. She returned his kisses, pressing her body hard against his. She stroked the back of his neck, ran her fingers through his hair, pulled his head down towards her, until he was kissing her neck, her face, her closed eyelids. Without a word, he began to push her towards the bed, and she was lying down and he on top of her. She shifted under his weight, turned her face away from him. 'No! I can't! You mustn't!'

'I must,' he said. 'I want you. I can't wait. I can tell you want me.'

'I do,' Breda said. 'All the time I do. But we can't.'

She turned her face away, wriggled her body from his grasp, and sat upright. He rolled over onto his back, his eyes closed, lying there without speaking, without moving. Breda watched him helplessly. She felt wretched. 'I'm sorry,' she whispered. 'I'm truly sorry! Please say you forgive me!'

Without a word, without looking at her, he jumped from the bed and walked out of the room.

Breda sat on the edge of the bed. She had seldom felt so deeply miserable, or so confused. He hated her, didn't he, because she had been prudish? Yet she wasn't a prude, she knew she wasn't, and when they were married she would show him that. If ever they *were* married, if he didn't tire of waiting.

Ten minutes later there was a sharp knock on the door and Graham came back into the room. Breda jumped to her feet and rushed to meet him. He held out his arms and she ran into them. 'Oh Graham, I'm sorry!' she cried. 'Please forgive me! Try to understand.'

'I do understand. And we'll forgive each other. We can't spend Christmas at loggerheads. So tidy yourself up and we'll go down and eat.'

He spoke in level tones of reason, as if devoid of feeling, yet Breda felt herself swamped by differing emotions fighting against each other: relief that he had come back to her, her own sexual frustration, which she was sure he did not understand, condemnation of herself that she had hurt him by her denial, and the underlying feeling that it had been right to do so, it had been all she could do.

She crossed to the dressing-table and surveyed herself in the mirror. She looked a mess. The ends of her hair were still damp and she was wearing her working clothes. Moreover, she would have to wear them right through Christmas Day. Hadn't she planned to wear something especially becoming – a red dress she had bought in Opal's, and about which she had told no-one, not even Auntie Josie? She had planned to make an appearance in it for Christmas dinner.

The thought of Christmas dinner reminded her that her aunt would not know where she was, and would be worried.

'I have to get in touch with Auntie Josie,' she said to Graham.

'That's not difficult,' Graham said. 'At least it won't be unless the lines are down. There's a phone in the house.'

The lines were not down. Josephine was relieved to hear from Breda, disappointed that she would not be with them all for Christmas and, by the tone of her voice, though nothing explicit was said, slightly disturbed that her niece would be spending Christmas as good as alone with Graham. But I'm glad I am, Breda thought. Other than spending Christmas as his wife, and in spite of the difficulties of the early part of the evening, she could think of nothing she would rather do.

It was clear enough, after they had eaten, that Mrs Wharton did not want them to linger in the dining room. She had preparations to make for the next day, when her family would be there in full force. 'Providing they can get here, though they live in Hebghyll, so I suppose they can walk,' she said. 'And the two of you are more than welcome to join us for our Christmas dinner.'

They thanked her, and went back upstairs. Graham had found a pack of cards, and for an hour they played various games, in an atmosphere fraught with physical longings and frustrations. In the end it was Breda who put an end to it.

'I'm really very tired,' she said. 'I'd like to go to bed, if you wouldn't mind.'

Their good-night kiss was chaste and hurried. Breda undressed, got into bed and put out the lamp. In spite of her fatigue, any hope she had of going swiftly to sleep was not fulfilled. She lay awake in the dark, hearing the sounds from downstairs, until even those ceased and the whole house was quiet. She felt as though she was the only person in the world lying awake. Her thoughts were wholly occupied with Graham, until at last she drifted into her first sleep.

It came as no surprise, therefore, when the bedroom door was quietly opened and Graham came towards her. Half waking, half sleeping, she made no demur when he climbed into her bed and lay down beside her. It was not until he began to take off her nightgown, hold her breast, that she became fully awake, and then there was no turning back for either of them.

They made love silently, as if it was happening in a dream, as if it carried no responsibility, no denial. It was

415

simply the most natural thing in the world, as if they had done it for ever. She was aware that at one moment she briefly cried out, but in ecstasy rather than in protest.

When it was over, Graham kissed her gently, and left her.

On Christmas Day the snow still lay deep. Breda got out of bed, crossed to the window and drew back the curtains. It was not quite daylight, but the brilliance of the snow took what light there was from the sky and offered back a white world. She would not, she thought, be able to get to Mass. The church lay down by the river; Mrs Wharton's house was at the top of a hilly road which led straight on to the moor. There was no way it could be done, though in her heart she knew that even if the church had been next door she could not have gone this morning.

She was thankful for the impassable snow. No-one except herself – and God, of course – would know what really kept her away. She doubted if even Graham would think of it. It was the first thing which had happened to her since she had met Graham which she would feel unable to share with him.

Her room faced the moor. She stared out at it. The thick, white blanket under which it lay was unbroken, unmarked. Pristine, pure. She could not face that word, and turned away, went back to bed until she could hear the rest of the house stirring.

By Monday the thaw had set in. Clearly the snow, having inconvenienced all except those who liked an old-fashioned, white Christmas, was going to be as swift in going as it had been in coming. Teetering down the hill from Mrs Wharton's house, Breda clung to Graham for fear of going flat on her back in the slush.

Christmas Day and Sunday had gone well enough. They had been warm and well fed – Mrs Wharton had seen to that, inviting them to join in the festivities with her family. Between Graham and Breda nothing had been said of their lovemaking on Christmas Eve, except that on first meeting the next morning Graham had said, 'Shall I say "I'm sorry", my love?' and Breda had shaken her head.

Nevertheless, she felt changed, felt that she must look different, and that everyone would notice this. Would it be apparent to the people at work?

Everyone who had promised to turn up for work that day did so, including Opal. She was accompanied by her ten-year-old daughter, Emmeline, and a tall, handsome young man whom she introduced as her son, Daniel.

'They're both here to work,' Opal explained. 'No passengers allowed. We've got exactly five days to give this place a new look, and most of what we're doing will have to be kept under wraps until Friday night, so as to keep the impact for the opening sale on Saturday.' She turned to Jim Sutcliffe. 'I thought Daniel might give you a hand on Display, he being the artistic one – if you can use him, that is. Emmeline can help to mark sale prices on everything.' She smiled fondly at her daughter. 'That should keep you quiet!'

'You'd better come with me and the Display lot and look at the plans,' Jim Sutcliffe said to Daniel. 'We'll decide where we go from there.'

It was the beginning of the busiest week of Breda's life. Every morning she arrived early, and every evening she caught the last possible train back to Akersfield, trudging up Waterloo Terrace, not knowing how to put one foot in front of the other. Sometimes she thought that the hot meal and the warm welcome which awaited her from her aunt, followed by her own comfortable bed, were all that enabled her to get as far as number 52.

But wasn't it all worthwhile, she thought, when Saturday came and the customers, eager to snap up the bargains they had seen temptingly displayed in the windows over the last three days, and advertised in the newspaper, rushed in the minute the doors were opened? She wondered how many of them knew it was Miss Opal herself who stood just inside the doorway, greeting them.

For her own part, Breda's work was largely over. For today she had to be on hand to take anything out of the windows, since only Display staff were allowed to do that. Apart from that, only small emergencies would claim her. As long as she could be found when wanted, she was free to wander around the store, to see the work in which she'd taken part actually on show. She eyed the intricate draping of materials on the Fabrics department, the colourful display of scarves and gloves, the piles of towels and bed linen, and the artistically designed sales cards, most of which had been done by herself and Daniel Carson.

Jim Sutcliffe came up to her. 'I reckon it looks good,' he said.

'I agree,' Breda said. 'And the tills are ringing. Won't that please Miss Opal!'

Half an hour before closing time Miss Opal sent for her. 'I want to thank you – as I have the others – for all the hard work you've put in over the last few weeks. You've done your part exceptionally well. I'd like to say that you and some of the others could have a day or two's holiday but I'm afraid it's not possible. I'm hoping you're going to be very busy here – and Mr Sutcliffe and the others from Leasfield have to be back there on Monday morning.'

'I don't expect a holiday—' Breda began.

Miss Opal interrupted her. 'You're going to have more responsibility. As time goes on perhaps more than you've bargained for. For that reason I'm giving you a pound a week rise as from Monday.'

Breda's eyes widened. A pound a week! It was far more than she'd expected. Now she *would* be able to take lodgings in Hebghyll! 'Thank you very much, Miss Opal,' she said. 'I'm very grateful.'

'Oh, I shall expect you to earn it,' Miss Opal said.

Isn't it the best New Year's Day I've ever known, Breda asked herself as she left Miss Opal's office. She would find Graham at once, and give him the news.

He was as excited by it as she was.

'You might be able to get a room at Mrs Wharton's,' he suggested.

'No!' Breda said quickly. 'No. I couldn't bear it, and nor could you.'

But wasn't the best thing of all about the New Year was that it was the one in which they'd be married? No more separate lodgings. They'd have their own place, and they'd be together for ever. Wasn't everything leading up to that?

But way down deep inside her there was one nagging worry which she wouldn't voice to Graham or to anyone. But for today she wouldn't let it nag at her. Just for today she would put it away from her.

Twenty-Three

Breda found lodgings easily enough. Graham enquired of Mrs Wharton, who recommended a Mrs Settle. 'Four houses down the road from me,' she said. 'Your young lady won't do better than Mrs Settle.'

If she wondered why Graham had not asked if *she* could accommodate his young lady, she did not say so. She would have refused anyway. She didn't hold with engaged couples lodging in the same house, especially when they looked as much in love as those two.

Mrs Settle offered breakfast and supper and a very small room with a single bed, an armchair, a wardrobe formed from a curtain hung across one corner, and a rickety dressing-table.

'Luxurious it is not,' Breda said to Graham, when they left after she had agreed to take it. 'But it's clean and it's cheap, and I can *just* see the moor from the window.'

It had to be cheap. Her wage, even with the increase, would only just run to it, taking into account that she would no longer have to pay her aunt. After she had paid for her lunches there would be little left to save towards her marriage, and she wanted to come to Graham with a decently filled bottom drawer.

Seeking lodgings was not her first priority in that week. Before another Sunday came she knew she must clear her conscience of the sin of Christmas Eve. On her first free dinner hour, telling Graham she had to do some shopping in the town, she sought out the church in Hebghyll and the priest heard her confession. She came away feeling relieved, though not totally. 'Are you pregnant?' he had asked her. She had to tell him she did not know. Now she longed for the days to pass so that she might be freed, yet dreaded their passing in case she was not. She had heard it said that it couldn't happen the first time you made love, but she had no idea whether that was an old wives' tale, and there was no-one she could ask, however obliquely.

She said nothing to Graham of her fears, nor of the fact that she had sought absolution for the act. He would be hurt by the thought that he had driven her to the priest, and as for the other matter, if it was so he would know soon enough. So, though she was sick with worry, and it would be more than two weeks before it could be resolved, she would try to put it out of her mind.

She arranged to move into her new lodgings on the following Monday. At the weekend, Graham went home with her to Akersfield, to help her to move her belongings.

'I'm right sorry you're leaving us, Breda love,' Josephine said. 'I've enjoyed having you here, and so has your Uncle Brendan. So you must promise us you'll come back often and visit. Think of it as your home.'

'Oh I will, Auntie Josie!' Breda said. It was an easy promise to make and she had every intention of keeping it. She would miss her aunt and uncle. Hadn't they made up, insofar as they could, for the family she'd left behind in Ireland?

'When the weather improves – and it won't be more than a couple of months now,' Graham said, 'we can walk over the moors to Akersfield and get the train back. We've done it often enough in the reverse direction.'

And then, on Sunday, the miracle happened. Father Delaney spoke to her after Mass. 'I was hoping you would be here this weekend,' he said. 'I heard only yesterday. Everything is all right!'

Breda stopped herself in time, remembering where she was, from shrieking with delight. 'Oh! You mean we can be married? At last?'

'That's what I mean, Breda.'

'Then I must rush back and tell Graham! Oh, thank you, thank you!'

She ran all the way back to Waterloo Terrace, burst into the house like a tornado. Graham, reading the Sunday paper, looked up, startled.

'What in the world . . . ?'

'It's happened! It's come! Everything's all right!' she gasped.

A broad smile broke across his face.

'You mean . . . ?'

'Yes! We can be married! Oh, Graham!'

He grabbed her around the waist and swung her around.

They were still in each other's arms when Josephine and Brendan, the latter supporting his mother, arrived back.

'Hello, hello! What's all this then?' Brendan asked.

Breda and Graham broke apart. 'We can be married!' Breda said. 'Isn't it wonderful?'

'Such a fuss!' Grandma Maguire said. 'I thought it was something important, you rushing off like the Devil was after you. Now will someone spare a minute to help me off with my coat? And I'd like a cup of tea.'

Breda bit back the retort which rose to her lips. She would let nothing and no-one spoil this moment. 'I'll make one,' she said. 'Do I take it you won't want to come to my wedding, Grandma?' Her tone was light and teasing.

'I'll think about it,' Grandma Maguire said.

From that moment it was all plans: fixing the date, fixing the place, deciding who would have to be invited and who could be left out.

'I'd be happy with just you and me,' Graham said.

'And so would I!' Breda agreed. 'We don't need anyone else. But 'tis not possible.'

'I should think not!' Josephine said. 'What would it look like, your family not there? A hole-and-corner affair to be sure. And I hope you're going to be married from here, Breda. It's your home in Yorkshire.'

'Of course I am,' Breda assured her. 'Where else?'

'I don't doubt my mother will offer to stage the whole thing in Reigate,' Graham said. 'She'll say it's a long way for all the friends she'll want to invite to travel to Yorkshire.' His words cast the first shadow over the joyful discussion. Transported by delight, Breda had not given a single thought to Graham's family.

'But it's just as far for my family and friends to travel to Reigate,' she said reasonably. 'And in any case we don't want a big wedding, do we? We can't afford it.'

'I don't think expense would be a problem,' Graham said.

'But Graham love, I don't want your family to pay for my wedding! That wouldn't be right.'

Breda heard a sharpness in her voice. Surely they weren't going to quarrel over the wedding, not when they'd waited what seemed half a lifetime to be allowed to have it. She reached out and touched Graham's hand.

'I'm sorry, love. Of course your parents will want to be at your wedding. And they'll be welcome. They'll have to stay in an hotel, of course, but they won't mind that, will they?'

They would deeply mind the whole thing, Graham thought. But he would not say so. It was his parents' problem, not his. They could solve it their own way.

The wedding was fixed, there and then, for the middle of February.

'I shall write to Mammy at once,' Breda said. 'Oh, I do hope she'll come! 'Twill not be the same without her.'

'A perishing cold month for a wedding,' Grandma remarked.

'Then I have to be thankful I don't intend to wear a flimsy white dress and a veil,' Breda said.

She would wear something new, of course, but something which would have a life after the wedding. Clothes were still rationed, though the rumour was that this wouldn't last much longer, and she couldn't afford to waste what coupons she had.

Graham proved right about his mother. On receiving the news of his wedding she wrote back by return of post, a charming, persuasive letter, suggesting that the whole affair would be far better carried out in Reigate. 'More space,' she wrote, 'for all your friends. I'm sure Breda will agree. I will be happy to arrange everything, and of course all expenses will be borne by your father, so no need to worry on that score.'

He handed the letter to Breda. She read it, then handed it back to him. 'I'm sorry,' she said quietly. 'It's very kind and generous of your parents, but I do really want to get married in Akersfield. Ideally, Kilbally would be my first choice, but failing that it must be Akersfield. Say you understand, Graham.'

'Of course I do.'

'Your parents, indeed anyone from Reigate, will be made welcome.'

'I'll write to my mother this evening,' Graham promised.

Into Breda's mind sprang the thought that since the wedding was to be in February there could be countrywide blizzards, and the roads and railways might be completely blocked and no-one would be able to get anywhere. 'Tis a sinful thought, she told herself, and pushed it away.

When Graham and Breda told Miss Opal about the wedding, as they were bound to do since they would need time off work, she provided a solution to at least one difficulty.

'But of course, Graham,' she said, 'your parents must stay with me. I wouldn't hear of anything else. And I shall expect to be invited to the wedding.'

'Just imagine,' Breda said afterwards. 'Miss Opal at my wedding! I can't believe it.'

For the intervening weeks it was difficult to think of anything not connected with the wedding, though Breda did her best, in working hours, to keep her mind on her job in the store. There was the other worry too, still with her. She tried even harder to keep it firmly out of her mind, allowing it in only last thing at night, when she lay awake in the darkness. If we're married in February, she asked herself desperately, and the baby is born in September, couldn't it seem like a premature birth? She would tell Graham, she had no thought of deceiving him, but need anyone else know? When the date for her period passed, with no sign, she could think of little else.

'There's something wrong,' Graham said. 'What is it? Or is it just wedding nerves, my darling?'

'It's not that,' she said.

'Then please tell me,' he insisted.

She told him.

'Oh Breda!' he said. 'Oh Breda, what have I done to you?'

'It takes two to make a baby,' she said miserably. 'And of course I want children, of course I do. But I wanted us to be married first.'

'But we will be,' Graham said. 'We'll be together. Whatever happens, we'll face it together!'

Then she wakened one morning, ten days later, days in which only sleep had driven the worry from her mind, and realized that what she had prayed for was happening. It was

425

all going to be all right. She slid out of bed and went down on her knees in thanksgiving. Then she dressed, and went to work with a heart as light as thistledown.

There was plenty to do in the store. The sale was now over, the garish displays which went with it had been dismantled and their places taken by ones more visually satisfying. The sales displays had been challenging and fun, and they had certainly brought in the trade, but to Breda's mind they'd offered little scope for artistry. Now it was different; now she could use her ideas and her imagination.

That she was able to do this was largely due to the temperament of her immediate boss, Leslie Bennett. 'He's an idle so-and-so,' Graham said. 'He's letting you do all the work while he looks for the credit.'

'Do you think I'm not knowing that,' Breda said. 'He's dull and he's lazy and he hasn't a creative idea in his head. Goodness knows how he got the job in the first place. But for those reasons he's happy to give me free rein.'

Her head abounded with schemes and new ones came to her all the time. Leslie Bennett had willingly allowed her the responsibility of changing one of the six store-front windows each day, so that there was always something new for passers-by to look at. If she was not too busy in other ways, she could manage two in a day, usually following a subject or a colour theme of her own devising.

'I've had what I think is a good notion,' she said to Graham one evening. She was sitting with him in the small chilly sitting room which Mrs Wharton set aside for her lodgers. Sometimes the two of them would occupy a similar room in Mrs Settle's house, though never for more than a few minutes did they stay in each other's bedrooms. Neither landlady would have approved of that. But it would not be long now, they told each other, before

426

they would have their own married quarters, either in furnished rooms or, ideally, in a small furnished house, though so far they had found nothing suitable.

'So what's your good idea, sweetheart?' Graham asked.

Breda bent down and turned up the gas fire. It would scorch her shins, while her back stayed frozen, but the cold was awful. 'I'd like to do one window as if it was a room in a house – any room, and not always the same. I'd furnish it as if it was lived in, even have a model or two so it would look occupied. And of course practically everything in the room would be on sale in the store. What do you think?'

'Sounds fine to me,' Graham said. 'I think you'd have to consult George Soames as well as Leslie Bennett.'

'Leslie Bennett will be no problem,' Breda said. 'If it works well he'll take the credit.'

'You shouldn't let him do that,' Graham objected.

Breda shrugged. 'If I didn't, he'd not let me do what I wanted.'

As she expected, Leslie Bennett raised no objections, though he insisted that he should be the one to put the idea to George Soames.

'It sounds interesting to me,' George Soames said. 'Go ahead and do it.'

'I thought I'd let Miss O'Connor have a stab at it,' Leslie Bennett said pleasantly. 'It will be good practice for her.'

It happened to be a day on which Miss Opal visited. She had decided to drop in once a week until the new business was firmly established. George told her of the suggestion. 'And I'll lay fifty to one it was Breda O'Connor's idea,' he added. 'Bennett is lazy and incompetent. I had hoped he'd leave, but he's got a cushy number here, so he won't.'

'I wouldn't take your bet,' Opal said. 'I'm sure you're right. I'd like to have a word with Breda myself while I'm here. As for Bennett, you'll catch him out sooner or later, and when you do, warn him! We can't afford passengers!'

When Breda came into the office, in answer to the summons she'd had, Opal looked up from the sales figures she was studying.

'I've been looking at the windows,' she said without preliminaries. 'They're very good.'

'Thank you, Miss Opal.'

'And Mr Soames tells me you've had an idea about doing a window each week as a room in a house. I take it it was your idea?'

Breda flushed. She wondered if Graham had said something, and hoped he hadn't. She could stand on her own feet. 'Actually, it was, Miss Opal.'

'Then go ahead and let's see what it looks like. But bear in mind that the purpose of the window displays is not only to be artistic, it's to bring people into the store and encourage them to buy.'

'I realize that, Miss Opal,' Breda said. 'I think this will do so. I'll show a wide spread of merchandise. But there is just one thing . . . ' she hesitated.

'And what might that be?'

'We don't sell furniture, and I would need some basic furniture. A sofa, some chairs; a sideboard so that I could display china and so on. And when I do a kitchen window I'll need a kitchen table. It doesn't have to be anything expensive because I'll mostly drape the furniture with fabrics.'

'Well, I quite see you can't have a room without furniture. I'll tell Mr Soames you're to have what you need, within reason. Liaise directly with him.' Opal made no mention of Leslie Bennett, but Breda recognized what was implied in the words.

'Thank you very much, Miss Opal,' she said.

Opal called her back as she reached the door. 'How are the plans for your wedding going?' she asked.

'Quite well. I've heard from my mother, and she's coming from Kilbally.'

'Have you found somewhere to live yet?'

'No, Miss Opal. That seems to be the most difficult thing of all.'

'Keep at it,' Opal said. 'I'm sure you will.'

What a pity, she thought as Breda left, that Henry Prince with all his money doesn't offer to put down the deposit so that they can buy a house. Goodness knows I'd be only too happy to do it for Daniel if he showed the slightest sign of getting married. And, of course, if Graham had fallen into line and was about to marry the girl of his parents' choice, no doubt that's what they would be doing.

Which only showed what fools they were. Given a chance of going into the business, Breda would have been an asset to Prince and Harper. Oh well! Now she would go a long way with Opal's, if she didn't allow herself to be swamped by domesticity.

She returned to the sales figures, which made pleasant reading.

Satisfying herself that Leslie Bennett was not to be found, while at the same time not trying too hard to find him, Breda felt justified in seeking out George Soames. He could be anywhere. He was well known for seldom being in his office but somewhere around the store, ever watchful, keeping an eye on things, stopping to speak to customers. 'On the prowl' the rest of the staff called it.

While searching for him she ran into Graham on the ground floor. She would normally not have stopped – they did not allow themselves the luxury of conversations in the store – but this time she couldn't resist. She stood in front of him, barring his way.

'Graham, I'm so excited! I've seen Miss Opal, she sent for me. She says I can go ahead!'

He smiled at her and she wanted to fling herself into his arms, to shout with joy. 'Good!' he said. 'I thought she would. And I've got something for you. Have you seen the *Record*?'

'Of course not. How could I? Why?'

'Furnished apartments,' Graham said. 'Maisie pointed it out to me.' Maisie was George Soames's secretary. 'Go up to the office and ask her to show it to you.'

All thoughts of window-dressing, of looking for George Soames, left Breda's head. Without actually breaking into a run, which was not permitted, she dashed up the stairs to the top-floor office, arriving breathless.

'Mr Prince says you'll let me look at the *Record*,' she said to Maisie. How absurd it seemed, speaking of Graham, to refer to him as Mr Prince. It was just another of the formalities which had to be observed.

Maisie broke off her typing and fetched the newspaper.

'It's near the bottom of the front page,' she said. 'It sounds just the job.'

Graham had marked it in pencil in the margin. 'To let, Hebghyll outskirts. Two rooms, part-furnished. Good position. Reasonable rent. Apply 23 River Road.'

'Glory be to God!' Breda cried. 'Isn't it just what we're wanting! And how will I get to it before anyone else does?'

'Ask Mr Soames if you can take an hour off and go and look at it,' Maisie suggested. 'Opal's won't fall down or catch fire while you're out!'

'Do you think he'd let me?'

'He can only say No. I don't suppose he will.'

'I suppose I'll have to see Mr Bennett first. Do you know where Mr Soames'll be?' Breda felt agitated, almost out of control with excitement.

'Not exactly. He set off for Dispatch. Something to sort out, he said.'

Breda found Graham though neither George Soames nor Leslie Bennett. 'It's perfect!' she cried. 'It's quite perfect!'

'Whoa!' Graham said. 'How can you know it's perfect? Though I'll admit it sounds promising.'

'Oh Graham, I just know it's going to be the one! I can feel it in my bones! Please can I take an hour off and go and look at it? If we wait until after work we might miss it. Oh Graham, you *are* the Deputy Manager. You can give me permission.'

She held her breath while he considered it. He was strict, and more so with her than he would have been with anyone else.

'Well,' he said. 'I'm not sure that's in my jurisdiction . . . '

'I can't find Leslie Bennett, nor Mr Soames,' Breda said quickly.

'In that case,' Graham said, 'I'll take responsibility. But for heaven's sake hurry! Don't dawdle.'

'As if I would!' Breda said – and was gone.

She knew River Road. It ran along the bottom of the valley, on the far side of the river bridge. Number 23 was a large, semi-detached house which had seen better days. The door was answered by a stout lady dressed from head to foot in black.

'I've come about the advertisement,' Breda said hurriedly. 'Two rooms to let, part-furnished. You see we're getting married and it sounds just right and my fiancé would have come with me only he's at work, which is where I should be only I asked for an hour off because we didn't want to miss it.'

431

She was babbling. She realized that when she saw the woman's stare.

'I'm sorry,' she said. 'We shall both be free at half-past five if you could keep it until then, give us first refusal. Is it in this house? Perhaps I could see it now and bring my fiancé back later.'

'It's not here,' the woman said. 'It's about as far from here as you can get in Hebghyll! It's on the edge of the moor.'

She watched a look of pleasure, followed by one of disappointment flit across the girl's face.

'Then it's too far for me to go now,' Breda said. 'I'm supposed to be at work. Could you possibly give us until after half-past five?'

The woman studied her. A pretty little thing, and anxious-looking. 'Well,' she said hesitantly, 'you wouldn't let me down, would you? You would come back? I mean, supposing someone else comes after it in the meantime?'

'Oh, we'll not let you down! Not for a minute! I promise faithfully! God's honour!'

There was another pause, then: 'Very well!' the woman said. 'I'll hold it until six o'clock. No longer, mind you!'

They were at the house in River Road by a quarter to six.

'You'll excuse me if I don't go with you,' the woman said. 'It's a fair walk, and I'm not at my best in the cold weather. Chesty, you see.'

She handed the keys to Graham. 'I'm sure I can trust you with them, and since you work for Opal's, I can always find you if need be. It's the two rooms on the top floor. The ground floor is let.'

'We'll return the keys this evening,' Graham promised. 'Let you know what we think.'

'Yes. Well, I'm not saying it won't need doing up a bit. The last tenant neglected it, but she was old.'

The woman was right. It was a lengthy walk, all of it uphill. When they reached the edge of the moor the houses ran out and they thought they must have missed it, but another five minutes skirting the edge of the moorland brought them to a small, solitary house.

'Heather Cottage,' Breda said. 'This is it! Oh, Graham!'

'It's quite isolated,' Graham said doubtfully.

'Does that matter?'

She pushed open the gate. Snow still lay on the short path which led to the front door. It's got to be right, Breda thought! It's just *got* to be right.

They rang the doorbell, but there was no reply from the ground-floor tenants.

'They must be out,' Breda said. 'We can let ourselves in.'

Steep, narrow stairs, uncarpeted, ran up from the small front hall and disappeared out of sight around a bend. Graham led the way.

The landlady had also been right about the condition of the rooms. They were shabby, and none too clean, with wallpaper peeling from the living room walls and distemper flaking from the tiny bedroom. The minute kitchen had a stone sink, an ancient gas cooker and one cupboard.

'But at least there *is* a kitchen,' Breda said. '*And* a small bathroom. We won't have to share, which is something.'

'Part-furnished,' was an accurate description. There was a sideboard, a shabby table, one armchair and three upright chairs in the living room, and in the bedroom a double bed with iron rails and brass knobs, and a chest of drawers. Nothing else.

'It's not exactly a palace!' Graham looked unimpressed. It's not what he's used to, Breda thought.

'But it will be a palace by the time we've finished with it!' she said. 'Our very own palace! Oh, Graham, there's so much we could do with it!' Already, she was teeming with ideas.

'We'd have to start right from scratch.'

'And isn't that better than living with someone else's choice?'

She crossed to the window, deep-set, with a seat built into the thickness of the walls.

'And look at the view, Graham! Will you just look at the view? Isn't it wonderful?'

Graham moved to her side.

'I'll grant you that,' he said. 'It's the best thing about the place.'

They looked out over the wide expanse of moor, still rising all the way to the horizon. Daylight had long gone, but there was a brilliant moon which lit up the snow. Rocks and great boulders thrust blackly through the white landscape like primeval sculptures.

'And in the spring it will be green, and in the summer, covered with heather!' Breda said. 'Oh, Graham, do say you like it! Do say you think it will do!'

Graham shook his head. 'I don't have your imagination, love. I don't have your eye . . . '

'Then trust me!' Breda begged. 'I *know* it will be all right! I promise you!'

He looked at her eager face, her shining eyes. She was irresistible to him and always would be.

'Very well!' he said. 'If you're sure?'

'I'm quite sure,' Breda said. She put her hands on his shoulders. 'Give me my first kiss in our new home.'

'With pleasure!'

'We're going to be *so* happy,' Breda sighed contentedly.

The time, which had dragged interminably while they had waited for the Bishop's dispensation, now took wings. Each day leading to the wedding seemed to have fewer hours in it than any previous one, and each day was crowded with things to be seen to. Breda gave up all idea of making her own wedding dress, though she had wanted to do that, and bought one in Opal's January sale.

'It will give me more time to work on Heather Cottage,' she said to Graham. 'I want to get it as perfect as possible so that we can live in our own place from the moment we're married.'

They had decided to forgo even the short honeymoon they had planned in favour of using the money to buy paint and whatever they could in the way of fabrics to smarten up their new rooms. Every evening saw them leaving Opal's and climbing up to the cottage, where they changed into old clothes and set to with paint brushes. Josephine ran up curtains and a few cushion covers on her sewing machine, and loaned them an armchair until they could afford to buy the sofa they wanted.

After ten days of cleaning and decorating Breda stood in the middle of the living room and looked around her. 'It's quite good,' she said. 'Not everything as I want it, but that will come later.'

'It's marvellous!' Graham said. 'It's a transformation! I'd like Miss Opal to see this, show her what you can do.'

The new window plan in the store had gone well and had attracted a lot of attention. Changing the 'room' windows week by week had also given Breda several ideas which she would use in their own home when there was enough money to do so.

'Perhaps she *will* see it,' Breda said. 'Who knows? I shall want Mammy to come while she's staying in England. Auntie Josie will bring her over.'

She wondered if Graham's parents would want to visit them here. They were coming to the wedding, having accepted Miss Opal's invitation to stay with her, so she supposed they might. It would be in sharp contrast to the house in Reigate. What would be her future mother-in-law's reaction to two tiny rooms in half a house? But nothing can spoil it for me, Breda thought. It's ours. It's mine and Graham's.

In the event, Henry and Miriam Prince announced their intention, if Opal would have them, of coming up to Yorkshire a day or two before the wedding. 'I've never been there,' Miriam said to Graham on the telephone. 'Naturally I want to see something of the place where you'll be living, and Opal seems quite pleased to have us a night or two longer.'

So, on the day before the wedding, Opal drove Mr and Mrs Prince to Hebghyll, and in the afternoon they went, together with Graham and Breda, to inspect Heather Cottage. The Akersfield family, plus Molly, planned to visit in a few days' time.

'It's very . . . compact,' Miriam Prince said.

Henry Prince squeezed his wife's arm. She was doing well. He knew her feelings, that she felt as though Graham was going to Outer Mongolia. He didn't share them, but they were real to her and he was proud of the way she had determined not to spoil anything by showing them.

Opal looked keenly at every bit of the rooms. 'It's splendid,' she said. 'Such clever ideas, such good use of space. And your colour schemes are exactly right.' She turned to Breda. 'Did you do all this yourself?'

'Graham helped,' Breda said. 'I couldn't have done it alone.'

'All I did was the donkey work,' Graham said. 'The ideas were all Breda's.'

'Very good indeed,' Opal said.

Breda smiled happily. 'Thank you, Miss Opal. It's what I like doing best.'

The day of the wedding was bright and clear. Breda wakened to the sun shining into her bedroom in her aunt's house, from which she was to be married. Graham would come over from Hebghyll during the morning and her first sight of him today would be when she went into church and saw him waiting there. It could not come too soon. She felt that the whole of her life had been a preparation for what was to happen this day.

Josephine came into the room, carrying a tray.

'Breakfast in bed for the bride!' she said happily. 'And it's a lovely day! Happy the bride the sun shines on!'

'Oh, Auntie, I feel as though all the rest of my life is going to be sunny!' Breda said.

'Well, I hope it will be,' Josephine said. 'But don't count on it altogether. There might be a shower of rain from time to time. But not today!'

Breda surveyed the breakfast tray: toast, marmalade, a boiled egg.

'I can't eat a thing,' she objected.

'Oh yes you can, and you will,' Josephine said firmly.

The small wedding party seemed lost in the vastness of St Peter's Church, especially as they were divided by the centre aisle, Mammy, Grandma Maguire, Auntie Josie and her family on one side; Mr and Mrs Prince, Mr Soames and Miss Opal on the other. But to Breda none of that mattered. She was aware only of Graham by her side, and Father Delaney speaking the words she had wanted to hear. Nothing else mattered. She made her responses loud and clear.

Afterwards they went back to Waterloo Terrace, where Josephine provided a cup of strong tea, sandwiches and wedding cake. Mrs Prince sat on the edge of a chair, smiling bravely, sipping her tea and eating nothing at all. Molly and Josephine, though they were clearly in awe of her, talked to Miss Opal while Henry Prince did his best to converse with Grandma.

'I don't like weddings,' Grandma told anyone who would listen. 'As an occasion, I mean. A good funeral beats a wedding hollow. And there's seldom a meal to compare with a funeral tea!'

She broke off to chase a piece of wedding cake which had lodged under her dental plate. Round and round her mouth she moved her tongue, clicking her false teeth from side to side. If she takes them out in front of Miss Opal I shall die of shame, Josephine thought!

'Perhaps we should be leaving, Opal,' Miriam Prince said presently. 'I expect you have things to do.'

'*I'm* taking the happy couple back to Hebghyll,' George Soames said, 'whenever they're ready.'

'Any minute now,' Graham said.

Shortly afterwards, Breda and Graham stepped into George Soames's car and he whisked them away, not stopping until they were at the gate of Heather Cottage. 'I'll not stay,' he said. 'Things to do!' He was gone like a puff of smoke.

Breda and Graham looked at each other. 'You have to carry me over the threshold,' she said.

'Whatever you say, Mrs Prince!' he replied.

Twenty-Four

'Shall we walk to the moor, or are you too tired?' Graham asked.

'I'm a little tired,' Breda acknowledged. 'But not too much. I'd like to walk.'

Now that spring was here again, and the evenings were all the time getting lighter, it was what they did almost every day. Home from the store, a very quick cup of tea, a change into casual clothes, and out again.

There was so much to see on the moor now, something new every day. Two winters of snow had melted and gone since they had moved into Heather Cottage. The first spring had given way to a warm summer, when all Breda's hopes of a purple, heather-clad moor had been fulfilled, and now they had come through the winter and emerged into the second spring. Fresh green bracken had uncurled itself on the slopes; birds were busy housekeeping.

'I wouldn't want you to tire yourself,' Graham said. 'You must take care.'

'I know,' Breda agreed. 'And I will. This baby is precious to me.'

'To both of us,' Graham corrected her.

'Of course! I know that!'

It had taken her almost a year to conceive, in spite of the fact that their sex life was full and vigorous; all, and more than all, that either of them had ever dreamt of. It was this which made Breda wonder if she would ever conceive, or if she was cruelly destined to remain childless. But now she was three months pregnant, and everything in the world was fine. The only cloud on the horizon, and it was daily growing closer, was that she would have to give up her job.

Graham, walking slightly ahead, turned around and offered Breda a hand up a steep and rocky part of the slope. She shook her head, smiling, and refused to take it.

'I can manage perfectly well, love. You mustn't coddle me!'

'Oh yes I must!' Graham contradicted. 'I would like to wrap you in cotton wool, wait on you hand and foot every minute until the baby's born.'

'Well, you're not going to,' Breda said. 'I won't allow it!'

He sat down on a flat rock, and pulled her down beside him.

'But you will take care? Promise?'

'Of course I will,' Breda said. 'Don't be so anxious.'

'I don't think you should go on working much longer.'

Breda shook her head. 'I don't agree, love. I'm absolutely fit and if I had my way, I'd go on working until the last minute. It won't be good for me, hanging around doing nothing. I'll get bored.'

Graham looked doubtful. 'What about . . . ?'

'If you mean what about how will I look, those smocks I wear are as good as any maternity dress. But I'll promise to give up working the minute I'm too tired.'

Privately, she couldn't imagine that happening for a long time. She had never felt fitter in her whole life.

'We must tell Mr Soames,' Graham said. 'It's only fair!'

'And Miss Opal,' Breda said.

Miss Opal would be on her side. Auntie Josie said that Miss Opal had worked in the Leasfield store almost up to the time of Emmeline's birth.

Two days later when Opal came to Hebghyll, Breda asked to speak with her privately.

'Well,' Opal said when she heard the news, 'I'm delighted for you, of course, though I had begun to think . . . ' She broke off.

'I'd also begun to think that I was never going to have a baby,' Breda said. 'So I'm especially pleased, and so is Graham.'

'Of course! In that case what I'd planned to say to you today isn't applicable any longer.'

'But I'd like to go on working for quite some time yet,' Breda said quickly. 'I don't want to leave before I must.'

Opal looked thoughtful. 'Well, I wonder? Yes, I *will* tell you. You see, a woman I know spoke to me last week. She said she'd been taking a great interest in the new windows you've been doing. "Though I still can't get my rooms to look as I want them. I don't seem to have the knack. I think I need advice," she said.'

Immediately, excitement ran through Breda's veins like fire. If her guess was right, and how could it not be, wasn't what Miss Opal was about to say the most wonderful, most incredible thing you ever heard? She leaned forward eagerly, perching on the very edge of her chair.

'So I thought about it over the weekend,' Opal continued. 'I've spoken with Mr Soames and he thinks it will work . . . '

Oh, do come to the point, Breda thought impatiently. Please say it!

'And what I wondered was, why shouldn't Opal's offer an advisory service on interior design and decorating. Every aspect – colour schemes, fabric, wallpapers, paint, lamps. All the things that go to make a room . . . '

Breda broke in, unable to contain herself another second. 'Rugs, cushions, china, ornaments . . . and preferably everything from this store!'

'Exactly! It's nearly five years now since the war ended. Everything's easier to get, no more coupons for materials. And people want a change, something new after all the years of austerity.'

'Oh, Miss Opal!' Breda could hardly control her voice. 'Oh, it would be wonderful!'

'There's the question of space,' Opal said. 'We don't have much room to spare.'

'It needn't take up much space,' Breda said. 'We'd work from books of fabric samples, colour charts, drawings and sketches. Most of the consultation would be in the client's own home, wouldn't it? It would have to be.'

Opal smiled at the growing pleasure in Breda's face, at her shining eyes and the excitement in her voice.

'You've got the idea exactly. And, of course, what I wanted was for you to head this. You're very young, but you have the talent. I believe, with the right backing, you could have done it.'

'Could have?' The words came to Breda like a blow, like an ice-cold shower.

'Well,' Opal said, 'haven't you just told me that you're going to have a baby? What I have in mind would be a big job, and so is having a child.'

There was a long silence, in which the two women looked at each other. I couldn't bear not to do it, Breda thought. And I couldn't bear not to have a baby.

It was Breda who broke the silence. 'Miss Opal, may I say something?'

'Of course!'

'I don't want to seem cheeky, Miss Opal, but *you* had a baby and kept on working.'

'I did,' Opal agreed. 'But it wasn't easy. In fact it was difficult, even though I had my sister to help me. I don't think I could have done it without her help, but who would you have?'

'I don't know,' Breda confessed. 'I've no idea. But I do know that I'd find someone, and I'd spend every penny of my wages on paying her!'

'Money might not be the problem,' Opal said. 'I had thought that I might put you on a small wage, plus commission, so a lot of it would be up to you. No, your problem would be finding the right person for your baby.'

'If I couldn't,' Breda said slowly, 'then I wouldn't do it. The baby's needs would have to come first.'

'Quite right,' Opal said. 'So I suggest you go away and think about it. Not so much about the job as about your personal life, yours and Graham's. I'm sure you could do the job, but there are more important matters to face.'

She stood up, a signal for Breda to leave. 'Come and see me when I'm in Hebghyll next week,' she suggested. 'But think about it all most carefully.'

Graham's reaction to the news was exactly what Breda had expected it to be. They had returned together from work, and were taking their usual walk. Not until they were sitting on the flat rock, with the whole of Hebghyll laid out below them, did Breda begin to tell Graham about her meeting with Opal.

He did not wait for her to finish before he spoke. 'It's a wonderful idea, and an honour for you to be asked. But of course you told her it was impossible.'

He was not asking a question, he was stating a fact; without heat, without emphasis. It was her answering silence which caused him to turn and face her. When her eyes met his, and he saw her look, he knew the answer to what he had not even thought worth asking.

'You did tell her?'

'I didn't tell her it was *impossible*. Not exactly.'

'What do you mean, Breda? Of course it's impossible!' His voice was slightly impatient, as if he was speaking to an awkward child.

'I said we'd think about it. I said we'd discuss it. I said that of course the baby came before everything!'

Don't I sound for all the world as if I'm begging, she thought? Perhaps I am? It was not at all the way she had planned it in her mind.

'Of *course* the baby comes first!' Graham said. 'That goes without saying, for both of us. So there's nothing to think about, darling. Nothing to discuss. I dare say you didn't like to tell her outright. But you must.'

'Would *you* be giving up your job to look after the baby?' she asked.

'But I don't have to! That's not the way things work, you know that. I earn the living, you look after the home and the children. Those are the facts of life.'

Again she didn't answer. He looked at her anxiously. Perhaps this was a pregnant woman's fancy. Perhaps there would be more of them in the months to come. He took her hand and began to stroke it, gently.

'You do want this baby, my love?'

'Oh, of course I do, Graham! You know I do. More than anything in the world. Truly!'

'And so do I. So everything will be all right. You'll see!'

Breda was not convinced, but she would not show her disappointment, she would not let his reception of her news lead to an argument. She could never bear to quarrel with Graham. She loved him too much.

'Come along, love! Time we were getting back. I don't want you to catch a chill.' There was always a breeze on the moor, and now, with the sun going down, the warmth had gone from the day.

444

'I'll not be catching a chill, silly,' Breda said. Nevertheless, she tucked her arm through his and they set off
together down the path to Heather Cottage.

'What's for supper?' Graham asked.

'Liver and onions.' How could he think about food?

'Good! My favourite!'

Didn't all the magazines say, if you wanted to ask
your husband a favour, then feed him his favourite food,
put on a pretty dress, seek the right moment? Breda
doubted if that would work with Graham, even if she
was prepared to get round him by such means. He had
made up his mind on the subject and as far as he was
concerned there was nothing more to be said.

She could not agree. To her mind there was a great deal
more to be discussed, no matter to what conclusion the
discussion led. But the magazines were partly right, she
would have to choose the moment.

In the event, it was Graham who chose it.

They had eaten, and cleared away. Breda went to the
window to draw the curtains against the dark night.
'There's a wind getting up.'

Graham, already immersed in his book, didn't
answer. Breda picked up her knitting and went and
sat in her armchair. It will be nice, she thought, when
we have our new sofa, which will be any day now, and we
can sit side by side. She felt the need for his physical
nearness.

Presently, he looked up from his book. 'What are you
knitting?'

'Vests, for the baby. I thought I'd better start on
something simple. I've always been good at sewing and
never much good at knitting.'

'One way and another you're going to be quite occupied,'
Graham said. 'Especially if we get the whole house to

445

ourselves. There'll be loads to do. You'll be glad not to have to go out to work.'

An elderly couple, who kept themselves to themselves, who were as quiet as mice and almost as seldom seen, had occupied the ground floor flat. Three months ago the husband had died as quietly as he had lived, and now his widow had packed her bags, been collected one Sunday morning by her son in his small car, and taken to live with him and his family in Derbyshire.

Graham and Breda had gone hotfoot to the landlady in River Road to ask if they might have the whole house. They would have liked to offer to buy it, but the time was not ripe. Though they, and Graham in particular, were now earning more money than when they had married, and could afford the increased rent, they could not afford to buy.

Breda knitted to the end of the row, then put down her needles. ' 'Tis not quite like that, Graham love. I am not after searching for an alternative to going out to work, a chance to stay at home. If I wanted that, the baby alone would provide it . . . '

'As it does for most women,' Graham interrupted.

'I know that. But I love my job, and even more I'd love the job Miss Opal has offered me. It's perfect for me.'

She left her chair and went and sat on the floor in front of his chair, leaning against him, taking his hand in hers.

'Oh, Graham, if only you'd just let me talk to you about it, about how I think it could work for all of us, you, me, *and* the baby! At least please listen, Graham!'

He sighed, closed his book and dropped it on the floor. It landed with a thud. 'I'm listening.' He sounded wary, reluctant.

'In the first place, no problem arises until much nearer the time for the baby's birth. I hope to work as long as I can, but I promise that if I'm not fit, or if the doctor

446

advises it, then I'll give up. I'll put our baby first at all times. So if I'm going to work, wouldn't it make sense to take on the new job? Physically, 'twould be easier. If we get the customers – and Miss Opal thinks we will – then I'll not be climbing in and out of windows much longer, dragging furniture about. I'll be visiting people in their homes, I'll be discussing and designing and advising. I'll not be doing the heavy work.'

'So that takes us up to before you have the baby,' Graham said. 'And what about afterwards? What about when the baby's here, a fact of life, a real person needing everything to be done for it? You'd have to give up the job then. So is it reasonable – even to Opal – to take it on for a few months and then drop it?'

'I would at least have set it up, got it going. That would be worth something to me, and I hope to her. Then if I had to drop it, if looking after you and the baby and our home was as much as I could manage, then sure, the job would go. And I'd make that plain to Miss Opal from the start.'

'You're asking a lot of Opal,' Graham said.

'And I'll give her a lot in return. Don't forget, it's *she* who wants me to do this. And having children did not stop her working. Will you just look at what *she's* achieved!'

Graham shook his head. 'Opal's a one-off. She's a law unto herself.'

'And you think I couldn't achieve what she has? Well, I dare say you're right and *I* don't have the ambition to own two stores. But I'd like to do what I think I'm capable of. I'd like, at least, to be having the chance to try.'

Graham began to stroke her hair. 'Breda love, I don't know what to say. You make it sound so reasonable, but all my instincts are against it.'

'Then please think about it,' Breda pleaded. 'We've got a week, and then I must see Miss Opal again.'

Two days later they received the news that they could indeed rent the whole house, on condition that they made no structural alterations without the permission of the landlady.

'She's safe enough!' Graham said. 'We couldn't afford to!'

They had already decided what they would do if the house became theirs. They would at once move their living quarters downstairs, leaving the two rooms upstairs for sleeping, the smaller of which would be for the baby. Downstairs there was a living-kitchen, a slightly larger sitting room and a bathroom.

'I should make an early start on the garden,' Graham said. 'We can make something of that, once we clear the weeds.'

Nothing more was said about Breda's job, present or future. It was as if the conversation they had had on that first night had never taken place. But we shall have to talk about it, Breda thought. I have to see Miss Opal on Monday. In any case, she found herself thinking about it most of the time, both when she was working in the store and when she was at home. Thoughts of the job mingled with thoughts of the baby, without, in her mind, any conflict at all. When Sunday came, without Graham having once mentioned the subject, Breda knew it was up to her.

From the minute she returned from Mass, the two of them worked on the rooms downstairs, stripping off layers of dingy wallpaper, sanding down doors. Everything was to be white.

'Are you sure it won't look cold?' Graham asked.

'Quite sure! There'll be warmth and colour from the curtains, the covers, the pictures on the wall. As much as ever we want.'

'If you say so,' Graham conceded. 'You're the expert!'

448

'I'm glad you say so,' Breda replied. 'You won't know this room when I've finished with it! And tomorrow I have to let Miss Opal know whether I'm going to make similar transformations in houses all over Hebghyll; perhaps even beyond.'

'Oh Breda!' Graham stopped in the act of scraping old paint from the window frame, and turned and faced her. 'Breda, I thought we'd decided all that!'

'*You* decided. I didn't.' She kept her voice calm.

'And I suppose you'd take the baby with you into all these houses you're thinking about?'

'I dare say that might be possible,' Breda said pleasantly. 'I hadn't thought so far ahead.'

'Then you should! Be serious about this, Breda!'

'I am. Quite serious. But I prefer to take one step at a time. If Miss Opal's idea takes off, it will do so quickly. Spring and early summer are the times everyone looks at their rooms and sees them as shabby, needing a change. If it doesn't take off, then she'll abandon it and that will be the end of the matter.'

'And if it does? I reckon Opal doesn't back many losers. If it does, where will you be then?'

'I don't know,' Breda confessed. ' 'Tis all to try for. But I've told you, and I mean it, love, I'll do whatever's best for the baby, both before it's born and after. All I want is a chance to start – just see how far I can take it.'

Graham looked at her. She stood in a room which was a shambles. Her face was dirty and there was a scrap of green wallpaper sticking to her hair. She was pink with exertion and her eyes were pleading. He had never loved her more.

'Oh my darling, I can refuse you nothing!' he said. 'Tell Miss Opal you'll give it a try. But don't make her any promises you can't keep.'

449

'Oh Graham!' She flung herself into his arms. 'Oh Graham, I do love you!'

The next morning she made an appointment to see Miss Opal as soon as possible after she arrived.

'Well,' Opal said. 'What did you decide?'

Breda told her. 'I realize it might not suit you,' she admitted. 'You see, I can't promise here and now to stay on after the baby's born. I shall have to see how things work out.'

'Of course you will!'

'And I wouldn't want to start something, and then leave you in the lurch.'

Opal looked long and hard at Breda. To be truthful, she didn't need this new venture, didn't she have enough with two stores? But there was something in her which wanted to take it on perhaps just because it *was* new, and a gamble, and there was something about this young woman who sat opposite her which made her feel that, between them, they could make it work. So it's my decision, she thought.

'Well,' she said, 'I can see the difficulties. But you don't win if you don't enter, so we'll do it! I have people to see now, but we'll talk later in the day, go into more detail.'

Breda stared at Miss Opal open mouthed. She couldn't believe it, nor could she find any words.

'We'll wish each other luck!' Opal said.

Breda pulled herself together, realized she had been given a signal to leave, and got up. 'Thank you, Miss Opal! Oh, thank you very much indeed. I can't tell you . . . '

'Tell me later,' Opal said.

The next person Opal saw was George Soames. She told him about her conversation with Breda.

'It's a risk,' he said. 'But when did you *not* take risks, Opal?'

'I know it is,' she admitted. 'I just think it might come off. And I hate to see talent going to waste. So what have you to tell me, George?'

'Not a great deal,' George said. 'Leslie Bennett has given in his notice. He came to ask me about promotion, and when he saw it wasn't forthcoming, he decided to leave. I grabbed at it, I can tell you! He'll probably change his mind, though, and ask for his job back.'

'But you'll not give it to him, I hope?'

'Definitely not. Though I'm not sure how we'll manage in the short term if you're taking Breda.'

'Ah!' Miss Opal said. 'Then I think I can help you there. I think I have only to say the word and Jim Sutcliffe would jump at the chance of coming to Hebghyll. He said something of the kind to me the other day. His wife, it seems, has always wanted to live here.'

'It wouldn't be as big a job as Leasfield,' George Soames said.

'I'd pay him the same. And the job would be what he made it. There's plenty of scope.'

'What about Leasfield?'

'He has a good deputy, waiting to step into his shoes. We'll be all right.'

'Well, that's that then,' George said. 'I wish everything could be settled so easily.'

Opal sent for Breda in the middle of the afternoon. This time the talk was all of how they would set up the new venture.

'You can cut your teeth on Mrs Alderton, the woman who gave me the idea,' Opal said. 'I'll offer her a special rate for being the first customer, and for your part I want you to do a really first-class job.'

'Oh, I will, Miss Opal!' Breda said eagerly. 'I can hardly wait to begin.'

'You'll have to wait a wee while, until we get fabric samples, paint charts and so on. Unless, of course, you can find most of what you want right here in the store – or perhaps in the Leasfield store.'

'I'll know better when I've seen the rooms she wants doing,' Breda said.

'Well, she lives right here in Hebghyll,' Opal said. 'And I reckon the first occasion or two I'll go with you. I'd like to see how you go about it. After that, you're on your own.'

'I'll be glad of your advice,' Breda said.

'Oh, I'm not coming along to advise,' Opal said. 'More to learn, to pick up the commercial side of it. The artistic bit is all yours. I've been thinking I shall advertise, use your name. "Mrs Breda Prince, Interior Design Consultant". How does that sound?'

'Wonderful!' Breda was ecstatic. She couldn't believe it was happening to her.

'The only thing is, you look too young,' Miss Opal said. 'But time will remedy that, won't it?'

Graham, when told, did his best to show enthusiasm. 'Design Consultant!' he said. 'You'll be passing me on your way up!'

'I'll never do that,' Breda said. 'You're Deputy Manager of the whole store.'

That was to change, and in a manner which no-one could foresee, or would have chosen. On a day towards the end of May, George Soames left the store, went home and ate his evening meal, and immediately afterwards collapsed with a heart attack.

Mary Soames acted quickly. Within twenty minutes George was in Hebghyll Hospital and Opal was speeding from Leasfield to be with her sister. Together, they sat by his bed all night, and in the morning knew that at least he would not die. When they knew that, Opal took her sister home, then went herself to the store.

The first person she sent for was Graham. 'You will have to take over,' she told him.

'I'll do my best, Miss Opal,' Graham said. He was white with shock.

'I know you will. You've been here since the start of Opal's of Hebghyll. You know how I like things done. And you've had the best of teachers in Mr Soames. We must do everything well for his sake. I don't want him to worry about a thing.'

'I'll do all I can,' Graham said. 'Everyone will. Mr Soames is very highly thought of. It will be a great shock.'

'I don't know how long this will last,' Opal said. She couldn't keep the worry out of her voice. There had been times in the night when she'd thought her brother-in-law would die. 'Come to me if there's anything I can do,' she said to Graham. 'And I'll be here as often as I can to begin with.'

In fact, George Soames's absence from the store was to be permanent.

'If you take this easy, then you could live a long time yet,' the doctor said to him. 'If you don't . . . ' He shrugged.

George gave in with good grace. If the truth were known, he would be glad to live a quieter life.

'And you'll do very well,' he said to Graham. 'I have every faith in you! You're a bit young to be Manager of the whole store, but I'm sure you'll do it.'

'Of course he will!' Mary Soames said.

Twenty-Five

Opal refused to consider promoting Graham to George Soames's job permanently until she was quite certain that George was ready to let go.

'It's quite possible,' she said to Mary, 'that when he feels better – and he *is* getting better, we can all see that – he'll want to come back. It wouldn't be fair either to him or to young Graham if I made a move too soon.'

'If it's anything to do with me he won't come back at all, so please don't encourage him,' Mary said. 'Oh, I know he's loved his job. He's lived for it all these years and it'll be a wrench to leave it. All the same, I think he will.'

'Well, just don't push him,' Opal cautioned. 'Let him decide in his own time.'

In the end, and in spite of advice from all directions, it was George who made his own decision. It was true he felt better every day – well, most days – but he knew he was no longer the man he had been. He thought of the hustle and bustle of the store at sale time, he remembered it in the Christmas season, and knew that it was beyond him. And as that knowledge grew so his desire to be in the store, in the thick of things, waned.

One day in July Opal called to see him, as she frequently did, keeping him in touch with what was going on. She found him sitting in his beautiful garden and he told her what he had decided.

'Why not take a little longer to think it over?' she suggested.

'I've done all that,' George said. 'I'm quite certain, Opal. I've enjoyed every minute of the years with you, but now it's time to lead a different life. Read all the books I've never had time for; sit in the garden. I shall enjoy it all, and I shall enjoy spending more time with Mary.'

'Well, if you're sure . . . '

He took her hand in his. Such capable hands she had: square palms, long fingers. 'I'm quite sure, love.'

'So the job of General Manager is yours,' Opal said to Graham next day. 'That is if you still want it, having had a taste of what it's like these last few weeks.'

'Oh I do! I do indeed,' Graham said. 'I just wish it could have come to me in happier circumstances.'

'I think George is happy to leave it,' Opal said. 'And remember this, you're not to do things just because it's how George always did them. You must follow your own bent, have the courage of your own convictions. George frequently followed his way rather than mine, and he was right to do so.'

Breda, though sad about George Soames, whom she had always liked and always would, was delighted for Graham.

'It's wonderful!' she said. 'And I know you'll be a success. In fact, Miss Opal wouldn't have offered you the job if she hadn't thought so too. The only thing is, my darling, don't work too hard.'

'You're a fine one to talk,' Graham said. 'Six months pregnant and still hard at it.' There was no anger in his words. Seeing how fit and well Breda was, how happy, he had become used to the situation. He trusted her to give it up when the right time came.

'I enjoy it so much,' Breda said. 'Every day is different.'

455

There was no shortage of clients – 'Let's call them clients, not customers,' Miss Opal had suggested. Mrs Alderton had been delighted by Breda's transformation of her drawing room and had immediately recommended her to two friends, but the woman Breda was to see this afternoon had telephoned in response to the announcement in the newspaper.

Breda received her in the alcove which had been chosen for the purpose, on the first floor. Opal had thought that an alcove was more suitable than an enclosed office. 'Let people get used to seeing you at work,' she said. It was furnished with two comfortable armchairs, a low table, swatches of fabrics, colour charts – and fresh flowers. The first meeting was always in the store, but it was no more than a preliminary.

'I think I've got the picture,' Breda said when they had talked for a while. 'The next thing is, I'd like to visit you in your home.'

Mrs Stevens hesitated. 'Is that necessary? I mean . . . I thought . . . '

'It really is,' Breda said. 'I can do a much better job for you that way. Is there some reason why not?'

'Not really. Only it's so awful, I wouldn't like you to think any of it was my taste. My late aunt lived there and I inherited the lot.'

Breda smiled. 'That's a wonderful starting point. Between us we can do so much. And, of course, this consultation and the first one in your own home are entirely free. Only if and when you decide to go ahead do you begin to pay. We'll discuss that then.'

'It sounds fair enough,' Mrs Stevens said. 'Could it be next week?'

Breda consulted her diary. 'Yes, Wednesday afternoon. I'll bring some of the patterns and charts we've looked at, but I'll also bring others as well. Don't be surprised if suggest something totally different once I've seen the room.'

She needed also to be able to see the house, *and* the view from the window. If the view was good she would work with it, incorporate it in her design; if it was bad then she would do all she could to minimize it. Also, in addition to recommending decorations, chair covers, curtains and so on, she would often suggest ornaments, china or glassware, a picture. Most of what she suggested would be obtainable in the store, but if it was not she would do her best to get it elsewhere. It was all part of the service.

She wrote down Mrs Stevens's address. 'Then I'll look forward to seeing you at two o'clock next Wednesday,' she said. 'And if you have any ideas about things you'd especially like, jot them down and we'll discuss them. It's important that you end up with what *you* want.'

'I'm looking forward to this one,' Breda said to Opal later. 'Mrs Stevens sounds as though she'd like to make a clean sweep.'

'I hope it goes well,' Opal said. 'But bear in mind that it won't always. One of these days you'll come up against a smart operator who'll pinch all your ideas, then carry them out herself instead of using *our* men and *our* goods.'

'I dare say I will,' Breda agreed. 'But what can I do about that?'

'Not much. Watch out for it. Don't leave too many loopholes. And if you lose, put it down to experience.'

'I don't think Mrs Stevens is in that category,' Breda said. 'I liked her.'

In fact, Opal was as pleased as punch with the way it was going. It was only the beginning, but people were starting to talk about it simply because there was nothing comparable in Hebghyll – or in Leasfield or Akersfield as far as she knew. And that being so, she felt confident that clients would eventually come from those places too.

The pity of it was that as each week passed she realized just how much the enterprise depended upon Breda's unique talent. What would she do if she lost her? It was very much on the cards but she must do all she could to prevent it happening.

Because of the fluid nature of the work Breda, encouraged by Opal, had been able to pace herself. On the rare days when the child inside her felt heavy, or the weather was too hot, she could work at home on designs. When she felt more vigorous she could, if she wanted to, put in more time at the store. The only thing she couldn't change, and would never try to, was her appointments with clients.

'The job's as tailor-made for me as my designs are for the clients,' she said to Graham.

'Well, that does seem to be the case,' he admitted. 'But just don't push yourself too far.'

'I won't,' Breda promised.

The baby was due early in October. With luck, and her present state of good health, she reckoned she might work until early September, though she would probably go less often into the store as time went on.

'I must say, the extra money from both of us is useful,' Graham remarked. He was earning a General Manager's salary now, and Breda a 2 ½ per cent commission on the fees of what were sizeable jobs, plus 2 per cent on extra items bought on her recommendation from Opal's.

'I reckon we could think of buying our own house,' Graham said.

'But do we want to?' Breda asked quickly. 'We've made this so nice now. I love living here. And it will be a healthy place for the baby; no traffic, no smoke.'

'Well, if it suits you, then it suits me,' Graham said. 'At least for the present.'

'I'm looking forward to this being our baby's first home. We've been so happy here. You do agree with that, don't you?'

'Of course I do, sweetheart,' he said.

Towards the end of August Breda sought out Opal. 'I think perhaps, Miss Opal, I shouldn't take on any more jobs now. I've got plenty of time to finish the ones in hand and on the list, but if I took on anything new, I might not be able to complete it.'

'Very sensible,' Opal said. 'I quite agree with you.'

'Can I ask you something else?'

'Of course!'

'Since I can't say for certain whether I can come back after the baby's born, do you mind telling me if you're going to take on someone else in my place?' It cut her to the quick to say the words, but she had to know. 'And if you are,' she continued, 'will you want me to teach her something of it before I go?'

Opal shook her head. 'No, Breda. I've already thought about that, and I'm not taking on anyone else. I'd rather suspend things for a time until I know what's going to happen. In any case, where would I find someone? It's not a question just of teaching someone to do what you do, it's a matter of finding someone with the talent.'

Breda felt weak at the knees with relief. At least the way was to be left open to her if she could come back. 'I would let you know as soon as I could,' she said.

'Well, yes, I would *have* to know,' Miss Opal said. 'Because if you're *never* coming back, then I shall have to look for someone else. I think the idea is too good just to let it go. So what I suggest is that I give you two months after the baby is born to see how you feel, and how Graham feels. By then I reckon you should be able to tell me something.'

'Oh, I will, Miss Opal!' Breda cried. 'Perhaps long before then. Almost everything will depend on whether I can get the right person to look after the baby for part of the day. I haven't anyone in mind at all, as yet.'

'It's an important decision. I'll ask around,' Miss Opal said. 'Whoever it was, she'd have to come very well recommended.'

It wouldn't be the only difficulty, Breda thought as she left Opal's office. There was Graham to consider. He had been very co-operative over the last few months, but that could change once the baby was here. Let's face it, she thought, it could change for me too. I don't know how I'm going to feel.

On the following Sunday Graham and Breda took the train to Akersfield to visit Josephine and Brendan.

Josephine embraced Breda warmly. 'How are you keeping, love?' she asked.

'Very well indeed.'

'You look it, I must say,' Josephine said. 'And no-one would know to look at you, you were more than six months gone! I don't know where you're keeping it!'

'I know she's there all right,' Breda said. 'She kicks!'

'So you've decided it's a "she"?'

'I had. Now I'm wondering if I haven't got a footballer in there!'

She wanted a girl, so did Graham, but she knew it wouldn't matter in the end. Just a lovely, healthy baby was all either of them asked.

It had already been arranged that Josephine would come to Hebghyll a day or two before the baby was due, so that she would be with Breda when her labour started.

'I don't like to think of you without another woman nearby,' Josephine had said. 'It's a lovely place you live in, but isolated.'

Breda was to have the baby in the Hebghyll Maternity Home. In the two weeks she would remain there, Josie would return to Brendan, and then come back again to give Breda a hand when she came home with the baby. Josephine was quite looking forward to it. She said as much now while they sat at dinner. 'I'm hoping you'll feed us every day on Yorkshire pudding,' Graham said. 'It's not the dish Breda does best in the world.'

'And what will I be eating while my wife's busy feeding you?' Brendan spoke with gruff good humour.

'It's very good of you to spare Auntie Josie,' Breda said. 'I do appreciate it.'

'He'll be well enough looked after,' Josephine said briskly. 'Kate and Maureen will fall over themselves to see to that!'

'And who will look after me?' Grandma Maguire demanded suddenly.

'The girls will,' Josephine said patiently. 'As you well know, it's all in hand. You'll not be neglected.' She won't let herself be neglected, Josephine thought. Part of the reason she was looking forward to going to Hebghyll was that for a spell she would be away from her mother-in-law.

'All this fuss!' Grandma said. 'There was none of this in my day. You just got on with it!'

'How are your mother and father?' Josephine said, turning to Graham. She had quite liked Henry Prince, and might have liked his wife, could she have got to know her better.

'They're both well, thank you,' Graham said. 'They'll come on a visit after the baby's born.'

The minute the Princes had heard of Breda's pregnancy, Miriam had wanted to arrange for the birth to take place in Reigate. 'We have a wonderful nursing home close by,' she'd written, 'and our doctor is simply splendid.'

461

Graham recalled it now, and laughed. 'My mother doesn't think there are any proper doctors north of Watford!' he said.

'I hope you told her it's got to be born in Yorkshire,' Brendan said. 'In case it's a lad. Otherwise he'd never get to play for the county!'

Breda and Graham left Akersfield by mid-afternoon. 'It's strange these days how I always want to get back home,' Breda said as they sat in the train. 'I'm sure it's to do with being pregnant.'

As they walked back from Hebghyll station to their cottage on the edge of the moor she took deep breaths, filling her lungs with the clean air. It had been hot and stuffy in Akersfield, but here the air was crisp and clear.

'I wouldn't want to be living anywhere other than Hebghyll,' Breda said as Graham turned the key in the lock.

'What about Kilbally?' he asked. He opened the door and stood aside while Breda entered the house.

'Ah!' she said. 'Now that's another matter! My first love. But Hebghyll feels like home now, and isn't that because it's *our* home? Wasn't it here you carried me over the threshold, then?'

'And I'd not like to do it now!' Graham said.

Mrs Stevens's house turned out to be a large, Victorian semi-detached, solidly built in local stone. She opened the door to Breda and led her through to the drawing room at the back of the house.

'This is the room I thought I'd have done,' she said.

It was dark and gloomy, but that was not so much to do with the windows, which were large, but with the fact that everything in it was dark: floors covered in close-patterned Turkey carpet, woodwork and furniture heavy oak, walls dark green embossed paper, and hung with sombre oil paintings. Whatever light came in through the windows, themselves closely curtained, first with Nottingham lace and then with crimson brocade, was at once absorbed by the dark surfaces.

Breda caught her breath at the sight of it. Her first impulse was to draw back the curtains as far as they would go, then tear down the Nottingham lace, let in more light.

'It *is* quite a challenge,' Mrs Stevens said nervously.

'I'm sure we can meet it,' Breda replied.

She felt less confident than she sounded. No doubt Mrs Stevens would want to keep all that heavy carved furniture, those overstuffed chairs and the monstrous sofa. She crossed to the window and looked out.

To her great surprise the window gave onto a walled garden, with a lawn, well-filled borders, roses and clematis in abundance climbing the walls, and a delicate birch tree in the far corner.

'Why, this is lovely!' she cried. 'We must certainly bring this into the room, and I suggest the very first thing we do is to take down the lace curtains. Would you agree to that?'

'I'd be happy to!'

Breda turned at the unexpected firmness in Mrs Stevens's voice. 'May I ask how long you've lived here?' she asked.

'Only three months,' Mrs Stevens replied. 'Since my aunt died. It's just as it came to me, and the rest of the house is the same. I didn't really know how to start, and then I saw the advertisement.'

Breda took off her shoes, stood on a chair, and unhooked the lace curtains, dropping them to the floor. 'You see the difference at once, don't you? I think that has to be the priority, to make the whole room light and fresh. Of course it's Victorian, and that's not fashionable now, but fashions go in cycles and it might well come back. Different covers and curtains, paler walls, would make a world of difference. Would you, for instance, be prepared to have a new carpet?'

'Anything! Absolutely anything!' Mrs Stevens said. 'My aunt left me some money, as well as the house, and I'm prepared to spend it.'

'Well then,' Breda said. 'Let's see where we start.'

They discussed every detail, down to the pictures on the wall, which Mrs Stevens declared herself more than ready to part with. She was a most amenable woman; not many ideas of her own, but willing to be guided. What more could I wish for, Breda thought?

'Well, I'll make some sketches,' she said in the end, 'sort out more fabrics, now that I know what's needed. Could I come again next Wednesday?'

'Certainly!' Mrs Stevens said. 'And may I ask you something?'

'Of course!'

'I can see you're having a baby – oh, it doesn't show much, but I can tell. So I just wondered when, and if you'd be giving up work. I mean, altogether, after the baby's born. You see, I'd like most of the house doing, a bit at a time of course.'

'My baby is due in October,' Breda said. 'I think I shall have to leave Opal's early in September, but of course I shall finish this room before then. I won't leave it half done, I promise you.'

'And afterwards?'

'I don't know,' Breda confessed. 'I *want* to take up my job again, at least part time, but it all depends on whether I can get the right person to look after the baby. It would have to be someone really special, someone I could trust absolutely.'

When Breda returned to the house on the following Wednesday, Mrs Stevens looked pleased and excited to see her. 'I've been thinking about what you said, about finding someone to help with the baby,' she said, taking Breda through to the drawing room. 'I just might have the answer!'

'Really?' Breda sounded non-committal. It was too quick, too good to be true, but Mrs Stevens was a client, she must at least listen to her.

'It's my niece. Her name's Grace Paterson and she was widowed in the war. Only nineteen, she was. She's been working as a nanny for the last four years, but now the family is emigrating to Australia. She doesn't want to go with them.'

'That sounds . . . promising,' Breda said.

'She's a very nice person, and she adores babies,' Mrs Stevens said. 'In fact, I took the liberty of inviting her here this afternoon. I thought you might like to meet her.'

Any reservations Breda had were swept aside almost from the moment she met Grace Paterson. She was everything she had imagined in the woman she had hoped to find: softly spoken, wholesome to look at, with her blonde hair, creamy skin and ready smile. She also had four years' experience of two children, from birth, and it was clear from the way she spoke that she was fond of them, unhappy that they were leaving.

'I think we might suit each other very well,' Breda said. 'Though you understand I'm not quite sure yet exactly what I want to do?'

'I understand that,' Grace Paterson said. 'It's a big decision.'

'And I'd want you to meet my husband.'

'Of course!'

How would Graham take it? Breda asked herself the question all the way home. When Graham came in she could not hold it back.

'It's all very sudden,' he said. 'Are you sure you're not just . . . well . . . clutching at straws?'

' 'Tis not like that at all,' Breda said. 'And I have not committed myself in any way. She knows she will have to wait until after the baby's born before I make any decision.'

'You really liked her?'

'I did so. But you'll have to meet her for yourself. It concerns us both. Will I ask her to come here?'

'Very well,' Graham said.

Breda finally left Opal's in the middle of September. She was sorry to go. 'I've enjoyed every minute of my time here,' she told Miss Opal on her last day. 'But especially the last few months.'

'You've done a good job,' Opal said. 'I dare say it's selfish of me, but I hope you come back to us.'

'We shall have to see,' Breda said.

In some ways it was a good time to go. She was clear of appointments. Mrs Stevens's room had gone very well, and the lady was delighted with it. 'It's unrecognizable!' she said. 'So light and fresh. You really are clever, and I wish you were doing the rest.'

But I'm really tired, Breda admitted to herself. I'm fit enough, but really tired. The doctor had advised her to take things more easily for the last few weeks and she was happy to heed his advice. Grace Paterson would be in from time to time to give her a hand when she needed it. Graham had met Grace twice by now.

'I have to confess, I like her,' he said. 'She seems a trustworthy person.'

Aunt Josephine arrived at Heather Cottage, as arranged, two days before the baby was due. 'They do say first babies are always late and second ones always early,' she said. 'But best be on the safe side. I'll help you pack what you need, so there's no rush at the last minute.'

' 'Tis all packed,' Breda said. 'Nightgowns, bedjackets, baby clothes, the lot. And two new books. Once it's over, I shall just lie back and read and sleep!'

'Make the most of it,' Josephine advised. 'You'll be too busy to read, once you're home! By the way, Grandma Maguire sent this for the baby.' She produced a small, bone teething ring. 'She says it belonged to Brendan when he was a baby. All I can say is, she never passed it on to me for any of mine, so count yourself honoured!'

'Oh I do!' Breda said. 'I'll write and thank her tomorrow.'

As it turned out, there was no chance to do that. At half-past midnight her labour started. Graham, in a lather of anxiety, far more so than she was, telephoned at once for the taxi, and took her to the maternity home.

'You can go home now, Mr Prince,' the sister in charge said after the first ten minutes. 'We'll take care of your wife. This is no place for a man.' She had no time for husbands hanging around.

'But when . . . ?'

'Oh, the baby won't be born for hours yet. They take their own time. Telephone around six in the morning and we'll let you know what's happening.'

At one minute after six o'clock, Graham telephoned.

'My wife,' he said hurriedly. 'My wife! Is she . . . I mean . . . '

'It would help if you told me who your wife was,' the nurse said gently.

'Oh! Mrs Breda Prince!'

'Just a moment. I'll find out, Mr Prince.'

'Why doesn't she *know*?' he demanded of Josephine. 'Why is she stalling? Is something wrong?'

He jumped as the voice sounded in his ear. 'You have a lovely little daughter, Mr Prince!'

'What did you say?'

'A daughter, Mr Prince!'

'Oh! Thank you! And my wife? What about my wife?'

'She's well. They're both well.'

'I'll be there at once!'

He put down the receiver, and turned to Josephine, tears streaming down his face. 'A daughter! I have a daughter!'

Twenty-Six

'Will you please give her to me, and I will bathe her,' Molly said.

'But Mammy . . . !'

'Do you not trust me to do the job, Breda?' she said. 'Have I not had seven children of my own?'

And where are they now, she asked herself? Scattered. Kieran busy in his parish in England, though next year he would come home for a visit; Kathleen as happy as a lark in her convent; Moira – well, who knew whether she was happy or not? She had enough of this world's goods to make her so, Barry had done well, but Moira had always wanted more of everything, right from a little girl. Patrick and Colum were doing all right in America, and now the both of them engaged to two sisters, who from their photographs looked nice girls. Little Maeve was in the churchyard, though she would never forget her. And now, thanks be to God, Breda back home in Kilbally, even though 'twas only for a week, for hadn't the pair of them, Breda and Graham alike, to be back at their jobs next Monday morning?

She held out her arms. 'Come to Grandma, then, and she'll give you a nice, warm, bubbly bath!'

Eileen put out her arms in reply. She liked this new woman in her life, she was round and soft, and spoke quietly. She smiled broadly, showing her eight front teeth, and uttered words which no-one understood but *she* knew said, 'I'd like you to bath me, Grandma!'

'You see!' Molly said triumphantly. 'She *wants* to come to me! Who's Grandma's darling, then?'

'You spoil her,' Breda said. 'Heaven knows what she'd be like if you had her here all the time.'

The accusation was good-tempered. What else could you expect when it was the first time Mammy had seen her granddaughter, and she almost a year old now.

' 'Twas a pity you could not come to Hebghyll this summer, Mammy,' she said. 'We've done a lot in the house. I'd like you to have seen it.'

'I would have. And I will next year. But someone had to look after Grandma Byrne – God rest her soul! – and who else but me? There was a lot to do for her towards the end.'

Josephine had come from Akersfield for her mother's funeral, bringing all the news of Breda and the baby which hadn't found its way into letters.

'She's a lovely child,' Josephine enthused. 'And Breda's a great little mother, in spite of the fact that she has her job and is getting quite well known for it. Did you know she had such talent?'

'I knew she had something special,' Molly said. 'I didn't know what it would turn out to be.'

Now she carried Eileen into the bathroom with Breda following behind. It being half-day closing in Kilbally, Graham had gone into Ennis with Luke, who needed to visit a wholesaler.

'Mammy can watch,' Molly said to Eileen. 'But Grandma is doing the deed!'

She lowered the child into the water and encouraged her to slap the surface with the flat of both hands. Eileen screamed with delight at the result.

'She's a bright one!' Molly said. 'Do you remember, that's what Dada used to call you? The Bright One!'

'I do,' Breda said. She remembered most things about Dada. She would never forget him, though Luke O'Reilly, she realized now, had been a better husband to Mammy than Dada had.

'Do you remember when he went off to Galway races and left you behind? My, but you were furious!'

'And he brought me back a hair slide. I have it still. I keep it in my treasure box, with my pebbles. Did you know I still had my treasure box?'

'I did not.'

'It was a wonderful idea you had there, Mammy. I shall give Eileen a treasure box as soon as she's old enough.'

'You chose a nice name – Eileen,' Molly said.

'If she had been a boy I would have called her James, after Dada,' Breda said.

'Next time, perhaps,' Molly said.

She lowered the child onto its back, its head resting on her arm while she gently lathered its hair. Bright auburn hair, it was. Exactly like Breda's.

'She's the spitting image of you,' Molly said.

Breda laughed. 'Grandma Prince says she's exactly like Graham when he was a baby!'

'Stuff and nonsense!' Molly said firmly.

'Well, if it makes her happy I don't mind,' Breda said. 'She's as soppy about Eileen as you are, though she doesn't see her often.'

'And what about this new job of yours? You've never said much in your letters, but Josephine was full of it when she was over.'

She rinsed the lather from the baby's hair, then pulled out the bath plug, lifted the child, and wrapped her in a warm towel.

' 'Tis not new,' Breda said. 'I was at it before I had Eileen. I had to give it up for a while, of course, and then

I went back to it. But you know all that.'

'I don't know how you do it,' Molly said. ' 'Twas all I could do to cope with the children and the home. I couldn't have done anything else.'

'But you did, Mammy!' Breda contradicted. 'Didn't you always help out at the Big House? Cleaning and polishing.'

'Oh, *that*!' Molly was dismissive. ' 'Twas not a *real* job, and only part time.'

'In a way, so is mine. I arrange my own hours, and I do a lot of it in my own home.'

And I have Grace, she thought. What would I do without Grace? Grace came whenever she was needed, looked after the baby as if it were her own, and vanished when she was no longer required so that Breda had the house back to herself. Grace was cheerful, sympathetic, capable – and she enjoyed her job. Eileen loved her, and her love was returned.

'I could have done none of it if I hadn't found Grace,' she said to her mother. 'And thankfully Graham took to her from the word go.'

Her first job, after she had returned to Opal's in the January of 1951 had been to redesign and refurbish every room in Mrs Stevens's house. 'I owe it to you for introducing me to Grace,' she'd said.

After that, commissions had flowed in, for Mrs Stevens, like Mrs Alderton before her, spread the gospel far and wide. 'If anyone wants to see what you can do, let them come and see *my* house!' she'd said. Since then, Breda had never been without work, and usually she had a waiting list. Miss Opal was cock-a-hoop.

'I think next year,' she said, 'you should spend one day a week in the Leasfield store, for consultations.'

It was Opal who had also suggested that they should tender for the refurbishing of the White Horse, an old hotel on the outskirts of Hebghyll which had changed hands and was to be completely renovated for reopening in the spring of the following year.

Breda had been doubtful. There would be great competition for the job from well beyond Hebghyll. Everything she had done so far had been intimate, for a single person, or a couple or family, in their own home. The White Horse, when it was finished, would be the best hotel for miles around.

'What could be better than bringing the feel of a really beautiful home into an hotel? Why not have a go?' Opal urged. 'If we win it, I'll see you have all the help you require. You'll have no need to do any part that isn't purely creative.' So Breda had let herself be persuaded, and now awaited the outcome.

Molly dressed Eileen in her nightclothes and carried her into the kitchen. 'A drink of warm milk,' Breda said. 'Then time for bed – though your Dada's going to be disappointed if you're asleep when he gets back.'

'So is Luke,' Molly said. 'He has fallen for her hook, line and sinker. 'Tis the greatest pity he never had children of his own. Wouldn't he have made the best of fathers!'

Half an hour later Luke came in, followed quickly by Graham. 'Where's my little girl?' Graham called out.

'Gone to bed, not ten minutes ago,' Breda said.

He bounded up the stairs. When he came down again, fifteen minutes later, he said: 'She was awake. She was pleased to see me. She's gone off to sleep now.'

'So what are you two going to do tomorrow?' Molly asked as they sat at supper. 'I've told you I'll look after Eileen all day, if you like. Luke can manage without me in the shop for once.'

'What I'd like best,' Breda said, 'is to go for a long walk along the cliffs. And afterwards down to the strand.' She looked across the table to Graham.

'A walk down memory lane,' he said. 'Well, it sounds just fine to me.'

It was fortunately a fine day. They set off mid-morning, taking a packed lunch. 'Where first?' Graham asked Breda.

'To the strand, I think. I'd like to walk on the beach.'

They did so, taking off their shoes. Graham tied his around his neck and carried Breda's in his hand. They strolled, not hurrying, stopping to look in small rock pools which the sea had left behind.

'We must bring Eileen here tomorrow,' Graham said. 'Show her how to dig holes in the sand.'

'She's much too young to do that!' Breda said, laughing.

'Then I'll do it for her,' Graham said. 'She'll enjoy it.'

'I wanted so much to bring her to Kilbally,' Breda said. 'I want her to know she's half-Irish. You don't mind that, do you?'

'Of course not! Wasn't it the Irish in you I fell for, the minute you opened your mouth?'

He bent down and picked up a pebble, small and round, smooth as silk, patterned in blue and grey. 'For your treasure box,' he said, handing it to Breda.

'Oh, isn't that beautiful!' Breda cried. 'And now will I find one for you. Even if you haven't a box, I can give you a treasure.'

Graham shook his head. 'You've already done that, my love. Didn't you give me yourself – and Eileen? That's treasure enough for me.'

She put the pebble in her pocket and slipped her hand through Graham's arm. 'Oh Graham, I do love you!' she said.

At the far end of the strand, they turned and walked back; then they put on their shoes and took the road which led to the high cliffs. The sun was high in the sky now, warm on their backs as they climbed. Breathless when they reached the top, they flung themselves down on the short grass near to the cliff edge.

The air was loud with the cries of seabirds, wailing and screeching like lost souls as they swooped around the black face of the cliffs. The sea, blue and green, white-topped with foam, banged and thudded rhythmically against the cliffs, the sound like the beat of deep bass drums punctuating the strident music of the birds. Breda watched a ferry boat heading for the Aran islands. And except for the islands, and behind them the long shape of Connemara, there was nothing but the sea.

'When I was a little girl I used to think about crossing the water to America,' she said to Graham. 'I thought about it whenever I was fed up. Once I told Kieran that I'd swim there. I reckoned everything would be good in America, and wouldn't Auntie Cassie and Uncle Fergal be waiting there on the beach to welcome me?'

'But you never made it,' Graham said.

'I never made it as far as Connemara,' she said, 'let alone America! I suppose, deep down, I didn't want to. I loved Kilbally.'

'But you left it,' Graham said. 'And I for one am glad you did.'

'And do you think I am not?' Breda said. ' 'Twas the best day's work I ever did, though I did not think so at the time. Wasn't my heart breaking as I sat on that boat?'

They sat for a while in silence, watching the sea.

Presently Breda spoke again. 'I shall always love Kilbally, but now I belong in Hebghyll. It's my home; it's where I want to be – with you, and Eileen and the other children we will have.'

Graham drew her close, and kissed her.

'And now,' she said cheerfully, 'what about our sandwiches? I'm starving!'

It was teatime when they arrived back at the house. Molly, seeing them approaching, rushed to the door to meet them.

'I'm so glad you're here! Miss Opal telephoned!' she said. 'You're to ring her back. She didn't say what she wanted. Oh, I do hope nothing's wrong! I hope you're not going to have to leave us!'

'It was probably Graham she wanted,' Breda said, 'not me.'

'No, 'twas not. She said *you*. I'm sure I got that right.'

The telephone was in the passage which led through to the shop.

'Come with me,' Breda said to Graham.

She gave the Hebghyll number to the operator in Kilbally, then waited through several clicks and signals on the line until, at last, she was connected to the Hebghyll store.

'It's Breda Prince,' she said. 'I had a message to phone Miss Opal.'

That pause, until she heard Opal's voice, seemed the longest of all. 'Breda! Breda, we've won! The White Horse. We've got the contract!'

Breda could think of nothing to say. No words came to fill the silence.

'Breda, can you hear me?'

Breda handed the telephone to Graham. 'I don't know what you've said to Breda,' he began, 'but she seems struck dumb by it! Can I help?'

'I told her we'd won the contract for the White Horse,' Opal said. 'I said "we", but really it's Breda who's done it! Aren't you proud of her?'

'Oh I *am*! I am indeed! But then, I'm not surprised. I always thought she would.'

'Put her back on the line,' Opal said. 'I want to congratulate her.'

Graham handed the receiver to Breda.

'Oh, Miss Opal, I couldn't think what to say! I'm so pleased. It's wonderful news,' Breda said.

'It most certainly is. I congratulate you most heartily. But I won't keep you from your family any longer. I'll see you next Monday morning at nine o'clock sharp, and we'll discuss the details. Goodbye – and thank you, Breda!'

They travelled home on Friday, by way of Dublin, where they visited Kathleen, and stayed overnight with Moira and Barry, leaving early next morning. It was still daylight when the taxi they had hired at Hebghyll station drove up the moor road to Heather Cottage.

The cab driver lifted the suitcases into the hall, while Graham carried Eileen, now fast asleep against his shoulder. When he had driven away, Breda looked around her. 'Home!' she said. 'Home! Oh, Graham love, it's so good to be back. The three of us in our own place, where we belong.'

THE END

THE RAINBOW THROUGH THE RAIN
by Elvi Rhodes

The Brogdens were one of Chalywell's most important families. Old Jacob had started the family antique business when he was nine years old, going round the big houses and buying small items of bric-à-brac for pennies. Now Brogden's was famous for its beautiful furniture and pictures. But the most beautiful – and valuable – thing in Jacob's life was his granddaughter, Lois – for Lois reminded him of the daughter he had lost so tragically many years ago.

When Lois fell in love with John Farrar, the whole family were dismayed, for between old Jacob and the Farrars was a deep and abiding feud that could never be mended. Lois, conscious of the storm clouds of war gathering over her future, was determined that nothing and no-one should come between her and her beloved John. But as war broke out, as families were torn apart, Lois found her life changing irrevocably. Loyalty, love, tragedy and hope were to direct her into a future she had never dreamed of.

0 552 13870 3

CARA'S LAND
by Elvi Rhodes

Cara Dunning first came to the wild and remote Beckwith Farm in the Yorkshire Dales as a young landgirl during the Second World War. Beckwith was isolated, sometimes beautiful, sometimes inhospitable, and had been owned by the Hendry family since 1700.

When Cara fell in love with Edward Hendry, it was not what her family had intended for her. Edward was fifteen years older than Cara, a pacifist, and a widower with two children, one of whom bitterly resented her new stepmother. But Cara was determined to make the marriage work, in spite of the hard life on the farm, in spite of Edward's reserved personality and the shadow of Nancy, his former wife.

Her greatest friend on the farm was Edward's mother. Edith Hendry, a loyal and wise daleswoman, was to see the young bride through many tragedies, many vicissitudes and the years of trying to run the wild sheep farm on her own. And as Cara's life began to change, so Cara changed too, finding a complete and utter happiness where she had never expected to.

0 552 13636 0

A SELECTED LIST OF FINE NOVELS
AVAILABLE FROM CORGI BOOKS

THE PRICES SHOWN BELOW WERE CORRECT AT THE TIME OF GOING TO PRESS. HOWEVER TRANSWORLD PUBLISHERS RESERVE THE RIGHT TO SHOW NEW RETAIL PRICES ON COVERS WHICH MAY DIFFER FROM THOSE PREVIOUSLY ADVERTISED IN THE TEXT OR ELSEWHERE.

☐	14058 9	MIST OVER THE MERSEY	*Lyn Andrews* £4.99
☐	13992 0	LIGHT ME THE MOON	*Angela Arney* £4.99
☐	14044 9	STARLIGHT	*Louise Brindley* £4.99
☐	13952 1	A DURABLE FIRE	*Brenda Clarke* £4.99
☐	13255 1	GARDEN OF LIES	*Eileen Goudge* £5.99
☐	13686 7	THE SHOEMAKER'S DAUGHTER	*Iris Gower* £4.99
☐	13688 3	THE OYSTER CATCHERS	*Iris Gower* £4.99
☐	13977 7	SPINNING JENNY	*Ruth Hamilton* £4.99
☐	14139 9	THE SEPTEMBER STARLINGS	*Ruth Hamilton* £4.99
☐	13872 X	LEGACY OF LOVE	*Caroline Harvey* £4.99
☐	13917 3	A SECOND LEGACY	*Caroline Harvey* £4.99
☐	14138 0	PROUD HARVEST	*Janet Haslam* £4.99
☐	14262 X	MARIANA	*Susannah Kearsley* £4.99
☐	13910 6	BLUEBIRDS	*Margaret Mayhew* £4.99
☐	10375 6	CSARDAS	*Diane Pearson* £5.99
☐	13987 4	ZADRUGA	*Margaret Pemberton* £4.99
☐	12607 1	DOCTOR ROSE	*Elvi Rhodes* £3.99
☐	13185 7	THE GOLDEN GIRLS	*Elvi Rhodes* £4.99
☐	13309 4	MADELEINE	*Elvi Rhodes* £4.99
☐	12367 6	OPAL	*Elvi Rhodes* £3.99
☐	12803 1	RUTH APPLEBY	*Elvi Rhodes* £4.99
☐	13738 3	SUMMER PROMISE AND OTHER STORIES	*Elvi Rhodes* £4.99
☐	13636 0	CARA'S LAND	*Elvi Rhodes* £4.99
☐	13870 3	THE RAINBOW THROUGH THE RAIN	*Elvi Rhodes* £4.99
☐	14162 3	SWEETER THAN WINE	*Susan Sallis* £4.99
☐	13951 3	SERGEANT JOE	*Mary Jane Staples* £3.99
☐	14230 1	MISSING PERSON	*Mary Jane Staples* £4.99
☐	14118 6	THE HUNGRY TIDE	*Valerie Wood* £4.99
☐	14263 8	ANNIE	*Valerie Wood* £4.99